Marybeth watches the mailman, awaits his quick glance up at her. She watches out the window a lot. Unlike many criminals, she has had a happy childhood, so she can spend time thinking about that. She has nothing else happy to occupy her mind. She has nothing to do until evenings, when she works.

Marybeth sees the postman step back a little. She sees the postman look longingly up at her, but he stirs no emotion in her. Living under an assumed name, she never gets any mail.

LYING LOW

Diane Johnson

FAWCETT CREST • NEW YORK

to Hilda de Souza, John Murray and Evelyn Paul

WEDNESDAY

1. Death in the Afternoon

California. August. The flat, hot Sacramento Valley; the town of Orris. Ashby Path. From the upper window of an old house a young woman watches the postman on his daily rounds. This is the point at which he always puts his pouch down on the curb, takes out a joint and smokes it, squatting in the shadow of his red, white and blue Jeep. Each day he smokes a joint and waits for a rendezvous with the principal mail truck, then he comes along Ashby Path. The young woman, Marybeth, never gets mail, but she hopes that Ouida will.

Ashby Path has the only big shade trees in all of Orris. When in the summer the temperature is over a hundred—which is most days in Orris in summer—Ashby Path affords the only respite from the heat, because the trees here are old like the houses, spreading and gracious, the only mature trees in town. The rest are saplings planted in front of tract houses. All Orris is perfectly flat and brown, except the lawns, which are kept green by sprinklers and in the dazzle of the heat appear red, Marybeth supposes, owing to some property of the human retina.

The beautiful old houses on Ashby Path are too big for single families any more and have been converted to lodgings for students at the University of California at Orris. They are all vacant now until the fall quarter ex-

cept this house, number 380. Nice gingerbread Victorian
houses of Midwestern design, with sleeping porches, fur-
nished with sagging wire-sprung beds, neatly covered
with thin chenille bedspreads of washed-out green or
coral, bare mattresses underneath awaiting students with
sheets. In the fall, the students will festoon the porches
with sheets painted with slogans. A decade ago, when
Marybeth was a student, college slogans read ''Fuck
War''; now they say ''Fuck Sacramento State.''

With the students gone, the postman can keep track of
everyone left on Ashby Path, and he feels a discreet
amount of interest in the permanent residents, just
enough to keep his feet moving along the burning street.
The Waits' house is the most commanding house, and
there are a few interesting things about the letters they
get there. Besides the regular bills and junk, there's a
foreigner and someone who gets no mail at all.

He turns up the walk at the Wait house. A dark hook-
nosed man in coveralls, seeing the postman approach,
steps behind a tree. The postman sorts through his hand-
ful of mail and arranges it:

> Occupant 380 Ashby Path
> Miss Theodora Wait
> Miss O. Senza
> Mr. Anton Wait
> Mr. A. M. Wait
> AntonwAit
> Srta. Ouida Senza
> *The New Republic*

He studies one, a foreign letter for Srta. Ouida Senza,
return receipt requested. Now self-consciousness arrests
him. He would like to look up to see if that girl is up
there watching him, not Ouida Senza but the other one,
who lives here but never gets any mail, has never gotten
a single letter and yet watches out the window day after

day. She's been here since May. The postman thinks of Rapunzel. She is a mystery to him. He loves her.

The foreign girl, Ouida, gets a lot of mail and she isn't half so pretty, just dumpy and dark and wears glasses, though when she gets a registered letter she smiles a smile of transforming beauty.

The Waits, Anton and Theo, are brother and sister. He gets more mail than she does, including a lot from abroad, but all the bills come to her. Miss Wait is the ballet teacher in Orris. The brother is younger and only lives here off and on. That's him jogging around the block.

Marybeth, watching him, awaits his quick glance up at her. She watches out the window a lot. Unlike many criminals, she has had a happy childhood, so she can spend time thinking about that, or wishfully about men touching her breasts, or wondering whether Ouida will get mail. She has nothing else happy to occupy her mind. When she can get grass without too much trouble, she smokes it, too, on these long forenoons, opening the window like a kid to let the telltale fumes out. She has nothing to do until evenings, when she works.

From her window Marybeth has been watching Ouida walking slowly along Ashby Path carrying a big sack. A strange and horrid stench floats up from Ouida's sack as she sets it on the porch and fumbles for her keys. Marybeth sees the postman step back a little.

* * *

Ouida carries her sack inside, down the hall through to the kitchen. In the sack she has treasure. She's spent her life savings on this, the contents of this sack, big chunks of unsavory meat as dry as stones. She dumps them into the sink, hoping Miss Wait won't come in just yet.

* * *

Miss Wait—Theo—notices crossly that the termite man is late and she wants to go out. But it is she who must await the termite man, because it is her house. Ouida and Marybeth are the lodgers. Theo hears the step on the porch and knows it can only be Ouida's, who is so heavy-footed. Theo has the thin person's impatience with the slow footsteps of the plump, the dancer's impatience with stumbling.

Marybeth has taught herself running stitch and cross-stitch, and now is learning French knots from a handbook. She sees the postman look longingly up at her, but he stirs no emotion in her. Living under an assumed name, she never gets any mail.

Ouida, running water in the kitchen sink, hears the leafy fall of letters through the mail slot. She dries her hands and goes to see, heart aleap, as every day, with fear and anticipation, for she is equally likely to get good letters and bad letters, and she has had a bad premonition since early morning.

Occupant. Theo gets to the hall first and picks that one up, and the other addressed to Miss Theodora Wait. It's from Friends Outside, one of the many charities with which she is reluctantly associated. She leaves all the other letters lying on the hall floor for someone else to pick up.

Ambivalent, the postman turns over the last letter, the registered one from Brazil for Srta. Ouida Senza, and wonders whether to bother ringing the bell. Return receipt requested. If they had any faith in the U.S. mails, they'd know they didn't need to register these weekly letters; and since they had no faith, they wouldn't really expect a return receipt; and he knows she's in there, and it is hot standing here on the step. He chucks it in the slot. It lands at Ouida's feet.

Ouida lovingly gathers the letters addressed to Anton Wait and puts them on the seat of the hall tree for Anton to find. Then she picks up her own, the one from Brazil (*"Estimada Irma"*), and—yes, it is—the one she's been dreading for so long. She has always hoped she would have enough philosophy to meet this terrible moment. Has she? She turns the official brownish envelope over and over, and then sticks it in her pocket, shocked, heart racing. She would like to ask Miss Wait to look at the letter, but Miss Wait has gone back into the library with such a dismissive click of the door. Never mind. Soon beautiful kind Lynn will come downstairs, and she would look and surely say something helpful.

Marybeth, whose name they have been led to believe is Lynn, still gazing out the window, now sees the neighbor woman, as usual letting her little kid, Chen-yu, stray off the curb, never minding about cars. Marybeth keeps her eye on this neighbor, who is known underground to be the one who sells false identities. Marybeth often watches her—her name is Julie—and has talked to her of other things. She couldn't tell if Julie knew about her or not, but Julie, looking sideways, seeming to talk of others, once said, "Yolo County is the safest place in the world, large population of people between eighteen and thirty who all look alike to cops and no one cares anyway. They pick up people much faster in Sacramento or even the

Bay Area. A person is wisest just to stay right around here.''

Marybeth is like hundreds of people in Yolo County, but she doesn't know the others, has left them, has needed to leave them and has found no life or faith to take their place.

Bloody hell, Theo says to herself in the library, reading the letter from Friends Outside, I'm too old to get mixed up in these things. Would Miss Wait supervise the dance program for the arts festival at Fontana Prison, per our telephone conversation? She will, she supposes. They all knew she would.

Ouida, her mind distracted with fear of deportation, runs cold water over the chunks of meat and watches them swell. She apportions them in three large crockery bowls and carries the bowls of swelling meat to the back pantry. They do not smell so good, she knows, and Miss Theo may object. The smell is a problem, and now the additional and much bigger problem of the letter. She touches it in her pocket, doesn't open it. She sighs.

Marybeth supposes she is by now the most perfect sitter-still in the world, really good at it, can sit still for hours, blank, heartsick, staring. In the eye of her heart she can see herself as the postman, daily glancing up, sees her, a heartsick young woman. From months, now years, of self-discipline, she can consider her life as if it belonged to someone else, to a person viewed flatly through a window. She is subject, though, to fits of despair as sudden as rainstorms; a terrible pain, as though a hand had come up out of the well of her heart bearing a knife and scraped and hacked at her brain and at the cords of her throat.

But by sitting very still, with a mind as blank as possible, she can diminish the likelihood that the bloody hand, the blinding pain, will seize her. She puts down the dishcloth of practice stitches and for a moment covers her face with her hands. She presses her eyes with her fingers. She turns her thoughts to others; what does Ouida have in her sack? How to explain to that mother how her little kid will get hit by a car someday if she doesn't watch him better?

Vain old woman, laughs Theo to herself, executing a plié and rising on her toes. Sixty but she can still dance, and not breathlessly, either. Vain old woman—she touches her flat belly—she knows hers is a harmless vanity. Nothing much on her conscience. She is a serene person who has given as much to the world, approximately, as she has gotten; that is, not too much from either side, because of mutual mistrust. She has not done things the regular way, quite. Has not wished to marry, for example. It is the prospect of a usual, an ordinary life, she supposes, that accounts for the suspended animation of the beautiful Lynn, struck with dismay at an age when most girls are full of hope, if somewhat fatuous hope. Which accounts for the unusual docility of poor Ouida when it came to dishes and vacuuming. Ouida, poor soul, must see what life has in store. Theo tries the pious thought that it is nice to be sixty and not worrying what the future has in store; but the thought, so untrue, fills her with a shudder, a terrible forewarning. For whom or what she doesn't know—maybe for the poor prisoners at Fontana, for all poor prisoners and creatures.

Glancing down the street, Marybeth sees the hook-nosed man, who seems to glide instead of walk, as if he were on wheels, sees him stop in front of the house and then roll around to the side. He is disguised as a termite man, in overalls, and carries a notebook in which he writes. Has he been looking up at her window? She draws back and peers from the edge of the curtain. Surely he's seen her? Terror contracts her fingers so that she jams the needle into the heel of her palm. Drops of blood redden the dishcloth. Now she sees Anton Wait jogging along the path in his blue warm-up suit and sees the strange watcher step out of the way. Anton goes through the side gate to the back yard where his studio is, in the garage. Handsome, white mane of hair, slightly abstracted expression as if he weren't aware that he was walking somewhere.

Slowly the long hours of the day pass.

Ouida takes her letters to her room, reads the one from her brother the lawyer in Rio. The other lies unread in the pocket of her pink nylon dress. She sits in her peeling Barcalounger and thinks of Brazil. It has a flatness to her memory, like pictures in a travel book. She can seldom hear or smell Brazil any longer. Her dictionary and her lesson, to be read for the religious gathering she will attend after dinner, lie on the table by her chair. She applies herself to the lesson:

It is clear that men of the modern world have lost the ability to solve their problems within themselves. Men of today are ready to give up ancient beliefs and accept new spiritual solutions. This is the dawn of the new age of indescribable beauty, spiritual radiance and human understanding. Peace will come upon the world everlastingly, and among the planets and all other civilizations of the universe. It is the end of the world as we know it, and as predicted in Holy books, and it is the Beginning under new teachers. Our first task is to discover or recognize the new Divine Mediators.

She has to look up "mediator." *Mediador.* She should have been able to guess that, she thinks, but English words are sometimes so resistant, so opaque, until you look at them sidewise or come upon them unaware.

In the back yard, all at once, Theo is screaming. The sounds of a snarling dog are heard, and strange cries, not human, not of a dog, and a cacophony of chicken noises from the coops. Mortal wails and shouts. Ouida rushes down the stairs and out back. The heat strikes like the heat of hell; it seems to rush upward from the glaring grass.

In the back yard Theo was beating back a dog—it was Mark, the Labrador from next door—and waving her arms and cursing at him, and he was backing off toward a hole he had dug under the fence. Crazed chickens ran in circles in their pen. At the rear of the yard, where they had planted sunflowers to hide the freeway, lay the corpse of a hen. In the golden August grass, in the late-afternoon sunshine, the hen lay like a swan in a painting, death a kind of gilding around the frame.

With the enemy driven off, Theo came to look down at the feathered corpse. She didn't walk too close lest she see the look of death, an expression of fear or resentment on the face of the hen. "It's Freda Hen," she said. "She got out again."

Ouida came running. "Perhaps—perhaps—" she cried, and squatted down like a village girl over the hen, and aimed her hand at her, waved the hand over her, the palm cupped to focus the supernatural rays at the limp head. "I pray it is not too late," Ouida said, in her travel-book English.

Theo, watching, felt faint with apprehension, found herself nearly choking with tension, for life was precious life. Poor Freda. Poor Theo. This fear—what's the matter with me? she thought. Yet she dared not speak or interrupt Ouida's stern spiritual trance. Instead her thought was hurry, hurry.

Ouida moved her hand to generate more waves and rays, and for an instant a little wind ruffling the feathers appeared like life returning. Theo shivered but dared not speak or ask. Could it not, she wished, be like the dying swan, able to rise again at the end of the performance? Whence this fear—I'm not a fearful person, Theo thought.

"Oh, what sadness. When we are truly gone, we cannot come ever again in the same body," Ouida said. "We must be reborn according to our just deserts."

"She's gone, then?" Theo asked, knowing, of course, all along, that Ouida couldn't save the poor thing. Just like that. Walking around clucking and pecking at seed, her beady little eyes open, the next minute . . .

"So it appears, yet we should not give up hope," said Ouida, whose life fed upon hopes of various sorts. Theo sat on the steps of the kitchen porch, eyes swimming with hope. A most agreeable hen, foolishly agreeable, with qualities not usually given to hens, and lovely feathers of speckled brown. Mark, the Labrador, pawed at the grape-stake fence and slavered at them unrepentantly. Their own dog, Carlyle, didn't bother chickens. Her screams—who would have thought a hen could scream?

"I didn't realize he had dug that hole," Theo said, apologizing without knowing to whom. They would have to plug it up. The wind ruffled the feathers of the dead hen.

"You see, I have not enough force when my own troubles are strong," Ouida explained. She lowered her radiant hand. "I cannot transmit, and instead I soak up all the power into my own body for my own needs; that is how it happens, and I cannot prevent it. We cannot help others so well when we have troubles of our own."

"No, it isn't your fault, it was too late when we got to her," Theo said. Like a black devil hound, that nice old

Labrador had come leaping and slashing. Sadness pressed the more heavily on her because of the sudden hopeful flutter of her heart. But the dead do not come back again in the same body after they are gone; and there wasn't any force in Ouida's hand anyway—they let Ouida direct her rays on them to humor her. And yet you never know.

Yes, you do know. Theo stood up. "Anton must be home by now; he can pluck her, we might as well eat her."

"Wait, wait," Ouida whispered, staring at Freda Hen. Leap, hearts. But no. Now Ouida stood sadly and with a crack of her knee. Theo saw disappointed tears standing in Ouida's brown eyes. Feeling, as usual, some irritation at Ouida's credulity, Theo put her arm around Ouida's shoulders.

"Never mind, never mind," she said, hugging the sweet soul and feeling a flush of comfort herself at Ouida's warm goodness, or perhaps it was the effect of the rays drawn from the cosmos which collected into the little cloth bag Ouida wore around her neck. The string covered the thin scar across her throat. Theo could never bring herself to ask Ouida whether she had had her throat cut once.

Theo went into the garage and called up the stairs to Anton in his studio.

"Is that you, Teddy? What? Come up," he said.

"The dog next door has gotten Freda Hen," Theo said, climbing the stairs, smelling the chemicals. Anton sat at his table outside the darkroom. He slid a small picture in a hurry under his blotter.

"Dead," Theo brought herself to say, cross to hear the quaver in her voice. "Ouida gave her one of her faith-healing treatments but she couldn't revive her. You know, Freda Hen was always getting out, the one hen that al-

ways got out. Anyway, I think she died from fright and
we might as well eat her."

"Okay," Anton said.

"Just sitting up here, it seems so inappropriate and
morose. Couldn't you do something in the garden?" Theo
said, beginning to feel angry at him. She had a fear of
his lassitude; she felt it as a reproach. Once their mother
had left him in her care when they were little, on a rainy
day, and he had broken his collarbone running to look at
the new kittens—splat, down he went on the wet cement.
That's how he was. People would blame her when his life
went wrong.

"I'm waiting for something to come out," Anton said,
waving at his darkroom.

"Poor Ouida really believes in her ability to detain the
fleeting ghost," Theo said, "and she believes not only
in the afterlife but in the forelife, too." How richly peo-
pled, how shadowed and dappled must the material world
be for Ouida. For Anton, too, for that matter. His view
of it was a masterpiece of topography covered with trees.
Perhaps it was only she whose grasp of life was theoretically unsound, whimsical, inconsistent. To her it was
made up of the sudden death of hens. You never knew
what it would do. Such a dependent and vulnerable view.
She wiped her hands along the front of her dress as if
she were an old henwife wearing an apron. She felt terrible about that chicken really.

"Everybody else seems to be waiting for something,
too," Anton remarked. "Ouida and the girl. Stare out
the windows. Coming home from my jog I noticed—the
house has the aspect of a brothel, a Middle Eastern
brothel, watchers from the open windows, harem maybe,
the watching faces of women . . ."

"Oh, you've never been to the Middle East," Theo
said. "Do something about the hen, please," and she
went down the stairs again, feeling angry at him. Those
were his chickens, after all; it was a hard thing that it

should be she, not he, who suffered the emotions of love and loss. How it is men seem to regulate their emotions so sensibly, no feelings wasted on poultry? Chickens for Anton were just a feeble gesture toward living off the land. Although she was fond of her brother, she preferred, on the whole, to live here without him, in their childhood home—without Anton and without chickens. He would always come home after his divorces, build coops, change the arrangement of her shelves. His income and his houses were neither one steady, as he was a photographer, and he took pictures not of living people but of shells and pine forests, and had spent years wandering in the Sierras with his old dog, Carlyle, as his only companion. Maybe that was why his wives divorced him.

Ouida stood in the kitchen gloomily making herself a cup of tea. "In God's eyes all creatures are valuable," she said to Theo when Theo came in from the garage. When Ouida first got to America, she called chickens "kitchens" and kitchens "chickens" indifferently. They sounded the same to her. English is so difficult, she would complain. But despite her difficulties with English, and her other difficulties, her face was now serene. Her other difficulties were a kidney trouble, a decision whether or not to marry her boyfriend—an unreliable-sounding man named Griggs, whom Theo had never seen—and the imminent difficulty with her passport.

"All the same, I am sorry I soak up the rays for myself," Ouida said. "Yet I must not be too sorry, either, for you must not allow the mind to wallow in vain apprehensions and unwholesome antipathies. And death, we know, is not the end."

"Oh, Ouida, your mind could never wallow in unwholesomeness," Theo reassured her, laughing a little at Ouida's phrase. She realized that Ouida's emotions

were more complex than her situation—stuck between
Portuguese and English—would allow her to express, and
she respected Ouida's passion to learn everything: English, the mysteries of life, maybe love, even death. But
she often laughed at her.

At the thought of death, Theo felt the first start of a tear
and hurried upstairs to her room to cry unseen. It was
the hour of the evening for the doves which lived in the
gingerbread of the eaves to flutter and come to life.

Theo knew her tears would pass off quickly if she just
let them come unrestrained, but of course hidden away up
here. She knew it was silly, crying for hens and for the
little families of doves. It was not for hens exactly that she
cried, but for whole orders of bald edible creatures that
had been optimistically furred or feathered against danger,
whose little artifices did not suffice, meager-brained but
trying to get along, against whom death would come slashing when it was not expected.

Hens. She knew it was silly to cry for hens. She knew
all there was to be thought and felt correctly on this subject, in a world full of dying children, of course she did,
and she also knew all there was to be said about foolish
weeping old maids. That was why she was in the habit
of hiding away in her room during these spurts of tears,
and in her heart she felt she was something rather decent
about this disinterested crying she was apt to do. It was
more than just tender-heartedness. ("Theo is so tender-
hearted," their mother had often said.) It was cosmic
work, you almost might say, crying for creatures who
have no one else to cry for them, and for the whole state
of things. While crying, she ran her bath, plucked her
hair from her hairbrush, dusted the powder from the
dresser scarf, enjoyed the fragrance of the powder.

* * *

Ouida was still in the kitchen when Anton came in the back door carrying Freda Hen, plucked and pitiful, a few feathers still clinging to her pink skin. As usual, seeing Anton, Ouida quailed with love. Ouida thought Anton looked like a conquistador, like paintings of *conquistadores* with their thin cheeks and high noses, their glaring eyes full of gold. "If they had taken off their helmets, the hair would be like Mr. Anton's hair, I think," she had told Marybeth once, "silver, like the helmets."

"Here, she's all yours, Ouida," Anton said, vaguely waving the pinkish naked hen by her dead yellow feet.

"Ah, good, you never can get the feet of the chicken at the Co-op. When I ask them, they tell me there is a law against selling the feet of chickens," Ouida said, smiling strangely and spreading her hands. "Can it be there is really such a law?"

Anton did not know about laws. He washed his hands at the sink and went back to his studio.

Marybeth was coming down the kitchen stairs for something to eat and noticed the usual shy look of love cross Ouida's face as she spoke to Anton. Marybeth, who understood the relation of power and sexual attraction and had once herself been in a phase of falling into bed with professors and the leaders of political groups, pitied poor Ouida, who did not understand, and was merely the victim of simple love, and whom Anton did not appear to notice at all. Marybeth worried a lot about Ouida. Ouida was the only third-world person Marybeth actually knew any more. Her past life, on the barricades, seemed as a dream to her now.

Ouida's loving look was altered now by some expression of shame or confusion, and Marybeth, arrested by an instinct of tact, some response to the curious secret scuttle of Ouida to the pantry, stopped unseen on the kitchen landing. She saw Ouida give Anton her smile,

but a less than usually forthright smile, and slink past
him as she sometimes did when she was planning to prepare something strange to eat—made out of mandioca
root, say, or palm leaves. She heard the insincerity of
Ouida's crafty small talk about chicken feet. Anton ig-
nored Ouida as usual, impervious to her beauty. At least,
Marybeth thought Ouida beautiful, though some of it was
in getting used to her. At first she merely seemed short
and plump, like a little pre-Columbian figure, one of
those clay-colored goddesses dug up from a field. Her
round fresco eyes made her look as if she had been
painted on a wall.

"I am Indian, white and Negro, all three, as are many
Brazilians," she once said to Marybeth. The beauty of
her face was mostly Indian, with high cheekbones and a
wide, sweet smile, teeth wonderfully strong, large and
white like the capped teeth of an actress. She had round
señorita eyes that rolled and flashed now at Anton's departing figure in a new, furtive way. Intrigued, Marybeth
lurked and watched.

At first, appearing to stifle some powerful impulse, Ouida
went to the refrigerator in the ordinary way and brought
back cabbage and tomatoes, then got onions and garlic
from the pantry.

Now, looking over her shoulders from left to right like
one engaged in a crime, and with a criminal's beating
heart, Ouida with her small sharp knife slit the throat of
the dead Freda Hen, whose blood still flowed a little.
Blood flowed over the drainboard into the sink. Quickly,
with a look to right and left, repeating some strange
words silently, for her lips were moving, as Marybeth
watched, she pulled out the last feathers from the tail of
Freda Hen and raked them through the bubbling blood.

Next she took paper towels and placed them on the
drainboard, and on them put the blood feathers, all the

while looking out and listening for any step. The potatoes were boiling competently on the stove. In the mortar she ground garlic and red peppers to spread on Freda Hen. When the feathers had drained a little, she wrapped them in a newspaper and started up the kitchen stairs. Seeing the fascinated Marybeth, she realized that she had been watched.

She laughed with embarrassment. "It is silly," she said. "I know that. I do not really believe in the old magic, but I have some memories of when I was a little girl, when the snake slid down the vine, and of my father crying because the snake had bit him. He was afraid. We were all afraid, my brothers crying also, and drums beating. Then the *macumbeira* came. People had called her.

"They were only ignorant people, you see, Catholics and people from the *favela* and people like that. My family was Protestant, though poor; all the same they went for the *macumbeira*. I can see her still, striding toward the house holding up the chicken with the blood dripping down. A chicken killed under auspicious circumstances, the feathers, it is thought by ignorant people, have a powerful magic. I do not really believe this. It is for Catholics and thieves and makers of political unrest, I know. And yet—and so—"

Marybeth pitied her confusion. "You never know," she said. "Why not? Still, what do you want feathers for now?"

Poor Ouida stood, still embarrassed. "Oh—I have many problems, you know, my dear Lynn. There is Colonel Pacific, who will not give me my passport, and can have me sent back to Brazil anytime, on a Brazilian army plane, too, and there is my boyfriend Mr. Griggs, and my kidneys, and—oh, secret things I cannot tell. And I might say a spell for the success of my *feijoada* on Saturday."

Marybeth wondered: Could Ouida really say spells? Could she shrivel the face and garble the words of Colo-

nel Pacific? What could she do to Mr. Griggs? Will she
say love spells about Anton Wait? Marybeth would have
liked to believe in spells.

"And today I have a letter which I fear very much,"
Ouida said. "Would you do me the favor of looking at
it?" She was carrying it in the pocket of her dress, and
pulled it out for Marybeth to see. It was from the Department of Immigration, and was unopened.

"What is it? Do you want me to open it?" Marybeth
asked. Ouida smiled, with a little chagrin, knowing how
Americans are unbelieving of signs. She took the letter
back again.

"This is not an auspicious day. Tomorrow may be more
auspicious. Anyway, I can wait to read this news."

"How do you know what it says?" Marybeth asked.

"I think it is a notice for me to appear to renew my
visa. I have a tourist visa, not a permanent visa. When
they discover I have no passport, they will send me back
to Brazil. If you are without passport, they will send you
away and put you in jail as well."

"But what happened to your passport?"

"Colonel Pacific keeps my passport. That one who
brought me to this country, as baby-sitter to his child. In
French you would say *au pair*. My wish was to learn
English and improve my life. In Brazil they have much
need for teachers of English. But Colonel Pacific took an
apartment so small that I had to sleep on the sofa, and
he wished me to do many things. So I said no, I will not
do these things, and then he said so you must go back to
Brazil, but on a Brazilian army plane—those are free at
no cost to him. I am very afraid of those planes. He
promised my brothers Pan Am for me. So when I continued to object to all these conditions, he took my passport, with the object of making me go at his control."

"But that's rotten! He could be reported, he can't steal
your passport, you could call the police."

Ouida shrugged. "I do not exactly wish to call myself

to the attention of the police, because I do not exactly wish to return to Brazil now, not even on Pan Am. Since I am here, I see that it is much more difficult to be an unmarried woman in Brazil than here. This is why I have the plan of the *feijoada*.''

''What's that?''

''Ah. In Brazil we make a wonderful food, *feijoada*, and everybody loves it very much, but it is unknown here, so that when Brazilian people are here they long forlornly. It has black beans, mandioca flour, collard—I think the collard here is the same as what we use, but we have another name—and it has various pork. In Brazil we would use the ears and the tail of the pig but here I will change that, for people are not so enthusiastic about those parts. And there are oranges on top, and sausages in, and with it you drink red wine. It is delicious.''

''Hearty,'' said Marybeth cautiously. Ouida nodded.

''So my plan is to make a benefit. I learn about benefits at the Presbyterian church. But it is to benefit me, this one. If I can get the money, I can try to buy my passport from Colonel Pacific. I think he cares only about money. I have already painted many signs and put them up at the church, and also at bus stops, and the people who will come will pay four dollars each, so that if thirty people come I will succeed in earning enough to buy the meats. If more come, there is the benefit.''

''Hope it works,'' Marybeth said. ''Do *they* know— Anton and Theo? Are you going to have it here? I'll help if you want.''

''Yes. Thank you, my dear Lynn.'' Ouida smiled suddenly. ''I feel your love and concern for me many times and I am thankful.''

Marybeth was disconcerted, for she did not like her feelings to be discovered, not the good ones any more than the bad ones. ''Well,'' she said, ''yeah, I do kind of worry about you. This country isn't as easy as you think.''

* * *

Marybeth waits till Ouida has gone up. She is so far law-abiding that she doesn't put her Tampax into the plumbing of this old house, but carries a neat paper sack to the pantry to deposit furtively beneath other things in the trash bin. Here Ouida has put the paper towel stenciled with the shapes of bloody feathers. For reasons she can't explain, Marybeth pulls them out and takes them, with their ominous but pleasing pattern, back to her room.

She is putting them up on her wall when the little folded paper is poked under her door. This no longer frightens her. At first it frightened her because she imagined it would say:

> We know you.
> We are coming to get you.
> This is the end of you.
> This is the real world, after all—

the genuine American now, with instruments of electronic surveillance, helicopter surveillance, telepathy, treachery. Your name is being whispered in trees this very moment. From bough to bough it shudders along its way. Soon they will know; they know already. Listen outside your window, and you can hear it in the wind, blowing in the wind, poor, poor Marybeth.

But this paper, in fact, will enclose words of love, as usual, from Anton Wait; written on the back of a pretty photograph of a plant or rock. Sometimes the inscriptions are exquisite, reminding her of poems. Sometimes they are rather inflaming, and make her cheeks redden, as she is in some ways an old-fashioned girl. If only these words, the exquisite and the inflaming ones, would come from someone besides that old man, because she sure could use some; she hadn't had anyone for a long time.

She opens the paper, looks at the picture and puts it

on top of the others in her drawer in a neat pile. Smell of chicken, so dinner must be ready; she'll have to hurry and dress, she has to be at work at eight in the evenings Tuesday through Saturday. Marybeth works at a camera shop called Photophobia.

She hears the others go downstairs. She cannot imagine what it would be like to be them. They are peculiar people, yet she has an affection for them which she cannot explain. Once she would have despised them as naïve old liberals, and now she thinks of them as them. It is she who has no longer any category. She used to be articulate, aflame. Now she puts on her uniform of a Photophobia chick. The feeling of apprehension, unexplained, which has been with her all day, heavy as thick clothes, makes her sweat.

2. *The Land of Plenty*

Demi-pension, Theo called it, only half facetiously. Breakfast and dinner. Unlike other keepers of boarding houses up and down Ashby Path or Olive Drive, who let their lodgers rummage in the kitchen at all hours, Theo had an image of order and harmony—these family meals. She disliked people rummaging in the refrigerator, disliked strange heads of lettuce turning brown, forlorn unclaimed asparagus, the crispening sour smell of someone else's hamburger spoiling in there.

They always had dinner in the dining room, always called the Redwood Dining Room because it was a local attraction, a landmark. Every few years a tenth-grade teacher would bring her class to see it, the Redwood Dining Room in the Wait house, designed by Julia Morgan, with a beautiful stained-glass window, after a design by Lucia Mathews. These artists had been sent for from San

Francisco by Theo and Anton's mother. The house was
tall and turreted. The freeway,whose path had in part
been dictated by public concern to Save the Wait House,
had cut off the view in the rear with an immense grass
embankment. The rush and roar of cars was unseen but
incessant.

The stained-glass window signified Plenty. Two girls
in Grecian robes communed among laden arbors of purple grapes. Goats on golden hills ranged behind them,
and the golden hills blazed with pale amber light in the
morning. At dinnertime the rosy, vinous light that
streamed through the window lit the room like a campfire
or a burning rose garden.

Marybeth, a Midwesterner, was always dazzled by this
light and didn't find it comforting. She thought the beauty
of California was strong and inhuman, though she did
like the farm look of the plowed fields around Orris when
the sun wasn't too hot. She knew that many people
thought that Orris was the ugliest place in California, but
she didn't mind it too much.

Ouida usually cooked dinner, but Theo seemed to like to
serve it, and to act bountiful, though to Marybeth she
looked like deprivation personified—she was so thin, and
her dresses were thin and flowing. She had the elegant
sharp features of an elderly actress worn thin by a lifetime of high-class parts. Her thin hair was cut short like
hair in old Greta Garbo movies, of photos of young Wal-
lis Warfield Simpson. Sometimes her pink scalp showed
through. The brother, as is always the way, had masses
of heavy white hair, the hair of a maestro, though he was
a famous photographer. Theo hadn't ever been pretty,
Marybeth guessed, with those surprised eyes, the long
column of her neck, the head turning on the end of it
like a periscope. But she must always have had presence
and style. Sort of odd for Orris.

Under Theo's lilac old eyes lay bands of gray, as though she had ringed them with charcoal, making her eyes look at you deeply as from out of an ash heap. Only the high color of her purple-specked bright cheeks bespoke bounty, and sometimes the expansive gestures of her long dancer arms, smooth-skinned as a girl's, as now when she came into the Redwood Dining Room in her flowing muslin gown, those thin arms coming out of the wide sleeves and encircling the big steaming hot casserole. She set it at her place, at the end of the table near the kitchen door, and began filling the plates.

"When it comes to 'offing,' " she was saying, continuing a conversation begun with Anton over their drinks, "in the sense of 'off the pigs,' and those other expressions—'offing' whomever—people who feel in favor of that sort of solution to social problems unfortunately never seem to feel as I do about whom to 'off,' that's what I complain of."

"Whom would you off?" Anton asked.

"Well, the really sinister people—the real-estate developers and anti-environmental judges; for instance, the one that let them continue dumping asbestos waste into the Great Lakes, did you read about that? And the doctors who testified that asbestos won't hurt you—I think that's shocking. I would off them. And the governor who told the National Guard to shoot the students. Also the Nevada members of the Tahoe Regional Planning Agency, and the people who want to build more casinos and high-rises up there at the lake; and the people who allow them to, and the timber people, and the freeway people. I don't see why people like that should live. Well, why should they? Society executes a man who shoots another man, but people who kill lakes and trees, they're allowed to live. Why? I ask. And people who oppose a sign ordinance, I would off them. But none of these bomb groups ever asks *me*."

Her brother just laughed at her, and Marybeth didn't

believe her either. Not even she, Marybeth, believed
things like that any more, she didn't think, though she
could remember the luxurious feeling of having beliefs.

Theo's wide lilac eyes did not disclose belief of any
sort. "No, no one ever asks *me* whom to bomb," she
said, in her sincere voice.

Poor Ouida looked worried by all this. Marybeth
minded the way they never seemed to pay attention to
Ouida, and never tried to speak more slowly for her; and
now she was hearing about bombs, it must sound very
strange to her. They didn't seem to care what impression
she got of things. Sometimes Marybeth tried to explain
matters to her later, but it would be hard to explain the
tone of this bomb talk. Ouida's eyes, behind her glasses,
were wide in puzzlement and despair.

"Oh, Teddy," Anton said.

Theo subsided, sensing that the ring of real conviction
that underlay what she imagined to be a joking tone had
begun to drown out fun, or so it must seem to the rest of
them, so reproachfully silent now, rosy-faced in the dinnertime light, the last sunset rays coming through the
window of Plenty, pouring forth as it were from the cor-
nucopias of the California shepherdesses, with little
specks of dust dancing on the rays. Rich odors of plenty
from the kitchen, from the casserole, wafting around this,
her little family, kind dear people—Ouida's gentle smile,
and the girl, and Anton—and women everywhere probably sitting down at this hour with this same sigh, she
hoped as contended as she in the main. A swelling in her
heart made her cry aloud.

"Oh! It's Freda Hen!"

"Very plump, too, for a back-yard chicken," Anton
observed.

"But," Theo said, "I'd forgotten! For a moment forgotten. Well, I'm not sentimental but you would imagine

that greediness would not have entirely obscured my ability to remember that this—oh, the poor thing.''

''Where is she now?'' Ouida said, in her—it seemed to Theo—rather Rosicrucian voice; or maybe, like Amneris, sepulchrally. ''Where is she now?'' With her smile a bit knowing, perhaps suggesting she had some private information. The whereabouts of the essential Freda Hen known only to the spiritually pure. Ouida's metaphysical interests were to Theo the least sympathetic thing about her, and yet she, too, had been moved by the flight of that little life. It had been there, and then it was not. Memories connected themselves up, floated in the room on the specks of bright dust.

''Well,'' Theo said, ''I've seen death before, seen a human being die before my eyes, who was alive and well the minute before. That's nothing, I suppose, for men, for people who've been to war, or a policeman or doctor, they see it, no doubt. But it was the most terrible thing—or the second most terrible thing—that ever happened to me.''

Marybeth noticed that Anton looked up in interest. Perhaps she had never told him the most terrible things that had happened to her. Perhaps everyone had secrets. They did not seem to know each other very well, this brother and sister.

''It was when I missed the train at Turku—that's in Finland. I was with a small ballet company traveling in northern Europe; this was just before the war, and I'd gone to Turku with some others just sightseeing. A funny little city, rather pretty, with wooden houses made to look like the fine ones in St. Petersburg. I'd gone out to the end of the busline to see a castle—I don't remember what castle—it wasn't much of a castle—and missed the bus coming back and hence the last train to Helsinki. I couldn't believe it. Someone had been imprisoned in that castle, I forget who.''

''White slavery really exists in Finland,'' Ouida said.

"I read that. People think it exists in Latin America alone, in Argentina."

"Oh?" said Theo. "Well. Anyway, I couldn't believe that my friends had gone, the train had gone and there wasn't another one till morning. It was now, oh, only six or so in the evening, and I wandered around planning to get a hotel later on, but it was so light, it was nearly midsummer, and you have no sense of impending night.

"So when I got to the hotel all the rooms were gone. The man at the desk spoke quite good English. Finnish is impossible. I think what had stunned me was that they, the other, would go back without me. Oh, I was a perfectly grown-up person—I was twenty-four or five, perfectly able to find my way, or so they must have thought. I came to see how it must have seemed to them natural enough to catch the train, but at the time I couldn't believe it.

"Well, eventually I found a kind of boarding house for the night. They spoke no English, but I think I got the address from the hotel. Anyway, they understood what I wanted, of course. In those days, though, it was more unusual for a woman alone, in a strange land— It was all neat and clean enough. The light of the sky—I suppose it never did get entirely dark at that time of year—the cast of the sky was like lavender neon in the room, as from lurid signs outside, for that's the kind of light that usually blights the sleep of ballet dancers in their cheap rooms. Anyway.

"In the light I woke up and saw, or suddenly saw, for I don't exactly remember falling asleep, an assailant in the room, a huge man, entirely naked, like an animal. And he was very hairy, covered all over with tufts of hair, and he was lavender in the light. Every detail of him was clearly in my view, and forever in my memory; he might be painted on the wall of my room to this day when I wake up suddenly, except then, of course, he was all too actual, breathing, making a loud snorting, growling sound—these might have been Finnish words, but when you are awakened by them, they sound like animal noises.

"Entirely naked and with a violent erection. Drunk perhaps, because he seemed to be lurching about, not coming directly toward me but kind of swaying as he stood, looking at me, and, well, pointing at me, and meaning to come closer. I didn't scream at first, but gathered myself up and tried to guess whether I could run around him out the door. He had a quality of incoherence—perhaps it was only that I couldn't understand him. He had a demanding, an important quality—I cannot explain to this day. My terror was not entirely for my personal situation, this rapist in the room, but the glare of his eyes—he was like a savage Nordic ghost returned from some glacial past, savage and purple—uttering these forgotten sounds. His outrage, his size, the ferocious slowness with which he staggered toward me . . ." Here Ouida gave a little cry of alarm, and then put her hand to her mouth.

"I simply gasped, shrank, quite like the victim in horror movies, pulling the covers up, no thought now of running. At the foot of the bed he put his hand out to drag the covers away, and caught at my toes as well. Then I began to scream, I think. Or maybe that was later. Then he gave a horrible cry, released my toes and pitched forward onto the bed, his body convulsed in horrible spasms, which, in my comparative innocence, I imagined to be some sort of, um, premature ejaculation. Well, men are so mysterious, the way they work—so my sensation was for an instant one of relief at this lucky outcome, or for the eccentricity of my attacker.

"I don't know. It can only have been seconds more before I realized that he was in pain. He was in fact dead, and slid slowly off my legs onto the floor. In those days one had a more final attitude about death, not knowing about closed-chest massage and those other heroic mea-

sures. So I didn't feel obliged to do anything. I wouldn't
have known what to do. But I screamed for certain.''

"How terrible," everyone said. What a shocking old
woman, Marybeth thought, talking of bombs and erec-
tions, trying to shock.

"No, or yes, but the truly terrible part comes later.
I'm sure I must have screamed; anyway, people came
running, making their Finnish language, grunts and
moans, as if you've been captured by some savage tribe.
These people then ran away. So odd, so cold.

"I stood in my slip in the strange Finnish boarding
house, quite alone with the corpse of the man, un-
moved—no one had moved him, I mean. Gone for the
police, I thought, and I also thought, they think I've killed
him, and how can I explain this, in this terrible language.
My thoughts were all for myself, you see, imagining jail,
Finnish jail, and now I did see that he had hit his head
somewhere as he fell, a cut across the forehead slowly
bleeding onto the floor.

"And a little dog came, a funny creature with a head
too large and a sort of snout. He came up to the body
and sniffed at the blood. He made noises not unlike Finish. Oh, and the man had clasped his genitals, had made
a sort of pathetic *cache-sexe* with his hand, almost as if
to defend himself against me. Very soon new people
came, and one appeared to be the widow or relative of
the dead man. She began to cry. That at least was an
unmistakable eternal sound, this poor woman's sobs. His
window—the odd thing, she was already wearing a black
dress, already in a widow costume.

"Others helped her roll him over, but her eyes never
left his half-closed eyes, seeking, I suppose, some change
of expression in them. With each passing moment, when
he didn't respond, her sobs deepened. I saw that she
thought of moving his hand—her hand had started toward
his, then she clasped her own breast. Someone else folded
his other hand on his breast, left the one modestly in

place. They lifted him onto the bed. No one looked at me or asked me what happened, and yet someone there, the man at the desk, knew me—we had exchanged signs and gestures when I came.

"No one had a care for me. Why should they? But I didn't know where to go. I couldn't put my clothes on, because people came noisily in and out to look at him. Oh, and they had put him down on top of my dress, which I had laid out there on the foot of the bed. All night long he lay there on my bed, on my dress. There hadn't been any hangers . . .'' Her voice trailed off as she suddenly couldn't remember how she'd got started on this.

"Oh, the poor man, the poor woman,'' Marybeth said.

"Maybe the man was having a heart attack, something like that, and staggered into your room for help, Teddy,'' Anton said. "Burst desperately into your room . . .''

"Well, I did think of that, of course, later. I have thought and wondered endlessly—what did he want? What had happened really? And what happened to the poor woman? Beside grief, was there shame? Was there some difficulty? Were they far from home perhaps, staying in this place? Where did they take him—for they did come at last and carry him away, and it became morning, and I'd pulled my dress out from under him little by little, when nobody would be there momentarily, and put it on and was dressed and went and got the train.''

Oh, God, she thought, I never did once think that he was looking for help. After all this time, to think of that now. "One thing I have never resolved in my mind,'' she said, "is whether I had locked my room. That is, how did he get in, and so quietly? I must have locked my room, one always does, so carefully, in hotels. Yet I can't to this day remember locking it. Suppose in fact I didn't?''

"Suppose what? What difference does it make?'' Anton said.

Theo smiled. "Well, it makes all the difference, in a way. From my point of view. But I simply cannot remember." But since the others did not understand this, a silence fell over them.

"I hope it isn't insensitive to, um, commend this chicken. It's delicious, even if . . ." said the girl, in her flat Midwestern voice. She rarely said anything, but it was always something courteous, which made, Theo thought, her conversation rather flat, too. Still, civility was an improvement on the hostility or indifference one often got from the young, though their student boarders had always, luckily, been nice. This girl didn't seem to match her little round wire-rimmed granny glasses, though in what way Theo could not say. She had dainty little unused hands. Theo never saw her doing anything. She had the pretty bowed lips of a silent-film star, except, of course, she wore no lipstick, and never permitted herself a teasing smile or pout. Poor girl, thought Theo, so luminous and limp, you wanted her to have some friends, some projects. At that same age she herself had had a purpose in life and spent six hours a day at the barre.

"Oh, no," she said. "But it's odd how it is harder to lose a creature if you've given it a name. I'm not going to name the hens after this. Oh, God—it's seven-thirty, I'll be late, it's a meeting night." Here she sighed, as she usually did, most nights being her meeting nights. The Co-op board. "Ouida, dear, I'll have to stick you with the dishes."

Ouida nodded, not upset. Poor Miss Theo, she was thinking, so nervous and thin, and no grandchildren. A lady of her age should have grandchildren and dress in black.

Marybeth tried to remember if Theo had ever once done the dishes. Anton sometimes did—that is, stuck them in the dishwasher. She couldn't remember Theo even having done that. The mother of Theo and Anton, an intellectual with books and books, even in her hatboxes, had imbued Theo with an ambivalent attitude toward domestic things. Though she wouldn't have accepted a view of herself as a shirker, someone who didn't do her share of the dishes, all the same she did have a lot of these meetings, just at the right time.

And poor Ouida, thought Marybeth, she looked tired, and had to go to meetings of her own most nights, and after a day of English classes, typing class, church visits, housework and trying to practice serenity. It was because she was dark-skinned and not good at English that they made Ouida do the dishes, without thinking about it; that was Marybeth's view. She wished that Ouida would protest just once. Yet she wouldn't have minded being Ouida, either, just sweet-spirited and unaware; knowing things for what they are is sure a curse.

"Lynn, hurry up or you'll be late for work," Theo said to Marybeth. "We can walk over together."

"You go ahead. I don't have to be at work until eight, and I have an errand," Marybeth said, intending to help Ouida with the dishes.

"Ah—well—I'd better run," Theo said, folding her napkin. They used cloth napkins, not paper, except occasionally, and then always from recycled paper. Theo took her sweater from the hall tree and strode off along Ashby Path in the twilight.

Marybeth and Ouida throw the dishes in the dishwasher. Ouida scours the casserole. "Amazing Grace," she sings aloud, in her beautiful voice. On the counter are arranged her plastic purse, umbrella, which she often carries although it has never been known to rain in Orris in August, a package of candles to take to her religious

ceremony. Once she took Marybeth with her, too; they
went to some little house in West Sacramento, neat and
pretty with a heavy lock on the door. The house belonged
to Ouida's friend Roberta, a Japanese woman married to
an American. The American was not there.

"He thinks Roberta's meetings are silly," Ouida confided at the time. "It is the only unhappiness in Roberta's
life." Roberta had actually been to the Foundation of the
Meishi-Sama, where Johrei originated, back in Japan, so
she was an important person to the others. Marybeth sat
in the ring of happy mild brown faces, feeling part bore-
dom and part regret for the condition of simple faith,
once available to her, though faith of another kind. Af-
terward there were brownies and oatmeal cookies.

"Would you like to come with me tonight?" Ouida
asks. "It is too bad that more Americans do not know
about Johrei and the Messianic Church. Many people in
Brazil are believers, but not enough here to fill a church,
only someone's little living room. Maybe on Saturday at
the *feijoada* we could put out *The Story of World Messianity*, do you think? That is a pamphlet written by the
Meishi-Sama."

Marybeth admires the way Ouida can speak of her faith
right out. "Well, I have to work tonight," she apolo-
gizes. "I'll come again sometime. I'll help you at the
feijoada. Oh, Ouida, the trouble is, I don't believe in
stuff like World Messianity."

"I know, many Americans do not. All the same it is
true. Through the love of the Meishi-Sama, in collabo-
ration with Jesus, of course, the purification of the body
will eventually purify all society."

"How can you believe in Johrei and Rosicrucians and
Presbyterians all at once? Don't they cancel each other
out?"

"Oh, no! Each is a different one, you see. Rosicrucians are more about history. They tell you to think of

history as a desert with—what do you call the green part of a desert where things grow up?''

"Oasis.''

"Well, with these green places, and the person must crawl along the desert in life searching for the green places, which are knowledge and love and studying—it is explained much better in the book they have. Also there is very good singing at Rosicrucian meetings. Also from them one can get a true picture of Jesus, the authentic portrait, and he is not like the pictures usually seen. Also they have knowledge of certain other matters of spirit and will—I cannot tell you. It is a secret, but Plato was a Rosicrucian, and also Jesus and others.''

"I don't like meetings,'' Marybeth says, remembering all those meetings she used to go to, all that passion knotted in the throat.

"Sometimes,'' says Ouida, taking her by the arm, "I am come over—''

"Overcome,'' says Marybeth. "We shall overcome.''

"Yes, overcome by a feeling of happiness and elation at just being me, Ouida Senza, on earth just now and not at some other time. I think to myself that it was good luck to come to America with the family of Colonel Pacific, even if now he steal my passport, and maybe it is even lucky I am a little fat, owing to an afflicition of my teeroid, or maybe the kidneys. And my eyes are not so good. But affliction can turn to good. I hope. It is written that some things help and other things admonish you. Admonish? Some things are rewards and punishments for matters that arose in past lives. You can do nothing about that.

"Perhaps some people would pity my life—but I think it is a miracle that Ouida, this one little sister here today, is connected to all those dead people way back into history, as far as Egypt, maybe farther. Oh, but I cannot explain so good in English.''

"Do you really think that people are punished for what they did in past lives?" says Marybeth.

"Oh, sure, I know it," Ouida says. They leave the pans because they are in a hurry.

> *"The Christian has a happy home*
> *For Christ is where the Christian is,*
> *On tossing wave, in foreign clime,*
> *No anguish in the trustful heart,"*

sings Ouida. "What is anguish?" she asks as they walk together along Ashby Path.

"Anguish? When you are sad and miserable."

"*Miserável*. That is a word similar in many languages, I believe," says Ouida.

3. Save the Whales

What will happen? was Theo's thought as she stepped outside, and then, in the low twilight, daringly, let anything happen. It affected her, and had always affected her, to get away from the house—momentarily frightening, and then, ever since she was young, she experienced this same immediate lifting of the heart, this sailing step upon leaving. The forces of peril and change seemed to do battle with the forces of duty and custom, weighting the door of the house to swing in either direction. Either going out or coming in had always been for Theo like managing the door of a vast, chill walk-in refrigerator. The night air outside was warm and welcoming.

"It's precisely because she's shy that she dances," she had heard their mother explain to someone once, but that was not it exactly. Who doesn't both love and fear danger?

Theo quite enjoyed these early summer evenings in this part of town. Just here, in this part of town, which was thought to be old-fashioned and now blighted by the freeway, there were trees, and moreover the trees and houses matched. Old Victorian houses like eccentric relations, with wry porches, painted unsuitable colors by graduate students, and large and venerable trees. Elsewhere in Orris the cheap tract houses were now ten years old and already deteriorated into seediness, while the saplings that had been stuck in the parking strip in front of each one still strained in their encircling chicken wire for mere establishment.

As she walked along, Theo noticed for the first time that all the older women were hugging their purses. Had this always been so? Theo's purse swung fearlessly from her shoulder, but some of the old friends she saw, who like her had grown up in Orris, clung to their purses fearfully. When had this happened? Theo had masses of old friends who had grown up in Orris, wearing leather headbands, their bosoms adorned with clay beads of their own firing, painting, stringing, their windowsills lined with pots. Many lives, like Anton's, spent in the service of the Sierra mountains or orphans or some political party. Not Theo, who was not political. But where were all the Communists any more, she suddenly thought.

At the corner of Third and A she met Buffy Swenson standing at the Texaco station, Buffy clinging to her purse.

"Going? I'm not going anywhere," Buffy said. "I do this every day, mail a letter to my daughter or granddaughter; then I wait here for the paper and I peek at the headlines to see if I dare buy it. Usually I'm afraid to buy it, there's always some horrible accident, or murders. So many murders. These Zodiac murders. I'm getting to the age now I'd rather not know."

Scared even to read a newspaper? We *are* getting to be timid old ladies. Possibility is what you ought to feel, joy and so on, whenever you leave the house, Theo thought or perhaps said.

"I still feel it a wonder, I feel it such a wonder," she had said to Anton once, even blushing, so that she had seemed like a girl to him, "that I'm let out alone, allowed to go places alone."

"It's sometimes a wonder to me, too, that you are allowed out alone," Anton had thought or perhaps said.

"Hullo, hullo, Miss Wait," called out the Australian boy from the hippie commune a few doors down— Alistair Burnham was his name—wearing aviator sunglasses and jeans decorated with scraps of Liberty print, rather a dandy of a young man. He kissed Theo's cheek and said he was on his way to the Co-op for Sure-Jell and paraffin. His wife was doing some preserving. He pedaled his bicycle slowly alongside Theo, weaving from side to side.

"Do some preserving," he said again, with a laugh. "If that's your conception of preservation."

As they walked, he tried to get Theo to buy something he was currently selling. "The Home Alert System, Miss Wait, you must have seen them, is an innovative way of putting you right in touch in case of emergency. Your address goes on the roof in large visible letters which can be seen by the police helicopter. Then a silent alarm—"

"Alistair, I do not think we should adopt such measures. Those people in New York with their double triple locks and metal doors. The fear mentality itself does something destructive, soul-destroying."

Alistair laughed. They crossed together along the overpass, Alistair walking his bike. It was still light, so the pickets were lolling outside the gun store, and the American flag was still set in its standard at the curb, hanging limply. Mr. Lopez, the owner, a fat man with a string tie, waved at Theo from inside as he talked on the phone and glared at the protesters, students mostly. In his window were cardboard models of Immortal Winchesters.

Theo waved back. She didn't approve of gun stores, but she felt inclined to overlook Mr. Lopez's. We have to forgive the Chicanos these lapses, she had said to Anton; there are so many things standing in the way of them getting their fair share of America.

Marybeth told Ouida good night at the bus stop and walked on alone, slowly, to avoid catching up with Theo and Alistair. Her solitude was more natural to her than companionable walks were. She watched Theo's tall figure lope along up ahead, Theo waving one arm like a flamenco dancer. What could they be talking about? Theo's arms were always waving, expressing things. Theo's nature was deeply mysterious to Marybeth; she seemed to have passed so many years to no purpose whatever, and so cheerfully. The idea of thirty more years of life imprisoned in your own meaningless head seemed unimaginable to Marybeth.

Marybeth was conspicuous in her orange uniform of a Photophobia chick. Observing her on other occasions, Theo had felt exasperated at her cringing sidle, as if she were trying to sink into the pavement. Inappropriate for a healthy girl of her age and nationality. If someone had asked Marybeth herself, What do you fear, she would have said, I fear someone seeing me, I fear being known.

Yet she did want terribly to be known. She constantly dreamed of seeing someone she knew, and these were not nightmares but joyful dreams. Sometimes they would be daydreams. She would be sitting behind the counter at the Photophobia and gazing out the window, and suddenly it would seem to her that some passerby was known to her. That looks like Lois, Lois what was her name— the same curly hair, that same color hair. Quite from nowhere such thoughts would come. People she hadn't seen or heard of since high school.

Marybeth came from Bettendorf, Iowa, and no one

from there could be here, not possibly. Yet she recognized people constantly—with joy, then terror. Then, when that hair, that chin belonged to someone else, she would sigh and her fear would drain away like water down a basin and she would feel safe again.

Marybeth was going to the Co-op, too, for another box of Tampax. The Co-op parking lot was filled with vehicles that looked like little houses built onto the back of pickup trucks. Some of the little houses even had stained-glass windows and louvered shutters. People lived in these, or in VW buses; there were lots of those, too. Marybeth would have liked to have a VW bus to live in; but having any kind of wheels just increases the likelihood of getting picked up. That was one of the first rules: no wheels. But she longed for a little house on wheels to hide in. And maybe a puppy.

She walked well behind Theo and Alistair Burnham, but she was close enough as they came near the Co-op to watch fearless Theo stride in through the ranks of mongrel dogs, each with collar, snarling outside, and through the ranks of snarling guardians of donation boxes; it was like a medieval courtyard, Marybeth thought, swarming with dogs and mendicants. Dogs and mendicants terrified Marybeth. Dog your footsteps, hound you.

No one ever bothered Theo for a dime or signature. Marybeth watched her sweep with a wave through the electric door which opened before her. Her boundless philanthropy opened doors. Kind smiles from dogs and mendicants.

"Got a quarter for the Free Clinic?" someone asked Marybeth, an ugly guy with ridiculous thin beard, red bandanna around his neck, one gold earring. Marybeth grimly deposited the dime she'd been clutching. Punks.

"Save the Stanislaus and other white-water rivers?" a nice plump housedressy woman sitting at a card table asked her, calling after her as she hurried in. Tears came to Marybeth's eyes. She would want to save the white-water rivers, of course she would, but she didn't want to spoil their petitions with her false names. What misery if Theo were ever to see her passing up these petitions for helping worthy causes.

"I'm going upstairs—we have matters of terrific moment to be decided tonight," Theo told Alistair, patting his arm. Alistair said good night and pulled out a shopping cart for himself. Theo, not one to shirk things, and not without a feeling of excitement, now climbed the stairs to the meeting room, pausing in mid-flight to look through the secret window used by the manager to keep tabs on things. She did this every Wednesday night, to estimate the number of shoppers and the look of things. Theo felt proprietary and pleased about this Co-op, which her mother had helped established around 1937. Theo liked the hushed cathedral atmosphere, the array, like offerings, of soul food, Oriental food, health food, diet food, display of inexpensive protein alternatives, food for the poor, and actually, when it came right down to it, quite a bit of food for the rich—Maine lobsters swimming in tanks, smoked salmon, Belgian endive, one hundred varieties of cheese—this rich-people's food slyly arranged here and there so that none need feel ostentatious about buying it or conspicuous about stealing it; it was just mixed in with everything else.

Theo watched Alistair push his cart to the paraffin counter and put six boxes in his cart. Strange, she thought; a lot of paraffin. She watched with interest as he pushed his cart to the candy display and put three large Cadbury bars into his cart and one into his pocket. Cadbury Fruit and Nut, Theo saw with her sharp eyes. Interested, she now watched him push his cart to the rear of the store where large crocks held Granola and other cereal compounds. Here Alistair met someone, a frail boy in his mid-twenties who looked desperate and frightened to Theo, though he was trying to be quiet and inconspicuous. Alistair pulled from his pocket a huge manila envelope and gave it to the boy. The poor boy, bare-chested, wore only a sleeveless vest. Where would he put the envelope? He put it under his arm and darted away. Alistair resumed pushing his cart, with his same insouciant air. Theo wondered if Alistair could be a dope pusher.

Theo saw, also, that Lynn was going to meet someone she knew. She saw Lynn walking along, and she saw another young man see Lynn, with galvanic effect, as though he had been plugged in. His hair seemed to stand on end. Clearly he would speak to her. That's nice, Theo thought, as poor Lynn seems to know no one and to have no social life. This has worried Theo.

Suddenly Theo felt like too much of a snoop, spying down this way on people she knew, a busybody watching the private deeds of people in a supermarket, and up she went to the meeting room at the top of the stairs.

Theo had attended these meetings all these years for a number of reasons—feelings of usefulness, habit, community and fellowship. Perhaps, even, noblesse oblige. But she was always conscious, just here at the door, of a certain reluctance. Really, it would be easier to not; and if she didn't, she would be spared knowing a good many things she hadn't wanted to know—about human nature, about Co-ops, about the wickedness of things in general.

Still, in she goes. The other eleven board members are there already, passing papers back and forth and talking in their New York voices, loudly, black and white faces alternating like the keys of a piano, all wearing glasses, either gold-rimmed or horn-rimmed. They are talking about whether to exclude from Co-op shelves pet food from companies which did not honor the Co-op request to sign an affidavit specifically renouncing the killing of whales and wild horses.

"Certainly exclude them," Theo says. "We want no pet food here from whales, none even tainted by a suspicion of whales." Upon this, as upon most matters of principle, Theo's position is inflexible and extreme. Extremism the privilege of advancing age.

Developers should be shot. Can we not dispense with plastic altogether? Have you read how the surface of the ocean is covered in plastic already? Plastic spherules shaped by the waves from the Baggies and the Handiwrap of the world?

"The thing is, Theo, the shoplifting problem gets so much worse when we switch to brown-paper bags for produce. We tried it. People stash steaks in the bottom. When we use clear plastic, we can see if broccoli is the only thing they have in there. Then the rate of shoplifting goes way down," explains Ted, the manager.

Does anyone here realize the agonies endured by the force-fed goose? Entrapped in a little cage, he has grain stuffed down his throat; he weeps tears of blood, it is said. Have you ever been in Périgord? Tears of blood, something about the way the food presses in the gullet, the tears are turned to blood. Can you really feel that we ought to sell pâté de foie gras?

Theo the voice of right unreason. Folding her thin hands; the luxury of rightness every Wednesday night, no sympathy for commercial interests, no pandering to the wants of the weak or thoughtless consumer, no quarter for human greed. Why should people not be saved from themselves? Why should wickedness be tolerated? In her heart she of course has sympathies, has weaknesses, forgives weaknesses in others. But as a matter of public policy?

Sometimes, standing on the Co-op staircase, Theo feels that she understands everything, can look into every life, into every shopping basket, can see the young mother clutching food stamps buying the best baby food, can see the youth stealthily secreting Tang beneath his dirty old bum's coat. How she loves them. At other times she feels that she understands nothing, has never understood a thing.

"We're already getting some static from the membership about the donation we're making to the Friends Outside, for the arts festival at Fontana Prison," someone reports.

"How wicked," says Theo, "for people to begrudge a few hundred dollars that might help a poor prisoner. Even if it brought into the life of one prisoner an idea of beauty or art . . ."

"No, no, they're complaining that we've been co-opted—ha, ha—by the prison establishment, in the service of half measures to pacify instead of rectify prison conditions. They say . . ."

"Oh, shame!" they all cry. They believe, variously, that painting and ceramics can mitigate crime. They believe in the richness of the inner life. Theo herself plans to direct the dance seminar workshop, which they've called Freedom Through Movement.

Well, why not? Those poor men. Theo, protégée and former partner of Feodor Koslov. Black men, graceful, in cages—whether an old woman could have anything to help them would remain to be seen; and yet the liberating, humanizing, refining discipline of dance can let any spirit live within its clay more harmoniously, more sweetly. In the temple of the body a gracious home. Theo believes this.

Marybeth is thinking of Theo and Anton and Ouida as she wanders along the aisles. All those charities and good works and they don't help the third-world person in their own house! All at once somebody says her real name in a loud voice: "Marybeth!" She cringes into a bread rack so that loaves of bread fall all around, and then her panic is replaced in a fleeting instant by a stern calm as she prepares for this next whatever it is to be.

Perhaps the dread moment itself. Calm certitude. The slight bitter smoky taste of the air all day, the ache around her eyes have been premonitory. She has the slight sensation of relief that she is confirmed in her dread. It was always going to happen and now it is happening. Like the moment that must come to everyone, when they realize that death is coming right at them and they just decide to face it. She decides to face this. Or maybe it is more like being transfixed in the glare of an oncoming train. Marybeth feels her rabbit eyes shining. He couldn't miss her. He couldn't not see her and rush toward her; she can't hide beneath a pyramid of Tide or in a bunker of sugar sacks.

Her face is calm, normal, smiles at him as he rushes up smiling broadly at her, hands out, excited and happy, saying "Marybeth, isn't it? Marybeth Howe?" in a loud voice that can be heard all through the vast hangar-sized building out into the streets, all around town. Chuck Sweet, a perfectly nice boy from Bettendorf, Iowa, recognizing her.

4. Night Thoughts

"Oh! Well! Chuck Sweet! For heaven's sake! Chuck!" Marybeth covered over her shivers of alarm with vivacious movements of welcome such as come naturally to sexy girls with wiles. But she was terrified, shocked, certain he would say her name again out loud. She wondered how he could help but see her terror. "Marybeth! Marybeth!" he was certain to say, as loud as the voice

of God booming out all over the store. And from the rapt
and radiant expression on his face she could see he wasn't
going to go quietly away. A joyous thing had happened
to him. They shook hands, they laughed, exclaimed.

"How amazing to see you here!" she said, with a sort
of rosiness to herself, too; she could feel it. She saw his
eyes notice the Tampax she was carrying and look discreetly away. He attended her to the checkstand and
waited while she paid. She thought of bolting, running,
but then he'd call out after her: "Marybeth! Marybeth!"
It had been years since she'd heard anybody say that name
out loud.

She suggested he walk her over to her job. What the
hell, she thought, they could talk there all right. She realized that she would kind of like to hear how things were
in Bettendorf.

It was funny, and scary, to think how quickly she'd
answered to her own name. She should have stared at
him and said "Who?" in puzzled tones. She'd practiced
that enough. Now, instead, she and Chuck were saying
"Imagine!" and "What are *you* doing here?" and "After all this time." She could hear her own laughter.

Marybeth worked nights from eight to twelve, four
hours and you got paid for six, probably because of the
danger at night, but nobody ever mentioned that. She
thought it was dumb for a photo shop to stay open until
midnight; people could damn well bring their film in before nine, say; but Photophobias were Open Till Midnite
Every Nite. Punks were all you got after about nine; it
was creepy after that. Usually she locked the door at
nine-thirty, the hell with them. She believed, rightly, that
the master of all Photophobias was not likely to come
around checking on her particular branch. So now she
locked the door right away when she and Chuck got there,
so no one could come in and hear him saying her name.
"Oh, Marybeth, what on earth are you doing here?"

What was Chuck doing here anyway, in Orris, of all

places? Lonely, like everyone who comes to California, and excited by this coincidence, running into somebody he went to high school with, in Orris, of all places. He was taking a course in summer school, on conserving paintings. He was interested in art.

Marybeth thought that was kind of funny. It made her feel stranger and farther away. She hadn't known that anyone from Bettendorf would be interested in art. Maybe they all were? How would she know? People who had seemed simple, the way everything had seemed simple—maybe they were all really as faceted as diamonds, how would she know? All she had thought about was war, and Wrong.

"God, I'm really glad to see you," Chuck said. "A familiar face in Orris—that's unbelievable." The expression on his beautiful countenance was awestruck and yet somehow deserving. Favored of the gods, he deserved to be sent a companion in this unlikely way in this strange place.

Marybeth could see he was a favorite all right. In high school, she remembered, he was this large kid always wearing strange padding and braces to do with various sports, and many kinds of headgear. He had sat next to her in Social Studies; and he always smelled of the liniment on his football sprains. Now he was interested in art.

And he had never heard about her! Evidently no one had ever said to him, "Did you hear about the Howe girl?" And now he was a man, richly bearded, differently fragrant and interested in art. And he had been to Europe, too. While she hid in cellars. Part of her said to herself, Get lost, Chuck, but part of her longed to sit here with him and hear all his news—new names popping into her mind, old faces, remembrances. Seals broke in her mind, covers came off. It was the first time in months or years she had felt connected to the world at all.

An orgy of reminiscence. Time flew by, then Chuck

remembered there was someplace he was supposed to be, and leapt up. But before he left he hugged her again, and said "Well, I know where to find you," in a way that made her know he'd be by the next night, too.

"Okay," she said. It seemed to her that her voice was a croak, the rusty unused croak of the long immured; but he noticed nothing odd about her voice.

And now I'll have to disappear again, she thought as she locked the door after him and looked out the window over the display cardboards at the late laundromat crowd. She felt as flat and fake as the cardboard Kodak girl smiling in the window. "Sure, Chuck, let's do get together, I'm always here. Oh, I live over on Ashby Path. Sure." Now where would she go next?

On the run again, so this would be her last night at Photophobia, the most recent of her dumb boring jobs. She ought to be grateful to leave it, but instead her heart suddenly swelled with love for the Photophobia. She walked in a daze among the stacks of Magicubes, wrist straps and greeting cards.

HAPPY BIRTHDAY. BET YOU FEEL LIKE A TWENTY-YEAR-OLD.
(With a little luck you might get one!)

She stole this card and put it in her purse to send anonymously to Anton Wait. She would have liked to steal a good camera, but decided it was too risky, on account of the serial number. She settled for a cheap Instamatic no one would miss. Then she wrote a little lying note to Mr. Barnes, the manager, about her sick mother, and then locked everything tidily up for the last time, and set off walking home along the quiet night street.

Theo was getting a ride home from Marty and Harold Frank, and as they detoured around the back of the park, Theo noticed, without quite knowing how, the dispirited dark huddle of Ouida in her lump tweed coat, waiting on the corner by the lumberyard. Theo shrieked for Harold to stop. Harold stopped and backed the car along to where Ouida was standing. Theo called to her. Ouida looked frightened for a moment, people shouting to her out of strange cars; then she understood and came and got in. She sat in back next to Theo, who began to scold her.

"You shouldn't be out alone," she said. Ouida didn't seem to realize things about America. They say that other cultures seem safer to you than your own does because you don't really know what's going on. And this is a bad corner, near the freeway exit, transients pulling off here, looking for liquor or gas or stranded teenage hitchhikers.

Perhaps, though, Ouida did realize she shouldn't be there, for she seemed plenty glad and relieved to see Theo. "I was waiting for my friend but he never came," she explained. "I feel so angry. Hungry?" When she was upset, her English faltered.

"Angry," Theo said.

"Yes. Why do someone say they will come and then they don't? I think that man forgets what he say."

"Perhaps he was delayed," Theo suggested, wondering for the first time what Ouida's friend was like, and why she was defending him. But it was easy to mistrust Ouida's understanding of agreements made in English. Theo could imagine Mr. Griggs waiting impatiently somewhere else in his dark car.

"He do this before," Ouida complained. "I think this is no good. I don't know why someone would do like that." She was shivering. Poor Ouida. She was wearing perfume. How must it be, putting on perfume, hoping to please, left on a street corner, shivering in the dark, strange English sounds everywhere, far away. Theo herself shivered at her sudden sense of human otherness, her relieved sense that only by chance she herself had not been left on the street corner.

Ouida sighed. "I was anguished standing there." She

smiled. Her wide, trustful smile did not reveal the nature
of her anguish, only a glimpse of her complexity.

"Your friend, what does he do?" Theo asked.

"Heedo?"

"What is his job?"

"Oh. He is a watch, I think. A watch?"

"A what? Oh, a watchman."

"*Segurança*. That is how I know he is an honest man,
he guards a big factory. Once in his car we drove by the
big factory where he goes at night to guard it."

"A man of what age?"

"He have I think fifty. He was a married man, but his
wife was no good. She went away, and he takes care of
the kids very good. He has six kids, and the youngest is
Lonnie, who have twelve years. Then there are some big
girls. He says these big girls are some trouble, but I think
they are good girls, only they need a mother. Girls that
age need a mother. A father cannot say what needs to be
said to them."

And what on earth innocent Ouida would know to say
to them Theo could not imagine. She suddenly thought
of her nieces, Anton's daughters, and wondered if she
should say something to them, to make up for Anton's
baffled silences with them. But what? And of course they
did have mothers, Sandra and Teri. She thought of Ouida
trying to talk to a rambunctious gaggle of big black girls.
Then she realized that she did not know whether Mr.
Griggs was black or white.

She didn't like to ask, but which would he be? Watch-
men were usually black, weren't they? On the other hand,
it was usually black mothers, not fathers, who were left
with big broods of children, so perhaps Mr. Griggs was
white. Of course, she hurriedly reminded herself, it didn't
really matter a bit. She thought of the high-spirited teenage girls in tight clothes she saw walking home from
Orris High School, girls of all colors, shrieking with
laughter and shoving each other and smoking, and she

could imagine poor Ouida hesitantly trying to speak to girls like that. It wouldn't do, it wasn't going to do. Six children; really, no wonder he was looking for an innocent defenseless person like Ouida. An American woman would have more sense than to marry a man with six children.

Or maybe Ouida would like a big family? The laughter, maybe it would sound more like Brazil to her. Sometimes she heard Ouida laughing with her friends on the phone, hilarious loud laughing—we never laugh like that. Yet we are happy, are we not? Loud laughter is just not our style? Ouida and her Brazilian friends get so excited, their voices get louder and louder, their laughter like whoops.

"One big boy in jail makes his father very sad," Ouida said. "A good boy but he got in with some bad people."

"You'd have to love him very much to take on a big family like that," Theo said in a cautionary way.

It was nearly midnight. Other residents of Ashby Path were coming home. A car pulled up in front of the hippie commune, formerly the home of Professor and Mrs. Truex, who had moved to Rossmoor, down in Walnut Creek. People carried boxes of Mason jars inside. Odd. Alistair's wife must be putting up a lot of something, Theo thought. Ideas of thrift and prudence the young had now, or was it mistrust of the world? She decided to go inside for some milk before bed: she always felt agitated by these meeting nights. Anton pulled up, waved and drove around to put the car in the garage.

Anton was contented; had spent the evening showing slides at the Greenbrae chapter of a Sierra Club fundraising event, then making love to an old friend from the Bay Area. Nonetheless he slowed his step a little outside the girl's bedroom on his way upstairs, thinking of how she was always in there, but never with a man. Why not? What was it? How beautiful she was. Behind the blue blandness of her gaze did she conceal thoughts—or no thoughts? He wondered what kinds of books she read. She had told them she was a history major, but he couldn't remember ever seeing any books about history. Once he saw her reading a child's book, *The Scarlet Pimpernel*.

Ouida followed Mr. Anton. She had recovered herself and once again could feel the beneficial effects of the elevating words and healing rays she had received at the religious service. She saw that purposeful good forces were at work; for instance, behind the arrival of Miss Theo to save her at the dark bus stop. That could be no accident.

As she climbed the stairs, however, her body, which had been warm, as was the air around her, from the divine light, began to feel the chill reality, the special chill that seemed to belong to this house. There were things in this house—the specter of her enemy Colonel Pacific hiding in the hallway. Immigration officers perhaps. Conquistadors in the upper corridors; the wraith, Miss Theo, unable to do dishes. She didn't understand the people in this house, though she did love Lynn, and Anton, and said prayers for them sometimes—not every night, for she had much else to pray about, but about as often as they deserved.

Poor little Lynn, she was thinking, needs prayers every night. There is a sadness around her you could see, like an aura. Ouida could sometimes see auras, and Lynn's was sick and yellow. Ouida's loving heart prompted her to stop before the shut door of Marybeth's room and uphold her palm, directing healing rays through the wood, which they were perfectly powerful enough to penetrate.

Thus, with radiant hand outstretched, Theo found

Ouida as Theo ran on tiptoe up the stairs. Ouida smiled at Theo with silent complicity. Theo contrived an approving smile and tiptoed on, wondering, though, if rays could travel through walls. It was somehow troubling to imagine Ouida irradiating you without your knowing it.

All in, everybody in now. Marybeth, lying in her bed, hears them all, recognizes each step: Anton's light brisk step, Ouida's clumsy clop—which mysteriously stops outside her room—and next the tripping skidding old Theo, who always runs up the stairs.

Marybeth lies in her bed listening to the footsteps and looking at the patterns of light and shadow on the white wall of her room, vague rays and dapplings of moonlight and streetlight. Ouida seems to be lurking outside her room an extra long time. What can she want? Is she listening or what? It doesn't exactly make her uncomfortable, but she's puzzled. There is Theo's brisk step whisking by. Ouida clops off at last.

Tonight's my last night in this room, she thinks. In the safe darkness, her bed and this room seem like the best places in the world. She has been changing rooms for—how many decades does it seem?—and each time she has to leave one, she gets this same yearning and love for it, as now. She wants to stay in it, unmoving and weighted down with warm blankets, as if sleeping hidden under a hill or in a grave. Over her bureau in the moonlight, the pattern of bloody feathers marches against the wall.

She feels glad that everyone else is home, back to the safety and chastity of this house, everyone lying singly in his narrow bed, as if they were all inmates of an asylum. She imagines all the footsteps and creakings of the narrow beds in each room as the sleepers climb silently into them. She imagines all the others to be too old and too innocent to be lying awake suffering—as she now

begins to suffer, and often suffers—sexual desire, which
will keep her awake.

It is always like this when life turns bad and she has
big problems and decisions; she stays awake worrying
about getting laid. It doesn't make sense. But it is against
nature, this sleeping alone; maybe nature overrides political problems. Maybe I'll just sleep around a little now,
she thinks; why should I live like some nun this way?
She wishes she had brought Chuck Sweet home with her.
Why didn't she—she isn't going to stay here now. She
can imagine making it with Chuck all right.

She turns her thoughts by reciting a litany which by
now has the soothing properties of a magic rhyme but
has no more meaning than that: I did what I thought was
right. If some people had not taken risks, all the war and
killing would have gone on. Many more people would
have died. It was the right thing to do. You have to act
on your beliefs. What good are beliefs if they have no
consequences? What kind of cheap beliefs are those? I
will abide by the consequences of my beliefs. But as usual
she can barely remember what her beliefs were, and the
recitation puts her to sleep.

Good night, good night. Ouida and Theo, in their rooms,
shake out their nighties, the dainty nightclothes of the
unmarried. Anton has slept in his underwear since the
Second World War. Ouida says her prayers, including
one for Mr. Griggs, an appeal to receive the ability to
understand his ways.

For this charitable prayer she is granted the realization
that maybe she oughtn't to care, maybe he is no good for
her anyway. One thing, he is so black-skinned. In Brazil
that does not matter, but darkness here is different; it is
not an advantage. Also American men treat women differently and leave them to stand on street corners. In
Brazil your brothers would not permit this, they would

come for you themselves. Two prayers for her brothers, one a pastor, one *advogado*.

I hope tonight I will not have to get up in the night, she thinks. It is the same thought she has every night, and has had since she was a little girl: maybe tonight I will not have to get up. Although here it is not a bad thing—only a few steps to the bathroom, and it is perfectly easy to put the light on—still the thought always comes to her.

When she was a little girl, how she hated creeping out into the darkness, sometimes two or three times in one night, back by the fence, afraid of the goat, afraid of the snake, afraid of the warm darkness itself.

My kidneys are much stronger now, with Johrei, in America, now that I am nearly thirty. Still the kidneys are not altogether strong. She has always to get up in the night, and always, when first walking, for a moment she feels the terror of the Brazilian darkness and her fear of the shadowy goat on his rope waiting unseen.

She adds a prayer that she will be able to understand Griggs, understand what he says, his pronunciation. "He speaks so different," she complained to Roberta once.

"How can you go out with him, then?" Roberta asked. "If you can't talk to him?"

"It is my fault, my English. I am just nice and polite when I don't understand. I smile and laugh, and he does not mind if I know or not. Well, he is so funny, he moves his head like this." She bobbed her head and shook it.

Maybe he had not actually said he would pick her up. Sometimes she got things wrong. Yet she had been so sure. On the corner by the bus. She can always understand what Mr. Anton says, as he speaks so clearly and distinctly, and is so *educado*. Not so good Miss Theo, who speaks too fast.

* * *

Theo, like an abbess, ticks everybody off in her mind, counting them all safely tucked in bed. This ritual of counting and thinking of them all every night is less from concern than from the need to calm herself with the idea that deep sleep lies ahead for them all, there are to be no more interruptions for eight hours. Once, some time ago, Anton made a noise, bringing home a woman friend, but Theo had settled that: it was one thing when he was nineteen, but now in his fifties, now really. No, it isn't sex I mind, idiot, it's the disturbance; I'm too old for that, be considerate, the horror of having to talk to some boring stranger in the morning; all right, even if it's someone I know, I don't want them here in the morning. All those years of being married—does he mind sleeping alone now? His bed has a little striped coverlet, like a child's bed, or a bed in a barrack.

The Co-op meeting hums in her head: whales, Japanese, geese, French, blowing up the Sutro Tower, Fontana Prison. Freedom Through Movement. She feels angry when she thinks of the people who say that programs like this are silly or condescending; speeches occur to her; she is addressing the membership, making impassioned defenses.

"Oh, really," she hears herself say aloud, "I'm not a fool, you know. Of course I understand that people don't get done over by attending a dance seminar or an art show or a play or a psychiatrist. I realize that."

But these poor people are poor cripples, she thinks. The world is full of the crippled. What are we to do? Mustn't we act on the chance that someday some ray, some shiver of beauty or healing will help them; if it only helped one person, it would still be worth it. What can it hurt to amuse people who otherwise have no amusement, even assuming it doesn't help them in any permanent way?

We must pass our lives somehow, Theo thinks. Each man is stuck with only himself to live with his whole life long; can't we help him see how to get along? Whether he cares, that's his own business. Maybe he doesn't care. Supposing he doesn't care . . .

Maybe I won't go, Theo thinks. Pride and foolishness. Image of meddlesome do-gooders. She remembers, with a taste like the taste of metal, that passion of frustration when, in spite of your best efforts, goodness and right do not ensue.

What great leaps they can make, men can, they can leap in the air like cats. Could you teach them to leap over walls? In the eye of her mind they are wearing purple leotards, like the character in the comic book, and they dance a *danse macabre*.

They are all good sleepers. Anton, now nearing sixty, notices he doesn't need as much sleep as he used to, so he gets up earlier, goes to bed the same time as before. When he goes to bed, he is asleep. Theo, too. Ouida sometimes will wake, for the bathroom, or with palpitations of the heart, a ricocheting and shuddering in her breast, as though she were sleeping over a mine. Then she will be frightened, as her mother died of her heart; also her half sister, while waiting for the bus in São Paulo, dropped down dead on the street corner. But if Ouida lies quiet on these wakeful nights, holding her fear like a tender egg, the horrid battering will cease and she will be able to slide back to sleep again.

Theo has always been a good sleeper, simple as that, can sleep on trains, in anterooms. That is a good characteristic for a performing artist. Marybeth is a constant sleeper, sleeps in afternoons, late in mornings, early the nights she doesn't work at Photophobia. She sleeps more than anyone alive, except sometimes at night, when she wakes oppressed with her bitter solitude. But most of the time she sleeps through, as if sunk into clay, already embalmed.

All are therefore sleeping soundly, each in his room in

his bed: Theo in the bed she has had since childhood;
Anton under his striped coverlet; Ouida, her head lying
trustfully under a heavy mirror hanging on the wall just
above it, the mirror she practices self-hypnotism in. Self-
hypnotism is part of her Rosicrucian study. Anton's bed
has a board in it for his back.

Now it is the middle of the night, or near morning; it
is that time in between, with the world still dark but
growing paler in the fields behind the house, and the
streetlights still on. All are awakened by screams,
screams, screams.

Theo sits up electric, thinking, as she has thought at
every nocturnal fright for thirty years, God, it is the Finn
in my room, and her stomach radiates with frizzles of
fear, as if sparklers had been lit inside it. Ouida sits up
muttering "*Meu Deus*, it is the goat"; Anton raises his
ear from his pillow to locate the direction of the shriek,
and gets up.

Marybeth wakes herself with her screams. Will they
come, did they hear? Their footsteps come scuffling down
the hall. Burglar, rapist, night knifist, they are all thinking, bravely coming along anyway.

"I'm sorry, I'm awfully sorry," she says through the
door. "I guess it was a dream. I guess it was me. I'm
okay, yes, I'm sorry." Then she lies awake a long time
after they've gone back to bed again, trying to remember
her dream.

THURSDAY

5. Farewells

Theo always woke seconds before the rooster did, in a terror that it had crowed. She had never gotten over worrying that the chickens were a bother to the neighbors, despite knowing that the real neighbors over the years had gone away, and strangers came, communes and boarding houses full of people philosophically committed to chickens. These big old houses.

Well, their life style is not our life style, Theo had said of communes; still and all we have to respect their way of being. I can see that communes are the wave of the future. People are being conditioned to accept diminished personal space.

But would they ever wish to endure chickens? Theo had sometimes thought of proposing an ordinance forbidding chickens, secretly, to escape these sensations of apprehension and guilt each morning. And Anton's insistence upon a rooster, such a boring psychological quirk, so obvious, fertility and virility, so predictable.

But she did rather enjoy getting up and going out to gather the eggs. She wore her apron to do this, stalking out through the low morning fog or beams of sunlight in the fresh grass to the ramshackle of coops, to bring the warm eggs in for breakfast; it was the nicest time of day, before the heat became too strong, before the wind blew.

Anton this morning, as usual, refused to eat the eggs, no doubt because of the cholesterol.

"I don't know why we have them, then," Theo said, also as usual.

They both commented on the strong smell, even in here in the breakfast room, not exactly a disagreeable smell, but a strong smell coming from the bowls of Ouida's *carne seca* soaking in the pantry.

Ouida came down, carrying her book, wearing her robe, which always somehow suited her better than her ordinary clothes did. In her robe she looked exotic, even glamorous, rather than plump. She looked like a dictator's wife, all kept and cruel. She went and stirred the *carne seca* before sitting down, then ate two eggs and put about half a ton of sugar into her coffee.

"This is the way we drink it in Brazil," she explained, as usual. The girl had not come down yet. Theo supposed she must be tired, after all that screaming in the night.

BUY GOLD PRUDENT INVESTORS ADVISED, said a headline on Anton's paper. For our golden years, Theo thought.

"Anton, you aren't happy," she said aloud, rather surprised to hear herself speak. It had only been her private thought. Anton looked at her. He was wearing a silk robe of deep blue, like a rich man in a movie.

"Women often say that, 'You aren't happy,' " he said. "It's usually a stratagem to reprove philandering. It's what they say when they want you to settle down. But, as you see, Teddy, here I am, settled down."

"Well, with your old-maid sister," Theo said, "a situation which hardly exists any more in the civilized world."

" 'You aren't happy.' A woman tries that idea out on you like ice on a pond," Anton went on, "trying to see where she will fall through into your secret self. But here you're not on very thin ice, Teddy, for I am happy.''

''That Meesis Aheem,'' Ouida burst out, ''she is all the time saying, about Brazil, how it is such a shame about all the poor there, that there is such a difference between the very rich and very poor. She never say this about India. I think people never criticize their own native land. Sometimes I want to say to her, 'What about India, there is many poor there, too, much poverty'—is that not so? Is Brazil the more advanced, would you say, or India?''

''Oh, Brazil, I'd say,'' Theo guessed. ''India has such a population problem.''

''Or you could say that women are like prospectors around a burnt-out mine, looking for the last traces of gold—if any—remaining in the slag,'' Anton was going on, composing his metaphor like a still photo. ''It's peculiar, though charming, how women always do want gold love if they can dig it out.''

''It makes me so hungry sometimes, how she talks that way about Brazil, and she has never been there. People talk much about places they have not been. Before I came here, I talked about here, too, with people who have also not been here, and they tell me how in America there are problems for a black person.''

''Angry. It makes you angry,'' Anton said, though he hadn't appeared to listen.

''Angry. Before I came, I was very worried about this, because people told me, 'Oh, there it is very dangerous for a black person to ride a bus and everything. They kill black people for riding on buses.' But this is not so, I find.''

''Oh, it is so,'' Theo cried. ''Terrible things are done here.''

Marybeth always slept soundly and late because of her state of constant dread, which made sleeping pref-

erable to waking. She never heard the rooster, or the
rising cackle from the coops, and her room was on the
west side of the house, where the sun came last. As
soon as one sunbeam pried itself in, then she would wake
up. Then the dread, like a stone incubus, would come
and sit on her belly. Every morning she would have
to battle its weight off, or she couldn't get out of bed at
all.

But sometimes, for a split second as the shaft of sunlight struck her eyelids or she heard a bird call, for a split
second before she remembered, then she would be happy,
with a vegetable sense of happy light. Then the memories, like stones, came rolling down again.

Like stones all the realizations this morning—that she
would have to go away, pack up, disappear, strew her
trail with lies. She remembered Chuck Sweet and the Co-
op and the long talk at Photophobia, delicious and beautiful, like a poison present. But now she would have to
move on. This always happened, it seemed to her, when
she became almost happy somewhere, got too uncomfortable; then the specter of discovery would loom and
she'd have to move on.

But she wouldn't have wanted to miss seeing Chuck,
that was the funny thing about it. She lay thinking about
him. A familiar face was a calming thing, a tremendous
luxury which is underappreciated by other people. The
sound of a familiar name is as wonder-giving as old stories, loved stories.

So now she just lay here, cherishing the still room,
feeling love for it. She had already decided that when she
got up she would go, at last, to consult Julie, the new-
identity person. She was beyond doing anything for herself any more, and lay awash in her bed as in a drifting
raft. She felt as tired as if she hadn't slept in the night at
all.

* * *

A real false identity, a thorough, papered, professionally prepared, written-in-gold one, had not come her way before. They were expensive, hard to get, and in a way she hadn't really wanted one, not really, had clung to what shreds of her true self were left. Even if you were layered with false names like scarves and shawls, you were still Marybeth at the naked core. It was another matter to begin life utterly anew, being someone else entirely. What if you screwed up your new life, too? It was like tearing yourself up into little bits and putting them down the garbage disposal, leaving nothing behind, to take a new identity through and through. From what do you construct your new self, ectoplasm?

Do you try to forget the real memories of your life: seeing the bear cub on the road, or finding the deserted house deep in the forest, with the food dried on the plates, petrified food; or the people you've made it with? Do you forget the sight of the dead man covered in tarp being carried out of the torn hole in the side of the building, though she had seen only photographs of this; she had been far away. But it was her memory, ineradicable; it was her deed.

What would the new self be called? Oh, shit, she thought, let them call me anything, Norma, Irma, let someone else decide. It would be nice to leave that up to someone else for a change, leave it up to Julie.

Julie, as Marybeth had known for a long time, was the person who found identities for people who needed them, usually draft avoiders wanting to come back from Canada, occasionally felons, often Alistair's Australian friends who had it in mind to come make their fortunes in the States but then went home again. Sometimes other sorts of illegal aliens, but not usually, because most illegal aliens were too innocent, too fundamentally honest, too dumb about the way things work. To take advantage of this kind of deal, you almost had to be American.

Julie had explained it all to Marybeth one day, had divined with the sixth or seventh sense she had by now that Marybeth was someone who could stand to know. She had stopped by the yard as Marybeth was mowing the lawn for Theo. She was dedicated to helping people, she told Marybeth. She had helped a lot of people to a life free of fear, she said.

"Of course people could do it for themselves, it's not some magic trick," she said, "it just takes time and research. I could tell them how to do it. You just look through old newspapers and find someone that died when they were little but if they'd lived they'd have been about your age. The best thing is when the whole family died— that way there's not much risk of relatives or whatever. Family of six wiped out at crossing, that's one I had once, and I got four sets of I.D. from that. Birth certificates, drivers' licenses, credit cards. You can completely change yourself. If it's a good I.D., that's the end of the matter forever, if they haven't got your fingerprints any-place." The rumor underground was that Julie had some supernatural talent for finding new identities. Other people could shuffle through old newspapers for weeks. Let her help me, Marybeth thought. I hope it won't cost too much.

She peeled off her thoughts, her enshrouding morning dread, and got up and put on her jeans and blue shirt, trying to feel resolute. She'd go down and see Theo and Anton one last time, and Ouida, if she hadn't left for school. She began to pack up the stuff she'd need in her new life.

In the top drawer she kept some old clothes from the thrift store which she'd never wear, and some books she would never read, and never touched with her bare hands, and a jar of oily-skin grains, though she had dry skin. She didn't know if this would put off real investigators,

but she felt the need to deceive and confuse even in her
dresser drawers. She left the dark red lipstick and the
odd china saucers she had bought to put under plants.
Then she had become afraid to commit herself to a plant.

From the bottom drawer she took the stuff she would
really use—underwear and another pair of jeans, and a
couple of headscarves. From the closet she took her disguises—sexy black dress, print housedress, books, comb,
little precious notebook. She wanted to take the pile of
Anton's photos—she looked a long time at them. But
never take things from one life to another, that is the
rule.

She put all these things into her backpack and took a
last look around her to make sure she wasn't leaving anything she would miss later, or any clues. It was too nice
a room; she should have known. A person in her position
can't have a nice room or a comfortable feeling. She went
downstairs, thrusting out the sad thoughts, and thinking
up her lies, choosing one from her big reliable storehouse
of lies.

At the breakfast table Theo was still thinking of the terrible things; the thought of terrible things battered in her
breast, elevating her pulse. Anton continued serenely to
read the paper, thinking no doubt of happiness, of gold,
of beautiful trees and rocks; while she was obliged by
her nature to think of people, prison, terrible things, resentfully. On the back page of Anton's paper, facing her,
was a picture of an elephant in a zoo. "That is how
prison must be," she said as she drank her coffee, prison
like a zoo, rows of cages but with men in them instead
of lions and elephants. The men would stand at the front
of the cages rattling the bars and snarling. Anton glanced
at the picture of the zoo and shrugged.

"Only the most docile, those having streaks of gentleness, will want to come to the dance seminar, no doubt.

The secret of their gentleness would not have been evident to the brutal prison guards, but perhaps to the chaplain or the psychologist, who chose them to come," Theo said. Anton made no reply.

What would they be wearing? Theo wondered. Not striped suits—how the brain is burdened with cartoon versions of life. Not zebra-striped suits, just some sort of baggy uniform which you couldn't dance in. They would have to wear leotards and tights, like any dancers. That would have to be arranged.

Can a life be changed, rescued, restored, enriched by art? That Theo did not know, and she did not know if anybody knew.

"I'm planning to participate in that dance program, after all," Theo said. "It's this Saturday." Anton looked up politely. Clearly he didn't remember.

"At Fontana Prison. The program the Quakers sponsor—Friends Outside—and the Co-op donates money and so on. They call the dance seminar Freedom Through Movement."

Recollection and possibly amusement altered his expression. He had a dim view of do-gooding. Theo had always wondered how he could have come to take people so little seriously and yet feel so fond of large inanimate objects, like redwood trees.

"If I were you, I would keep away from here yourself, on Saturday," she advised, "unless you mean to help Ouida with her *feijoada* fête. Hundreds of people in our back yard, isn't that so, Ouida?"

"Oh, I hope so, it is very important to my life," Ouida said.

"Maybe I'll stay. I'm very fond of Ouida's *feijoada*," Anton said.

Theo poured more coffee, contemplated more toast. "I really do feel that the dance can give meaning to otherwise restricted, embittered lives, and also think of the talent, the potential, of these young men, many of them such fine athletes. It will be interesting, worthwhile.''

''It's worthwhile, of course,'' Anton said.

''But,'' said Theo, ''I didn't think they'd have asked me if I were a young woman.''

''Of course they would. You're the best teacher in this area, a talented, qualified woman . . .''

''But you see, if I were young and beautiful they couldn't ask me to go there, into a prison among all those men. I know.'' A little bitter this pot of coffee tasted, a little salty.

''You won't be among them exactly, Teddy. There are special areas, every precaution.'' Of course he didn't un-derstand the sudden salty taste of her coffee.

''Art may go among them, but not love. Does it make sense, one without the other?'' Theo wondered aloud. This remark for some reason made Anton laugh, and that put an end to it. Theo had never been able to anticipate what would start Anton laughing.

''Art has soothing and elevating properties,'' Anton said, ''which nobody has ever been able to prove of love.''

''Nijinsky himself could be in Fontana and no one would know until someone gives these young men a chance!'' cried Theo.

Ouida here leaned forward with her book, to ask for help with something as she often did. ''Does 'man' mean 'woman' also, in English, in this case?'' Theo read the phrase and assured her that it did. It was time for Ouida to go dress for her English class, at the Orris Community Adult School, where she also studied beginning typing.

Ouida had once explained to them her theory about typing: ''I have read that typing is the avenue through which the consciousness is bound to the universe. When you type, it seems, the words flow from the fingers, in through the eyes and out through the fingers, but they do not pass through the brain, so that sometimes the words that appear are unexpected and strange, dictated by outside forces, do you think?''

''What about this, 'aspiration'?'' Ouida asked now. '' 'Aspiration,' like *'aspirador'*? That is confusing.''

''Hopes, struggles,'' Theo said.

Ouida laughed. ''*'Aspirador'* is the vacuum cleaner in Portuguese. And here is another thing I do not understand today,'' she said, tracing a line with her brown finger: ''God is a Number endowed with motion which is felt but not demonstrated. Balzac.''

Theo read it over, aloud. ''That is metaphysics,'' she said severely, ''which I never understand.'' All the same, she looked at Ouida's book when Ouida had gone upstairs to dress.

· Do not be deceived by false philosophy. Millions of humans try to excuse their perplexity and helplessness within this vale of tears by saying that they are victims of FATE. The FATALIST believes that human beings are the mere puppets of fate. They do not believe in the very powers of reason and will that make man human, and distinguish man from the brute. They do not believe in human aspirations, wherein man strives toward perfection.

''Your life would have more meaning if you helped others, Anton,'' Theo said.

''Oh? No, I've given up on people. I don't mind contributing to the preservation of the physical environment. I think I do my part there. Nothing else seems worthwhile.''

Deeply shocked, Theo pressed her knuckles and stared. Given up on people! What can have happened to him, in his life, that he should think in such a way? How little she knew him, or anybody.

''Oh, Anton,'' she said. ''The children of migrant farm workers, think of them. Think of the handicapped!''

* * *

Just then the girl came down, wearing her flushed, pretty morning look, wrapped in her silence, her long hair done up today in a prim way. They gave her jam and toast.

"I heard from my brother last night, in Wyoming," she told them. "He has a job doing something on a ranch—a farm or ranch—and he says if I come right away I could work until school starts, doing seasonal work, and you can make up to three hundred dollars a week." Her blue eyes swept them like the eyes of a Siamese cat and with the same expression. "So I think I'll go. You can rent my room while I'm gone. I packed my stuff. I'll be back before school starts."

Theo and Anton sat surprised, Theo feeling pained at the idea of a new girl, and hurt that she should think they were the kind of greedy boarding-house keepers who rent a person's room with the person's spirit still flitting around in it and the bed still warm. Of course there was really nothing to be sorry about at the idea of Lynn visiting her nice decent young brother and making a lot of money climbing ladders in some orchard or whatever it was you picked in Wyoming. Surely there was nothing to pick in Wyoming?

"If you'll be back before school starts and still want your room here, dear, you might as well leave things as they are," Theo said. "Take some coffee, have some more toast." She and Anton sat like anxious parents watching the girl eat.

"I won't mind leaving Orris at this time of year," the girl said. "It's so hot, I hate the heat." She sighed. She would have liked to talk to them, and speak in her real voice, but she'd long since give up real conversations, maybe didn't even know how to have them any more. Though hadn't she talked to Chuck?

* * *

It was a funny fate, Marybeth thought, for someone who believed in saying what you thought and felt, to have to conceal everything you thought and felt, for all time. She could imagine a world in which everyone had so much to hide that no one could really say anything at all. Civilities only. It would be the new ice age. Some days she thought only in civilities; she had found when you lose the chance of saying what you think and feel you stop thinking and feeling, sort of.

"I just want to thank you for everything," she said civilly. "You've been very kind." Mr. Wait glanced at her over his paper, and she remembered his notes and thought she might be blushing slightly at the ambiguity of her little speech of thanks. But now he was reading again.

She ate as long as she could; then she'd finished and there didn't seem anything left to do but tell them goodbye again and go. She waited in the hall until Ouida came down, dressed for school and carrying her letter. Ouida held it out, still unopened, to Marybeth.

"Would you read it for me now? For it must be opened, though I do not think today is a particularly auspicious day either."

Marybeth took the letter, opened it and looked at it. It was a notice for Ouida to appear for a review of her visa. BRING YOUR PASSPORT, it said. Maybe, thought Marybeth, maybe I could get Julie to do something for Ouida, too. Or maybe she should just ignore this. Would they come get her?

"Well, it's just what you thought, but I wouldn't do anything yet," she instructed Ouida. "Pretend you were away on vacation and didn't get the letter, if they should come looking for you." Marybeth would ask Julie what to do.

"I do not think they will give me another visa," Ouida

admitted. "Even with a passport. They will say I must go when the school is over at the end of August. With a student visa, a visitor visa, either one, they make you go back. The only way to stay is to marry an American. And then they send you back anyway, even if married, if they think you have a false marriage for the purpose of staying here. One girl I know, Aparacida, they came upon her at five in the morning with flashlights. She was in her bed. They wanted to see if Carlos, her husband, was in the bed with her. They think she have married him because he has a green card, but it was not only that. She really loves Carlos. The love, however, is what they wanted to make certain about."

"Oh," cried Marybeth furiously, "they spy on everybody! They even spy into your bedroom. Well," she added, thinking about it, "I'm surprised they would do that to your friend, though—I thought they would only spy with flashlights like that on other Americans."

"Americans also. I find it confusing, because one other girl I know, at my school, is American, is a black girl, Leona, and they come upon her in the night, too, but in her case they wish to make sure that her husband is *not* living with her there. I do not understand this fully, but if he was there they would take away her money, something like that?"

"Oh, Ouida!" cried Marybeth. "You ought to go back to Brazil where your family is, where people love you."

"No, I never will, I think, if only I can escape it, for there I am a prisoner—all women are prisoners to the ideas of their brothers."

"Oh, I don't understand that, you could just tell your brothers to go screw," Marybeth said, wishing that a few brothers were all she had to worry about. "Ouida, I have to be gone for a while. Take care of yourself, take care," she said. Ouida put her arms around Marybeth and pressed her round cheek against Marybeth's.

"I will see you when you get back," said Ouida, "if they have not sent me away."

6. *Strange Gods*

Theo knew it was silly, this little gust of sadness wafting across the breakfast table, this little draft of regret. She knew the girl would come back in a few weeks, but she felt sad. She did not like changes; that was it, she knew. Anton buried in the paper that way, no wonder women kept divorcing him. She looked again at Ouida's book, left hopefully open on the table.

Man cannot change the wind. But his power of mind can help him to use the wind. Like the wind, like lightning, there are many forces in the universe. Some, believing them to be directed by FATE, do not resist them. But the true man can harness the forces of the universe, even as the wind and lightning. Men must learn to use their human powers. First they must learn what they are. . . .

Well, art must surely be one, she thought, feeling cheered by that, so that she stood up and would go dress and be happy that no one needed her today; she was not like other women, thank heavens, who drooped and saddened when no one needed them. Freedom and energy were the things. She would give ballet lessons in the afternoon and she would feed the chickens at dusk—Anton's chickens—but these were not activities that bother and gnaw.

She ran lightly up the stairs. It was a rule with her to run upstairs, but occasionally she was obliged to pause for breath on the landing—well, sixty years old; and now, while pausing just an instant, she happened to smell a sort of burning smell coming from Ouida's room.

She stood closer outside Ouida's door sniffing, and it

was undeniably a burning smoky smell, but no smoke appeared. No heat to her palm pressed flat against Ouida's door. She knocked to make sure it wasn't Ouida herself in there burning, or straightening her hair with a curling iron. It wasn't a hair smell exactly, and it was very faint, even imaginary. She drew hesitantly away when Ouida didn't answer. Perhaps there was no smell.

But then, at the top of the stairs, it seemed more distinct—it was maybe no more than the slightest warming of the air, but it was something, and she went back to stand in front of Ouida's door again. She'd better check.

Feeling really very abashed, she did just open Ouida's door and peek in. The smell was more intense but no sight of blaze or billow of smoke. Theo stepped hesitantly in. The blue eyes of Jesus reproached her, watching her from the wall over Ouida's bed. Theo knew it was Jesus, though she hadn't ever seen this picture. Blue eyes. She faltered, arrested by the look on his pale, lamb-like face. She had never seen this picture before but recognized Jesus watching her. She avoided his glance and looked around for the fire.

Ouida had moved the heavy plate mirror from its place over the dresser to the wall above where her head would lie on its pillow. Trusting, reverent soul, to imagine it wouldn't decapitate her in her sleep. Why had she done this? Tidy coverlet tucked up, brushes and bits of jewelry and letters neatly arranged on dresser, and no sign of the source of the faint—What was it? Where was it? Theo looked in the bathroom but found nothing there but a rather horrid mess of bloody chicken feathers in the tooth glass. The smell had to be coming from the closet.

Perhaps some pipe or heating duct ran through there? Theo opened the door. A little squat candle melting in a dish on the closet shelf, with aluminum foil spread underneath the dish, no doubt a precaution, and the candle flame reverently illuminating a sort of printed design involving triangles thumbtacked on the wall. The top of the closet was streaked with smoke, though this candle was not smoking; it was inoffensively burning itself and itself only. The flame didn't come near Ouida's clothing or anything made of paper or anything flammable. Still . . .

Theo's eyes in the gloom of the candlelit closet picked out several pairs of Ouida's rather wide shoes, a suitcase or two in back, a box of candles. Ouida's altar, evidently. Theo was stricken. She closed the door and hurried out of Ouida's room.

Her first impulse was to go down and tell Anton. He would just deal with it in a straightforward, obvious way, like telling Ouida to put out her candle. But she hated admitting she'd gone into Ouida's room that way, like a snoop, like a landlady. Or she could tell the truth, that she'd smelled something burning; anyone would go check up on something burning. But nothing was burning really. It had been what? Only a little trick of a draft or crack in the wall that sent a little—She couldn't even smell it herself now, as she stood taking deep breaths on the landing. It would be obvious to anyone that she'd been snooping on Ouida's room.

And yet Ouida couldn't be allowed to keep an open flame burning in an enclosed space in this old wooden house; that was out of the question!

Her religion, no doubt, Theo realized, as she went on up to her own room. Or one of her religions, she seemed to have so many, a funny thing considering Ouida was so intelligent and pleasant; odd that she should be so credulous.

Of course an open flame in a closet was not intelligent; it was awfully stupid. Theo could imagine the insidious crackling flames stealing over them as they slept, the smoke perhaps overcoming them before they woke at all; or maybe they would experience some awareness before death. Flames leaping around them, searing throats of smoke, scorching skin, the shrieks of sirens helpless below the windows, the glorious window in the Redwood Dining Room illumined blood red. Apocalypse.

She thought as she dressed. What to do? The only thing she could think of to do was to creep into Ouida's room herself, and set fire to Ouida's clothes on the sly, to account for discovering her candle. The absurdity of this made her laugh. Fighting fire with fire. No, there must be something more sensible. In a way she wished that Ouida would move away, too, now the girl was moving away, and she and Anton could travel. How peaceful to have no one to care for day after day after day.

As she went downstairs again, she breathed deeply by Ouida's room and smelled nothing. In a way it would be a relief, would be lovely to be as simple as Ouida, as clear and bright as winter air. How could Ouida be a marvel of complexity and deep-hearted as a Piranesi person, as Theo believed all people must be—and also a simple truster of lit candles? Perhaps there's a moment in the history of a person, or of his line, she thinks, where faith is officially dropped, lost like a family fortune.

Faith. She and Anton never had been given any. Someone must have lost it; it must have been Mother, she thought. One day while singing Episcopal hymns she must have got a suspicion, or some prayer she really meant didn't come through and her heart hardened. And then, too, a lot of women of Mother's generation thought they couldn't have both religion and the deep love of a man, in the sexual way, though this was not something Mother had ever discussed. "Our family was always Episcopalian," she would say as they walked past the church, in a voice regretful but brisk, like Satan cast out. Theo and Anton had never gone to Sunday School.

Nobody our age believes in God any more, Theo thought. I suppose we're getting to the age to get religion again, that belated piety that comes over people, though it never came over Mother, and I don't feel any piety coming over me. Really it's the young, with their moist hopeful hearts, their trustfulness, who take up piety. Like Ouida. The old are indifferent or know better. Still, she thinks, I'd try to clear my heart if I could.

She can. She has always been able to make her heart clear and trusting the minute she gets out of the house, the minute she steps out on the porch and begins to un-chain her bicycle, leaving the piety to Ouida, maybe even to Marybeth; also the housework.

If only it hadn't worked out like this, Marybeth was thinking as she walked over to Julie's house. Could I have guessed I'd screw up my life so bad? Me who nothing ever happened to, I never expected anything to happen to me.

She darted along the sidewalk, wearing her pack, look-ing wishfully up and down Ashby Path for Chuck, wish-fully and a little fearfully, as if she expected him to be hovering nearby with cohorts of Feds; as if they would jump out from behind the big walnut trees. But no one was to be seen.

If only it was true that somebody, a big shadow or other presence, could jump out at you out of your child-hood and grab you and say, "All's canceled, I'm taking you back with me. Look here, what's done is done; now back we go to Bettendorf, Iowa." Chuck the agent of reclaim. But of course he wasn't there. Then she realized she *was* being followed; it was Carlyle, happy about an outing, trotting along at her heels. Carlyle, a skin-colored short-haired dog, really ugly, with a spotted blue eye. Marybeth sent him home with stern remonstrances.

At Julie's house, the Australian guy, Alistair, Julie's old man, greeted her in the hall. "Julie's in there in the kitchen," he said. "In theeaah," he said, in his way.

Julie was pasting labels on jars and writing neatly on them "Plum 1975," in a little hand: "Plum + Apple 1975."

"You mentioned once something about—about knowing somebody who could set up a new set of I.D.," Marybeth said at once.

"That's right, me,"Julie said.

"I think that's the best thing for me now, in my circumstances, just a whole new person, new birth certificate, new karma, everything."

"Aw, I can't guarantee the karma," Julie said.

"Not that I acknowledge the validity of licenses and papers issued by the corporate state," Marybeth said facetiously. "Is it expensive?"

"Yes, it is." Julie sounded sorry. "The thing is, there aren't that many identities to be had, there's just a finite number, so they cost a lot; it's like diamonds or pearls. Plus there's a certain amount of risk for me, or for whoever actually procures the documents—it's using the mails and all that. I have to get about seven hundred fifty."

"I haven't got that now, I've got maybe a hundred dollars. I'd be getting a job, though."

"There's a limited quantity, after all, and that makes it expensive. These are the actual identities of formerly living people, properly recorded in the files of public agencies and so on. These aren't forged or fake and that's the difference. With my method you can expect to live a hassle-free undetected life, no knocks on the door. It's taken me a long time to work out the refinements of my method."

"Oh, I understand that," Marybeth said humbly.

"I've got a few names in the works but nothing definite yet. As a matter of fact, I was planning to go to Reno today, to do some research there, and maybe I'll have something you could use when I get back. I have some leads to follow up on in Reno. Anyway, names from around here are riskier, if you mean to stay in this area."

"It doesn't matter where I go."

"Look, are you working now?"

"No, I had to quit. The thing is, I think someone knows I'm here. I can't stay around here, that's the whole point. This is like the last place for me, and I can't stay here either; you should hear where I've been, how long I've been . . ."

"It would have to wait until I got back from Reno in any case, and I have a problem about getting up there today, and anyway, it might be as long as three weeks even, assuming I get something suitable.

"I want it to be perfect, forever. I would forever have to become this new person, and I accept that. I can't stand being a hundred people any more, I can't even remember all my names any more," said Marybeth, hearing her voice rise and tremble.

"I don't like to hear the details of a person's reasons," Julie said. "That way if I ever get asked, it's true when I say I don't know who people are. Would you like some coffee?"

"Thank you," Marybeth said anxiously. "And could you ever get anything for Latinos? For a woman about thirty?"

"Hardly ever," Julie said. "Latinos are much harder because the records kept are so bad. No one bothers to keep track of them, as if they didn't even exist."

"That's what you'd expect, I guess," Marybeth said, "of this society."

"As a matter of fact," said Julie presently to the silent and abject Marybeth, "you *could* help me out. There's a way that you could help and that way I could help *you* quicker."

"All right, sure."

"My problems is my kid, Chen-yu. I usually leave him in the day care center, but it turns out he cries the whole time he's there. I just found this out. I've been taking him there for months and he's been crying for months and they just told me. So I have to get a sitter. But if you could baby-sit him, just take him to the park or wherever each day for a couple of days, till I get back, I'd go to Reno today and get started. I mean, I've just been waiting until I could make some arrangements."

"What about—where would he sleep? I don't have a place right now. I told them . . ."

"You'd bring him home here. Alistair—his father—is home at night, or someone's here. He has to sleep in his own bed or he cries all the time, and you could get his supper for him here. He's used to this routine, having supper here. Just keep him away from here until about five o'clock today and tomorrow both, and I could probably be back Friday night, or Saturday night at the latest."

"Let me come with you," Marybeth said. "I'll come along to Reno and watch him there, and we can stay in a motel or something like that. That'd at least get me away from here. I think this guy lives right around here—somebody from my home town, he knows me perfectly well."

"Chen-yu throws up in the car," Julie said. "Anyway, if something went out on you, Interstate 80 is the first place they'd watch. It'd be dumb for you to come along. You'd better just stay right around here. Change your hair."

"Look," said Marybeth, "could I stay here, too? When I bring him back at night? I haven't got a place. I told the people where I was staying that I was leaving for Wyoming."

Julie looked at her thoughtfully, the sort of undressing look you usually got from men.

"No," she said. "Um, it's my policy with people I'm fixing up that they shouldn't be associated with us at all. You could stay in Sacramento, at the Y."

Thinks I'd try to make it with Alistair, Marybeth saw. Thinks I'm that dumb. "You'll have to tell me what he eats and all that," she said, shot with misgivings. Why couldn't the kid stay with his own father? What about the other people in this place? It was funny that among all those people they couldn't watch one little kid.

"I'll pay you," Julie went on. "Same rate as the day care center—no, like a sitter, one seventy-five an hour. You wait here and I'll go get his stuff together. Whatever you do, don't let him touch that jam."

Rows and rows of neat jelly glasses with the jam a funny color, unappetizing. A funny smell on the air, not jam.

"In fact, let's go in the other room and get out of here with this stuff," Julie said, carefully taking Chen-yu's hand. She closed the kitchen door after them, and left Marybeth and Chen-yu standing in the dining room. The dining room had a piano and a single bed covered with a Madras spread and the usual sorts of Mao posters, so that many things came back to Marybeth all at once, estranging her more than ever from her past self, her fierce and caring self.

She and Chen-yu stared at each other. A little kid of about three or four. He did not try to touch anything. Presently Julie came back with a brown plastic airlines satchel, containing, as she demonstrated, a pair of pants, some graham crackers, a can of orange juice, a wooden locomotive, a bib and shirt. She explained what they were for, and all about Chen-yu's habits. She was a very straight mother, it seemed to Marybeth, for someone in such a dangerous and crooked business: but maternal carefulness was something you wanted in the person you had to trust your secrets with.

"You and he should go out before I do," Julie said. "He cries if I leave him, but if *he* goes off with someone else he's fine."

"That's how men are," Marybeth said.

"Going bye-bye! Chen-yu going bye-bye!" Julie said brightly. Chen-yu watched them both alertly.

Marybeth took him by the hand. "Chen-yu and Marybeth going bye-bye," she said. Then Julie looked at her with a strange look, and Marybeth realized that she had spoken her own name, and her stomach turned sickly, a practiced response to fear. See—she couldn't trust anyone—not even herself.

7. Precautionary Measures

Theo had put on her black leotards and tights, and her full, calf-length black skirt with the ruffle at the bottom, and was pedaling her way along, knowing how she looked, like the witch in her witch costume on a hot summer day, but people in Orris were quite used to her bicycling along with ballet shoes dangling in a little bag from the handlebars, old bike with balloon tires and foot brakes she'd had since the fifties. As she passed the Orris Community Adult School, there were Ouida and Ouida's friend Roberta coming out on their morning break. Theo, in no rush, couldn't not stop. She'd met Roberta other times, a thin little Japanese person whose baby, Theo remembered, had a shriveled arm. She greeted them.

Ouida and Roberta planned to walk as far as the shops. Ouida was going to buy collard for the *feijoada* and, she said, kale and cabbage, for her kidneys bothered her a little. Kale and cabbage were believed by the Meishi-Sama to be efficacious to health. Health in turn efficacious to spiritual harmony. Looking at Ouida, Theo thought, you wouldn't guess about her deep strangeness; she just looked like any plump dark young woman hopefully swaying her hips as she walked along with her plastic shopping bag.

"If spiritual harmony included everybody, it could mean perfect peace in the universe," Ouida said. "Even the arrival of eternal light. One disorder—say, in the kidneys—leads to another, leads to another, and thus to all things, all things being connected. Many people do not believe this, nevertheless it is true."

"Well, in a way," Theo agreed. "That's in a way why I'm going to Fontana to help those poor men."

"It is a strange day for me," Ouida said. "It is either propitious or not propitious, but I am not clear. First the letter, and the pain in my back, not propitious, but then something happened in my typing class that is perhaps propitious. Tell me what you think."

"Most days are neither the one thing or the other," Roberta said. "There are days of equal proportion, too."

"Yes, that is true. I don't know. I arrive in the typing class a little late this morning, but the teacher does not glare at me, and I suppose that is good. Then I push on the keys of the typewriter and instantly a miraculous thing occurs. The words come alive, suddenly, around and behind me, and I can understand everything that is being said. It was like the gift of tongues. Before, every day, I sit there and hear the noise of the typewriters, and I write the words, and hear the speech in whispers of the girls who sit behind me, and understand nothing. But today the sounds organized themselves into words."

"That's wonderful!" said Theo thankfully.

"Yes and no. For do you know what they were saying? It was the Chinese girls behind me, who always before sounded to me like reeds and rushes. I thought they were speaking Chinese. I don't see how they could learn to type, those girls, because they were whispering all the time. But now I hear them say, 'Oooh, it's too funny, that fat girl, she's a voodoo. If you look close, you can see the outline of the voodoo charm she wears under her sweater.' I understood them plain as plain. They were talking of me, you see. 'It's a bagful of something,' they said, 'maybe human bones.' They were talking of the Focal Point, you see. 'It gives me the creeps. I wish they wouldn't let these people come here.' Talking of me. 'Think of the Arab who raped the girl on Elm Street, and the Arab consul just got him off. These people. These people.' ''

"Is that true, about the Arab on Elm Street? I live on Elm Street," Roberta asked Theo.

"Probably," Theo said.

"Then they began to talk of Sirhan Sirhan. At first I was so pleased at my new English I didn't care. It was like once when my teacher took out of my ear a huge ball of wax, when I was a little girl, like a miracle."

Suddenly up next to them in the street, driving a Dodge Dart, a man stuck his head out of the car window, whole arm and shoulder, too; perhaps this was the erring Mr. Griggs, for Ouida seemed to know him. "Good day to you," he said, in pleasantest tones. His voice was rich and thick. Ouida and Roberta greeted him, and Theo stared.

"Can I have a private conversation with you?" he said to Ouida. Roberta and Ouida looked at each other. Clearly Ouida was remembering her long wait in the dark the night before. Still, her sense of Mr. Griggs's interest showed on her pleased face. Theo thought of stern things for Ouida to say, but Ouida did not say them.

"You can come for me after school at Roberta's house," Ouida said. "Now I go to the market, and then we are going to our driver's training class, which is very important. Today is the day we take the written test and get our learner's permit."

First Griggs frowned, then smiled. "Okay, then," he said, and lifted his hand for goodbye, making a lot of noise with the engine of his car. Quite a nice-looking new car, green. Mr. Griggs was older-looking than Theo had expected.

"If you marry with that boy," Roberta said to Ouida,

"you could stay here. I know a lot of people who do that, marry an American. Like I did!" Then she clapped her hand over her mouth and giggled.

"Roberta has a very nice American husband, who she truly loves," Ouida hastily explained to Theo. "I have thought of it. But anyway I don't know if Griggs wants to marry. Once he asked me to help him in his house—he has a son, Lonnie, twelve, who is sick. And once he asked me to go to Reno and see the shows. I am thinking of doing that. Such a thing would not be possible for a modest woman in Brazil, but Americans are more free, and I would like to see the shows."

"Be sure to get separate rooms in the motel," Roberta said.

"I told him that already, and he said, 'Don't worry, I'm going to occupy my time with gambolin the whole time.' However, I could not find 'gambolin' in the dictionary."

"I hope Mr. Griggs doesn't gamble a lot," said Theo severely.

Marybeth was afraid of being seen by them, walking so near Ouida's school, but what could she do—here she was with a child, readymade motherhood. She hadn't a clue what to do. The schemes that had occurred to her—flight, hiding—didn't seem possible now. And you couldn't take a little kid to the library, or with you to hunt for a new job, or to the supermarkets checking notices on bulletin boards. What did you do with them?

On the other hand, Chen-yu toddling along at her side would be a kind of disguise. It was the kind of thing an FBI agent would never think of. They suppose you go around in a wig, bristling with guns. Marybeth thought Chen-yu was a game little kid, a good uncomplaining walker for one so young.

They walked slowly down B Street, past the dental

building with the boarded-up windows, past the health-food store on the corner. She looked for signs in the windows that might concern a job or a room. In the health-food store there was a sign that said "Let Your Friend Massage Your Feet Tonight," together with a diagram of feet, with directional arrows and pressure points.

Marybeth found something worrisome about this, but couldn't say what. A foot rub would be a nice thing—why should it upset her? She would buy some Earth Shoes if Earth Shoes didn't cost so much and make you look conspicuous. Feet were important things, to be taken care of. She guessed she was really on the thin edge, really the thin edge now, that tears shot to her eyes over the idea of Earth Shoes and foot rubs. She hadn't expected her mind to give out before her luck. Chen-yu never talked; he just solemnly trudged along barefooted. Marybeth wondered if it was good for his feet or bad for his feet for him to go barefoot all the time. There was something wrong about Let Your Friend Massage Your Feet, but what?

I can't get over it, Marybeth, seeing you here, of all places, Chuck Sweet had said. All this way from home. I never heard what became of you—yes, he had said that, she remembered it clearly. I never heard what became of you. I supposed you'd gotten married, that's what most people in our class have done by now—all the girls, at least. But you're here! Do you go to U.C.O. ?

Yes, she had said coolly, I'm a graduate student. What are you doing here, Chuck? Now, suddenly, she imagined massaging and kissing his feet; what a funny, degrading thing to imagine.

What a beautiful woman you've turned into, Marybeth, he had said with a certain assurance, with a certain awareness of how this would be taken, or of what a beau-

tiful woman is. This suggested to Marybeth that a few
things had happened to Chuck Sweet, too, since they left
Bettendorf. But what? Chuck had large brown eyes, like
a man in a magazine ad. Marybeth, leading Chen-yu by
the hand, continued along Fourth Street, fearing and
hoping as she looked up and down to see Chuck Sweet
dart out at them from behind a parked car or a tree. But
he didn't.

At the next corner she became aware that a green car,
a Dodge Dart, was driving slowly on the other side, with
the driver watching them closely. She was instantly seized
by her reflex fear, the feeling that someone had laid ice
to the nape of her neck. Walk naturally, look unconcerned. It couldn't be someone looking for her, it just
couldn't; it was only last night she had met Chuck. I
never heard what happened to you, he had said.

Hurry, come this way, Chen-yu. Why did they call him
Chen-yu? If police or Feds had staked out the Photophobia, they would have seen her walking in the block
between Ashby Path and A Street. Marybeth pulled
Chen-yu into the Phillips 66 station they were just passing by.

"My little boy needs to use the bathroom," she said,
and the man gave her a key. In the ladies' room she tied
her black hair up in her red bandanna so none of it
showed. Chen-yu stood in front of the toilet without
complaint but without peeing either, staring from it to
Marybeth and shuffling his feet. Marybeth did not know
whether she should aim his penis for him or what. She
could imagine him talking volubly when he was home
with his mother: "And then she molested me. She's a
child-molester." She didn't touch it. But if he peed now,
he'd pee on his foot. He wasn't circumcised, his penis
was like a little pod. Abruptly she pulled his overalls up.

"You've had your chance, buddy, we can't stay in here
all day," she said. "You tell me when you need to go,
okay?"

Pasted on the door, where she noticed it as they left, a sign read:

Are you happy with *your* body?

Polarity treatments are a way to give Your Body the care it deserves. Polarity offers an alternative to merely accepting tension, pain and disease, which are often considered the price of life. Polarity Therapy is the Science of Balancing the life energy in the human body. Various physical manipulations, both simple and gentle, are used to alleviate these unwanted accumulations of pain and tension. For treatments call Vanayana, 841-7945.

The tears came to her eyes again.

They went outside. The green car had driven away. I'm just being paranoid, she thought. But the feeling, which could seize her anytime in its ravaging jaws, was breathing close now, the feeling that the tap on the shoulder would come today. She supposed it was because she had lost the security of Photophobia that she had this premonition that it would come today. That's why my stomach is crawling this way, the tap; it's all up with me, I know. I should be trying to do something to save myself, these prescient feelings should be obeyed.

Or maybe it's just my period. She was always prey to these fears around the time of her period. But her period was about over. Whatever it was, she knew she had to struggle against low spirits, because low spirits and discouragement are themselves a signal, an announcement drawing eyes and suspicions. Smiles, an expression of serene happiness—those were an impenetrable disguise. Someone had told her you have a better—a worse—a greater chance of being raped if you are in low spirits; rapists got these signals of misery off you like radar, and possibly so do the Feds.

Marybeth always studied the fate of other people. A couple of weeks ago there had been one called Sharon

Armbrewster, who'd been caught back East. Marybeth devoured these stories like saint's legends. The tap on the shoulder came for Armbrewster when she was buying raw milk at an alternative dairy in Evanston, Illinois. Marybeth had read every word of every account of it, and tuned in on every channel, though there was nothing till the eleven-o'clock news and then not very much, just this wide surly girl saying she would continue to fight, and no way at all to tell what she was feeling. Marybeth hadn't planned out what she would say when the tap came for her.

Part of her had always expected they would kill her in the process of catching her, as so often happened, and she wouldn't have to say anything. Because she wouldn't know what to say. I believe. I still believe. Our duty as Americans. But all that would be a lie, because of course she didn't believe in anything any more.

The thing was to keep your spirits up. But it heavily oppressed her, this sense that the tap, the strong fingers on her upper arm, the low voice would come today. She ought to get out of here. Young mother walking with her little boy, no one would notice anything funny about that.

Or maybe this racy feeling of fear and change wasn't a true premonition about the FBI, but was owing to Chen-yu instead, this new slow-moving appendage for one seventy-five an hour. At Photophobia you got two fifty and could sit around thinking your own thoughts most of the time, whereas, Marybeth found, now she had to try to think Chen-yu's thoughts, to guess when he would want to dash in front of a car, or seize and swallow a piece of broken glass, fall, be hurt, cry. She feared he would cry.

It must be a drag to have a child and have to do this all the time, she thought. It seemed amazing to her to remember that when she had first gone to college she had expected to major in early-childhood education. Think of that. It almost made her laugh. Compared to the things she'd done, this was nothing—it didn't make sense to feel so powerless and frightened at the task of following Chen-yu around for a couple of days, and the stake was a whole new future, maybe freedom, a new name at the least.

Well, she knew it was her whole life that was defeated, it was not just that baby-sitting was hard; she had had the usual amount of experience baby-sitting. How did Julie know she wasn't a child-murderer, anyway, trustfully sending her little boy off with Marybeth this way?

"Have you had your invitation yet?" said a woman on the corner. She stood near a card table with papers Scotch-taped around the edge. She got Marybeth with eye contact and moved toward her. She had the abashed pallor of a Salvation Army worker, but she wore a vinyl leather jacket. She smiled and her eyes never wavered. "We want to invite you to a party. There'll be food and wine."

Marybeth clung to Chen-yu and backed up a step, and the woman stepped forward, waving a brochure.

"Then there'll be a little talk and a slide show. We want to tell you about how we live and the things we believe in."

"No, thank you, I wouldn't come," Marybeth said, feeling scorn for people who had beliefs, feeling past and above all that. But she accepted the brochure. The woman stared into her eyes as if trying to catch her with looks.

Kids, thought Marybeth, how slowly they walked, how many things they seemed to see, noticing that she had walked right by things that Chen-yu stopped to look at, peeling paint on wooden steps, falling petals from hydrangeas. She had heard from a lot of people, without believing it, that having a child changes your perspective. Expands your mind, people said. Girls said that back in Bettendorf, the ones who got married right away, and

girls in college had said so, too; also women you talked
to in the Co-op or sprawled on the grass in parks. Marybeth had never believed it.

But now she noticed that it was true. She was newly
and intensely aware of all the other people with small
children, she felt part of them. She was always yearning
for community, and now she felt it for people with small
children, that was unexpected. She saw how they daw-
dled along, the way she and Chen-yu did, and she saw
how you carry a small child. She saw babies in back-
packs, and a man with his child strapped on his front in
a kind of harness, the child leaning against his father's
chest like a stone or an albatross, his little arms sleepily
around the father's neck.

Marybeth could remember a kind of pushcart you could
push a child in, but she didn't see any now. Her brother
had been pushed in a cart like that, also perhaps she
herself, but now she didn't see any. Nonetheless the world
to her eyes seemed suddenly full of slow-moving people
pushing and pulling little stone children.

She fitted in, indistinguishable, she knew. Of course
she used to baby-sit like other girls, of course she did.
She hadn't always been a murderer—the tears now shot
to her eyes in the way they had been doing, always at the
ready. There had been nothing about her to alarm the
mothers on her block, of course there hadn't. Even so,
she been connected to a death, even then.

While baby-sitting. The mouse in the trap. "We've set a
trap," Dr. Foley had told her, "so if you hear a snap,
don't worry."

I'll never have children, she had said to herself, hearing that snap, thinking of the little dead mouse. But the
mouse wasn't dead then; it could be heard dragging itself
in pain around behind the refrigerator, dragging its trap.

Sometimes the dragging, scraping pain would stop.

Now it's dead, it's really dead now, she had thought in relief. But it was resting and then would try again.

That's like my life now, dragging along in a trap and sometimes feeling dead, sometimes resting, she thought, clinging to Chen-yu's hand.

Then she had been afraid to kill a little mouse. But she'd been afraid to free it, too. She'd been afraid to look at it, had tried to call her father, but he had gone to the basketball game.

I'll never have children, she had thought, and turned up the television to blot out the sound of the dragging trap, hoping the little kid wouldn't wake or cry, and hoping the Foleys would come home early; but they wouldn't, they never did. "I'm cooped up here all day"—that was Mrs. Foley's phrase. It was she who liked night life. Lambie was what Mrs. Foley had called Dr. Foley; Marybeth could remember that, Lambie.

"Come on, Chen-yu," said Marybeth, helping him up the curb, lifting him by one arm, and up he came like something pulled from underwater, all in a rush. He laughed. It was the first time he'd laughed or smiled. What had the name of the Foley's little boy been? She couldn't remember; all she could remember was the sound of the dragging of the trap. Between her eyes, deep in her head, she felt the pressure of clotted tears.

Holding tight to Chen-yu so he wouldn't go into the street, waiting at the bus stop, looking up, Marybeth saw a bus go by, and someone in it was waving at her. Her first impulse to cringe and turn her face was replaced by the feeling of belovedness and safety that being waved at gives you. It was Ouida in the bus, in a whole busload of people like a prison van. For a frightened second Marybeth thought they'd caught Ouida and were deporting her.

Then she thought of getting on the bus with Ouida and pretending to be a wetback and getting herself sent to Mexico. Through the window of the bus, faces—brown, black and yellow faces—were smiling or wore expressions of preoccupied concern, but you could see it wasn't a death or deportation bus.

Ouida kept waving till Marybeth waved back. Marybeth took Chen-yu's hand and wigwagged it at the bus, and arms, many arms and hands, wigwagged back at the little boy waving. Then the light changed and Ouida was carted off.

"Bye-bye, bye-bye," Chen-yu began to scream excitedly.

Oh, what's going to become of Ouida? Marybeth thought. She would become a cleaning lady, the world will make her into a cleaning lady when she should be happy, dancing and singing. Instead she would falter and slow, and push vacuum cleaners for other people; no one would love her. If I don't do something, thought Marybeth; but what can I do? Oh, please let me think of something.

Marybeth and Chen-yu sat on the bench at the bus stop and she fell into thoughts about Chuck Sweet again.

Do you go home much? he had asked.

That was when she realized he must not know about her, or was pretending not to. No, my folks moved away from there a few years ago, so there's no reason, she told him. He hadn't been back himself in a long time, he said.

But I *want* to go back, Marybeth had said. I hate the idea of forgetting it. I forget the names of the places— the place we all used to get ice cream—remember? Everybody used to get ice cream there, and it was shaped like a castle.

"The Prince Castle?"

"Yes, the Prince Castle! The Prince Castle! The other day I was trying to think of the name of the Girl Scout camp—I was a counselor there when I was a senior, and camper there three summers and I forgot it—remember, on the Rock River?''

"Camp Archie Allen," Chuck said. "We would go across the river to visit in canoes, from Camp Harvey Dodd.''

"Yes, yes—see? I feel like I'm losing my entire past.'' But she saw then that she shouldn't betray her panic. He watched her, his small smile bemused or surprised.

"You might not relate to Bettendorf if you saw it now," Chuck said. "It's changed a lot. I went back after the service, but I couldn't stay. It's changed and I'd changed.''

Marybeth had stared at him, stricken. *The service!* Was he some returned POW or some nut thing like that, junkie, raper? Had he *been* to Vietnam?

"It—Bettendorf—it's gotten bigger, housing tracts and old nice things torn down," Chuck went on, supposing her silence to be encouraging of further explanation.

"What about you?" she asked.

"How did I change? Besides getting bigger?" He laughed.

"Oh, we all changed," Marybeth said.

"Europe. Europe is what changed me. History. Ages past. All that stuff that didn't happen in Bettendorf, Iowa. It's hard to explain.''

"Country boy?"

"Little me and all that history. Dark complications of the human spirit unknown in Bettendorf. Michelangelo. Medici tombs, Lord Nelson on his column.''

"Who?"

"Before that my idea of a statue was the Statue of Liberty, right? 'Merican. Nice American statues.''

"Yeah, I see," Marybeth said. But she had never been to Europe. He'd probably been a lot of fantastic places.

"Anyway, it ruined me for Bettendorf," Chuck said. "You can't predict how your life can change, can

you?'' Marybeth said, struck as usual with how some
bitter lessons of life was to be extracted from the most
casual discourse. Still, Chuck didn't look embittered by
life; he looked in charge of it. Something about him gave
the appearance of someone grown, strengthened, enriched by it; this was plain from something, maybe the
Apollonian color of his beard. He was finishing a Ph.D.
in art history and had a Fulbright to Europe next fall.
She remembered he had played football. She had never
been to Europe. She had majored in political science,
she had told him, less a lie than most she told.

Theo did not see Ouida on the bus, did not see Marybeth; her eyes were on her pupils dawdling along, eight-
year-old slowpokes with their bathing suits in little bags
together with their ballet shoes. She rode past them
smartly with a curt ballet mistress nod, was waiting in
the upstairs practice room of the Methodist Students'
Center when they began to stray in.

They would rather be swimming, they take a little while
to settle down. Tap, tap, with her cane Theo lightly re-
proved them, coaxed them into a wiggly row, fat little
girls, skinny little girls, and one little boy, kind of a
concern to Theo, who had confided to Anton that she
feared his mother was making a fairy out of him.

"I think he loathes and dreads ballet class, poor little
thing," she had said. "What does he want to be there
with all those girls for? They're in his regular class at
school, and how they laugh at him. I deeply respect male
dancers—a life of sacrifice—but poor Charles, who is to
say at the age of eight that he has a vocation? Of course
you do have to start them young. But his mother is so
dreadful—so bitter and tough . . .''

Here was Charles, stoically at the barre, his feet in
little girls' ballet shoes. Mrs. Madison was trilling and
tinkling up and down the piano. It occurred to Theo that

because Charles was a Negro maybe he was wise to take up dancing after all, as a way of success. This was to look at the matter in a more cheerful way. You wouldn't find successful dancers in Fontana Prison. Maybe his mother had thought the matter through.

"*Ronds de jambe,*" said Theo. "Dum dum dum dum dum de *dum.*" Would black prisoners at Fontana be, for instance, like Finns? The rain in Finland, how it had rained. How cold, all the dear little wooden houses red and yellow painted, boarded up against the rain.

Perhaps she wouldn't go to Fontana. Pride and foolishness. Image of meddlesome do-gooder. In spite of one's effort, goodness and right do not ensue. What great leaps they would make, she cheered herself, leaping in the air like great cats. How men could leap! Teach them to leap over walls. Leaping, capering figures in black, making patterns against walls, against sky. Little Charles leapt at the touch of her stick. Dum dum dum dum de *dum.* The powerful sense of pity, the poor little child doomed to a future of he knew not what, and it was not going to work out for him, she foresaw that, watching him now making solemn pliés, his baby eyes straight ahead, his small bony knees quivering a little.

No, it was not going to work out for him. Blinded with tears, she had to go open the window, pretending the practice room had gotten too hot.

Going home, Theo stops in the electrical store.

"It's silly for me, I suppose," she says, explaining it to the man.

"Not at all—these old houses," the man says.

"Even a trace of smoke will set it off?"

"Allow me," says the electrical-store man, lighting a cigarette. Poof, says his mouth to the smoke-and-fire sensor. It screams. Quickly he waves the smoke away. "See?"

"Our old house," says Theo. "I often worry."

"It may be the wisest thirty dollars you ever spent," says the man, and Theo writes him a check. She puts the little heavy box in the basket of her bicycle. There are things you can provide against, there are things you can do, she thinks.

8. Bus Rides

Ouida, going by on the school bus, waved at Theo, but Theo, pedaling briskly, didn't see her. Then Ouida waved at Marybeth, and at a little child. They waved back, and she was happy for the encouraging waves, for she was on her way to the Division of Motor Vehicles, and she was nervous. So were all the others, though they had studied the charts and learned the street signs and the meaning of the little arrows describing turns. But would the teacher, Mr. Hawkes, have let them come so far if he wasn't sure they could all succeed? He walked the aisles of the bus radiating his confidence in them.

He'd also made sure that everyone had his four-dollar application fee. Only Mrs. Aheem did not, as the teacher appeared to have expected. He lent it to her. In the bus there was an air of general excitement, the camaraderie of mass certification; also inside the Division, a plain building of cement block. The students smiled helpfully at one another as they formed into two lines behind the people who were already there, as they had been instructed to do.

Ouida waited her turn with patience. Waiting in lines was more interesting than it would have been even yesterday, for today she had her new gift of understanding the English words that sparkled in the air all around her.

She felt so much more—so much more *in* the world, she told Roberta.

"They found his head in a paper sack and the rest of him stuffed behind the refrigerator," a man was saying in the next line, very clearly.

"Sounds like another one of those Zebra killings," said someone else.

"He was only thirty-seven years old."

"The wife and children were shot to death upstairs."

Ouida gasped sympathetically and moved forward in her line, her plastic sacks rattling, her ears straining. She tried to keep her mind on the facts of traffic safety. Up ahead, a black girl with cheeks painted orange was directing people at the eye chart. They stood gazing up with a piece of cardboard held first over one eye, then the other. Ouida could see the letters very well, even this far away, and was reassured.

"Yes, it's a good idea to make sure everyone has good vision before they drive," whispered Roberta from the next line. "For the protection of passengers and other drivers."

Ouida nodded. She was thankful she had new glasses, though they had been expensive. Now it was her turn. The girl took her hands and rolled them in ink and printed them on a paper. This frightened Ouida—would the passport people now be able to find her the more easily? However, it was too late to object. Now the girl put a pencil in her hand and pointed at places on a piece of paper where she was to write her name. Then she handed Ouida a white cardboard square.

"Put this over your right eye—*right* eye—and look at the chart," said the girl. "Read the top line."

Ouida looked at the chart. A, Z, M. "Ah, zhay, emmy," she said. The girl frowned.

"Try the next line," she said.

"Erry, pay, effy," Ouida said. The girl lowered her pointer and took up another little white card, which she wrote on and handed to Ouida. She had put Ouida's name on it, but it was not conferred with the festive and congratulatory manner appropriate to the newly certified. Rather censoriously, instead.

"This must be filled in by your eye doctor affirming that your vision has been checked and your corrective lenses are adequate," the girl said.

"I have new glasses," Ouida said. "They are good. I see very good." The girl made an impatient fist. Her fingernails were long and shiny and pearlescent.

"Like ah *said*, this card must be filled in by your eye specialist and presented to us before we can issue you a learner's permit," the girl said, and Ouida was obliged to back away, confused, and let someone else step up for his turn. Nearby, Roberta stepped forward, and read the chart—the very same letters—A, Z, M, R, P, F: Ouida read along with her. Roberta was given her learner's permit with no difficulty.

Suddenly the explanation occurred to Ouida, and chilled her blood; the *soldados* will have told them not to give her one, for she has no passport and they are watching her. Ouida's palms began to sweat, but no *soldados* detained her right then.

Seeing Ouida on the bus made Marybeth think a bus was a good idea, so when the Greyhound came along they took it. She didn't care. It was something to do with Chen-yu anyway—an hour-and-a-half ride to San Francisco, and they could have a look around and come right back. After they were on, though, she saw it was a mistake to take a small child on a long bus ride. Chen-yu mauled her, and got filthy sitting on the floor of the aisles. He wouldn't sit on the seat. Nobody paid any attention anyway; that was one good thing. Chen-yu seemed happiest standing up on the seat looking at the people behind them. Marybeth put her hand lightly on his behind to brace him, afraid he'd fall over backward if the bus stopped quickly.

She must have been crazy to come on a long bus ride with a small kid, a wiggly little kid. Otherwise it would be just the thing, anonymous and soporific. No one was anyone on a bus; it was a kind of legitimate limbo or sanctuary, like a church. No Feds would come onto a bus to get you, they would wait till the next stop. She wondered if you could hide in churches any more.

Chen-yu clutched himself between the legs and old ladies looked significantly at Marybeth. I didn't tell him to do that, she thought; why were they looking at her? Then she got the idea: he needed to go to the toilet. She dragged him along down the aisle to the toilet in the rear and jammed them both into the smelly, lurching little stall. She had to pull his pants down and then hold him against her at an angle high enough so that he could aim. They went thunk together against the wall as the bus took a curve. On the wall, scratched in the paint, it said TRACY MORRIS AND GREG GARCIA WILL FUCK FOREVER.

Nothing happened; nuts, Chen-yu didn't pee. They stood there as long as they decently could, and she could hear feet outside, scuffling anxiously. So she did him up again and took him back to their seat. Nuts, she was getting thin-edgy again, tears springing to her eyes at the dumbest things, now because of those nutty words "will fuck forever"; what an idea, what vanity, what hopefulness, what sweetness there was in the world, must be, somewhere. Poor Tracy Morris, poor dopey little teenybopper, scratching talisman words on walls.

It was a relief when the bus ride came to an end, that was one thing about a bus ride with a little kid. In the bus station, people walked around, all looking more or less miserable, which was a comfort, in a way. Marybeth bought Chen-yu a candy bar out of a machine. This is San Francisco, little friend—do you like it? She couldn't tell. He watched it all and had no opinion.

She noticed she had four dollars left and some change.
⏴ They went outside and wandered along Mission Street,
Marybeth thinking what to do. She bought Chen-yu an
Orange Julius. He was so silent. He drank it intently,
with dirty little hands clutching the cup and his eyes
looking down into it, watching it disappear as his little
cheeks worked, eyes never raised until he had seen the
last drop, and Marybeth watching him. She couldn't imagine how she had thought of majoring in early-childhood
education, wasn't that weird? What would happen to
Chen-yu when he grew up, she wondered. What if he
died and didn't grow up? "Watch your space, Chen-yu,"
she told him, guiding him from tripping up strangers.

The sun was bright but a cold summer wind sped down
Mission Street between the camera stores, lunch-o-mat-
ics, Hong Kong tailors; blew briskly in the electric lines
the trolleys ran on. Chen-yu in his little shirt didn't seem
cold, but Marybeth shivered. The chill felt good, in a
way, after the Valley heat, but she shivered.

"I can't talk to you here, I'm underground" is what she
should have told Chuck Sweet, it suddenly comes to her.
Or, "I'll come to live with you if you never say my
name," like a charmed person in a fairy tale.

"When you say my name, I'll go up in a puff of green
smoke," whispers Princess Marybeth, the frog girl, and
beautiful sweet Chuck never does say it, but loves her
and embraces her, and they do it twenty times a night.
But then sometime, groaning in passion, he says,
"Marybeth, I love you," and poof.

So it's no use anyway; nothing's any use. I don't want
the new name, I don't want a new place, I don't want
anything. It is I, here I am, it is I, she thinks of shouting
as they walk along.

* * *

A black man wearing an apron full of magazines walked in front of her. He was portly, his face was seamed with weals. His eyes were scanning the crowd and he picked her; she must have seemed weakest, was weakest.

"Do you hate black people?" he asked her when he had her eye. He stepped closer. "You don't hate black people, now, do you? A pretty young lady like you?" Voice like syrup, dripping hate; hate and fear flowed into Marybeth's veins as if he were injecting them. He waiting, smiling, reaching for his periodical. Why did they have to do this, she thought, he doesn't want fifty cents that much.

"No, of course not," she said primly. That was true of course. For God's sake, she had done her bit for the modern world. Still her heart pounded as if she were taking a lie detector test.

"That a pretty little child you got there. Wouldn't you like to make me a donation for this newspaper, all the proceeds go to help black youth don't have a good chance like your little baby there. Help them to learn pride in their race, also get a good breakfast."

Fucker, she thought, resenting his malice, his power. She got out her coin purse. He looked into it with her. "You got a dollar there," he said. She took it out with limp fingers; he took it and smiled at her cowardice. Their eyes met in hate. "If you feel you can give more, this is a good cause to help people that don't have such a good chance as yourself."

"Fucker," she said, but not so he could hear her, backing off, getting behind someone; let him get someone else, why did he have to lay her bare? Ah, well, poor them, was there any use in anything?

Walking up Powell, she started crying again, for about the ninetieth time that day. Honestly, I must really be wasted, this is too dumb, she thought, standing sniffling away on a street corner in a midday. The tears shone on her cheeks; people looked away quickly. She couldn't explain why she was crying, but maybe it was because a woman had walked by carrying a little plant in a pot, and this just brought out the tears and made her throat swell up, she couldn't explain why. Tracy Morris and Greg Garcia will fuck forever.

Well, it was that woman so happy with her plant, carrying it grandly before her—a spindly sort of plant, too, with floppy leaves in a hospital-looking foil wrapping, but the woman loved it. They weren't going to or from a hospital, this woman and her plant; they looked too happy for that. Her face was lighted with contentment, just a plain dumpy woman who had nothing special to be pleased about, in this society, that Marybeth could see.

She'd forgotten, she'd been caught off guard; now she was reminded that sometimes people are happy. It was a possibility. Not often, but sometimes you saw a pinpoint gleam of happiness beam out of somebody, just somebody walking along. It always caught you right in the eye, like a dart of sudden sun through the trees. Blinking back tears, blotting her cheeks on the backs of her hands, Marybeth said, "Stand still, Chen-yu, wait a minute," Then she watched the woman and her plant until they turned a corner, the plant still nodding its head like an idiot child. Marybeth grabbed hold of Chen-yu's hand and they tried to step, merge, inconspicuously into the stream of people.

The house will seem empty, thought Theo. Bicycling home, she saw a friend who didn't see her. Ha. Alfreda doesn't expect to see her old friend still riding bikes, Theo thought, a little self-satisfied. Other women my age looking so much older really don't need to: permanents and girdles age them; it's all a matter of staying in shape. Some people look old at forty, I do not look sixty. She was not vain, but she was pleased about that. The smoke alarm was heavier than it had seemed, so that she wobbled slightly when it rolled in the basket as she turned up Ashby Path. Soon the cedar waxwings will eat the pyracantha, she thought, catching sight of her house and the berried bushes in front. As she was wheeling her bike, here came a visitor up her front steps, a youth of heavenly beauty. He looked, she realized, familiar. She could not say why.

Theo nearly spoke aloud at the ravishing sight. Her weakness for beautiful young men was a weakness she forgave herself. Merciful heavens, to be oneself so large and strong, like a Michelangelo. What could it be like? How strange to have no breasts. Her breasts tingled with fear at the thought. And you might not want that hair on your face. On the other hand, hair on the chest, hair curling on great brown legs—she had always thought it wonderful. She parked her bicycle against the front steps and fastened the chain.

The legs of this young man, who waited quietly for her to finish, were, however, covered by blue jeans. Masses of golden hair waved around his head. He had a quite apostolic golden beard. The voice was a wonderful resonant bass. What could it be like to speak thus, as if you were buried deep in earth with a head cold, or howling out from a cave; how wonderful, voices like drums.

She wouldn't rent him a room, though; it would make her uncomfortable to have such a masculine person around; that was a policy she had decided on long ere this. You never knew when you would get one with an extra Y chromosome—or was it X, the one that turned them violent and criminal. You avoided this risk in part by not taking the large, manly-looking ones, precisely like this boy; and then, too, they had said they would keep Lynn's room for her until the new quarter started.

"Excuse me," the young man said.

"Yes?" Theo supposed she'd been gaping. She opened the front door and stood in the doorway, symbolizing her ownership of this house.

"Is there a woman named Marybeth Howe here? Is this where she lives? She said she lived on Ashby Path, but I've tried all the other houses."

"What?" Theo said. She was startled. She'd been thinking up her regretful speech about having no room. But now she remembered. This was Lynn's friend from the Co-op.

"Marybeth Howe. She's—she's quite beautiful, with black hair and blue eyes, and she said she lived on Ashby Path," he said.

"Oh, I see," Theo said, quick mind set awhirl, and beneath the whirls a deep calm feeling of unsurprise. She would piece together the particulars later. "Yes, she does live here—I'm sorry to have been woolgathering. But she's gone for a while, to Wyoming, I think, or Idaho, I forget just which."

He looked sorry, disappointed, uncertain. "To see her mother? Idaho? She left a note where she works that her mother was sick."

"Oh? Perhaps she thought—Well, she said she'd be back before school starts. Would you care to leave a message?"

"Oh, I guess not. I'll check back," he said, and went away. Theo pressed the door closed after him. Delight prickled her skin, the feeling of something strange, a mystery. She went along to find Anton.

Ouida went home with Roberta to give Johrei to Roberta's baby. They believed his arm was getting better; it seemed to be better. Roberta was sure he was moving it some.

Ouida waited for Mr. Griggs, but he didn't come. She was certain he knew where Roberta's house was, yet he never came, and so at last she took the bus home, though she could have walked—it was not far. But the day had made her tired, somehow, and her legs ached, and the place in her lower back again, too.

On the bus, as had happened all day, she could understand all the words that anyone said all around her, all the words had come alive, and she was glad she was riding along listening, and she began to cheer up some.

"I stand four, five hours in the fuckin line, then the palce is closed, *now* what am I supposed to do, what my kids supposed to do?" a woman was saying plaintively but clearly behind her.

This gave Ouida more confidence about talking to strangers than she might have had even yesterday. The woman next to her was very friendly, so Ouida told her about Brazil. "It is very beautiful. You must go to see Copacabana someday. It is even more beautiful than San Francisco. But I prefer America. In Brazil we must spend many hours and much money in the beauty parlor. The hair must be done, the nails, the make-up. It is very expensive. Here—you can see—I have a natural." She laughed. "In Brazil only the rich people dare to have a natural; the lower people are ashamed if the hair is curly like this." Her companion, who had limp taffy-colored hair, admired and envied her natural.

"Oh! It is my stop!" Ouida stood up suddenly and spilled her sacks of collard and kale. A man across the aisle helped her gather everything up. The bus driver waited kindly until it was reassembled and she was safely off.

America, adopted land, thought Ouida lovingly as she walked up Ashby Path, and could almost put out of her mind her disappointment about the Division of Motor Vehicles and her other fears.

Marybeth Howe, Marybeth Howe, who? Theo was thinking about this as she changed her clothes. She was unable to stop thinking about it. Marybeth Howe was a familiar name to her, and yet she was sure that Lynn had never mentioned it. Lynn who had told the young man she was Marybeth or Marybeth who told him she was Lynn. Which way? If only Theo could quite remember why the pretty name danced so teasingly beyond the reach of her memory, promising to surprise and horrify them.

Marybeth and Chen-yu stepped along the city street. People all around them wore expressions of vagueness or strain. Suppose—it occurred to Marybeth for the first time—suppose it isn't natural for people to be happy? Suppose they aren't meant to be happy? At all?

Oh, of course they are. Isn't that why we want them to have enough to eat, and freedom, and equal opportunity, so they can live happily? Mere life is nothing, is not enough, without happiness.

But maybe—she thought, stricken—maybe there's a class of people who aren't meant to be happy, who are just agents of happiness, who sign away their own happiness as one of the conditions of happiness for others. Maybe I'm one of those.

She felt herself to be on the brink of asking a dangerous—*the* dangerous—question. She tried to turn her thoughts.

But the question cried out to be asked, like a voice entrapped inside a casket, thumping and peremptory: Are you, Marybeth, never to be happy, but to live your whole life of seventy or eighty years in your present frame of mind; that is, in fear, solitude, subjection and apathy?

Shame flushed her at the nakedness and self-interest of this thought. She had been brought up to believe that a person ought not to inquire into his own personal happiness. Happiness just went along with you as you briskly went about your business of helping and making and doing; it stepped faithfully, smartly at your side. But if you spun around and tried to fix it with your gaze, if you *tried* to find happiness, it would be nowhere to be found. This was well known.

How frightened she was, in thinking these forbidden thoughts about happiness, that she had already scared it away. Certainly it was nowhere to be found.

A lifetime in this condition of worn pain. In or out of prison wouldn't make any difference.

She had used to think that when the war was over, the world—and she had meant to include herself—the world and she would both be happy. But the war was over, and it and she were not happy.

Oh, I'm just depressed, she thought. I have to struggle against these low spirits. I just had my period. Anyone would feel depressed if they might go to prison. If I could be safe, be free . . . Or if the *world* would clear up.

But suppose, she thought suddenly, for the first time, suppose it did clear up, and *all* the prisoners and victims were free, and had school breakfasts and all the stuff you wanted and worked for, and the system was changed—and all wars over for always—would you, Marybeth, then be happy?

Oh, God, how she wished she hadn't gotten to thinking like this. Her heart pounded, dreading the answer to this question she had long been afraid to put. The answer was no, of course not, no. She couldn't imagine herself happy under any circumstances. It was impossible. She felt as if her blood were draining away into the street. If you can't be happy, whatever happy is, then why should you live?

This confrontation with animal selfishness, this wish to live happy, this sudden sense that altruism was a lie, confounded her. She buried her face in her hands. She wasn't good at ideas, she wished she'd stop having them. She'd been better as a leader, all energy and rhetoric and no thoughts at all.

"Is that your little boy, Miss?" someone said to her.

"Oh, Chen-yu, God damn it, come back here." The

kid just toddles off in any direction, he doesn't know
about cars, he's surely going to get killed one of these
days.

We need lunch, she thought, it's nearly two. They
found a sandwich shop. Marybeth, looking at her three
dollars, saw that they didn't have enough to get them
home on the Greyhound. So what the hell, they'd blow it
on lunch. No good trying to remember things head on.
You have to put them out of your mind. Marybeth Howe.
It would pop out, Theo knew, if she could just put it out
of her mind.

With the new name from Julie, Marybeth reflected, she
could get a new job; maybe she'd try to find one that paid
something decent, and get a Social Security number.
Would a Social Security number make her happy? Maybe
she could just turn up at Photophobia again and say her
mother had recovered, and when she ran into Chuck she'd
cool him somehow.

No, impossible. You can't trust the Chuck Sweets, you
can't trust anyone; that is another rule and never to be
forgotten. She'd been warned a million times that trust
is the first temptation: you want to relate to people normally; you want to forget and start trusting them. But
you must not.

The waitress brought them something, cheese sandwiches. Anyway, the thought returned, what does it really matter if one person is happy? The world doesn't
care. If you made a list of all the people in the world
who aren't happy, she thought, this list would be so long,
so endless a list, you would be ashamed not to be on it,
among your comrades the rest of mankind. These spores
of happiness that float and try to root in your flesh are a
kind of fungus; the good person scrapes them off. Marybeth, sunk in animal hunger, consumed her cheese
sandwich and tried to shake or scrape off this rooted wish

to be happy, just for a short time, this ignoble animal wish.

Just for a short time? Just long enough to make love to someone, as short a time as that, and time to eat a steak? But she's ashamed. What does it matter if one person is happy, when you consider all the misery of the world?

It's funny, she thought, looking at Chen-yu—kids are just little people; they eat hamburgers and drink Orange Julius and look at the world through their eyes. They see the same things you do, cars and stuff. But what are their brains saying? Marybeth, looking at Chen-yu for signs of happiness, saw urine trickling down the pedestal of his lunch-counter stool, forming a puddle at the bottom.

Marybeth Howe! the thought excited Theo as she hurried down the hall to find Anton. He and Ouida were watching TV; strange, for it was early, only four o'clock. On the television screen a man and a woman crouched by a campfire. The man was a cowboy, you could tell by his gun and wide hat, and the girl was pretty, with a long flowered dress on, and a pinafore apron.

Their words were plain as plain to Ouida.

"I cooked breakfast because you were still asleep, not because I thought I had to. I don't have to do nothing around here that I don't want to do," said this country girl with a toss of her pretty curls and a flutter of lashes.

The cowboy grabbed hold of her wrist roughly. Ouida's heart stopped.

"And now you can wash up, and hurry up, because you're coming along with me," he said. "Get ready." There were glances between them, direct and smoldering. The girl wiggled her arm and then tried to get her whole body free as the cowboy captured her with his arms, and they lurched to their feet, and he held her against him and she exerted herself but could not get free.

"Yeah, I guess you're takin me along because I'm such a good cook, right?" said the television girl in a soft defiant tone, a knowing tone, seeming to Ouida as if she ought to be angry, but with a smile of a funny kid as she stared up into the cowboy's stern face, like the face of a conquistador.

"Oh, I understand!" Ouida said. "They are really in love despite their talk of cooking—am I understanding right?"

"Adult Western," Anton said.

"I'm taking you back to your family where you belong," said the cowboy.

"Oh," cried Ouida in disappointment. Anton and Theo looked at her.

"I'm sorry about the way it's going," she explained, "because I thought he would now say that he loved her."

"Cowboys never say such things, even when they think them," Anton explained.

"That's true," Theo agreed. "It's a convention of the genre." How sad but how touching that Ouida's mind should be on love, poor girl. It drifted into Theo's own mind, rather independently of her preoccupation like Marybeth—Lynn; it drifted across her consciousness like an English subtitle: Ouida loves Anton. Of course. Poor girl, Theo thought, why didn't I notice this before?

"No words of love and no kissing in cowboy movies of this era," Anton said, "but they always get married in the end."

"Woman's proper destiny," Theo said.

"Yes," Ouida sighed. "When I thought I could not marry, in Brazil, after my operation for the teeroid, I believed my life was over. Now I do not care so much for getting married. Oh, I do and I don't; it is hard to say."

"*Teeroid?* Oh, thyroid." Thyroid, they understood, when she drew her finger along the thin line of scar where her throat had once been cut open.

"It was a very dangerous operation, but cost me nothing because it was done by the training doctors in Brazil. My family could not afford it otherwise—it would cost thousands of cruzieros—dollars—for this, and it was *muito delicado*."

"What was the matter with your thyroid?"

"I was always so fat, so I thought perhaps an operation of the glands, or of the kidneys, so I went to them, and they said, well, we could cut the thyroid. But afterwards I was still fat—this was before I learned about World Messianity. Now I know that sickness is the toxins of the body going out, and it is sickness that makes you healthy, so I avoid doctors and I am much better—thinner, too— and I think I could marry."

We never knew—Theo went back to the thinking of Marybeth-Lynn—we just didn't notice a thing. Police and neighbors and friends would ask about this when the story got out. Of course we never knew. How can you know? We've had dozens of students here, most more trouble than this girl, none nicer.

Yet the feeling grew on her along with a feeling of glee that they had known all along. Something seemed to reward or confirm her; right along there'd been something. She grew flushed with pleasure; she was sure she was right, this was the kind of thing she was good at remembering. Why does something shocking make you feel happy, something shocking but not mortal, exhilarating? And shall I tell Anton? Of course I'll have to; anyway, things like this were no pleasure to keep to yourself.

"If I were to fall in love," Ouida went on.

Love, I almost feel for that brave girl, to bring excitement to us like this. I always knew there was a mystery—because there was something so guarded, fatal, highly colored for a modern girl, cheeks apt to stain, bright pink patches appear at odd times in response to you knew not what remark. It sometimes seemed to Theo, though she had hardly dared to say it before now, that she had seen in the girl's eyes the one expression which she was herself most expert at recognizing; but she couldn't quite think what it was. She felt a deep affinity.

9. Realizations

No, there's no denying, Theo thought, with her cheeks heating up pinkly like a girl's, no denying that a sensation of gladness comes over you when you learn of the unexpected mystery and wickedness of someone you know. There's no denying the attractive bravery of wickedness. Bravery, however, ill-advised, makes the heart pound. Her feeling of affinity for this girl was, she knew, illicit, but it was there: relish, admiration. Theo thought of the brave women of the French Resistance. She could imagine Marybeth, smudged and beautiful, lurking in a cellar and the booted men outside, and bombers going over. If I had stayed in France, been caught there somehow by the war, as almost happened, then would I have been in the Resistance?

But I didn't, I came back to Orris, not that I ever regretted it. But perhaps it was cowardly and life-denying. This girl has taken chances. Theo tried to remember, but could not, just what it was the girl had taken chances about.

I myself, she thought, well, I took a chance on leading a plain life, an ordinary unsung life, like most people. That's a big chance, it's the biggest risk of all. What if you don't turn out to have the inner strength to support it undisappointed?

"Anton, just come into the kitchen a minute," she said. There was no use in Ouida knowing about this. Was she really glad Ouida's English had gotten better with a bang? It might turn out to be inconvenient.

"As I was coming home, a young man was coming up our steps, I thought at first hoping to rent a room, but he wasn't, he was looking for a friend of his—Lynn, obviously, by his description, but he called her by another name—Lynn isn't her name at all."

"Oh?" Anton said, not understanding. "It's interesting about Ouida, isn't it? Suddenly she understands everything, perhaps not idioms, but she hears the words correctly. Lynn—well, maybe she doesn't like her real name. Would you like a sherry?"

"Yes, please," Theo said. "Now listen, I know I'm right, it's just the kind of thing I remember accurately and in detail, and it's just the kind of thing you always refuse to believe. And there may be implications. I'm sure there'll be implications. Of course this boy could have been mistaken about Lynn—seen her at a distance and mistaken her, or something like that."

Anton handed her the sherry and was wearing his expression of patience, as when he would watch at a hole for hours with his camera waiting for the rat or whatever it would turn out to be.

"You don't believe me, I can see," said Theo. "Men never do seem to believe that things can be drastic, can be horrible. They expect life to unfold as a series of predictable events. But it doesn't—and here's proof: this lovely girl living in our house, a boarder among boarders, quiet and good, really a murderess living under an assumed name. Life can never be predicted and is always upsetting.

"He told me the real name, Marybeth Howe, and I remembered almost immediately," she went on. "It's just the kind of thing I happen to remember. I know you think that's morbid. So Marybeth Howe is some kind of dangerous criminal—a murderess, I suppose. A murder is the kind of thing I would be most likely to remember."

Anton knitted his forehead to disguise his unbelief.

Theo seemed to glow with life, almost joy; it seemed to him ghoulish of her.

"Maybe one of these FBI most-wanted girls. I'm an obsessive reader of post office notices; the lines are so long now, it's the only thing to do while you stand there. But this would have been some time ago—several years ago perhaps—because I no longer remember what it was—political conspiracy or mail fraud, then, maybe—I don't think murder is a federal crime. It explains a lot about Lynn, Anton. Why she is always guarded, and why she seems to have no friends. She is *wanted*."

"A celebrated crime of passion perhaps?" Anton suggested. Theo did not think he was serious. Did he believe her? Was he teasing? "Or one of those scary murderesses from cults? A Manson girl? No, I can't believe it."

"It's very curious that I can't remember," Theo said, thinking back on moments, shadows, flickers of dementia or malice which might have seemed to cross the girl's face—an unnatural stoniness of expression concealing her real ability to carve gashes in living people or hack their heads off.

Women don't do these things, Anton was thinking, and Theo was thinking that they might.

They were enjoying the discussion, especially Theo. How like Teddy this is, Anton thought, looking at the excited brightness of her eyes, her sharpened teeth showing like a dear old stoat. Who could believe it? Who could have thought it?

Now they saw Ouida standing in the kitchen doorway smiling her pretty formal smile, the one that meant she hadn't been able to follow their fast American talk.

"Excuse me, but if you will be sitting in here a little, I will vacuum the dining room and library," she said.

They nodded. "I prefer to vacuum when the news is on." She laughed.

"It's all academic, since she's gone anyway," Anton said of Marybeth.

"It may have been a sympathetic sort of crime—perhaps she was a rape victim. Yet I've a notion it was not a sympathetic crime or I'd be able to remember. Surely I'm trying to forget. She's such a lovely girl."

"It'll drive you crazy either way, not knowing," Anton said.

"Anton, promise you won't call the police about this," Theo said, suddenly scared. From the dining room came the reassuring sounds of Ouida and the vacuum. The orderly daily humming of life all around you, and you discover a murderess has been living in your house.

The murderess was stunned for a moment, viewing the puddle. Had forgotten that they have to be tended every moment, have to be fed, have to be distracted with sights and comforts and taken to pee. "Oh, nuts, come on, Chen-yu," she whispered, and dragged him out of the restaurant before anyone saw. Chen-yu. She wondered what he'd change his name to when he grew up. She could advise him. Making up names was one thing she knew she was good at. This made her wonder about her own new name, coming from Julie; it would be the first new name she had no control over, except for her own real name. Of course she hadn't had any control over that.

He looked as if he were going to cry; maybe he hadn't finished his sandwich. She clutched him tightly. "Come on, Chen-yu. Chen-yu and Marybeth going on the cable car, okay? Nice, nice cable car? Like a train. Chen-yu see it?" They walked up Market Street a few steps to where the cable car was pulling in. He smiled radiantly and Marybeth felt proud, rather, for a minute, to have accomplished this.

The rush of air, the clatter of the cable car were exhilarating for a minute or two. They got off at the top of the hill near those big hotels. She hopped off at the stop and held out her arms, and a man handed Chen-yu down to her. The man was looking at her, sexy and hopeful, and then flinched when he came into contact with Chen-yu's sopping bottom. Marybeth laughed. Chen-yu's legs flopped like a little doll's as she carried him over to the sidewalk and set him down.

One of the hotels had a glass elevator running up and down its side, with ant people staring out. Chen-yu nodded in fascination when she asked him if he wanted to ride on that. She was beginning to catch on. You just have to keep them moving and distracted with sights. She wondered if the hotel would even let them on the elevator in their old clothes. The people in the glass elevator went up and down the outside face of the building like mercury in a thermometer. I can become an elevator operator in my next life, she thought.

The doorman looked at them disgustedly. Marybeth tried to appear confident, as if they belonged to someone who stayed in this hotel, daughter and baby in from Marin County hippie commune come to visit dowager mother, who is upstairs crying, from Detroit. Marybeth could invent whole pasts at the merest wink of a doorman. Here we are, Mama, she practiced in her mind, without thinking of her real mother, who seemed not to belong to her any more. Nobody stopped them from getting into the glass elevator.

Chen-yu didn't like it much. He looked out the glass at all the city and at all the world, and didn't seem to care about the distance and immensity. Maybe their eyes didn't distinguish things like detail and depth until they got a certain age. Marybeth loved the elevator. She wanted to rise and rise and rise and just escape out the top into air. She relished the appalled swoop of her own stomach, proof she wasn't dead.

She drew Chen-yu out behind her at the top, where she had expected an observation room. But it was a white-walled gallery. Perhaps they had gotten off on the wrong floor. She looked around all the same. On high white diagonal walls hung enormous photographs. Usually she only liked photographs of people—say of old wizened women staring out of the doors of shacks, or of prostitutes in faraway cities with their bright lips and bold smirking faces. These pictures instead showed the still world—ripples on sand, a pine cone, mountains with snow on them. There were no people. Each was a composition of light and shadow; the menace of shadow elucidated the shining form.

Struck, even moved, Marybeth dragged Chen-yu along, studying the prayerful shapes of mountains, tunnels of waves. They walked along staring into pine needles. Chen-yu laughed at a squirrel on a branch. Marybeth noticed that she was breathing quickly, as if she'd been running or making love. The gallery opened out into a broad foyer where a woman sat at a table with a stack of catalogues, and behind her on the white wall were the words "ANTON MUIR WAIT: Retrospective 1938–1975."

"Oh!" said Marybeth in surprise, aloud, not quite knowing why, but it was so especially surprising to know a person whose name was up in large letters. Oh, so this is what he does! He's famous, then. Someone who is permitted to interpret the world.

"From his tonalist beginnings in the thirties, Wait showed an increasing impatience with the potentiality of traditional soft-focus for the hard surface of . . ." said a placard by a photograph of the great brown visage of a cliff.

"Would you like to see the catalogue?" said the woman, so that they had to retreat again along the corridor, afraid of having to buy a ticket. Marybeth found herself thinking of the love notes Anton sent her. Perhaps he did know something about love. Now it was too late. Just for a minute—before telling herself it was silly, how hard up can you be—just for a minute she felt the wish to sleep with Anton under the tall pine tree, lapped by the pounding waves.

A stairway at the exit led up or down. They climbed. It was easy just to keep trudging and climbing. And wasn't it normal to try to climb up to a high place, where you received inspiration and assurance, the way people in the Bible went up mountains, and pilgrims in other stories? They found themselves entering a great lounge with a bar in the center, with people lounging at it, and windows all around where people stared down at the world looking for assurance. She and Chen-yu found a spot to look down from.

Down below to the east the sun was striking the windows of the hillsides houses in Berkeley and Oakland, making squares of flame. The calm water of the Bay stretched southward along the peninsula. Ships steamed in and out, sailboats skirted here and there, tilted. On all the ships, piers, porches, in all the rooms behind the sunlit windows, people lived, think of that. People crawling along in all the tiny cars she saw. Down there were a million places she could go; the world was a hive of cells and cars and rooms for people to live and hide in. An infinitude of new names, combinations, new doorbells and new cards on mailboxes could be imagined. The world went on in every direction as far as you could see, entirely intersected with lines representing rods, streets, avenues leading to the unseen but indisputably present rest of the world—leading to, say, Canada, where, however there's an extradition treaty, but on, on to Alaska, over into Russia, roads even across trackless wastes—probably there was some way across land masses to Brazil, home of Ouida, into the Amazon there and get adopted by primitive tribes.

And it seemed to her that a great sigh was coming up, as if all the people in all the houses had sighed at once. An anguished, a defeated, a plaintive sigh of resignation, reedy and thin to the ear; she could just hear it: It is not possible to be happy, it seemed to say. It is necessary to be good. You can't be happy, but you can be good. A great sigh, like a wind, carrying the whole message of the world.

Unaccountably, tears came to Marybeth's eyes again, and at the same time her stomach began to churn. She felt in her purse for a Kleenex. Her mouth watered evilly. Dear God, was she going to throw up? That would certainly attract attention; that would be even better than tears for making people look at you and then look away in frantic hate, remembering you. Christ, where do all these tears come from and please don't let me throw up here.

Her fingers groping in her purse encountered a comb, the camera, a scarf, a plastic compact of birth control pills. She pulled the scarf out and pressed it against her lips until her stomach stopped. No one was looking at them, she must look all right, but she felt dead white and her hand shook. When she looked down at the world again, her stomach took another turn. She looked away and took deep breaths. Then she reached in her purse again and pulled out the birth control pills and stuffed them into the sand-filled cylinder by the elevator, she couldn't say why.

She'd never been afraid of heights before. Her face was wet and sweaty. Chen-yu watched her. The idea came over her, as it had several times that day, and often did in moments of fatigue or despair or when she got her period, or when it was her birthday or Christmas or when something made her think of her mother and father: they were going to catch her today. She had always shaken off this cowardly and dangerous feeling before, with various admonitions, but now her stomach was so queer. When she thought she looked okay, she took Chen-yu's hand and went off to find the inside elevator, where you didn't have to look down.

* * *

You didn't have to look, Ouida thought, averting her eyes from the television as soon as the news came on. She'd vacuum instead. When the somber faces of the newsmen came on, looking out with earnest exasperation, she always turned the set off and did something else. Let the others injure themselves nightly with the poisonous toxins. The vacuum made a restful sound, rushing up to fill her ears, her poor ears which had been assaulted all day long by the newly understandable English, as well as by the noise of automobiles, planes and chickens. She could see that English comprehension was not an unmixed blessing—once you understood it, you couldn't switch it off.

But with the vacuum on, her thoughts could come back in Portuguese, clearer, more concentrated. It seemed clear that the driver's license people had been alerted by the immigration people to be on the lookout for her. It had to be something like that, because her eyes were perfect with her new glasses. But if the immigration people knew she was going to turn up at the driver's license bureau, why had they not seized her there? Was it because they did not know that she did not intend to come to them of her own volition?

Meu Deus. Marriage—the word came to her in English—seemed the only safe thing, especially if the *feijoada* benefit was not a success. If only Mr. Griggs was not so late with his car all the time.

Suddenly a flicker behind her caused her to whirl around lightly—and she could lightly dance at the *carnaval*, too. She glimpsed the darting of a giant shadow on the wall, a huge shadow, three times the size of Griggs and darker, more profound; human, cloaked. It flickered and then vanished so suddenly that she wondered if she had somehow inhaled it with the wand of the vacuum cleaner that she held, uselessly whooshing, in her startled hand. Yet it was only by the racing of her agitated heart that she could be sure it had been there at all.

Her heart stopped, turned, braking sickeningly with fright, and her mother and half sister had both died of their hearts. She pulled out a chair and sat down until her own heart calmed, and tried to guess the meaning of this portent, which had come hard on the heels of her reflection about Mr. Griggs and many other things. It was so large, it could almost portend the Federal Government; it was too large for Griggs, even for Colonel Pacific, of that she was sure, and it was trapped inside the *aspirador*.

She reached over to turn off the vacuum, so as not to waste electricity. Of course he was not really inside there. A dusty sweet smell filled the space around her; the particles floating looked brighter than specks had ever looked before. One shadow that comes to people of course, she thought, is the shadow of death. This did not seem like the shadow of death, or if it was, it had not come for her; it had not laid its hand at her throat as it was said to do. Yet it was menacing, that one, ugly, *feio*, the lumplike shape of its back, the toss of its cloak, a crabbed line of chin and nose; it was the profit of ugliness. Certainly it was the embodiment of the dim feeling of fear that had lain about her since yesterday, which she had thought then to have to do with Colonel Pacific. Now that was not so clear. It had indeed looked like descriptions she had heard of the shadow of death.

She was being a foolish girl, she knew, but she turned the vacuum back on, hoping perhaps to suck the shadow up again and chew it up in its entrails, pulverize this bad shadow. It was silly; but it really seemed that the shadows had not come for her at all, but for someone else, and she knew that when her heart got back to beating normally, then she had better go and warn Miss Theo. Even though she knew that Miss Theo would not believe her.

* * *

''Why would you think I would have to call the police?''
Anton is saying, these two still standing in the kitchen
where Ouida left them, taking sips from their little
glasses.

''Men are generally more law-abiding than women,''
Theo says. ''Women have a feeling that since they didn't
make the rules, the rules have nothing to do with them.
I have this feeling myself. Men, on the other hand, care
about rules and forms. At meetings—for instance, at the
Co-op meetings—it is always the men who say things like
'point of order,' and 'matter of precedent.' Men use
logic to justify wickedness. I've noticed it time and
again.''

''But you think I would turn in a poor, pretty girl?''
says Anton, his face redder than usual, his eyes astonished.

''Well, of course 'pretty.' When you say pretty, I have
to qualify my prediction. Pretty makes a difference. I
suppose it makes crime harder to believe. Pretty does
not have to resort to crime. Pretty cannot have meant it,
in any case. But if I convinced you that pretty did, then
I would expect you to say, well, of course we love *this*
pretty murderer, but if everyone made exceptions for the
murderers they know, then what kind of society would
we have? And then turn her in.''

''Well, perhaps some men would, but, Teddy, I'm not
men, after all.''

''You aren't going to turn her in?''

''Teddy, she isn't even here. But I wouldn't, no.''

''That's because you don't believe she's done anything,'' Theo says in a fury. ''You don't believe she could
have, because she's pretty and young and a woman. It
must have been an accident. Women do not come
equipped with malice and volition both, isn't that what
you think? If they have one, they don't have the other.''

Anton shrugs. His beliefs are as she says. "But I read that female crime is on the increase," he consoles her, and they both laugh.

"Miss Theo, there is something I have to tell you," Ouida said, so conspiratorially that Theo imagined that Ouida, too, had found out the identity of Marybeth. They had not noticed Ouida standing there.

"It is not easy for me to tell you this, because I know that in America everything is reason, reason and not much faith."

"That would not be my construction of the American consciousness, not at all," Theo said, mostly to Anton.

"In Brazil, for instance, there are many believers in World Messianity, and here hardly any. What is plain in Brazil is not believed here because people have not the habit of belief. I am not explaining this very well."

"Oh, Ouida, darling, Americans have enough problems of faith without World Messianity, too," Theo said.

"Well, signs, portents—I know you do not believe in them, but I must tell you something, a great feeling that came over me that the shadow of death is in this house. At first I thought it was for me, of course, but no; and yet I am afraid, and I think you should know. These things can be averted; sometimes they come as a warning."

"Well," Theo said, disconcerted, impressed in spite of herself. "In fact, something has happened, so you're both right and wrong. It's poor Lynn, she is in some difficulty. She's been in some difficulty with the police." How could Ouida have known this?

"Perhaps that is it," Ouida said, relieved. The police were one thing that could be averted. Someone who does wrong can make reparations and avert horrors. "If she has done a wrong thing, then she must go to the police. Then, after some time, she will be sorry and her heart become pure again.'' Theo and Anton did not seem to understand her. Their faces were aloof and blank.

"We must pay a price for all that we do, and then when we have paid it we can be again as we were.''

"Go to the police?'' Theo said in drifting tones, as if she had remembered leaving her handbag somewhere else.

"Also, if she is a bad person, then it is better for everyone that she go to jail; that is what jails are for. We do not always agree when the police take someone to jail, but they are usually right.''

"The police?'' Theo said again.

"Many times we disagree in Brazil, for there the police are also political and may take people away for their beliefs. That is not true in America, I know. But criminals, they must be punished. That is a law everywhere and always has been.'' Why did they seem so astonished? It was a law in America, too, surely, as also in Brazil and down through history. "It is in the Bible.''

At this Theo and Anton betrayed a flicker of understanding. Oh, they thought, it is a religious idea; it is not that gentle Ouida is especially vindictive.

"We must worry about society but also the soul of the bad person. If he pays in this life, then he can go on to another life without bad suffering. I will tell you a story about the woman who was going to be hanged in Londrina, in Brazil; this was when I was younger, and a minister in our church went to talk to her and he told us about her. In her jail cell she had a very bad dream which she told to the minister and he explained it to us. In this dream she was herself in another life before, and there she was a woman who drowned a little boy. She said in her dream she know—knowed—know? . . .''

"Knew,'' said Theo and Anton.

"In her dream she knew her name but when she wake she cannot remember, but she remembered it was in Germany.''

"Why did she drown the little boy?" Theo asked.

"Because he was the child of someone else, and she cannot herself have a child, something like that. Some people came in a boat and tried to pull the little boy out, but he was dead. So in this life she must die a terrible death by hanging and in this way pay for that other."

"It seems so unfair!" cried Theo. "Why should you be responsible for what you did in another life when you can't help it, it wasn't really you!"

"Oh, yes, it was really you," Ouida said.

"The thing with the little boy, that's a little like something that happened to me once," Theo said, with a dart of pain across her abdomen which she couldn't explain; it was, almost, a memory of pain.

"However that may be, Teddy, I think we have a present problem on our hands," Anton reminded her with a look. "Ouida, you are under no circumstances to tell the police or anything like that."

"Oh, no, I would not myself do that," Ouida said. "I do not like the idea of someone going to jail. Only I know it is just, and it is a way to make people safe also." Then she smiled, remembering something. "I am no one to go looking for police, remember."

"Ouida's views on jail are just the normal views that everybody used to have forty years ago. How greatly things have changed," Theo said. "And we think there's no progress."

"Did she," Ouida wondered suddenly, "did she perhaps murder her lover? Then I do not think anything bad would happen, for the law understands that love, and jealousy, sometimes the passions . . ."

"No, I don't think that was it," Theo said.

"No? Well, I *have* noticed that is true, that ladies do not kill men in America as often as in Brazil. I think that ladies are better-natured here. In Brazil women often kill men if they are jealous; but they are forgiven, for the law understands certain things about human nature. If a man kills a woman, they are not forgiven so often. But death, of course, is never condoned!''

10. Simple Justice

Ouida, heavy-hearted to think of trouble for her pretty American friend, went back to the dining room and dragged the vacuum cleaner into the living room. The evil influence was gone or remained inside the machine this time and did not infect the room. She had just begun pushing the long-handled brush along the top of the curtains, her thoughts sinking gratefully into Portuguese, when the doorbell rang. Two strangers stood at the door— a woman with a baby in a stroller and a man companion. They smiled at her in a friendly manner. The man had on a very fine suit and he was white, and the woman was a black woman, and the baby in the middle was light brown—so, was her first thought, even in America sometimes a black woman marries with a white man. This couple was dressed up as if they were going to church.

The men held out a paper to Ouida. ''Have you heard the good news?'' he and the woman said together, in gladdened tones; then they looked at each other and laughed with apparent pleasure at the accord that had directed them to speak in chorus.

''Have you heard the good news?'' the man resumed, still holding the paper, which Ouida now took. *Good News*, the paper was called.

''We'd like to tell you about the blessed news sent by Jesus Christ regarding the coming,'' the woman said. Ouida looked at their beautiful clothes and pleasant open faces. The little child waved her rattle.

''Come in,'' Ouida said politely. Politely the visitors came in. ''Please sit down.'' It was plain that they wanted to talk to her, and had not come for Miss Theo or Mr. Anton. Beaming, they sat down, and Ouida did, too, but with confusion about whether to ask them if they would like some tea or coffee, as would certainly be offered in Brazil. She inched forward with hostesslike alertness on her chair.

"Have you ever asked yourself why most of today's news is bad? Why there is war, and crime, and violence? Why not peace and plenty? Pure air and fertile land?" said the woman.

"And yet," added the man, "the world spends twenty-seven million dollars an *hour* for war. Pollution blights the land, air and water. Millions live in hunger and poverty. Why do we have reason to think that things will get any better?" He spoke very clearly and was easy to understand.

"Yes," Ouida agreed, "terrible things happen, especially in India, but also in my country, Brazil, and also here. Yet I know we are on the eve of a great change for mankind." It occurred to her that these were almost the only visitors she had had in America, though Roberta would often stop in for a moment when she called for her to go to a meeting. These new visitors paused, a slightly startled pause, before beginning their discourse again. Ouida felt worried about her accent. Perhaps they had not understood her.

"Why should we expect the Creator to come to man's rescue?" the woman went on.

"Excuse me, but can I offer you some tea?" Ouida suggested. Again the exchange of glances.

"A glass of water?" the woman said. "Thank you," the man said. Ouida went off quickly to the kitchen. Her heart threatened palpitation, yet she was not unhappy but rather pleased and excited—she examined her emotions—and encouraged. There might be something propitious and mitigating about this visit, after the various ill omens coming so thick and fast—the letter yesterday, and the bad event at the Division of Motor Vehicles, and then the shadow of death on top of that.

As she was filling the kettle, into the kitchen flew Miss Theo, looking like death herself, pale, her long arms clutching the front of her blouse as if she had a pain in her own heart there.

"Ouida!" cried Theo. "I suppose I shouldn't have screamed at them, I frightened them out of their pants, but they frightened *me*. There are so many strange things happening here today, and then to encounter these sinister strangers in the living room."

"Religious people, I am making them some tea," Ouida said.

"Oh," Theo sighed. "Oh. Well, get them out, can you? I'm afraid of strangers—never let anyone like that in, one just doesn't. You don't know those people, they could be—they could be—how do you know . . ." She flapped her arms, quite absurdly distressed.

It was strange, this behavior, even from the excitable Miss Theo. She was puffing a little, exactly as if she had the heart trouble so distinctly prefigured by the shadowy presence; her large eyes rolled, she seemed to flap like a dying hen, her feathers on edge. Ouida set her kettle down in case she might have to support Miss Theo, and felt obscurely angry at her, and fearful that she had caused a fatal difficulty. Theo waved her into the living room: "Get rid of them, get rid of them."

When Ouida got to the living room, her visitors were fleeing anyway. They had left a paper on the seat of the chair where the woman sat. "Many people find it hard to understand the ways of God," it said. "They ask themselves certain questions, questions which human beings have asked themselves for centuries, without listening for the answers.

Why is evil allowed to remain in the world? If God cares about people, why does he let them suffer? Why do some people suffer and others prosper? Why does it often seem it is the Godless who prosper?

If you have asked yourself these questions, you are like many people. Perhaps you may not know the answers, yet the answers are very simple and available to all. There is but one answer. The answer is one word. The answer is: FAITH.

Sometimes we feel that we are alone. God has forgotten us. Other people do not understand us. Is FAITH alone enough to bear us up over the turbulent waves of pain and sorrow that are man's lot?

"Oh," Ouida said to herself, "that is the question, there is the very question that I ask myself. What wise people have left this paper!" And without meaning to, for she was a strong and sensible young woman, she uttered a cry, something between a sob and a sigh. It was as involuntary as if a spirit hand had pressed on her, there, expressing it.

She ran up to her room, always her impulse when she had an ache or a pain, and now upon feeling a strange unfamiliar sensation, as of swallowing something too large. In her room she realized she was angry, that it was a knot of anger beneath her breastbone, hurting her. It was bad of Miss Theo to shout at the religious people and make them unwelcome, and it was disconcerting to realize that beneath her brisk kindness Miss Theo was a mean woman ready to screech, something that was true of many *brancas*—in Brazil, too—and true of many women who are not married. Also true of those who are not religious, for with no faith to guide them they fear strangers in their houses, they fear the future altogether. Oh, but did she not fear it herself?

The pale blue unsympathetic eyes of Jesus watched her. The chill candle flickered in its dish on the closet shelf. She walked in a square around the prison cell of her room, clasping her hands. Through the open window sounds came up from the yard, Mr. Anton feeding the chickens.

Mortification. Mr. Griggs. The Division of Motor Vehicles. The Department of Immigration. Miss Theo had not ought to have screeched at them, them rising, gathering their papers, gasping, and the poor baby in the stroller being clattered over the sill of the door with a hurtful bump, shame blazing in all their cheeks.

Yet they had left sympathy and consolation for Ouida on the chair, their paper, what a kindness. Unconsoled, bitter, she sat on the edge of her bed and tried to form a soothing prayer. She thought of Mr. Anton, of his kindly nature and his occupation making beautiful pictures of God's handiwork, so that in the next life he could expect to be a priest. She could imagine Anton a priest, putting his hands on her head, on her cheeks, putting his hands on her, perhaps her shoulders, on her . . . He had never touched her or taken her hand. Ouida stared into the pinkness of her palm and did not know why she felt so strange, so forlorn, so longing. What would become of her?

She had stuck the hen feathers on her mirror, around the frame one by one. They drew her gaze now. What had she wanted them for? Those feathers had potent properties, could heat the blood with burning love, or kill an enemy, but only if you believed in them. She, Ouida, of course did not. She looked at her reflection to see if her eyes were swollen. Her face did not show her grief. Her face in grief became just the impassive face of all Brazilian women, more familiar to her in a strange way than when signalized by smiles. She ran her finger along the serrated edge of a dried, powerful feather, stiff crusted symbol of something. She plucked it and drew it along her cheek in the path of a tear.

She tried to think how these feathers worked. Though she herself did not believe in them, might they not be of help to the girl—Lynn—in trouble with the police? Perhaps someone coming to the *feijoada* would know the spells—some Brazilian from the *favela* or from the country. You hear of marvelous cures and spells. She clasped the feather to her, without faith in it, all alone, alone, far from home.

A thought of home overwhelmed her, not from the middle distance of her life in Londrina, but from childhood, from her own village. She could remember leaning against the sun-warmed cement-block wall of her house, or standing in the shadow of the thatch; watching the pigs in the muddy ruts of the street, and the little naked children crowding in all the doorways.

What had she thought about then, when she did not know about America, or even about Londrina or São Paulo, and it was as if there were just this one street in the world, a street of huts and on one end Marco's Cantina where the men went, and the store with a big bright glass window, the coffin store. Inside on racks the little coffins stacked, little white coffins of graduated sizes, and, at the bottom, the black coffins. How had it been decided, she tried to remember, that you got a black coffin instead of a white?

Well, they would put her in a black coffin now; now that anger had entered her body, there was a poison stain on her.

She didn't often let herself remember her village. She had liked to believe that her life had somehow begun with the smart civilized rituals of the missionary school, as if her first memory were lifting out the sheets, pounds and pounds of wet sheets, from the automatic washing machine that sang day and night outside under the tin eaves of the lean-to; and with the spider monkey watching her, and the coatimundi, and in the distance the little singing voices of the children in their white smocks, the saved children who wore white smocks instead of grave-clothes.

How far they had come, *ela e Arturo e Edgardo!* But to what purpose, she wondered now. Indian girls in her

village got babies from nature, not from marriage. She
had thought that shocking once.

"I was a fool to think they would give me a driver's
license before they give me a visa," she told herself
aloud. "I thought they could not tell I have no visa."
Her tears would not stop. "I was a fool to think that they
will give me anything. There is nothing in this world for
me."

Up from the yard came Anton's voice, talking to Theo:
"Calm down, Teddy. I object to your being excited by
all this, it's horrible somehow. She's gone, anyhow. Go
look in her room, see if she took her things."

"I couldn't. We said we'd keep her room for her. I
couldn't look in someone's room."

All at once, without warning, Chen-yu began to cry, un-
controllably, like a whistle at noon. He planted his feet
and wailed like a factory chimney. Marybeth was dumb-
struck.

"Chen-yu, honey, what's the matter?" she asked him
over and over, whispering, and then more loudly to reassure passersby who stared that she was concerned, was
trying to help. He shrieked. "What's the matter, tell me,
can't you? What's the matter?" She said it loudly.

She felt him all over to see if a pin was sticking into
him. But he was all right except for dampness. She lifted
him up; he leaned against her and wailed. She put him
down.

He was attracting attention. "Come on, Chen-yu, shut
up," she said. It seemed to her that that made him louder.
Marybeth looked at the women who looked at her. They
didn't seem sympathetic. Do something, said the glances
of the passersby.

Marybeth didn't know what to do. "Do you want
candy? Ice cream?" His tears were tears of misery, there
was no doubt. Some deep source of misery, personal to

him, some pain or sorrow. "Can you talk or not?" she cried. The cold glances of the passing woman frightened her. Perhaps she would be arrested for child abuse.

He wants to go home, why wouldn't he? He wants his mother, anyone would. Dragged around by this strange woman. On an impulse of remorse she kissed him, and, mysteriously, he stopped, maybe with surprise. Marybeth gathered him up as if he were a ticking bomb and stood teetering on the curb with her thumb stuck out, wanting to get out of there as quickly as they could.

In a minute she realized she wasn't even standing on the right side of the street; you have to stand on the south side to catch the cars heading back over the Bay Bridge. She crossed over, and, mind of ice, climbed into the first car that stopped, a guy about thirty in jeans and dumb yokel straw-colored hair.

"Yeah, Fairfield or as far as you're going up Highway 80," she said. He nodded.

"Lovely day," he said.

"Cold," Marybeth said, "kind of cold." He glanced around at them.

"Your kid ain't got no sweater—aren't you 'fraid he'll catch cold?"

"He's all right," Marybeth said, looking to see if that was solicitude in his face. A mean, narrow little face; she didn't like it. She looked away, looked so as not to meet his eyes if he looked at her again.

Almost at once she saw the shiny handle of blue metal hidden in the fold of the jacket lying between his legs on the seat. The handle of a gun? Her eyes fell on it but he didn't see her see it. She stared out the window ahead of them. It made sense to her in a strange way, like a mystery solved; this was the tangible menace that had been stalking her. He had a gun.

"Too cold for a kid not to have no sweater," he said.

Nuts, Marybeth thought, I'm always jittery hitchhiking. That could be anything—a wrench, a stapler. This guy's all right. She tried to think of something to ask him, something predictive, some test question. Nothing came to her.

His driving was all right. Did his eyes slew round to look at her? She was afraid to look at his jacket, too much like staring at his crotch, or at his gun—either way. She stared straight ahead, toward the on-ramp, a crazy confluence of arches where the freeway joined the bridge.

Chen-yu suddenly leaned against the seat back and slid down it, plumply, with a giggle, jiggling the guy's elbow. Marybeth wrestled his wiggling little body onto her lap. The car drew neatly into place in a line of other cars going over the bridge.

On either side of them the world was a pretty blue, like a blue tablecloth spread out for a nice picnic, the little sailboats like folded napkins. The world always looked more festive when you were sad or scared; it was everyone else's picnic. The car smelled funny, she thought, nothing identifiable, but funny, familiar. All cars have some funny smell of their own. There weren't any seat belts. The driver swerved into another lane, abruptly, so that she and Chen-yu slid toward him. She tightened her hold on Chen-yu and moved away.

"Do you live around here?" he asked.

"Yes," she said, unable to think of what the right thing to say was. "No, I'm staying here right now. I live in Wyoming."

"Yeah?"

Marybeth quickly saw that that was wrong. She had said the wrong thing. She looked away out across the water, at the steel railings of the bridge. She thought of people walking along them, and thought of their legs being crushed by cars. You should never say you're from out of town; you say your father, the police chief, is expecting you. "I'm staying with my aunt and uncle in Albany. He's with the—the water district."

"All that way from Wyoming, that's pretty far away, ain't it?" he said.

"You ever been there?"

"Not me," he said, but he had a hick Wyoming accent, Idaho, someplace like that.

He sounded all right. So what if he had a gun, a lot of people do. Her eyes tried to pry at it again. Who knows what he's into—that doesn't mean he's going to hurt us. Chen-yu began to sway sleepily and bump gently against her breast. He was probably used to taking a nap; poor little bastard, has to go through life with a name like Chen-yu and he doesn't even know it yet.

She'd been scared before and nothing ever came of it. I'm a bad hitchhiker, ought never to do it, she thought. Ought to know better. The story of my life. She'd even been hitchhiking with male companions and got scared, they had all got scared; it's the situation, maybe built in—everybody gets paranoid. She got the idea of calling to people driving along next to them; just something, as if she knew them, or calling "Watch me, keep an eye on me here." Gunpowder was what the car smelled of, explosive, that bitter smoky smell of cordite, a smell she knew perfectly well. Julie's plum jelly. This redneck with his gun.

A new idea scalded her; as if someone had poured it from a kettle, it splashed searingly against her brain: this is the pattern. This is what I've been bound to do all along. This is going to end my problems. This guy is destined to kill me.

Yes, clear, that was how it would be. Kill me, dump me somewhere. Someday they'll find me, body of unknown, half clothed, half decomposed; they'll look at my teeth and figure out it's me. They'll put it all together.

That's what happens to people like you, living and dying by violence. Her mind's ear hears this intoned by the priestly voices of television sheriffs, ministers, school principals, her father and mother. She believed them.

From the corner of her eye it seemed that the gun had enlarged, a bulge, increasing.

She sighed, it must have been out loud. The guy looked over at her abruptly. He must have been watching her all along. He must be able to watch her in the mirror. Look, whatever you do to me, she thought of saying, please don't hurt Chen-yu. But she knew she mustn't acknowledge the danger, she must be serene as long as possible. Yet she could feel the imploring cries battering in her throat to be cried.

In a way she was glad the mystery was over, the mystery of what was going to happen to her. Things had been up in the air so long. How could she feel glad about something like this? With this mortal fear flowing up, would she struggle and resist when the time came? Rotten that Chen-yu was along, God, Christ.

"I'm Marybeth," she said, the second time she'd spoken her name aloud that day.

"Sadler," he said.

Her mind worked on the idea of jumping. She'd done that before, jumped out of a truck, a time when she had thought truck drivers were safe nice people and it was all right to ride with them, and he'd grabbed her hair and pulled her toward him, all the time driving this huge truck, and looking down from his imprisoning grasp she saw his big purple prick—God knows what he had in mind, driving along at sixty. But then they had come to a construction ditch and had to slow down, and she just jumped, wriggled away and jumped; her scalp ached where he had clung to her hair.

Some men in hard hats and bright orange vests laughed to see her alight, crazily tumbling out of that big truck, and one gave her a sandwich.

Maybe she could grab the keys out of the ignition and throw them out the window. But he could catch her hand, she'd have to be quick, he'd have to be looking away during that instant. Some keys you have to turn before you can pull them out, some come right out—which was this?

His eyes, kind of bluish yellow, watched her in his mirror.

A young woman yet, intoned the voices of television newscasters, not so much to live for—even so, it's a shame. Would she really miss anything? Hadn't she messed it up already? It was clear that there were to be no babies, no lying all night in the arms of lovers; she was past all that. Was she young or was she old? Little hot Chen-yu throbbed in her arms.

"Sadler is my name. I have to stop off and do something in Albany," he said. His voice drained away. Nervous. He's nervous as me, Marybeth thought from a distance, like an audience.

"You're from Albany?" she asked in a bright social voice, making him like her, so he'd have to kill her liking her. It was easy to make men like you.

"I didn't say that," he said.

Would Chen-yu understand to run, when they got out of the car, if she whispered at him *"Run!"* as frighteningly as she could? He had a warm orange smell, which she clung to.

A man in a big Buick pulling up next to them seemed to know them. Could it be Chuck Sweet? But it wasn't; he pulled ahead. Her killer made a mistake shifting; his gears ground, his car leapt as though shot.

"What do you do?" Marybeth asked. "Are you interested in art?" He seemed amazed. He remained silent. "I wanted to be a painter," she said, knowing this was useless, but the words just came drooling out of her as if her head had come unplugged. "Or rather, I was expected to be a painter, my mother was artistic, she went to the Art Institute, but really I'm not artistic, not to speak of. I really wanted to be a guerrilla, I . . ."

"I wanted to be an engineer," he said. What do you know. Her heart raced with hope: engineer; finer sensibilities; education. Oh, shit, maybe he means a train engineer, all boys want to be engineers.

"Are you married? Do you have children?" But here the quality of his silence became more impenetrable; her words bounced off him like little showers of gravel. This was the wrong thing to ask about.

Maybe she could put out her hand quickly and draw the gun from the folds of his jacket; could lean forward quickly imprisoning his right hand on the wheel and with her left hand draw the gun, and if the car crashed, that would be good, too. People would crowd around. Maybe he was stoned, his face was so stony and rapt.

What if she told him, "I am a wanted killer myself"? What would that do to his face? I am a well-known axe-murderess, a poisoner, too, she could say.

It was easier to think about him than about herself.

She was sweating, that was the smell: it was herself. He could smell it, too. They all smell alike, he would be thinking, stinking afraid. If she could clear her smell out.

She reached for the window crank and moved it, watching him. He allowed it. Maybe I could offer to screw him, she thought. But maybe that's what he means to have anyway. I give head, she could say. Or, It's my birthday, she could say.

Now they were coming off the bridge, and out into the wide lanes opposite the toll plaza, a good place for jumping out. If she didn't jump out here, they'd move out into Interstate 80. She should say, right here, "Please let me out at the Emeryville exit."

She should say it so he would say no, or say nothing, and drive on. "Let me out at University Avenue," she should say, or, "Let me out at Gilman Street," provoking the moment he would say no and they would understand each other and understand what he meant to do.

"Horsie, horsie, horsie!" screamed Chen-yu, so that their eyes leapt around looking. Yes, a horse looked back, up ahead of them from his horse trailer. Chen-yu laughed and waved.

"Your kid wanna be a cowboy, looks like," her killer said.

He's leaving it to me, he's leaving it to me, thought Marybeth. I have to be the one to say let me out. Then he'll say no.

Maybe it was an oil smell. Inside the car it was hot, the air seemed to move before them with the purple shimmer of oil. Maybe the car was leaking oil and would leak it all out, and they would come to a halt. A car bleeding to death. If you could just pull a plug on a car and stop it some way.

She sighed deeply and said aloud, "Just let me out at the Emeryville exit will be fine."

"I thought you said you wanted to go up Highway 80?"

"We want to catch a bus into Oakland. I forgot, I have to meet my aunt."

He didn't say anything but he didn't slow down, either. Her heart, which she had not thought could race any harder, began to be heard through her breast. He would be thinking of what to say. His own thoughts would be scattered, high-pitched, she knew this from experience, the shapes of words all crazy and distorted, bouncing off the inside of the head. She tried to hear them through the walls of his head. Probably he could not hear her words either.

He said nothing; maybe he hadn't heard her, hemmed in by his own words. She'd better speak again. It's always up to the woman to talk; that's not fair, she thought. What if I say nothing more and am silent like a man—then what?

They went past the Emeryville exit, past the University

exit, so what need was there of words? He was going seventy; maybe a cop would pick them up.

What use of words? Marybeth sank into her thoughts. Maybe you'd like to come back to my house, she thought of saying. You know, you turn me on.

No, that was not the tack to take; make no suggestion of sex, sex a kind of smear on the windshield. Still, if they rape you they don't always kill you. Why do you think this is a killer? Well, it's those eyes, those eyes in the newspaper police-artist drawings, this is the Zebra killer, or the Zodiac killer, seen him someplace.

Did you ever fall in love? she thought of saying. Immediate love at first sight, love just takes you over, it isn't something you can help. That's what happened to me, Sadler, I've fallen in love with you; my little boy here, too. He loves you, we'd like to go home with you, we'd like to buy you a new car, my uncle the Buick dealer, you mustn't think this has ever happened to me before.

He had slowed the car down and moved over two lanes to the right. Marybeth stiffened and watched.

You're terrific, Sadler, she wanted to scream; I just have this feeling of love and devotion to you, nothing like this has ever happened to me before—with the funny feeling coming over her that these hard weapons, love ideas, would sting him someplace.

Her throat too dry and constricted to speak, as if dust poured in on them.

He was pulling off the right-hand exit by the race track. God—she saw where he meant to go, down along the Bay, through the parking lots by the race track, with no one around there today, and the swampy ground would soak up her blood; it would mingle with the oil slick off the Bay, that is if blood and oil do mix, and she'd say to Chen-yu, *"Run, run!"* All the same he couldn't get away on those little short legs across the wild cement acres;

Sadler could just drive over him and crush him down under the wheels.

There was no time to think about it any more. Mary-beth closed her arm around Chen-yu and leaned on the door handle, and they splattered out against the chain fence along the freeway exit. She didn't know if he lunged at them. He cried out something. Now the car skidded and passed them.

"Oh, Christ," she cried, her thoughts slopping and washing inside her jarred head.

She must have closed her eyes a second or two. She was on the ground staring into a pile of paper cups and leaves and wads clogging the fence and plastered over her eyes. She got up.

Chen-yu seemed crushed into the interstices of the chain links. Clinging to the wire, she slid along the fence to gather him up. She heard a car stopping, turning. Then her knees buckled again and she sagged against the fence.

Some man's face is near hers. He has pinned her down on soft cushions or they are in a coach traveling fast somewhere. She wants and doesn't want him to do what he is going to do. He passes his hands over her breasts, he will force her thighs apart. His face is beautiful but ruthless. He wears his uniform of the Forty-ninth Hussars. He always does what he wants to do; he always has his will.

In her belly deep inside she feels a tremble of excitement and dread. She is tense in expectation of his strong hand on her thighs. The softness of the cushions is welcome; welcome, too, will be the thrust of his body. She waits for the feel of his huge, hard cock. She swallows. Her head clears.

The men are still leaning over her. "What's happened?" "Are you all right?" "Were you in that car?" "Where's your car?" "Accident, accident," their voices are saying. Marybeth stares up at the faces, follows their eyes, looks at her forearms covered with blood. They catch at her and help her up; she feels their hands all over her shoulders. They've caught me, she thinks.

Now, somehow, they are sitting in their car. She is in the front seat. Her head is quite clear now. In the back seat, she becomes aware, is a blanket heap, a little heap of Chen-yu. And these are cops.

She has a dream, her head sinking against the car seat, of the whole thing happening again, the cold uprush of air as the door opened, the scream and the scraping. "Did I do something to offend you?" she seems to hear the voice of Sadler say.

She shakes her head to clear it. "Are you all right?" the patrolman is saying. Another cop, a wide old cop, is speaking on their radio. She tries to think but cannot.

Presently she says, "We fell out of a moving car."

"Was there trouble? What car? Did you get the license? Was it a green Chevy?"

"No, no trouble," she says. "My little boy leaned against the door handle and we fell out."

Why do they not speak of Chen-yu? Perhaps there are regulations, forms for speaking of dead heaps of blankets. Humbly Marybeth waits for them to tell her.

"There was no trouble," she says, in a convincing normal way. "I'm kind of shaken up. It was a hard fall, but, you know—Yeah, I know, seat belts."

They say nothing. The blanket heap is perhaps stirring. She realizes that she does not know if the Chen-yu she snatched from the fence was living. Perhaps he was a dead floppy doll already.

"Why didn't the bastard stop? Leaving the scene of an accident. Put out a description on that," the wide policeman says into his radio.

They would be speaking of Chen-yu's death on their radios, wouldn't they?

Could she bring him back to life by telling them who

she is? Could she exchange herself for him? Now's the chance. They've caught me, I must tell them. But she can't say any of this.

Now the little heap begins to make a sound, long and high like a radio signal. He isn't dead. No, she says, the man didn't scare us; no, we don't know his name, he picked us up in San Francisco; no, we didn't notice the license; no, it wasn't his fault; no, she didn't want to go to the emergency room; they were all right, could they go home?

"What's your name?" asks the one policeman. Her throat constricts.

"Lynn Lord," she says. "I, um, live in Orris, at 380 Ashby Path."

"Any I.D. ?"

Now is my chance, she thinks, now is my chance to tell them who I am and get it all over with. It's all over with anyway. You can't be happy but you can be good.

Still she sits dumply. "Oh, my purse! I guess it's still in that guy's car!" Her lies are undamaged by her fall. They believe this, of course. Why can't they tell lies from truth? Why can't everyone? Why don't they peer into her eyes and say, "Who are you really?" But they don't. They lecture her about hitchhiking. Do me a favor, do yourself a favor.

I won't tell them tonight, she thinks. Tomorrow is soon enough. I have to get Chen-yu home.

She feels so grateful, she almost loves them, handsome big men, one has a mustache, a Gay Nineties mustache. She thought cops were not allowed to have mustaches.

"We can send you home, you can ride up 80 in the sheriff's patrol. Christ, you dumb broads, hitchhiking. Don't you know what the world is like?"

11. More Ghostly Visitors

Sometimes after dinner, if she didn't have a meeting, Theo would sit in the Redwood Dining Room, reading until last light in the rosy animating presence of the nymphs of the window. She would do this if Anton was going out, and she had done it all the year she had lived there without him; a companionable room.

But tonight something was wrong in there, a shadow on her book, a color not the accustomed sunset rose but bleached gray, as if something obstructed the light coming through the stained glass. The expressions on the faces of the Graces, newly pensive, as it seemed, met Theo's own mood of unease and regret. Why had the girl felt obliged to go? Could she not tell that here was a place of sympathy and protection? A sudden dread of loss, of change, of the shadows that loom up altering peaceful accustomed ways, made Theo get up.

Maybe the windows were just dusty, maybe they needed professional cleaning. Something was wrong in here, anyway. She went to read in the kitchen instead, where she could spread out her papers on the kitchen table. She was making some notes for her remarks on the dance, to accompany her demonstration for the prisoners, a few little remarks, nothing complicated, but must be cast just right, must be provocative and convincing but must also be simple and short.

With the world so full of strangers and fugitive murderers and weird events, it frightened but hardly surprised her to hear a rustle, fugitive and mysterious, at the corner of the kitchen porch and a flurry of barking from Carlyle. She glared out into the dusk expecting an excited killer with a shotgun, and instead there was the girl, really called Marybeth, crouched like a half-tame something with her hand extended, about to tap on the door. Theo waved at her to come in.

She kept, she hoped, a calm demeanor, but her mind raced with plans, tactful strategies, that would be required here, decisions. Should she reveal that she knows Lynn's true identity? What will Anton do if he finds her come home?

Theo wished to reassure and not to frighten the girl, who was frightened already, as was apparent as she stepped into the light. Here was their usual Lynn, but altered almost into another person, face all dirty and shining with anguish, and clutching a little bloody child.

"Theo," she began. "I didn't really, well, you can see—I—can I come back again, just for tonight?"

"Of course, come in," Theo said calmly. Little child battered but alert, eyes wide open, staring like a starved child in an appeal poster, and his face all matted with blood, so that Theo had to look away, stomach lurching, as she was someone who couldn't bear the sight of blood. "Isn't that Alistair Burnham's little boy?"

"Yes, I was with him, sort of baby-sitting him, and we were in a car accident. See, I didn't go to Idaho, I . . ."

"Oh, how dreadful, the poor little thing. Are *you* all right? You did right to bring him home here, dear," Theo said, "but where is his mother?" She took Chen-yu from Marybeth's arms and tried to think of soothing, reassuring things, as if they were fearful wild animals she wanted to lure safely into their cages. In Theo's arms the child felt heavy, felt wrong some way. Brisk competence welled up in her. I can cope with this. "Never mind," she said, "we'll wash him and call his mother."

"I didn't know where else to come," Marybeth said, then suddenly slid down the wall to the floor, thump, and began to cry, just like a child herself, sniffing and squishing the tears against her cheeks with the palms of her hands.

Theo locked the outside door with Chen-yu clinging to her neck, and moved slowly around the kitchen, half afraid that a sudden movement would startle Marybeth away. Marybeth gave long deep sighs and brought herself under control. She watched Theo, it seemed to Theo, with a certain directness she hadn't seen before, her mouth not pinched shut tightly but full and red.

"There are certain things I have to tell you," Marybeth began.

"I'll just wash his face off a little," Theo hurried to say, setting Chen-yu down on the kitchen table. Her stomach turned again when she really looked at the raw, scraped little face. He swayed like a limp flower; Theo gathered him up again.

A new sense of reality coldly overcame her. Something was wrong and bad here. Why was the girl back, and why this blood? The child was bludgeoned; he was as tiny and frail as a hen. Theo wished Anton would come in just now, and deal with this.

Marybeth got up and went over to the sink. She began to run water on her hands, and then withdrew them. Her wrists were raw and bloody, too, and she winced. In the better light, Theo saw that she was all dirty, as if she had been charcoaled for a play. Theo wished for Ouida to come and deal with all this.

"We must see to this little boy," she said.

"I tried to wash him. I can't take him home this way. It was my fault. They must wonder where he is; how can I take him home like this?" Marybeth said.

"Let's see if he wants something to eat." That's what one always did, wasn't it? "Ice cream? Hamburger?"

"Look, I need to talk to you, I have to explain about all this," Marybeth said, frightening Theo by her passionate tone and hysterical quaver. Theo didn't want to hear about it yet; she wanted to hear about it calmly, somehow to cherish—was that the word?—cherish it?

"Later," she said. "While you were gone, a young man came looking for you. He seemed to know you by another name than Lynn."

The girl's eyes snapped open wide. Then she said firmly, "Marybeth Howe, that's my real name."

"Yes, that was the name," Theo said.

"Was it Chuck?"

"He didn't leave a name. A handsome young man with a golden beard."

"Yes, Chuck," Marybeth said. "He didn't leave his phone number or anything?"

"No."

Then Marybeth remembered that her life was different now, bruised, discovered, ended. It didn't matter about Chuck. Tall Theo stood in the middle of the kitchen holding Chen-yu, who looked too heavy for her long stick arms. Marybeth took him from her and he brightened. Stupid little guy, now wanting Marybeth, trusting her.

"What does he eat?" Theo asked.

"We can try ice cream," Marybeth said. "He likes that."

They would have to call his parents. Theo asked about this while Marybeth fed Chen-yu the ice cream; she ascertained the details, then went to use the telephone in the library.

"This is Miss Wait, at number 380," she said, uncertain to whom she was talking. "We have Chen-yu here. Is this Chen-yu's mother?"

"No, she's not here. His father is here," said a voice, and went away.

"Hello," said Alistair. "Miss Wait?"

"Hello, we have Chen-yu here; he can sleep here, or will you come after him?"

"Uh? Well, if you can get him to go to sleep there," Alistair said.

"When do you expect Julie?"

"Probably tomorrow. It depends," Alistair said.

"Chen-yu fell down today and got a little skinned up,"

Theo said carefully, in an unconcerned voice. "Be sure you tell Julie so she won't be too shocked. He looks grisly, but he's fine really."

"Ah, poor little chap," Alistair said. "Lynn is looking after him, right?"

"Yes, she's here, too," Theo said, more reluctantly. "He'll have some supper and sleep here."

"Ah, right," said Alistair. Fathers, Theo thought crossly.

Theo, mistress and protector of the house, of Marybeth and her child, standing there with a strong exhilarating sense of intrigue, was all at once aware of a man's voice sounding through the library wall from the living room. The law coming for Marybeth was Theo's first thought, or, peering through the door, the law come for Ouida. She'd forgotten Ouida's jeopardy, and now here was a tall black man in a uniform. Stifling a scream, she realized this must be Ouida's friend, the Mr. Griggs she had seen that morning in his car, a burly man of uncertain age in a khaki uniform, grizzled hair. She peered more closely. He had a manner that seemed polite. Ouida looked distracted. Does she love him?

Theo discreetly withdrew from the door. The house seemed warmer, full of secrets and hum, as if little secret radios were turned on in every room. She would go back to the center, the kitchen, she thought, but for a moment listened.

"Now I know you ain't got nothin to do every day," says Griggs. "What about Friday night?"

"I had planned to go to Roberta's house, for a church meeting."

"Well, you ain't got to be in some church every minute. Saturday? I works in the afternoon, but you could come over in the evening. If you was a nice friend, that's what you'd do, if you was any friend to me.''

"I wish to be a friend,'' Ouida says, distressed that her affection and good wishes for him are not understood by him. ''But Saturday is my *festa*, the *feijoada*.''

"I'll come get you after that.''

"You never come when you say,'' bursts out Ouida without intending to, this reproach, however, lying so long so close to her lips it just slips out. ''Many times I wait—sometimes it is dark—it is not good that you do me that way. If you tell me you will come, then come.''

"I'm tellin you! I'll be around after your school tomorrow; you can go to Roberta's house anytime.''

"Yes, okay,'' says Ouida. ''It is not that I don't wish to help you.'' She wonders how it would be to marry with this man, and is glad to see him moving toward the front door now and saying goodbye in a manner nice and polite, so maybe he is only difficult about coming in the car, and reliable in other aspects. She thinks of Brazilian men, walking in groups, smoking cigarettes, with mustaches, in their striped suits; she thinks of their strong perfume.

It occurs to her that if Griggs would pick her up at school and drive her to Alonzo's Specialty Market in Sacramento, where she must go to buy black beans and mandioca flour, then it would save her many hours on the bus. He could do this before the housecleaning. She will firmly insist.

Good, there he goes, thought Theo; we mustn't let people in here, we have a fugitive here. Ouida's friends or not, they must not come in here now. She thought fleetingly of her responsibility for Ouida. She ought to see to it that Ouida didn't make a mistake. But what was the mistake—to marry or not to marry? Theo had always known that her own decision not to marry wouldn't suit most women, and, moreover, that strange accommodations were made.

"In Brazil," Ouida had said, "the man is boss but woman is queen of the house." Suppose this Griggs beat her but allowed her to be queen of the house—would that be an okay deal by Ouida? It was not as if she had a tall house with a beautiful Redwood Dining Room of her own to be queen of.

And would Ouida like lovemaking? Did she even know about it? Innocent mild Latin virgins—what did they know? Or perhaps she would like the embraces of a man—hot Latin blood, and so on. Even she, Theo, thinking of herself as cold and composed, had liked them quite well.

And she would also have to see that Marybeth didn't make a mistake. And that the prison men didn't make mistakes—that they might have a chance to see what the dance could do to repair mistakes already made, that is. Anton—well, to hell with Anton, he'd had enough chances, let him make mistakes if he cared to. But Theo felt tired, suddenly, and entangled. It was as if little strings were tied to each girl baby that she would be garnished with through life, invisible strings, she never knowing when one will tug and pull with a mean, painful peremptory twitch. Theo rubbed her arms, trying to get disentangled. Tears came to her eyes as she thought of all the little tangled girl children coming daily into the world. Oh, how did people get through their lives, especially in Brazil and India; wasn't that the central mystery, how they even got through?

Sitting at the kitchen table, the girl made a pretty picture. All her strings were invisible. Such a charming-looking girl, the skin so clear, hair never hung in oily strings the way the hair of most girls now did. It was hard to imagine that such a clean-looking girl could be so soiled by events, experiences. Of what sort? She had, Theo supposed, slept with a lot of different men, which Theo didn't disapprove of exactly, or even rather admired, the unconcern and largesse. We were so mean with our bodies, she thought. Women, even my crowd, and we were artists—fast, people thought—even we were so mean and cautious, sneaking, always mortified tears afterwards. Well, my friend Ariadne died, though, of an abortion in Tijuana. Nothing came free. Well, what if you found yourself pregnant on tour, what would you do? You had to be careful.

Hard to imagine her with men, though—with blacks maybe; her voice so sweet as she spooned ice cream into little Chen-yu's bird mouth. They didn't feel themselves soiled at all by a man; they were asserting their rights, girls now. They're lucky, Theo thought, and then thought it was a strange idea to have about a battered girl, wanted by the police, that she was lucky.

Anton must feel that he's lucky, too, Theo went on thinking; a man is still desirable at age sixty, to some people at least, a famous man lucky to be still on the prowl among all these liberated girls, whereas no one wants an old woman. Only an old man would take Ouida; perhaps no one in Brazil would take her—she must be nearly thirty, which is, nonetheless, but half of sixty. Theo sighed.

Soon Ouida came into the room to join them, wearing her bewildered look that usually meant that something was passing her understanding, something American and strange. "I am going to make tea," she said. "Shall I for all?" While the kettle boiled, she sat at the table opposite Marybeth, yet without appearing to notice Marybeth's scratched face, and said, in the clumsy way she had of introducing conversations in English, for she knew no graceful transitions: "I am thinking of bridals."

"Of getting married?" Theo asked, drawing near, interested. "To Mr. Griggs, then?"

"No, or yes, but I mean I am thinking of bridals generally. I am thinking of my friends in Brazil, of the little happy grooms. Everyone has much happiness at a wedding, which is a strange thing, for everyone knows that much unhappiness will follow. My sister-in-law have nine daughters, with my brother the pastor. He is so serious, and he sing like an angel. He loves his wife, but another man might be angry with her to give him so many daughters, and treat her cruelly. That is what you don't know before the bridals begin, I mean."

Marybeth rolled her big eyes in dismay, as she always did when Ouida revealed all the sexist racist things that went on in Brazil. She wished Ouida could have a better perspective. "Nine daughters and it's *her* fault?"

"Oh, well, I am thinking of me, too," Ouida admitted. "Without a passport I will have to marry. They do not make you show your passport at a marriage, right?"

"Right," Marybeth agreed, appearing to welcome this distraction, wiping goo off Chen-yu's chin, thinking about Ouida. "Do you *want* to get married, Ouida?"

"Do you know what you'd be getting into?" Theo asked.

"Oh, I know about mating of course. Remember I was a child on a farm," Ouida said. "I am not against the natural functions. We consider them pure and holy. I will do them if I must be married. I know about that.

"But I do worry about marrying someone black. It is not a way of thinking I am used to. In Brazil there is no racial discimination, discrimination is by social class only. White may marry with black or brown. For instance, Colonel Pacific is pale, but his wife, Isabelita, is quite dark, and also the eldest daughter, Carmela. Here it is not so usual."

"Why, of course it is," objected Theo. "You can marry a person of any color you please in California. I don't know about some of those Southern states. Here you see interracial couples all the time. Personally, I think that's the way to solve the whole difficulty . . ."

"I have not seen too many instances," Ouida said, "but alas, the problem is myself. I do not know if I really wish to marry with a black person. But since I am black myself that is what people expect. I do not get along so good with black people here as with white, and I do not understand what they say sometimes."

"Oh, Ouida!" cried Marybeth and Theo together, dismayed by various things. How can Ouida be a third-world person if she is a bigot, thought Marybeth.

She's learned English, thought Theo; now she'll have to learn what not to say in it.

"Also I think I am old to be married. But yet I want to stay in this country," Ouida went on. "It is wonderful here. Also life here is more possible for a not married woman. In Brazil she cannot live alone, she must live in her family. One who is not married helps the brothers and sisters-in-law with their children and their housework. Your life is not your own. But I am caught, for if I stay I must marry and then it does not matter what life is like for the unmarried." She laughed at the logic.

"Just tell your brothers to go . . . I don't see why you are afraid of your brothers," Marybeth said.

"Why do you think you're too old, Ouida?" Theo asked. "You could still give birth."

"For Brazil anyway, I am too old. A girl may buy high-heeled shoes when she is twelve there. It is funny— then, too, is much laughing, as at bridals, and she steps proudly on the arm of her father, with no one looking ahead. Oh, they look far ahead. When I had drawing lessons at the lycée, they talked of the middle distance. You can look far ahead but not into the middle distance, which is when the nine daughters come."

She was really upset, they saw, twisting and wringing her fingers. She saw Griggs in her future.

"I'm sure Mr. Griggs is basically a nice person, and you aren't too old," Marybeth said, to reassure her.

"Yes, he is very nice," Ouida said, and stared into her cup.

"We can put this poor little boy to sleep in your room," Theo said to Marybeth. "If you push your bed against the wall, he won't roll off. His mother or father or someone can come for him tomorrow, but he'll sleep here tonight."

Marybeth nodded and wiped Chen-yu's chin with the dishtowel. "Come on, buddy." She picked him up. "I think he's pretty sleepy. He practically dozed off in the middle of eating."

"You must be tired, too," Theo said. "You can sleep on the library sofa, if you like. Take some blankets from your room."

"Yeah, okay, I think I will," Marybeth said, her tiredness becoming apparent to her, rather as if someone had turned down the lights on her, or started a hum in her head, a voice saying "Future, future," draining away her attention and will. She gathered Chen-yu up and carried him. She stopped in the doorway.

"Don't be alarmed or anything, but I think I should tell you I'm someone wanted by the police. Tomorrow I'm going to give myself up to them. I've decided to give myself up."

Theo gave her a knowing smile, brisk and motherly. "I know, we know about it; everything is going to be all right."

The girl looked shocked and unbelieving and carried Chen-yu off upstairs. Theo, listening after her, heard her slip or stumble on the stairs.

Ouida looked at Theo. "It is too bad that such a girl must go to jail," she said, "so young and beautiful, she should be married, not me."

"Ouida, don't you tell anyone she's here, don't speak of this to any of your friends," Theo said. "Don't say any public prayers about it. We want to save her from the police, of course.''

"Oh, I would not reveal her, any more than I would reveal myself to the immigration authorities, but it will come in time. Things reveal themselves.'' She sighed. "There is a will, a force of justice, which we none of us can escape, and I know this is true, so I know she will be caught. Perhaps I, too.''

"Good night,'' Theo said crossly as Ouida rose to take her tea upstairs. Theo did not at this moment wish to discuss cosmic justice. "And please don't mention fate and things like that to her. Her situation must be difficult enough.'' Ouida nodded and said good night.

Theo sat alone in the kitchen, at the center. She wished for Anton to come home. She rehearsed speeches in her mind to say to the girl the next day: It doesn't make any difference to us what you've done. We don't care. We don't want to know.

One is bound to wonder, though. She thought of herself at the prison on Saturday, looking at the men, thinking, It doesn't make any difference to me what you've done. It doesn't make any difference to art.

But one is bound to wonder. She thought particularly of their hands—hands on guns, hands on a victim's throat, hearts thrilling. Still that isn't my concern, we're here about art. Dancers are the greatest athletes: a great male dancer is one of the most accomplished of all athletes; he must be faster, stronger, more agile than a runner or a pole-vaulter or a football player. Now, our object here— we can't expect to become great dancers or stars, but the dance is a way of conditioning our bodies and expressing ourselves.

Theo felt a wish to talk to Marybeth. "I had half expected to be a great dancer,'' she wished to say. "Every ballerina normally does expect this, and really I almost was, or was for a short time, but in those days, a woman far from home—I didn't have the heart for it." She had thought this many times before, and felt no resentment that she hadn't had the heart for it really. "No, of course the world didn't suppress me," she would explain to Marybeth; "it was just that in the long run it wasn't something for me, hotel rooms, all the boring waiting, the quick feel in the passageways."

The man in prison: can I depend on it that they will be interested in self-improvement? Perhaps they only want parole. What do they care about conditioning their bodies—if they were interested in self-improvement, they wouldn't be in prison. Or did that necessarily follow?

Anton comes home to find Theo sitting up waiting in the kitchen.

"Lynn alias Marybeth is back," she says. "It's all true—she is in some kind of trouble and intends to go to the police tomorrow."

"Where is she now? Did you find out what kind of trouble?" Anton asks.

"I don't know, I still can't remember her crime, and she didn't volunteer to explain. She's asleep in the study— we had to put Chen-yu in her room, Alistair Burnham's baby. She was watching him and they fell out of a car."

"Sounds a bit peculiar."

"There is much here that has not been explained," Theo says. "I've been thinking about it. After all, it's so seldom that life demands of one to think sensibly and thoroughly; I've been sitting here trying to think and waiting for you, and what happens is, I get very sleepy."

"What is required of you, my dear? If she goes to the police tomorrow." Though Anton cannot help but think that is a shame.

"I don't think we should let her," Theo says. "I've been thinking of all the things she could possibly have done, one by one in my mind: hit-and-run drunk driving; axe murder of her mother and father; crazed baby-sitter in manslaughter leap from car; bank teller embezzles large sum—and I can't think of a single thing that I think she should go turn herself in for.''

"Brutal slaying of gas-station attendant in holdup?''

"Well, impossible. I suppose she might have been with a boyfriend, something like that, but in that case it wasn't she, it was he.''

"What happened to the girl who went along with her boyfriend wildly thrill murdering, what was his name—Starkwell or something?''

"I don't know, I suppose she's in prison, as she properly should be, but she isn't Marybeth.''

"I think we'd better find out tomorrow,'' Anton says.

"But does it matter? Is it a decision which is ours to make?''

"Her decision, but we can make suggestions.''

"No, I mean, theoretically, as law-abiding citizens, we ought to feel that she ought to give herself up for any crime whatever, pay her debt to society, throw herself on the mercy of the courts, you know the phrases. Whereas, in fact, we don't feel that way. We want to decide. If it came out, we'd have to say—to police or the neighbors—we never knew. The Waits, those models of percipience, a murderer living in their house and they never knew. But you know, Anton, I feel in a way as if I'd known all along. It explains so much. Of course, you say to yourself. Isn't it obvious? . . .'' She spreads her hands.

"Teddy, you seem so pleased. It isn't—it doesn't seem like something to be happy about. It's not amusing, it's serious and terrible.''

Oh, Anton, Theo thinks. How stupid. Of course it's serious and terrible; how can you say happy, happy is not it.

"I'm not happy, I'm concerned,'' she says. "I'm going to bed.''

"We'll talk to the girl tomorrow, figure out what to do with her," Anton says. "Christ, what a stench in here; is that Ouida's *carne seca* stinking? It's getting goddamned high."

I must talk to her, thinks Theo, pausing outside the library door where the girl has gone to sleep. Oh, Anton doesn't feel the sadness at all, or how ravishing, how beautiful the lineaments of secrets are on a girl. No wonder she's beautiful, the deep secrets, the political passions. I'll just ask her. She can tell and trust me.

Her heart beats to think of the story, of what it might be. It's wonderful to hear of brave women. She thinks of the dances of China, with fierce women in blue trousers dancing up revolution and danger. She thinks, Marybeth is like a pirate crawling among riggings with a knife in her teeth, wearing a torn blouse—that must be from some old movie I saw. She is as beautiful as an actress; why is she not an underground heroine? That's what they usually want, the papers and newsreels—someone beautiful. She thinks of all this, then does not tap on the girl's door.

We can none of us talk to each other, she thinks, running up the stairs while Anton remains behind in the kitchen, probably mixing himself a drink. We can none of us talk, we might as well be deaf. What would they all do if I did really tell them what I know about them? I know your feelings of desire for that girl, Anton, and I know you're getting fat, too; don't I see you pushing the fat part of the chop to the side of the plate? Don't I see you push the little pieces of paper under the blotter if I come by? Don't I know that Ouida thinks I am aloof and too skinny? She pauses, as is her new habit, to sniff out smoke on the stairwell nearest Ouida's room.

Crossly she takes off her necklace and hangs it on the corner of her mirror. She brushes her hair. It's possible, she thinks, that Anton doesn't know anything about anything; he lives in another world. In his way generally considered a great artist, at least by those who consider photography an art, which does not include me. He puts his eye to his lens and moves his finger. Great snowy shapes, dappled trees, waves result. It is peculiar.

She lies on her back in bed and thinks of their childhood, of picnics, when they both were given little cameras; only from Anton's would emerge some stone or shell she had stepped right over. She wasn't visual. Perhaps his tendency to take up with beautiful women rather than women of character was a consequence of being visual. Many people are not visual at all, or they wouldn't live in ugly rooms, she thinks. Or perhaps beauty can be learned, like the dance.

She spies the smoke alarm on her dresser, still in its box. Oh, silly, she thinks, it isn't doing any good like that. She gets out of bed and unwraps it. She plugs it in with a guilty feeling. Tomorrow she will put it in the hallway where it will benefit everyone. In the darkness the tiny red eye of its light reassures her some.

Ouida tiptoes back down the stairs and taps at the library door, feeling a little afraid of Lynn, a girl so in trouble that she must surrender to police. She thinks of the beauty of the wild *favela* girls, who did not care about anything and laughed when the police took them; they stole or lay with men for money. They had about them burnished auras of glamour, like singers in a club with the spotlight on them. Lynn now has this aura, but because her skin is not so dark her teeth do not shine out from a heartless, careless smile.

"I'm turning in, I'm wiped out," Marybeth whispers at the door. Ouida wishes to embrace her.

"I do not care what crime it is, my dear Lynn, and I will say endless prayers," Ouida says. "When you have paid the cost, your heart will be cleared and nothing will be held against you for the next life. I . . .''

"Oh, Ouida! My name is not Lynn, it's Marybeth," cries Marybeth. "Don't talk to me about the next life— what do I care, I haven't finished messing up this one."

When she has closed the door again, Ouida stands there a minute with her hand upraised, luminous palm concentrating the healing rays.

Marybeth spreads the blankets on the sofa and wraps herself in them. She aches and hurts. She reviews the strange events of the day and begins to wonder if she has made them up. Has she really escaped death today? Maybe she just panicked, made the danger up. She's not sure. The pale, mild features of her killer are now like melted wax, his tones as soft, the deranged purposefulness of his small pinched face perhaps no more than preoccupation with some care of his own. Her convictions flicker. What did he do or say, really, to warrant leaping from a moving car?

She can scare herself by thinking what might have happened. What if Chen-yu had been killed? She ought to feel blessed that she didn't kill him, recklessly tearing him from a moving car; she was crazy, had no judgment, thank God she didn't have to pay for that craziness, that panic, with his death. Thankful is what she ought to feel, does feel.

Yet the force of the fear of death is something to be reckoned with when it comes over you with such imperative. She has been afraid of death almost continually for how long—nearly six years now—she should be used to the feeling by now, a feeling like wearing an ass's head around, something stifling and ridiculous, afflicting her movements, affecting the faces of all who looked at her. But today it was as if death had snatched off the mask, set the cold wind swirling around her naked face, whispering, "Look, look, here I am, you haven't really seen me until now."

Now death has gone dancing away again, and here she is lying in her same house, sunk in patience, limply acquiescent. It is as if the fates were off somewhere arguing among themselves, some pulling for a gory rape-murder at the side of the road to put an end to her; others, more sophisticated, advocating long legal process as more exquisite, more excruciating. You should always hang yourself in your cell, she thinks.

Still, she's not going to wait for the fates to decide; she has made up her own mind. She will get up tomorrow and go to some police station and go ahead and end it all herself.

She has expended all her resources. Destiny lurks behind all the metaphors: pay, debt, owe, cost, nothing is free. She will pay her debt. She feels calmer at coming to a decision she must always have known she would make.

Tomorrow. Or in a couple of days. A couple of days can't make any difference when you're thinking about the lifetime of prison ahead. She thinks of newspaper stories about dying children being taken to Disneyland, and she thinks of the qualified nature of happiness that must be finite and whose end is in sight. But pain, she thinks, is finite, too. She falls asleep thinking about that, and sleeps well.

In the night she awakes, conscious that she has heard a sigh or cry. That little kid, she thinks; I must be crazy, I just went off to sleep without looking after him, where is he? Then she remembers that she is in the library on the sofa, and Chen-yu was put in her room directly above.

Has he cried out? Perhaps something is wrong, perhaps internal injuries. Her heart pounds. The house is in blackness, the odor of something they had for dinner, vaguely onions and cabbage, lies on the air, one of Oui-da's dishes. And the unfamiliar wood smell of the library, and the smell of wax. She switches on the study lamp and creeps along the hall and up the stairs to her old room, afraid. What has she heard? Is he still in there? She pushes open the door.

Little mound on the bed. She approaches. His eyes are closed—has he cried out? She leans close to see if he is breathing. She can't tell. She leans closer, and then can hear the fragile aspirations; such a frail stirring, it would not move a leaf or the merest butterfly.

Perhaps it is not even so, and he is not breathing but dead, for the difference seems inconsequential. She touches the cover to see if it moves.

Then he stretches an arm, alive, warm. Marybeth wishes to snatch him up and kiss him and thank him, but of course does not, and instead steps pensively back.

Now she has the sensation that someone—others—are in the room with her. A host of silent presences, making her feel watched. But not police eyes, not the dead eyes of the professor, or the other malign eyes that sometimes watch at her bedside. Now she is stifled with the sense that they are female presences, female and solemn.

She shivers, it is terrible, she doesn't understand. She has waked up because she heard Chen-yu cry out, that's all, and now insomniac female ghosts breathe their chill gusts on her, whispering with evil satisfaction, Women do not sleep, women do not sleep.

12. Empty Beds

Morning. Ouida awoke early because she had a busy day ahead. She hadn't slept well—too many currents and buzzings in this house, a palpitation in her breast, the unyielding knot of anger, the shadow of the goat.

The young girl had come back in the evening, and that was strange, and now, about Miss Theo, the quality of a cat with the hair standing on end. Words drifting up which she could not understand despite her new understanding, words mysteriously entangled, darkly rising and falling, a sea of hints, a stumbling on the stairs. Theo's voice had taken on a rushed and thrilled rapid way of running along, as when she shouted at the religious people. The memory of the religious people was not so deeply humiliating this morning, yet it still warmed and stirred her.

She performed her spiritual exercises. She stared into the mirror until her lids fluttered. She knelt and whispered. Then she went downstairs to the kitchen to get busy making a cake to take to her school. She was worried about this because she had no real understanding of American flour and had many baking failures. Here was Mr. Anton, already up and had made the coffee.

"You're up early," he said. "What are you doing?"

"This is the day I go to the children's elementary

161

school, I and the others from the adult school. We are all going to share with the children items from our native country. Meesis Aheem will tell about India, Sachiko about Japan, oh, and some others. I about Brazil. It is our project, and we go to a poor school in Sacramento. See here."

She pulled out things from a plastic shopping bag and piled them on the kitchen table. A gourd on little silver legs, and two tiny, tiny coffee cups.

"The coffee is drunk very much stronger there than here, in these small cups. This other is for maté, which is like tea."

"That should be very interesting for the schoolchildren," Anton said.

"Yes, for me, too, but I worry that my English will go in the middle."

"No, it won't," said Theo, coming in, like the others dressed already to go out. "Remember to speak slowly. Anton! I've thought of it—she's only one of those interminable silly college girls that went around blowing people up, and whom the FBI keeps most wanting. Isn't it a relief? The sort that nobody particularly wants to be caught, and when they catch them you always think, Wouldn't it be nice if the FBI could concentrate on someone really dangerous?"

"It is really dangerous, blowing people up, for the people who get blown up. Was it a person? Or just a building?" Anton asked.

"A building, a draft board or something. I can't remember. I suppose it had a person in it. I'm sure she's very sorry. You wish the FBI and the police and so on would have some sense of proportion and go after the really wicked people, the murderers and so on. They don't seem to have any common sense."

"Suppose the FBI did come," Anton asked, "and showed you a picture of Marybeth and asked you if you'd seen this girl—what would you do?"

"Well, I'd say it looked a little like our boarder but the nose was wrong, something like that."

"Perjury?"

"I'd just be vague. They can't track you into the depths of your subjective mind. How do they know what your eyes can distinguish?"

"And would you be vague for anyone, or just for Marybeth?"

"Oh, for anyone, more or less, unless it were a corporate criminal or a thrill murderer. Or a government official. But the FBI never looks for them."

Ouida pulled out something else from her sack, with a shy smile, carefully, like a delicate cake. It was a hat covered with bananas, Brazil nuts and oranges roped on and tied together in various ways. She set it on her head and laughed at their surprise.

"It's a *carnaval* hat," she said. "I made it. You think it will amaze them?"

"Oh, yes!" said Theo and Anton, amazed. Ouida began to wiggle her hips, then remembered Anton and stopped. "I am a very good dancer at the *carnaval*, but I will not dance for the children, they would laugh too much because I am fat."

"Remember Carmen Miranda?" Theo said.

"And José Iturbi," said Anton. "And Xavier Cugat."

"Children love chocolate best," said Ouida, looking in the oven, "but those I am not so good at, and that is funny, no, because cocoa comes from Brazil, too."

It is the smell of warm fragrant cake that wakes Marybeth up. That and the voluptuous pleasure of the soft sofa cushions and warm afghan, the pleasure of sleeping in a new place, content her for a moment. She stretches and gathers her thoughts. The dread does not rush down upon her this morning. It is curiously suspended above her like a canopy, allowing her time to look around. Heavy morn-

ing sun gilds the edges of the thick drawn library curtains. Each morning brings this fragile moment of
happiness, precarious as a welling tear, only momentary
before the canopy descends, shroudlike, as every other
day—how long? Six years.

This is the day she will go to the police. It is all decided. Her life of a fugitive, all life, is over; her life is
over. She lies as lead.

Other people lose their lives in their twenties, they OD,
or get cancer, get in wrecks—no need to think you can
avoid it. Would she rather be dead or in prison? She's
considered this before, over and over, but she can never
get anywhere with it, because she can't imagine either
one.

You can always kill yourself. In her warm cocoon, her
body seems too present to think of killing it. She can
wiggle its toes; she can feel, as usual, the prompting to
love suffuse her body. I'm like a headless body, she
thinks; my brain has bled to death.

But she still has memories. They seem, if anything, a
little clearer to her this morning, perhaps in the way the
drowning person reviews his life.

She can remember all her previous beliefs. Once as a
child she actually heard the hooves of reindeer on the
roof of her aunt's house, at Christmas. No one has ever
believed her about this. In the old days, she was never
able to talk about her early memories with the others,
because they had nothing happy to remember, they said;
and they looked at people who had with mockery and
distaste. What had they done with their memories? She
has learned to keep hers quiet, poor little shreds. How
used, how worn-out they will be at the last, when she is
an old woman in prison, nattering over her shreds of
memories.

In bed it is lovely and warm. You just naturally want
to wait as long as possible to hear the prison doors close
behind you and your breasts fill with lead. She has always

imagined she will die when she gets to prison. She knows, but cannot really understand, that the people inside are actually alive. She has read all the books, about George Jackson, about Attica; she has seen the film of naked men with hands clasped behind their heads being marched in rings with guns waved over them, but she is not a strong naked man marching around, eyes glittering hate. She doesn't know what she is, or what kind of prison they will send her to.

She's afraid there is a special kind of prison, a kind of brothel prison for girls such as she, where priests and guards come. She wiggles her toes. Or, in a way, she is afraid it won't be a brothel prison; at least there the priests and guards would come, that would keep you alive. She's afraid it will be a sewing prison, a broom-making prison, with scary sadist dyke guards, and you and the rest would scream shrilly from the walls at any stray man walking by, all screaming hag-calls for love. Meantime your breasts shrivel up. No one has told her what happens to girls in prison. She hasn't been able to find out.

She'd like at least to get laid before she gives herself up to torture and desiccation, even if it was Anton. That wouldn't be so bad. She thinks about Chuck Sweet. She wonders how big his cock is. She thinks about other times, men she has slept with, but it's no use thinking about it; it's something that you have to do, over and over again. How amazing that you don't get tired of it.

Framed on the library wall are large photographs—a ridge of sand, gleaming black mussels on rocks, clouds. Marybeth thinks about Anton, a handsome man, distinguished, who has written her notes of love. She sighs. She wants to sleep with revolutionary leaders; the two policemen, especially the one with the mustache; football players. She is swollen as a bud.

She sighs, heavy with dread of the day, languorous with desire. She imagines some sort of chemical saturating her skin with desire. Perhaps she's been poisoned. Maybe in prison they poison you, so you are continually sopping with desire, and the air so thick you can't breathe, like this; it's part of the torture, and no man ever comes near you, so your life evaporates out your skin until you shrivel up and die.

She guesses she'd better get up and just get on with it. She's dead already.

Her jeans and shirt, stained and dusty, lay by the sofa. She'd have to get something from her kit of respectable clothes left at Julie's, something really straight. She could do that this afternoon. She put the dirty clothes on. She heard Ouida's step in the hall. Innumerable little tasks crowded her mind, last words and actions.

"Normally the police and FBI do concern themselves with dangerous criminals," Anton was saying in the kitchen.

"Oh, really, Anton, by whose definition dangerous? My idea of a dangerous criminal is never the same as the government's, and Lynn is not my idea of one. The government cares only about things which threaten it, they don't care about *people*. Surely you wouldn't turn in someone you know, great heavens, Anton. Perhaps you'd turn in Ouida over her difficulty with her passport?"

Marybeth stopped, heart pounding, in the hallway.

"She must start life over again under another name," Theo said.

"Of course," Anton agreed. Then Marybeth realized they must know everything.

They looked at her almost as if they expected her to be carrying a little suitcase to take to prison with her. She felt embarrassed. It was as if, with their kind, poised smiles, they were waiting for her to dive. Her face grew red, she could feel it.

"Good morning," she said.

"Toast, coffee, eggs, my dear?"

"Today I'm—this is the day, I've decided," Marybeth began at once. "Later today I'll—"

"So you said yesterday," Theo broke in, "but do you really think you should? Whatever it was, I'm sure you're sorry now, and I don't see the point of involving yourself in—all that."

Marybeth thought, It's kind of funny, calling it "all that," but she did not laugh.

"They never give up on you," she explained. "People get caught decades later. They have a special person somewhere assigned to just you, thinks about just you; any report that comes in from anywhere, this person evaluates it, wonders if it could be you; he reads all the things that dentists send in. All the dentists have to report every year."

"Oh, surely not," protested Theo.

"And if your evaluator dies, they just turn over your files to someone else. They don't give up until they find your body on some cold road, or your teeth amongst the ashes, or until they find you."

"God, what a waste of time," said Theo.

"You can be however old. I've thought and thought about this."

"You give them credit for more resolution than they have," Anton said.

"So you see," cried Marybeth, "you just have to get it over with! I just wish I knew what 'it' was. You can't escape, I wish I'd faced this before, but it takes a while to get your nerve up. I'm the last one. Oh, but why didn't anyone tell me you can't avoid it . . ."

She's excited, Theo was thinking, she's self-dramatizing. I know that temperament. She shouldn't do anything at all till she's calmed down.

"What interests me," Anton said, "is how you happened to get into all this. Women never seem to imagine that their actions will have consequences."

"Their actions never do have any consequences," Theo pointed out.

"Oh!" cried Marybeth. "That's it, I was so surprised. That's still my main feeling, I think. Even though I would do everything again."

"There are many things I'd be glad to do and take the consequences for," Theo said. "If someone came to me and asked me to blow up that terrible-looking television tower in San Francisco, I'd say 'Certainly,' of course I would. I'd make the bombs or whatever they wanted."

"Teddy, you would not," said Anton, exasperated, finally, at Theo's talking silly like this, in front of this girl in particular.

"Oh, but I would. That's the trouble with me; they are equivocal, without fixed principles. They live in conspiracy. I'll let you build your eyesore if you let me raise the electricity rates, it seems to work like that. When you reproach them, they say, 'That's the way the world works.'"

Theo thought of men as blind baby birds, chirping "That is the way the world works" with every gape of their hungry beaks. A sizzle of indignation began in her. She looked to see if the girl—would they ever learn to call her by her real name?—shared her indignation. Did her eyes snap, cheeks redden?

No, she sat in a dispirited huddle. She has been made to accept the imperatives of her situation, Theo thought. The imperatives of her situation compel acceptance.

"Even you, Anton," Theo said, "a life devoted to nature in all its beauty—you think it would be wicked to blow up that Sutro Tower, an evil blight on the landscape for hundreds of miles put there merely to improve television reception."

"It isn't that I think it's wicked," Anton said, "it's that I wouldn't have thought of it at all." But he was aware of feeling rather charmed at the idea of blowing up the Sutro Tower. It must have occurred to everyone but him. He felt guilty, as though he had dozed at a public occasion. But some things are not done; blowing things up is not done.

"People who do blow things up seem so stupid, the things they choose—" Theo was clacking.

"What Marybeth says is quite true, Teddy," Anton interrupted. "They don't give up on fugitives. The smartest thing for her to do is turn herself in, but I don't think she should just walk into a police station. She should get a lawyer and he should contact the police. That's the way it's done. That way she doesn't get her head blown off. And they make deals of various kinds— the police and the lawyer—so she can have an idea of what's in store. Of course, she can't change her mind if she doesn't like it—she has to take her chances. But she's already taken her chances. I'll make inquiries about a lawyer. Nothing to be done till Monday, probably."

"I have no sympathy with giving up," Theo said, in a sudden sharp tone. "There's something sullen about it. Nothing works out the way you expect, yet you can't just plant your feet and say, 'Very well then, I won't go on.' "

It was the sharpness of her tone that struck them silent. What was she thinking of, back in her own life? When did she plant her feet, over what? Marybeth could see that Anton did not know. Theo's long nose cast a shadow along her cheek, like a witch.

"Well, I'm going to run an errand," she said. "I'll have my second cup when I get back. Anton, don't answer the door or anything—you know. I'll be back in twenty minutes or so." She glared them into silence and went out by the front hall, together with Ouida, who had wrapped her warm cake in a bath towel.

Marybeth and Anton were left alone at the table. It was the first time they had ever been alone; she had always been careful to avoid it. Marybeth, who had been think-

ing of Ouida—what would become of Ouida, too innocent for America, when she, Marybeth, was locked
away—felt her eyes fill, and pretended to drop something
so as to bend her head and wipe her tear; she didn't want
Anton to think it was for herself.

"Don't worry," he said, "Theo will think of something, she always does; she pays reality no regard, never
has, and I guess in a way reality pays no attention to her,
either; that's the deal *she* made."

Marybeth straightened, and sighed, and accepted
more toast. "Can people make a deal?" she wondered
aloud. "Isn't it too late for me? I haven't disregarded
reality, I've borne it in mind ever since I discovered it
existed."

"You thought you could outwit it, evidently," he said.

"Well," she cried in a defensive way, "I *did* think that
someone had to try to change the world, that people had
to try! It was a natural mistake. A lot of people thought
that way. The war . . ."

Here she broke off, afflicted with the amnesia, the sense
she always had when she tried to explain what had happened back then, that she was talking about someone
else, some vital, bright-cheeked girl she might have seen
laughing or fighting along some street or in a newsreel,
nothing to do with her now. Anton got up, a tall shape
standing above her.

She wished he would kiss her. Why did he not? Those
little notes, the pretty snapshots—what had he meant by
them? But what it was in his power to give he now with-
held, so that she burned for an instant with the passionate
wish, then with shame. He excused himself and went
outside, so he couldn't see the red splotches of despair
that rose on her throat. She was too damaged now, too
compromised by fate, she saw. No man would want her,
a girl bound for prison, Monday at the latest.

* * *

Finding Marybeth's friend proved easier than Theo had thought it would. He had left his name at the Photophobia, with an address, for Marybeth to find if she came back there.

"How's her mother?" asked the clerk at Photophobia.

"I haven't heard," Theo said, and hurried off. Marybeth's friend—Charles was his name—wasn't home, but the other young people at the house took a message. Theo felt cross, disappointed at the young man for not being there, sitting waiting. Her heart was rosy with the flush of romantic mission; she had half expected to see Charles swim up on the back of a swan, with bows and arrows for saving Marybeth; instead he wasn't home.

Well, she couldn't wait around for him. She wrote out a message, tantalizingly urgent, and left. She wasn't really sure what she had hoped this Charles could do anyway. Talk Marybeth out of giving herself up, of course, and also represent or personify freedom and love.

He caught up with her before she was halfway home.

"Were you looking for me?" he asked. "Charles Sweet? Is it me you want?"

"Yes," Theo said, and told him about Marybeth. She told him all she knew, that Marybeth had committed a crime, and about how this was the day she meant to deliver herself to justice. You, her friend, someone she used to know, can surely prevail upon her not to give herself up.

It didn't occur to Theo that he might be a police informer or an agent, or a believer in law and order, or in cause and effect. Theo was a believer in a sort of physiognomic theory which couldn't attribute undesirable or momentarily inconvenient behavior to someone so beautiful. His smile was the smile of an angel, or the heart-stopping reckless doomed beauty about to fly his last mission—the kind of looking man she had never trusted, as a matter of fact.

But he seemed to have a beautiful nature, too, his face luminous with concern. He would rush to Marybeth's side; he would be there almost immediately; they were old friends from Bettendorf, Iowa. He would save her. Theo wouldn't let her go anywhere until he got there. "Don't worry," he said reassuringly.

"One thing, though, would it be okay if I came along in a couple of hours? I have an appointment, um . . ." He looked uncertain, stricken, unresolved.

"Appointment?" Theo repeated, slightly shocked. Frivolous.

"Dentist . . ."

"Oh. Well. Whenever you can," she said. "I'm sure she's not going to rush off to the police this morning."

Then, as she comes in the front door, Theo chillingly remembers, wonders why they haven't heard from Chen-yu. He can't still be asleep. Concussions, she thinks of, and of vomiting blood and strangling on it. She tries not to hurry, tries to walk up the stairs, controlled.

Marybeth's room is a litter of clothes and books and things pulled out of drawers. Theo stoops to pick up a thing or two—a sweater, a photo inscribed in Anton's handwriting—she cannot help seeing this. It says "snowy mounds" and then is folded. Theo of course forbears to unfold it; she drops it into an open drawer. Her eye falls on another of these photos, on the floor, which says something about "exquisite breasts." What fatal magnetism attaches to such phrases that the eye is drawn to them, amongst hundreds of other words, amongst volumes. In Anton's hand. She feels guilty that she has spied on Anton.

Now she brings herself to look toward Marybeth's bed. She has always felt a strong aversion to looking at other people's unmade beds, reluctant to discover the secrets of their sleep. She sees, as she expects, a dead mound of bedclothes, then sees that it is not Chen-yu. He is not in the bed. No explanations for this occur to Theo. She doesn't consider that he might have gone to the toilet. She knows little about small children and what they do. Instead, horrors chime around her from every direction, as if she were chained in a bell tower. Her head clashes and rings, she covers her ears and slumps to the floor in a strange faint.

Her own crash brings her back to consciousness. In the seconds of unconsciousness, she dreams of the legs and arms of a child being stuffed into a sack. When she comes to, on the floor, amid the litter of books and underwear, she is icy cold. She gets up, avoiding another look at the unmade bed, and goes out of the room, along the hall to her own room, and closes the door tightly behind her.

When she comes to herself again, she is lying on her bed, with the feeling of holding tight against panic, of sliding and teetering but holding fast. What has happened?

It is the unexpected thing that knocks you for a loop, she tells herself; it's the dark objects floating just under the surface, suddenly clouting you at the crest of the next innocent-looking wave. She thinks of other explanations for an ordinary woman not given to fainting to hit the floor: a stroke, a woman of her age had to be aware of the possibility of that. But all her limbs move, and she can speak.

"Overtired," she says aloud. But she knows she is not overtired; she is perfectly fit, a dancer, unusually vigorous for a woman of her age. It was a second of terror that put her under, terror and premonition.

Downstairs the mantel clock that can sometimes be heard and sometimes not be heard strikes ten as clearly as if it ticked on her own bureau. She flings her arm over her eyes, pressing images out of them which glare against the blackness of her lids. She sees glaring eyes, round-ringed pupils with the peculiar dilation of people deranged with fear and anguish such as she has actually seen and can never forget, and the wide frightened eyes

of Chen-yu last night. Last night? Has she seen him more
recently than that?

She opens her eyes to banish the wild eyes in her memory. Where is the line between memory and sight, she
wonders, for she can still see them. It is in a way wonderful, but terrible, the sly gluey quality of memory
sticking eyes to eyes, all the frightened eyes she has ever
seen, laminated together in her brain.

13. *Something Nasty in the Shed*

Sometime later, Theo can hear Marybeth clatter on the
stairs, shouting that Chen-yu is gone. "Where is he? He's
gone! Oh, my God," she cries, "he isn't in his bed, he
isn't here!" As if raising this cry will help him. Theo,
lying on her bed, sunk in her strange lassitude, hears the
racket. The most animation we'll ever see in that silent
girl, she thinks. She attends the commotion through her
closed door with weary certitude. Death is in the air,
definitely. They will have to endure so much, panic and
nausea, pounding hearts, turning over the brush, calling
down holes, sick dissolving terror opening the old refrigerator door. She hears the door slam down in the yard,
Anton's studio door in the garage. He has been alerted
by Marybeth's cries.

"I don't know where Theo is; I think she's in her room,
she wouldn't answer, I'm sure he isn't with her," Marybeth is saying to Anton. Soon they will come and pound
on the door.

Her body feels limp, exhausted with her premonition
of their suffering. When the moment comes that you cannot bear any more, why, you know it; it's perfectly clear.
She knows they'll never find him; she cannot bear it. She
tries to prepare her mind, which is still moving around

at the helm of her tired body like the agitated captain of a doomed ship.

"He's easily old enough to have just got up and gone home," Anton says to Marybeth down in the yard. "He knows where his house is; he's been over here by himself dozens of times."

"That's true of course," Marybeth agrees. Theo, hearing, agrees.

Presently, from outside the window, down in the yard, on the stairs, their shouts: "Well, he isn't here," the bathroom, "or here," the chicken coop. Theo hears them stamping through the house, slamming doors and closets. She wonders, What will they think of Ouida's flame?

Now the rushing and stamping through the house again. Theo feels impatient with them still. Why don't they see, accept, the tragedy inherent in—in what? Just that it has happened, tragedy has entered her life again—or at last, as she had always expected. The only difference is that it has not come by telephone, as she had expected.

She'd always imagined that tragedy comes by telephone, but perhaps it never really does. Looking back on her life, thinking of the Finn, and of the little girl Esther Lundberg, and of her friend Ariadne, it becomes clear that it has never actually come by telephone. Surely they are looking in all the places they've already looked? Why don't they try the holes, the old refrigerator?

"Well, we mustn't go to pieces," Anton is saying somewhere. How clear the voices on the summer air, through the flung-open windows, voices floating more freely in summer, except to other residents of Orris, sealed up by their air conditioners, inured to pain.

"Does Theo know?" Anton asks. "She's probably gone to pieces."

How do they know I'm gone to pieces, thinks Theo. How do they know what I'll do? I may yet do something.

I may have my face lifted and give some recitals. But her mind is sunk.

"He's probably just wandered off," Anton says. "I've known cases of children wandered off in the mountains for as long as four days and are found."

"But this is civilization, and that's so much worse!" cries Marybeth. "There are murderers, there's the freeway. And he's always going in the street—she's just never impressed upon him about the street." She tries to calm herself by remembering his unblinking, staring sort of competence. But the idea of the freeway keeps coming back.

"I'll call his house and see if he's gone home there," Anton says.

"No! Then they'll know I've—I've lost him. It'll just scare them to death. Let's wait till we know something for sure."

"This is Anton Wait," he says cagily on the phone. "Lynn, the student who lives with us? She's been minding Chen-yu? Has she by any chance brought him back there? I'm trying to find her." Not there, he is told, and the father out, and the mother gone to Reno. You never know who you are talking to over there, there are always so many people around, sneaking in and out, with strange expressions.

"Teddy, Teddy!" Anton calls outside Theo's shut door. "We've lost that little boy. Come help us look for him. He's bound to be somewhere near. He must have wandered off. Is something the matter? Are you resting or what?"

"Yes, I know, it's the strangest thing," Theo says from her bed. "I went in to get him up, and he was gone, and the shock or something—I think I fainted. Now I'm lying down. I'll come out presently. I'm quite all right really, but a little shocked."

"Doctor," "stroke," "concussion"—words Anton begins to say, in tones of anxiety that rather touch her.

She reassures him, anxious that he not rush into her room. Anyone looking at me could guess my secret, my dread; it must show as clearly as if I wore a grinning skull or a death mask.

"I'm quite all right really, Anton, but just rather knocked out—the sudden strain, on top of last night and so on."

"You can't go to pieces over something like this," he says, with the return of his usual acerbity.

Marybeth could not forget as she rushed down Olive Drive, could not forget the sound of Chen-yu's tears, the keening sound of sorrow. She tuned her ears for it as one might attune to woodland birds amid city noises. Cars rushed by. But there wasn't any crying.

For an hour, maybe longer, she looked in things, walked along by garages, peered in back yards, listened, listened. She peered down railings and gratings. Some children were playing in a back yard that smelled of daisies. They climbed on a green wooden swing frame built by some father, tottery and splintery. "Have you seen a little boy go along here looking lost?" she asked them.

"Who?" they asked.

"Chen-yu, his name is. Little, with blond hair."

"Chen-yu Burnham? No, he hasn't been here," they said. "He never comes here now, he goes to the day center."

They thought of Chen-yu as a person, as a separate person, with habits; how could that be, thought Marybeth. Yet of course they're right. But he's so small!

"Sometimes he gets a Frosty down on B Street," they said. Marybeth noticed them looking at her face, at her skinned arms. She thanked them and went along, sickening with every step. Streets he would have to cross, caverns and shadowy crevices to every building, every place the maniac could hide his little corpse. The soapy stink of an apartment laundry came at her, and the rotting vegetables in boxes in back of the Chinese restaurant.

If he'd been hit by a car and the driver stopped, they'd take him to a hospital, but they wouldn't know whom to call, he'd just be there, Baby X. After a while she decided to go back and call the hospital. Where was he? Where was he? His death was to be her punishment, after all. It was too soon, or too late, for tears; she couldn't cry. There was just the pain of low headache.

Walking home, she looked at the notices pinned to the telephone pole. Couldn't one say "Lost Child," the way some said "Lost Dog," "Lost Kitten"? One notice said:

Atenção Brasileiros

Todos estao convidados para uma deliciosa feijoada da completa, a mesma sera servida num quintal maravilhoso com árvores a gramado. Davido os preços altos do tudo, estamos pedindo uma oferta de $4.00 por pessoa, itemos servir as 1:30 horas da tarde

Quem estivar interassado, e favoar enviar sua oferta para Ouida Senza, 380 Ashby Path, Orris, CA 95616

It rushed into Marybeth's mind that maybe Ouida had taken him. Those odd religions, those old superstitions. Embarrassed at her own disloyalty, she thrust the thought away.

There was no notice on the telephone post about a lost child. She walked back to Ashby Path, but slowly, in case they had already heard the worst, were there waiting to tell her.

Ouida's teacher, Mrs. Clausen, drove them to Sacramento: Ouida, Mrs. Aheem, Sachiko Kitano in their finery. Dainty Sachiko had to sit just on the edge of the car seat to avoid crushing the sash of her kimono. Ouida carried the fruited hat in her sack, carefully on her lap. Mrs. Aheem, superior as ever, lounged comfortably in her strange wrappings. Ouida wondered what would happen if you caught the end of them—would they all unwind? What would Meesis Aheem have on underneath?

There were things about the Sacramento Union Junior High School that Ouida didn't understand, but she was humble about her ignorance, and had even become used to the cloud of unknowing that seemed to hang over her head, a kind of fog that had seemed to descend, even to thicken, since her English had improved, making people and Americans more difficult than ever to understand.

"Americans go home" was written on a wall of the school. Now was that not odd, on a wall of an American school? Who had written this? Where could Americans go, since they were already here? And "gloo is peace," and she could not even find the word "gloo" in her little dictionary.

They stood in the hall, a dark gloomy hallway painted a green depressing, one would think, to the spirits of children. The children, who could be seen through the small windows in the heavy classroom doors, wore clothes of every color instead of neat uniforms, and their faces were of many colors, too. They did not seem interested when the teacher brought in their guests. Dull rustles, laughs.

Ouida's teacher whispered to the real teacher of the children, and the real teacher rapped on the desk with her paperweight. The children laughed louder. It seemed to Ouida, suddenly, that there were millions of these children in the room, hordes. They could be the children of Mr. Griggs, or some of them could, and if she could speak to these ones here, she could speak to those children of his. A few were smiling. Perhaps it would not be so bad; people, even children, are not basically bad.

"Here are some ladies from faraway lands we have studied—they're going to show you some things and tell you about their native lands, and I'll be asking you some questions after, so pay attention," the teacher told the class.

Marybeth came into the empty house. Silence. She stood, crushed in the kitchen; then Anton came in, spreading his hands.

"Not anywhere," he said. "Is Theo down yet? I'm worried about her. It isn't like her to stay in her room like this. The fright has done her in, I guess, the fright and the excitement. She can't take it, Theo can't; that's why she hasn't ever done anything with her life—talks tough but she can't really take it."

Marybeth's stomach curled to hear him judge another person's life like that, and she thought of her own life being judged and written off in the minds of her parents and sisters and brother, their saying of her, "Marybeth got into a bad crowd at college, that was during the Vietnam War, and so she's never done anything with her life. Knits place mats in prison."

"It's too bad," Anton went on, taking a beer from the refrigerator, "because she had every talent, every chance. Our mother expended every resource available to her on Theo. It's usually that way in families, I guess, that one child seems to the parent more promising than the others. Do you have brothers and sisters?"

"Two sisters and a brother," Marybeth said. "I'm the youngest. They don't know where I am or anything; we aren't in touch."

"Isn't there anyone you keep in touch with—someone who sends them word and so on?"

Ah, *he* has killed Chen-yu, and he means to kill me, Marybeth realized. Needs to know whether anyone will miss me. A sex killer—those messages, why didn't I see it before?

But she answered truthfully. "No, no one will miss me. I'm underground, right? If my folks were dead, how would I know? How would anyone find me to tell me?"

"I would have thought plenty of sympathizers. Everyone sympathized."

"You would think so. Well, there are, but it only lasts until it gets inconvenient. You learn not to trust anybody. Once I was sold out because this other girl wanted an apartment I had."

Oh, stupid, she thought, he's not going to kill you. But did he murder Chen-yu? He's definitely a strange man, sends those weird little pictures. Or maybe he's covering up for Theo. She's excitable and strange. Or maybe I murdered him myself.

"Do you—does anyone here sleepwalk?" Anton asked her. "Does Chen-yu sleepwalk? Children often do. My youngest daughter did, we would find her in the back yard in her pajamas. Once we found her on top of the garage. They outgrow it."

"I can sympathize with those old bums that leave home and never ask about where their wives and children are any more. It's kind of peaceful not knowing," Marybeth said, thinking about her own life. But then her own words shot Chen-yu into her mind. "Oh! What are we going to do! We have to find him," she cried.

"Did you see Ouida this morning—could he have gone off with her?" Anton wondered aloud.

Ah, Marybeth thought again. Ouida. Is that possible? A woman Ouida's age, not married, maybe gone mad longing for a child. Is that a myth? Once she told me she wished she was married with children—she said that. Marybeth looked at Anton to see if this was what he was thinking, too, but he was just drinking his beer and looking out the window. Marybeth felt as exhausted as if she had never slept at all.

"She went off this morning with all those—um—toys—
in a plastic sack, and she baked a cake, remember?"
Marybeth's heart speeded up as she remembered this.
Ouida has kidnapped him, that's clear, but at least she
won't hurt him. He's all right, she's just put him somewhere.

Anton shook his head over the whole thing. "He's just
wandered off someplace on his own," he said.

Well, they'll never find him, Theo was thinking upstairs.
She wished she could keep out of her mind the recollection of how she had lost their mother's diamond locket,
and she'd never dared tell Anton. The locket which always encircled their mother's neck and now was gone,
like her. Should she tell Anton? No, she could never tell
him. Loss, loss, so unendurable, and yet endured by other
human beings with such fortitude. How could they? How
can they be so brave? How glad I am to be safely here in
my room. Let the others look for that poor little boy, the
others with their sturdier pysches, and let me shirk a little
just this once.

How grievously mortal things engrave the brain. The
Finn, naked and blue, as vivid to her mind as he had
been thirty years ago—no, thirty-five now. Her fear of
him a secret thing, and now all her secrets and fears
floated up in a lump, a sort of nacreous clot or sharp
thing, like a bit of tooth. Did I somehow do that child in
myself? There was something—she couldn't remember.

Did I perhaps—I myself—push that little girl Esther
Lundberg into the sea? Have I put Chen-yu into a well?
Had she seen him out of the corner of her eye in the
hallway that morning?

She thought again of Marybeth's room, of the tumbled
bed, of an odor vivid to her even yet—just some cheap
peach bubble bath, the sheets thrown around, the stain
of blood from some skinned place on the poor child's

body. The bed so narrow, the pillow—her breath came fast in gasps, the faintness, the fear returning.

The child, she thought. Return your thoughts to the child and to philosophy. For that's how it happens, we are here and then gone. Only tiny bubbles rising to the surface brimming from the gasping lips, or the remnant of an echo, the echo of a soft cry, up from a ravine, which, like the crashing of the tree in the forest, does not exist if there's no one to hear.

No one hears him. He does not exist. Only last night he was eating ice cream—Rocky Road—his little lips bright with cold; now he is nowhere, that's how swiftly it happens.

When you are used to it, she thought, you feel calm about the little child, by an early death spared so much suffering. But she felt pity for the sick despair lying at the heart of the frightened girl, creeping into her room in the morning, finding him dead, and panicking, going through the motions down there of searching, hunting, lying, having herself stuffed the limp little body in some garbage can, with the resolution of the damned, being damned anyway on account of that other business, that prior deed of miscalculation. It was Marybeth who did it, of course.

It is the sadness and waste of this that she minds. The lovely vital girl. All the people in prison like that once, vital, all were small children once, with joyous and expectant hearts. She thinks of Charles, her little ballet pupil, thinks of how once he said, "Man, I threw my dog outta the window and he died." And yet Charles is a sweet little boy, an adorable little boy, and his heart still hopeful. She will take him out for a sundae one of these days after class and talk to him about the sanctity of life. She also thinks of that other little girl, Esther

Lundberg, long ago. The defeated sorry tears sting her eyes.

Who should come to the front door but Chuck Sweet? Marybeth felt grateful joy, not fear at all, at the way he came in, large, in a denim work shirt, looming confidence, not at all like someone who'd turn her in, but with the white smile of a savior instead. In a way she wasn't even surprised to see him. She must have been sending out yearning signals, like a transmitter.

"I heard about it," he said. "I came as soon as I could."

"How did you hear?" Marybeth asked, thinking of Chen-yu.

"Charles Sweet," he said, holding out his hand to Anton, and to Marybeth he said, "I heard from Miss Wait. She came after me this morning and told me all about it."

"Anton Wait," said Anton, shaking Chuck's hand.

"Oh. Oh? It's an honor to meet you, sir," Chuck said.

"You mean she told you about me." Marybeth suddenly understood. "She didn't tell you about Chen-yu?"

"Yes, about you," Chuck said. He had large sincere brown eyes, concern in them. "What's Chen-yu?"

"Something terrible has happened," Marybeth told him. "We've lost a little boy." She explained it all to him. "And he's only about three or four—say, four—and he hardly talks at all. We might walk right by him and he wouldn't call out. And we've looked everywhere, we've looked all morning. I think we should call the police."

"How long's he been gone?" he asked.

"I don't know, we missed him about ten," Marybeth said. "I think we should call the police."

Anton and Chuck both shook their heads.

"Obviously we want to avoid that," Chuck said.

"Yes, call them," Marybeth said. Things would just be out of her hands.

"I don't see any point to the police," Chuck said. "They'd ask how long he'd been gone, we'd say a couple of hours and they'd tell us to go look some more. Or they might put something out on their radio, but the likelihood that would do any good doesn't equal the risk to you. There's just no reason to fear. He's just wandered off somewhere, and he may have gone home by now. Look— I'll go into town and check at the day care center and around the schoolyard. He may have followed older kids from there. I can do the asking around more safely than you can. Mr. Wait, why don't you go over and try to find out something at his house? See if he shows up there, without alarming them."

"Oh, what are we going to say to his mother and father," Marybeth wailed. "I keep thinking of that. What can we say to them when we have to tell them?" The mortal dread welled up in her with new intensity. She could picture his little white fingers clinging desperately on somewhere, if only they could get to him in time. "He's tenacious, he's strong. He's really a strong little kid," she said, trying to think of hopeful things. "He went everywhere with me yesterday, and he never got tired and he never complained."

"Right, it's very unlikely that he met with a serious accident," Chuck said. "A person of four is quite sophisticated, you know. He probably has somewhere in mind to go."

This calmed her. Chuck was right. And yet she could imagine him clinging to a ledge, to the side of a well or jagged and fatal chasm, or in a culvert by the side of a freeway, clinging to the fence and buffeted by the forces of great trucks and cars hurtling by, not seeing his tiny clinging form. He would float like a little log, she thought, then he would melt, pale and formless, without eyes, with limbs like drowned sails.

"Highway 80, the freeway—he hasn't got any sense about streets," she said.

"He has the sense to see cars coming. Why would he go on the freeway? There are plenty of more interesting places to go. Look, you walk away from town on the side of the freeway, on the frontage road, and then cut across the field toward Sawnee Creek. I'll go to town, like I said. Is there anything special about him? Is he blond, dark, what?"

"Blond." Marybeth hesitated. "He's battered and skinned up," she admitted. She couldn't confide her real fear—amnesia, brain damage. "He fell out of a car yesterday."

Now a shadow crossed Chuck's face. Battered child. He thinks I've done it, Marybeth saw. Probably they all think that. Wasn't she the only documented murderess here?

"Well," said Anton, "I'll go over to his house," and picked up his camera. When he had gone, Chuck held Marybeth for a moment comfortingly in his arms. "Don't worry," he assured her, "everything is going to be all right," with such authority that she almost felt, for a second, that it was.

Ouida noticed that the laughter of the children did not seem to cheer Sachiko. Her little voice shook, Ouida didn't know why, since some of the children, one could plainly see, were Japanese like Sachiko. Whereas none were Brazilian, that was plain to Ouida. How could they be? Then Sachiko showed them a block of wood and told them it was her pillow, and they laughed with more affection for her, and she smiled happily, too.

Amazement! Now Meesis Aheem was unwinding her wrappings! She stood before the class in a YWCA T-shirt and an ordinary skirt. What amazement. Ouida could not understand it at all. What good was it to swaddle yourself like that if underneath you had to wear ordinary clothes as well?

"Now I will show you how to tie the sari," said Mrs. Aheem to the class, in her crisp imperious voice. They applauded when she had done it. Ouida still could not see what prevented it from coming off; there were no pins or ties for security.

When it came to her turn, Ouida drew the maté cup out of her sack and set it on the palm of her hand. She spoke of it. Miraculously the words emerged—English words. Comprehension. She saw comprehension, though not interest on their faces. She was grateful.

"It is for a kind of tea, is polite to drink it, but coffee, too, and most Brazilians prefer the coffee. Coffee is grown in Brazil, after all. We put more sugar in than you do here."

For some reason—she did not know why—some of them laughed at this. But it was not unkind.

"And here is the hat we wear for *carnaval*," she said, with resolution, and set it on her head, and was rewarded with applause.

She told them about *carnaval*. She did not mean to, but she mentioned the poor people of Brazil. "Even poor people, they save for a fine *carnaval* costume, and spend much money they cannot afford—they would rather have a fine costume than bread or beans. In Brazil the beans we eat are black . . ." Then she began to fear she was talking too long a time, or that the words had turned into Portuguese, so she stopped.

It seemed like forever before the teacher stepped forward, the children's own teacher, and said, "You wanna ask these ladies some questions?" Yes, they wanted Meesis Aheem to wrap and unwrap again, and they wanted Sachiko to untie her bow.

"In Brazil, the little kids there, do they turn tricks? The kids with no homes?" asked one girl of Ouida.

"Tricks? Tricks? Tricks?" repeated Ouida, trying to

remember this word. Had she been talking of the children with no homes? Why did they not talk to Meesis Aheem about this; in India there are many children with no homes.

"She means, do you have child prostitution in Brazil? We have been studying child prostitution in Social Studies," said a neat little girl in the front row.

Bewildered, Ouida could think only of white coffins and black coffins; she thought of the little children playing before the doorways with no pants on, and of the tiny mothers coming out of jungle patches carrying their heavy babies. Prostitution?

"I do not know," she said. What sort of teacher is this, she wondered, speaking of such matters to American children aged eleven? She looked to her own teacher, Mrs. Clausen, who smiled uncomprehending, unjudging encouragement, like a mother.

"I do not know," said Ouida. She did not know. Who knew what contracts were made among people in the jungle patches, along the rubble streets where no one dared to walk? She did not know. The sum of things she did not know seemed now before the wide gazes of the children to press on her head like a clay pot of water, producing the slight headache of ignorance. She blinked in the imperative brightness of all the wide eyes.

"In Japan do they wrap up the feet of the girl babies and make them little and scrunched up so you can't walk?" someone asked of Sachiko, who grew flushed with the strain of understanding and looked at Mrs. Clausen and said to the children that she did not know.

"No, no, of course not," Mrs. Clausen said. "Ancient China. That was ancient China. Horrible things like that are not done any more."

Marybeth set off south, down to the end of Ashby Path, then over the barbed-wire fence that bordered a field, and across the field. The land, flat and low, could scarcely conceal a child. Presently she would come to Sawnee Creek, where a child might very well play, but could not drown unless he was injured. She sought for comforts. The embankment to the side of the frontage road was high, fenced at the top along the freeway. He wouldn't climb up there. This made her hopes rise. There was hope even though the poor little kid hadn't had supper last night, hadn't had anything but junk food, like ice cream and Orange Julius, and maybe he'd starve. How long can they survive without food?

Dear God, she thought, as she had as a child, just let him turn up all right, then I won't mind what happens to me. Somewhere a panic of brakes chilled her; was that the moment he stepped into the path of the truck? The hot sun burned the back of her neck as she stared into thickets and shrubs, her own voice calling, high and tentative, and unanswered.

For an hour she stumbled on. She watched, leaned against fences. Now she sat on a stone and watched birds flutter from branch to patch of weed to bramble or fence post, seeming purposeless. It occurred to her that she could talk out loud to birds and birds would not tell. Among birds no one bird could tell the other birds the things it thought or knew. Like taciturn mutes, each must live his own life unshared, as she must, too. Can't you say "Chen-yu," damn you—can't you look down and see where he is? She remembered the birds who covered the babes in the woods with leaves. The babes in the woods were dead. Trembling, she got to her feet again.

Now it was four, that meant he'd been gone six hours. Can a child of four live for six hours unsupervised? Can they? God, how was she supposed to know—they are so small and silent. She stumbled on the clods burnt into rocks in the dry field.

Beyond this field, beyond two cows standing, who would have to be walked by, lay a slope, a shed and a few live-oak trees, seeming in the flat agricultural land-scape, in the burning heat, to be an oasis, a destination. Marybeth headed over that way without thinking, but with a feeling of excitement, a flutter of certainty. That was where Chen-yu was bound to be.

As she came closer, the dry pounding of her pulses, the sensation of sickness set in again. She thought she saw movement, down close to the ground, a swaying head. Please, God. She approached quietly, so if it was a cat or a dog it would not run away. All her thoughts teetered on a fence of true/not true.

Then they were resolved with a plunge. Not true. Death, peril are not true. There he was, safe and actual, as she had surely known he would be. Human beings are sturdy and smart. A warm milky grateful taste rose in her mouth. She started to rush, to shriek—but something in his composure stopped her.

He was sitting on the ground, wide-legged, making a row of twigs stuck in the hard earth in front of him. Each twig was about two inches long and meticulously placed an inch or so from the next. He had a purpose, a plan. While Marybeth watched, he climbed to his feet and went to look for another long stick, and began to break that into little pieces, too, to make more little standards for his game.

She watched. She could remember being a little kid like that. For some reason, her child self was vividly present to her. Her feet must have been as small as Chen-yu's—maybe only five inches long—yet they had felt as solid, personal, occupying space in the world and hold-ing her up as well as now. She could remember looking down at her feet, icy white in the cold shallow water of a stream, dappled feet with little twigs floating over them making shadows, and the water around the toes broke as around pebbles, and she had had no sense of her feet being five inches long.

That was the stream she had made the great dam in.

She'd played in streams a lot, alone along banks, down in thick vine clumps, first with brush, then stones and mud; an excellent dam, and she could understand Chen-yu's pride and concentration. What exultation—it could still quicken the heart to think of it—exultation when the little stream, coming along as it always had, before it met her, bringing its nest and branches along, found it needed to turn aside, needed to change and run another course. Thus a small girl can change a stream.

Other emotions as inevitable as waves now rushed over her—anger, relief. The world collected itself into normal objects, planes, and surfaces naturally arranged, no longer crazily disarranged by panic—trees, little shed, cozy oasis indeed, out here miles from everywhere; how in hell did he get out here? She rushed toward him.

He didn't seem surprised to see her. He seemed at home, in fact, as if he had come here often. He got up and trotted to her like a little host, and pointed to his work

"How did you get out here, Chen-yu? How did you know the way?" she snapped. "Aren't you hungry?" She saw banana skins. He must have found bananas in Theo's kitchen. "What did you figure on drinking? How did you figure on getting home?" She didn't really expect him to answer or talk to her, but at least he smiled.

She stared around her as at a new world. Funny smell in the air again. She looked in the window of the shed, and tried the door. It was a funny place for a shed, was maybe built for tools or for irrigation paraphernalia. The hot window was dusty and rain-spattered. She rubbed it.

The shed was filled with things that surprised her, things obviously brought out here. She had expected rusty pump dials or something, but here was the tidy and admirable stash of a scientific farmer—various sacks of fertilizers, nitrates, potash, gasoline for tractors, boxes on boxes of things unstained and new.

She looked closer. Boxes of ammunition, lengths of

pipe, glycerine, plastic bottles of distilled water, empty
jugs—wine jugs and old Clorox bottles, and, on a high
shelf, neat boxes that were marked "Mason" and contained jelly jars. Rings and lids set on the workbench,
and even a packet of labels.

Marybeth realized what all this was. She laughed and
hugged Chen-yu and led him away, frightened all over
again, even in her relief. "You shouldn't come out here
by yourself, Chen-yu, buddy," feeling thankful he didn't
play with matches, with enough stuff in there to blow up
every power station between here and Redding, or the
Banks of America, or whatever these people, whoever
they were, were into blowing up.

Walking back across the hot field, Chen-yu—barefoot,
not even minding the stubble—showed her his little-
accustomed path, and made, it seemed to her, a little
hum of happiness, holding in his hands the sticks he had
used. Chen-yu's hum expanded in her ears, in her throat,
into almost a roar of relief and joy. At first, she thought,
her joy was just for him. With every crackle of his step—
safe, sound, it said—she exulted. They had been through
a lot together, she and Chen-yu. Some things you could
never have forgiven yourself for, if anything had happened. But now Chen-yu would go on ahead. In a way,
she thought, she herself was saved no matter what happened next.

14. Innocence

Marybeth and Chen-yu walked home across the field.
Marybeth chattered to Chen-yu; he was her only friend,
silent and therefore trustworthy, and the habit of talking
to Chen-yu had crept up on her. Now she was all happiness, like a disembodied benign ghost, watching ev-

erything going well among the living and feeling glad about it. And feeling glad that there were still people around who objected to things. She felt the familiar stirring of passionate satisfaction that there were still people who were willing to take all the rotten things and blow them up, and never mind that her own life was over.

"Chen-yu, honey, be careful, there's broken glass there," she said, steering him along.

In the long run, she told herself, what does one person matter; there will be more and more, like in China. It doesn't matter about me.

Maybe that's what she'd say as they dragged her off: I'm happy. Or, I'm not happy, but I'm not sorry. I suppose they want you to be sorry, she thought. Unrepentance makes people mad, especially if you're a girl.

Violence is not the answer. That's what they want you to say. But she wasn't going to say it. You have to save yourself a little bit.

What if they have some sort of graph, she thought. Some sort of meter that can detect the swell of joy, the strong beating of an enthusiastic heart when you think of all that explosive and all that useful locked-up rage. There are still people out there raging, even when your own rage is gone.

Even when her own rage was gone, and she almost felt happy. And Chen-yu was safe.

When they got in sight of the house, they saw Chuck watching out for them, and when he saw them he raised both arms over his head and began running toward them. He'd done track, too. Now he had something to do with art, so it wasn't true, as she had used to think, about dumb jocks. God, had he really been in the army? How could he? How can that be? Could she tell him about the shed full of bombs? On the whole, no, she didn't think so. With safety, her wariness returned.

Chuck held Chen-yu against his chest, and brushed his cheek against the child's hair, an unconscious gesture of tenderness that Marybeth noticed. Chen-yu snuggled against Chuck's blue work shirt and smiled up at him with astonishing confidence and spoke, actually spoke: "I builded a city, and it was San Francisco."

"We were worried about you, kid," Chuck said. "We're glad to see you." Carrying the little boy in his strong arms. Chuck's arms were brown and covered with a light down of golden hair, and they were so large—Marybeth's throat burned with sudden love for both Chuck and Chen-yu, and with the peaceful sense that she herself was not there at all, was just a loving bystander, invisible, a watcher with no name, the incarnation of burning selfless love, rid of herself, futureless. Oh, oh, she sighed, in this rapture of selfless peace.

"You're all scratched up, too, and bruised like him," Chuck said to Marybeth.

"I fell out of the car, too," she said.

"Kind of trouble-prone, aren't you?" Chuck said.

"We were running away from you, Chuck. That's what you have to do. In case you were a member of the CIA."

"How do you know I'm not?"

"Now I don't care," Marybeth said. They walked along.

"*Why* are you doing this, anyway?" she asked presently.

"This?"

"Came over here this afternoon."

"Oh." He appeared not quite to know. To help, of course.

"*I* know," Marybeth said. "You're still the quarter-back, aren't you?"

"Yeah," he said. "Eagle Scout."

"Head counselor," said Marybeth. "Altar boy. Class president."

"Yeah, that's right," said Chuck. "Monitor. Honor camper."

"Why you, though?" Marybeth asked. Why anybody? Why some and not others? Was Chuck a designated agent of happiness?

"Oh, well," he said. "Why not?" They walked along.

Of course I'll get up, Theo thought, even before she could hear, by the pitch and cadence of the voices in the yard, that they'd found him, found him unhurt. Her vision seemed to clear. Her eye fell on an old sign, pried off a building by some former lover, attached to her wall for how many years, how silly of her to have kept it all these years: *"Prière de ne pas stationner."* Her wall was like the wall of a teenage girl, the posters and ballet announcements all over it. She felt embarrassed for herself.

The trouble is, I have no philosophy, she thought, no more than a chicken or a goose. To come in out of the rain, that's about all I do know. She'd valued recklessness. A cautious woman would have married and settled down and had children. Or is *that* the way of the reckless? Well, there are traps and webs and mines wherever you look.

She thought of old Cosmo Wrightsman, the clerk at the 7-Eleven. Whenever she went in there and there were no other customers, he would talk, and often would say, "Well, I've paid my dues," adverting to goodness knows what, for he was a plain old man who had had no adventures that she knew of. "I've paid my dues." Now what could he mean?

Would Anton consider that *he* had paid his dues? Those marriages, or perhaps in the war. But surely divorces are a way of not paying your dues? But he's paying them now, staying home with his old-maid sister.

Of course a person gets up. She felt silly. Panic is another of those emotions you can't recover when it's gone; just like strangeness of your own behavior remains, incarnate fact, like a garden bench. "Theo, come out of there." She could remember her mother saying that, the small Theo sitting up on the closet shelf hugging her knees. She had always left the closet door open a little peek so that whereas inside was dark repose, the real world outside could be glimpsed, too, and whiffs of clear air. "A child on a closet shelf!" Mother would say.

She'd come out now and go apologize for not being more helpful about that baby: thank God they'd found him. She had so much to do, and the lecture to prepare for tomorrow even though it was a lecture she had done dozens of times; still certain new things must be said, certain things omitted. And they would have to talk about what to do for Lynn—no, for Marybeth. Marybeth the prisoner. There is little enough a person can do; all one does is nothing. Even so, one does; one must. So. She got up and combed her hair.

She crept downstairs, ashamed, paused to sniff at Ouida's door and then went the rest of the way down. The doorbell rang, so she hurried the last few steps to answer it. When she peeked out, the door open the tiniest crack, her mind leapt with cautionary alarm; here was another man in a uniform. Perhaps they were being watched—detectives investigating them, wearing these disguises, meterman, postman, termite man.

"Registered letter for Ouida Senza," said the uniformed man. "Sign here."

She shivered. Immigration. We just want to keep to ourselves, let us alone, let us alone, she thought of saying.

"I'll sign," she said instead, briskly. "Miss Senza isn't here right now."

She read the envelope. It was only another letter from one of Ouida's brothers—either the pastor or the lawyer.

The brothers sent their letters registered because that's what you had to do in Brazil or the letter never got delivered. Things are so different here, why can't they realize that, was Theo's usual thought. At least the mail was all right here.

She laid the letter on the hall table regretfully. It would make Ouida sniff a little sadly; she would press her fingers to her mouth to stifle sighs; these letters always did. Darling sister, when are you coming home? All your family wishes you to come home. "I think they will never understand," Ouida would say, tears brimming her large eyes.

Anton was coming through the kitchen door from the back yard. He took a beer from the refrigerator, without speaking to Theo. She could see that he was angry with her. Anton is an old man, wearing that old plaid shirt, she thought, just a beer-drinking old man.

It was that he'd been worried. He frowned at her, made her say over and over that she was all right, not ill, not failing.

"Honestly. I think it was an emotional thing, I can't explain it," she told him. "Oh, I can explain it of course. It sounds silly in retrospect, but when, just for a moment, I thought the child was dead, it brought back memories very vividly, and a certain fear I've always had about myself. I've always been afraid that I'm—oh, somehow—the angel of death."

Anton merely stared, said nothing.

"You know, the kiss of death, as they say. I have always been afraid it is I, it is I who bring on death. I have to be kept out of the way, I have to be careful or I bring it on others." She was just trying to explain how it had seemed to her, she'd been so uncertain, so defeated by the conviction. She knew Anton wouldn't understand this, his commitment to life was so, well, simple-minded was how it had always seemed to her: chipmunks in logs, tadpoles in ponds.

"You're just crazy, you've always been a hysteric," he said.

"I've had this feeling off and on for a long time. It's torture, it's terrible, when it comes on."

"It's vanity, it's neurotic thinking of a particularly futile kind, egocentric in a childish way," Anton snapped.

"So I just knew they would not bring that child back alive; I had kissed him, I had fed him," she said.

"Teddy, are you being serious? You can't possibly believe that. What a disorder. Of course bad things do happen in the world, in some cases to people we know, but we don't cause them."

Why is he so upset? she wondered. I'm not being so silly as he thinks. "I myself arranged the abortion of Ariadne Neff—a boyfriend of mine knew a doctor in Tijuana—and she died. And you, when you broke your collarbone and when you broke your arm, both times I was watching you. I was home with Mother when she died, and there's plenty more—the little girl on the ship, and the Finn in the room, and then I supposed that this little boy. I can't explain."

"I think he needs real food," Marybeth was saying as she came into the kitchen with Chuck and Chen-yu. How beautiful they looked, like a beautiful family, Theo thought—the golden young man, ravishing dark girl, scruffy tot looking none the worse for whatever had happened to him.

"He's only had junk food for two days, plus two bananas he had the sense to get for himself," Marybeth went on.

"What's his real name? Chen-yu? He isn't Chinese or anything," Chuck said. "You hear a lot of kids called Mao, or Chou, but you can understand that."

"It's the name of a brand of nail polish we had when I was your age," Theo said. "I've wondered myself, why on earth name a child after nail polish."

Chuck and Marybeth asked Theo if she was feeling better. She watched to see if they were going to punish her for her odd behavior in not helping in the crisis. But she could soon tell that they hadn't judged her at all, considered her at an age where they had no right to, or had no interest in judging her. Old women did what they did.

"There's some hamburger," Theo said. "Ouida was going to use it to stuff a cabbage for dinner, but use a little of it, make him a hamburger."

Ouida came in just then, as if they had called her name. She was carrying her sack of Brazilian treasures and wore a look of pleasure, and the carnival hat, trailed by fruit flies. The presentation at the school had been a success, she said, and the trip home even more successful.

"It is a most curious thing, on the bus, and also walking along, everywhere," Ouida said.

"What happened?" asked Marybeth, who was patting the little hamburger for Chen-yu.

"My horoscope said today is an auspicious day, and it is turning true. Everyone is courteous in America as a regular thing, but today they were very happy to me, full of affection and cheer. Yesterday my English became clear, and today I receive the love of the world!" She laughed, to show she didn't quite believe this. "Everyone smiles and laughs wherever I go," she explained.

"It's your hat," Theo said. "It's unusual, you must admit."

"Yes, partly the *carnaval* hat, and there's more. See, I also wear a *carnaval* dress." She threw open her loose smock, and under it they saw a ruffled flowered skirt and blouse cut high, showing her bare midriff of firm brown skin.

"It was not my hat and dress directly, I know, but what they signify. In fact, it is puzzling, because when I wear these Brazilian clothes, people treat me more nice. More nice than when I wear American clothes, I mean. It is a joke on me that I spend much time trying to appear American and to be American in my speech and in every way, and now I discover that people treat me better when they think I am not American. Is it not surprising? Is it not a great secret?"

"It's not surprising," Marybeth said. "Americans don't mind foreigners, it's other Americans they're afraid of."

Ouida shrugged as if this passed her understanding. "This is a busy day for me, as well as an auspicious one," she said, shaking the cake crumbs out of her bath towel. "I will not be home for supper, because I am going to help Mr. Griggs at his house. I think it is okay to do so. I know he is not married, because here the men tell you if they are married."

"If he were married, would you go more reluctantly, or more confidently?" Anton asked. He had not appeared to be listening.

"I would not go at all to the house of a married man," Ouida said. "In Brazil sometimes men come around and become a fiancé to a girl when they have a wife already, which they do not mention to the girl or her family. Then when it is discovered, there is much shame and disgrace. I am very careful in Brazil, and my brothers are careful. The policy of my brothers is that the man must show his documents."

"His documents?" said the fascinated Anton.

"Their *cartão oficial*—their official card. It says on it whether married or single. If they reserve their *cartão* and will not show it to you, then I say no, I do not wish any further acquaintance. Cheaper women do not care, and do not regard the document, but I would not wish to be the friend of another woman's husband. I would not wish another woman to make me unhappy that way, that is simply the Christian philosophy. But anyway, in America things are better, because if they are married they tell you. They don't expect it to make any difference.''

"Is Mr. Griggs divorced? Can he legally marry you?" Theo asked, with a sudden suspicion.

"I think so. But you see the importance of finding out. In Brazil, where there is no divorce, sometimes people have an arrangement from the court. My friend Pilar goes with a nice man who has such an arrangement from the court, separate arrangement, but he cannot marry Pilar. Sometimes people go to Uruguay to marry, but they are not married in the mind of Brazil. The mother and father of Pilar are upset. Things are more honest and straight-forward here.''

"Oh, you always think things are better here when they aren't," Marybeth said, thinking at the same time, Brazil, why not? She could gain some weight and pretend to be Ouida; that's if Ouida ever got her passport back, and Ouida could stay here. Brazil would be okay.

"In Brazil they torture the prisoners, here they just send you back home," Ouida said. "Although my brother the pastor says it is better now, not so much torture. He says when the government has got rid of all the Communists and bad people, then the bad things will not be done at all. Sometimes it is necessary at first, the way purification of the body sometimes produces coughing. The poison must first be removed from the body.''

"Really!" objected Theo. "Is there no such thing as principle in Brazil?" Ouida was so accepting of things.

"A legitimate government would have nothing to hide," Marybeth objected, too. "The people should rise up, they shouldn't just turn the other way.''

"My brother says things are better now, more peace, and the lower people have more money than before, so

that everyone is more happy. Strictness is necessary
sometimes. When my nephew in the army smoked mari-
juana, he have a strict sentence, for this is illegal, but
when he is finished he is better and more mature, even
my brother's wife agree with this.''

"Oh, Ouida, how can you say such things, a good person like you? Think of people going to jail for nothing,
for a little thing like smoking grass!" Marybeth cried.

Ouida went to wait for Mr. Griggs, and Anton went to
his studio. Chuck said, suddenly "Chen-yu wants to go
to the bathroom. Where is it?" Marybeth wondered how
on earth he knew; the kid hadn't said anything.

Then she and Theo were alone, and Theo suddenly
seized her arm and spoke urgently, her old eyes aglow
like violet coals: "What did you want to be when you
grew up? I mean, when you were little? A dancer? A
painter?" Hopes of a young girl like wildflowers, new,
bruisable, frail and liable to be trodden. She wanted to
hear about them.

Marybeth was shocked by this sudden question; it was
too personal, after these years immured and protected
against a probe into her life.

"I don't know," she said. "I can't remember. I didn't
have any aims or ambitions. Not until I went to college.
I don't know. Nobody told me I *should* have any."

"Well, what did you think became of people?" Theo
said, sounding strangely cross.

"I don't know," Marybeth said. "I can't imagine. I
don't know." She wondered herself. "I was—I guess I
was just unconscious. I just wandered around and played.
I was like Chen-yu, I guess. I suppose I thought about
paper dolls, or I read stories."

"But your burning desire to help the world?" Theo
persisted. "You had a burning desire to help the world?"
She leaned closer to Marybeth.

"If I did, I can't remember," Marybeth said, and pressed her lips together as if she wouldn't talk about it any more. It was true; she couldn't remember.

If only I could remember, thought Theo. Were Marybeth's the delicate hands that poured the gasoline on the soaked rags, set alight around the helpless scientist? Or however it had been done. Now Marybeth with delicate fingers was shredding up a paper towel and piling the bits on the kitchen table. If Theo could only remember. But she found it impossible to ask. Had there been others with Marybeth? Boys she at other times slept with? Had they tied the man up and danced around jeering, or had he just accidentally been standing there at the Bunsen burner when the bomb went off, or however it had been done? Or was it Marybeth alone, looking through the window from her hiding place in the hedge, aiming at the evil scientist, pulling the trigger with her delicate fingers? Perhaps Theo would go look the case up in the library.

"I was somebody who believed in everything," Marybeth added. "In this country, in abstractions, in God, even, and I thought that truth always wins out, all that stuff, so when I found out otherwise, I just went over with a crash."

Ordinary people, Theo thought, embarrassed at the sudden flush in her cheeks, of her feeling for this girl. Something, the smell of peach bubble bath. She turned away, opened the refrigerator door, moving the milk to one side, piling the margarine box on top of the butter box and rearranging the bottles—ketchup, chili sauce, barbecue sauce, *salsa verde*—on the shelf in the door, the tallest to the left, in order of size. Ordinary people, an ordinary woman like me, she thought.

"Just like so many people in the sixties," she said to

Marybeth. "Those were terrible times, everybody understands that."

"In fact," said Marybeth, going on as if she hadn't heard, "I didn't even know there was anything wrong with the world."

"You didn't know?" Theo turned.

"Well, some things. A boy in our class had a harelip, my uncle died, one of our cats ate her kitten—Christ, only things like that. I didn't notice the other things."

"And yet, when you saw, you took action. How I admire that," Theo said. "But"—remembering something—"did you never see films of the death camps? When you were little?"

"Well, no, but I saw plenty of films about Vietnam."

"It's not the same. Not even Vietnam," said Theo.

"I wouldn't want to see them," Marybeth said. "Oh, I couldn't."

Theo realized that she didn't know how old Marybeth was. How old would she be? She could be any age. Why had life not marked and stained her?

"What I mind," Marybeth said, "is finding out that I'm like everybody else. When I was little, it never occurred to me I was like other people. Now I know I am not going to make any difference. Nobody does. It's stupid to think that anything you've done will make any difference. But I do mind that."

Theo could not help putting out her hand and touching the bruise on the girl's cheek. She expected it to burn to the touch, like a brand, but the cheek was smooth and cool.

"Yes, sometimes I'm ashamed of my life, ashamed of having cared about art and order, of not having wanted a messy life. You should be glad, you should not underrate your life," Theo said.

* * *

Suddenly there was Julie Burnham tapping furtively on the kitchen door, peering through the window at them. Theo waved her in. Julie slipped inside, looked around like a spy and, with meaningful looks at Marybeth, put a long fat envelope behind the flour and sugar canisters. She was wearing Marybeth's backpack, which Marybeth helped lift off.

"Is Chen-yu here?" Julie asked. "They told me he slept here last night. Was it all right? He hates not to sleep in his own bed. Did he go to sleep all right?" Evidently Anton had not told her. Best to confess.

"Yes, he got up this morning, though, and went outside, and we couldn't find him. We were really scared." Bound to confess everything. "Also he fell down, and he looks kind of skinned up—did they tell you that?"

That girl isn't as young as she looks, Theo thought, looking as closely as she could at Marybeth without seeming rude. How old would she be? I suppose she's been a fugitive since the sixties. Those people are not so young any more. Little lines at the corners of her eyes, the face tired. She could almost have been that little girl on the ship—how old would *she* have been? Not a bad idea. Could almost *be* the little girl on the ship.

"Chuck took him to the john," Marybeth said. "They should be right back."

Then they heard Chen-yu's little piping voice in the hall, talking to Chuck. When they came in, Marybeth held her breath to see if Julie would shriek and gasp to see his skinned nose and the long scratch on his cheek. Julie did. She screamed, then seized him, covered him with kisses.

Whereas Chen-yu had been calm, holding Chuck's hand and actually speaking; now he began to cry.

"Oh, I'd better take him home," his mother said. "He wants to go home. I'll talk to you later, Lynn," and bore

Chen-yu away. Chen-yu didn't even look back at Marybeth.

"Is this for you, this envelope?" asked Theo in the quiet.

"Yes, I know what that is," Marybeth said. "It's my
new identity."

"Oh, open it, open it!" Theo cried, filled with a rush
of fear. Let her open it quickly and settle the new identity
over her like a mantle, like a Tarnhelm, like an invisi-
bility cloak before some policeman, some FBI man
should come to the door.

They looked at Marybeth. She held the envelope from
the corner, as if it reeked.

"I don't want it," she said. "I don't even want to see
it. I'm not going to take it, it isn't any use."

Theo denied this, protested, scolded. "No," Marybeth said. "Too many people know. Julie and who knows
who else at her house. What do I know about that name?
Maybe it's just a rip-off. I would always be wondering
and waiting for someone to find out, just like I do now.
It's no better than a name I make up myself; it's no
stronger, it might be weaker and it's costly—let someone
have it who can afford it. Besides, I've made up my
mind."

"New identity!" cried Theo, entranced. "To think it
can be done. Oh, do open it! You could get a new everything—driver's license, a birth certificate, a passport.
What's to become of you otherwise?"

"Look, please don't talk to me about it. I've accepted
that there's a hold over my life, and I've got to get free
the only way I can. Realistically I figure I'll have to serve
about a five-year sentence, that's the least, up to life im-
prisonment, but not too many people have gotten that,
and then—I don't know—it doesn't matter."

Oh, how terrible, Theo thought, just a young girl, her
spirit in shards, what could they do? Marybeth threw the

envelope on the counter. Chuck picked it up, then slid it back behind the canisters again. It seemed that he hadn't yet made up his mind; his lovely face was rather severe, and he said nothing.

"Well, we'll talk about it later," said Theo, wanting to shake the danger off, clear it away. "Let's have dinner. I guess we'll have to have stuffed cabbage another night; Ouida isn't here."

"I've made the hamburger up into patties," Marybeth said. "I'll cook them. Please. I want to."

15. Experience

The hamburgers were rather shrunken and charred; perhaps Marybeth had consulted some cookbook, or *Sunset* magazine, for there were runny pats of blue cheese on top. Theo was sure Anton would have preferred to skip the blue cheese. They sat in the Redwood Dining Room, and it might have been any dinner all these months, except that Ouida wasn't there, and Carlyle, strangely, refused to enter the dining room but sat in the hallway making reproachful complaining whines. But the rest of them sat chatting, and the addition of this nice young man was pleasant; he was well-spoken, Theo thought, and had views of art, had, no doubt, views of life, too; and had conversation! Unlike so many young men. His views of art were in fact confounding; he was interested, he said, in seventeenth-century French painting. The School of Versailles, he said, and Theo said she was afraid she had no conversation about that.

Anton brought up a trip he had taken to the foothills of the Himalayas, with the Sierra Club. Now there was something men could talk about. "How like men," said Theo, "that although you made this trip five years ago, you have never told me all these details. As if you imagined I would not be interested in Sherpas and crevasses, whereas I am. Women are. Are we not?'' she asked Marybeth. Marybeth only nodded.

Chuck had done some climbing, too, but only in the Alps. ''Basically I'm no climber.'' He smiled. ''I'm too forgetful and too self-conscious both.''

''Serious climbing concentrates the mind wonderfully,'' Anton said.

''You talk about it so vividly, one might almost be there,'' Theo said, whether with or without irony no one could tell.

''I have a story to tell, myself,'' she said presently. ''It was much on my mind today, with that little boy missing, but I wonder if the same idea will strike you as struck me. This was on board ship going to Europe, after the war. I was going to Copenhagen. I was going to dance. My heart—my state of mind—is somehow important. There's a way in which I was never the same after this. But then I was happy.'' But perhaps, she thought, my state of mind is not important to this story, and anyway there is no way to suggest the frissons of possibility, or joy, the shivers of freedom and thrill I felt then, compared to the old woman I suppose I am now.

''I was not a girl then, by no means. I'd been in Europe a good deal before the war, but only in the corps de ballet, and now I had better parts. I thought of myself as alone on stage, but of course I was with a company.''

''You said at the time you had no continuing aspirations, you were only going back the once,'' Anton said.

''Did I? Well. Anyway, on the ship with me was a young family—a woman and husband, and a baby, and a little daughter about three or four. The father would carry the baby along the deck, and the mother kept the hand of the little girl, stately and fond, daily on their walk; everyone admired them. I, as well as everyone else. They were Swedes, and had been in America during the war, and now were going back to Sweden. Their English was charming, so elaborate and crooning, the way Swedes talk. The little girl and baby were born in this country— in Minnesota, I learned, talking to the mother one day. The child always held her mother's hand or walked alongside, on their walks, and they always dressed charmingly, in the prewar fashion, the child in Mary Janes and pinafore and so on. We had sailed from the East Coast—I had taken the train across. I'd been visiting home that summer. But of course that has nothing to do with it.

"Then there was a storm at sea, it lasted almost two days, and you scarcely saw a soul, everyone stayed down. I myself was not seasick, but sat in the salon for nearly the whole two days, reluctant to lurch along the passages, hurtle against the railings; I was afraid of breaking an ankle or a wrist or a rib more than anything. There would be almost no one at meals, it was as if cholera had swept away human life, the stewards forcedly jolly—but of course it wasn't a serious storm, I've been in worse; heavy weather was the worst you could call it.

"Later I did venture out, when it was calmer, and there was a terrible agitation, a swarm of people, and the young mother of this family sitting on a chair, people running up to her; she sat there much like a queen with courtiers all around, but so strangely. Such a strange silent swishing of sailors and people up gangways, whispers, the pulling of heavy doors. This young woman was wearing a sort of orange negligée, terribly blown, for the wind was still high, and I saw her staring crazily around her, but not moving from her chair, and it was then that something, a knife of pity, struck at my heart, to see her eyes, though I didn't know what had happened. The horror, I remember, preceded my knowing.

"I was overcome with fear, and I began to scream. It is the only time in my life I screamed. I'm not a screamer, but I began screaming. 'What's happened! What is it?' It was as though something had me by the throat, some form of communicable dread. But *before* I found out what it was, that is the point.''

"You screamed at the Finn in your room," Anton said. "You often scream.''

"But what had happened?'' Marybeth said, eyes round.

"What had happened was that the little girl was gone, she was nowhere to be found, she was never found. There was no explanation, there was no reason; the parents had got on board with their charming little daughter and got off without one, as though the child had never been.''

"But what had happened?''

"They presumed she had fallen overboard in the storm. Or perhaps some—somebody—the things that happen to little girls—no one knows, but I couldn't help but think of her, I couldn't get her out of my mind, I suppose I've never got her out of my mind, perishing alone in the water, her mother not there to save her, wondering, not wishing it to happen and yet it was happening. I've never been sure I didn't see her myself, on the deck, I could have sent her below, I should have made her go below. If I saw her. The mother is an old woman now, I suppose, and she must still wake up at night, knowing that she shouldn't have let the child get out of bed, or go for the newspaper, or whatever it was. I wonder if she still wakes? Perhaps by now she has forgotten that she ever had a little girl.''

And yet, Theo saw, they didn't know what she meant. Their eyes were sympathetic, curious, uncomprehending.

"Think of all the people there were, who are no more,'' she said, trying to explain, theatrically flapping her arms.

In her eyes Marybeth could see real enough terror, as if Theo felt it clear into her soul, for everybody who ever was. It seemed to Marybeth that that was taking a lot on yourself.

* * *

Oh, thought Theo, they don't see of course. How can they be so calm? In the light of all that has happened here and all that will happen? No shadow of dread or doom clouding their faces at all. Is it only I? For she felt restive still, wary, cross with them, perhaps unreasonably, that they should be so unresponsive to the great troubles passed through and awaiting—awaiting the girl, who now seemed to have recovered her indifferent manner, a certain lassitude—perhaps she used drugs? And her eyes were different. How without drugs could anyone be calm, if they really meant what they said: Tomorrow I'll do it. Well—she must mean Monday—so there was still time for someone to think of something. Lawyers the first step anyway.

Chuck is so tall, thought Marybeth. I think he's grown or something since we were in high school. I wonder what I look like now, compared to then. I must look awful. He doesn't even look at me.

Chuck so coolly eating his dessert, drinking his wine. Marybeth wanted to touch him with her foot. What the hell. One last chance to make her last wishes known. Only chance to have any wishes, and then an end to wishing. But she didn't touch him; she sat like a sheep and tried to think of Theo's story. She felt her throat get dry looking at Chuck, and Chuck wasn't even looking at her; he was looking full of interest at Theo, and they were talking about the fate of the little girl.

"I'll make coffee, but let's have it in the living room," Theo suggested, rising graciously as at a dinner party. Strangely, Anton agreed, sounded pleased, though he usually refused coffee in the evenings and normally would be going out, even just out to his studio, and the girl would usually have to go to her job at Photophobia, or otherwise just up to her room, and she to her room; but tonight they had a guest, this Chuck, who was evidently happy not to be going back to his boarding house just yet, and they'd asked him to dinner, so it was like a dinner party, maybe a dinner party in a bomb shelter.

Chuck followed her out to the kitchen, which Theo found momentarily irritating; did he think she was too old to carry a tray of coffee? But she soon realized from the hovering of his shadow at her heel, the bright triviality of his well-brought-up compliments upon the meal, that he wanted to say something privately when they were out of earshot of the others. Carlyle, waiting in the hall, followed after Chuck.

"I think I'm in a good situation to help her," Chuck said. "I'm leaving the country in September with a Fulbright to France. With a passport she could go along, as my wife, and once abroad she'd be quite a lot safer."

"That would be wonderful," Theo agreed, "but how will you convince her? I think she wants to have it over with. I've read that about fugitives. They get so anything is better than the suspense, the unresolved flatness of their waiting, the paranoia . . ."

"I understand that perfectly well," Chuck interrupted briskly, as if Marybeth were going to burst in on them.

"We'll have to sit on her or something, do something to dissuade her. But that's what I thought you could do," Theo said.

"Yes, she should give up the idea of surrender."

"Yes. Surrender," Theo agreed. "Terrible."

"She must never surrender," Chuck repeated in this same resolute way, and then turned on her his blazing sudden smile, so that Theo heated with resistance to him, and poured the coffee. Was he reproaching her for something in particular, saying *"surrender,"* such a shocking word really, in that portentous tone?

"You were thinking, why couldn't she become that little girl on the ship?" Chuck said. "Use her identity."

"Yes. Of course, Julie has already brought her a new name, too. Marybeth has explained it. It's Julie's profession, she's an expert. What an age of specialization we live in. It is done all the time."

"The ship would have made a report, but here or abroad? In Copenhagen? Was it an American ship."

"A Dutch ship," Theo said. "Yes. Without a trace. Her birth recorded in Minnesota or wherever it was, her death—nowhere."

"I'd have to know exactly where and when she was born, to get the birth certificate."

"Tomorrow I'll look in my old journal of that trip, it might mention something about it. Wisconsin, or Minnesota? I'll have to look."

He took the tray from her. He's in love, I suppose, thought Theo. Or is a childish romantic—to the rescue, maidens in distress. She'd almost forgotten it was she who had put him up to all this.

"You could get into trouble over all this," she said. "We all could."

"I doubt it," Chuck said.

"Take the cups in, and the sugar from the table there. I'll come along with the coffee in a second," Theo said, and turned her attention to the stove. Standing over a stove was, she had learned, the one situation in the world when no one would intrude upon a woman's thoughts.

This young man has not been to Everest, Theo was thinking; has he been to Vietnam? She wondered. Did he like it? A fighter, knife blade in his teeth. Men like going to war—I really think they do—because it gives them secrets. No woman can imagine war. Well, I suppose those Israeli girls can, and nurses, nurses see the things. Still, do you really want to see them? Aren't you grateful not to have to see them? Theo could not decide. It wasn't fair for others to have secrets; yet there were things you would rather not know. She could understand that Mary-beth would not want to see the death camps.

Anton had done just photography in the war, photographing roads and lines of trees and clumps of bushes from the air, and there were no secrets in that. She had seen the pictures, also pictures of climbing on Everest. No secrets in that. She could imagine Anton in war, strapping on his helmet, the jokes, the tears for someone's plane seen disappearing downward in a trail of smoke. For him the smells, the hush, the camaraderie, sounds; for her the newsreel image.

How is it, she wondered, peering in the top of the pot to see if it had all dripped through, how is it girls nowadays would put themselves in jeopardy—a lifetime in prison, imagine; perhaps they are just trying to share the secrets, trying to pry. Meddlesome. Or do they have more imagination than I?

Or less? Do they foolishly think if they go out there and march and throw bombs, the boys are going to let them in on the secrets? Oh, no.

A small knot which Theo wore in her bosom—she could almost touch the place beneath which it lay, like a cherished locket containing, but in very small quantities, petulance and disappointment, and which had been mislaid beneath her worries for Chen-yu and Marybeth—now swung and knocked reassuringly against her thin breast.

Chuck had set out the little cups of random design collected in England and Canada by Theo's mother. Anton had brought out the brandy.

"Well, we could have a game of something," he said, in a jocular holiday way. He took, Theo noticed, the white Limoges, rose-sprigged. She took the deep blue English cup with gold, a vulgar little cup; she always took this one. She shot her hand out because Marybeth was reaching for it, too.

Yes, Theo thought, a kind of bomb-shelter spirit here, none of us wishing to leave; we stick together. She suggested bridge. Marybeth had not learned to play bridge, though Chuck had learned it in the army, in Germany, he said.

"Monopoly," Anton said, and got out the old Monopoly board, bought sometime when his daughters were little and came to visit Theo and Mother here. An awkwardness became immediately apparent over the place on the board that said "Jail" and the cards that said "Go Directly to Jail," but Marybeth only laughed.

"I don't mind. When I woke up this morning thinking I would be in jail today, it was a relief. This morning was the first morning in six years it was a relief to wake up. Instead of things being worse than your sleeping self thought, they were better, they were over. I just felt tremendous relief." Her voice was confiding and strong, her color somewhat up, probably from the wine and brandy. There was something strange about her wide blue, somewhat smudgy eyes. Does she put mascara on her lashes, Theo wondered, noticing for the first time that the girl no longer wore her round wire-rimmed granny glasses. Perhaps they had been part of her disguise, which she had now left off.

"Your sanctuary need not be jail, you know," Chuck said.

"It's just that being in jail will be so easy, compared to being underground. I know that seems irrational, but what nobody could possibly understand but me is how I can't stand it any more. I've been underground six years. Realistically speaking, I might not be in jail that long, taking into consideration what other women have got."

"Have you no comrades? There must be hundreds of people like you," Theo said.

"Oh, sure, when you first go underground it's kind of

companionable, you're a hero, people take care of you. Friends, and money—from sympathetic campus groups and so on—filters along. Hundreds of people are willing to help and you'll meet them and they'll take care of you and it feels okay. But nobody tells you how long it's going to go on. The people drift away, their own lives take them over, yours doesn't fit in. You are just this dangerous person in their attic or their basement. I lived for three months in the basement of a professor and his wife. What's the difference between that and jail?''

"You can get out," Chuck said.

"Well, yeah. You leave, you get to feeling safer away from the people like you, you think of a new name, dye your hair, get stupid jobs, you almost turn back into a real person in time, with a new reality. But you can't get a job doing anything where people might ask about your education or your brain or your past, and that means you work in the laundromat or the Photophobia or the coffee shop. And the world changes, the time has gone by.

"Well, eventually you catch on that this is it. If you ever meant to do anything with your life, forget it, you did it already; now you have to look backwards—oh, I don't know how to make anything out of my life this way. I feel like Sunyo Yukomo—did you read about him? That Japanese soldier that lived for thirty years in the jungle? He sort of came out blinking and the world welcomed him. I read all about him. The world went by him.''

"Couldn't you go to Canada?'' Anton asked. "I thought Canada.''

"Not with this felony. They'll take draft avoiders and deserters, but not with serious felonies.''

Serious felonies, Theo thought. Oh, it had, inexplicably, a ravishing sound.

From the living room they could hear noise at the front door—Ouida coming home. Ouida, or perhaps *two* people at the door, someone with her, sounds of movement, perhaps of embrace, or of clumsy resistance to an embrace, and Ouida saying good night. Then she came distractedly down the hall and put her head in at the living-room door to greet them. She seemed surprised to see them all sitting so sociably there at this hour. Something stirred in her, a wish to tell them of her experiences, which were so difficult for her to evaluate by herself. She set down her big sack of oranges, and accepted a cup of coffee.

"Though I should not, because then my heart pounds so bad in the night. I know it is from the coffee, but in my family there are weak hearts."

"You've been helping your friend Mr. Griggs?" Theo asked.

His hands are so huge and strong, Marybeth thinks. I wonder if he has a big cock? No matter what they say, big ones are better. Oh—if only we could just crawl under this table, if only these people would go away—maybe we could go over to Chuck's place. But we can't. Anyway, maybe Chuck won't want to make it with somebody in my situation.

Chuck is so cool-headed—making a little row of his hotels. He has already got everybody's hotels. Again she wants to rub her foot against his, but she doesn't; she still sits like a sheep, and tries to listen to Ouida's outpouring. It is important, she cares about Ouida, the others don't care about her enough. But she keeps thinking about Chuck. Ouida trusts everybody, anybody, she is such a trusting person. A trusting person needs a suspicious person to look after them, that's for sure. She tries her best to pay attention to Ouida.

"I don't know, I think it is okay, the house of Griggs," Ouida was saying. "I'm afraid it was very dirty. It is true that he needs a friend to help him. His house is not so big or pretty as this house, but he has some nice furniture. He has chairs with flowers on, and a round table, and many pictures of flowers on the wall, and an amazing lamp which goes all the way from the floor up to the ceiling with various lights along the stem. It is very pretty. I had not expected that he would like flowers, but that is good, isn't it? Brazilians are all fond of flowers. And he has color TV in a big cabinet, more big than ours here, and a rug of that color—'' she indicated a turquoise flower on a cup.

"So you went over there and cleaned for him," Marybeth said.

"Not too much. I did what I can. It needs vacuuming very much, but he has no vacuum. He says his daughter has taken it, so tomorrow I will go over there after the *feijoada* with the vacuum from here, if that is okay, and give him a good vacuuming. It's not very clean there, but I think that is what happens when a man takes care of a house, and his children are not much help to him.''

Marybeth gave an angry sniff. "No wonder the wife split.''

"In a way," Ouida added, "his house is like a Brazilian house. The sofa has rough cloth with little gold stripes, very pretty, like I have seen in Brazil. I think the world is not so very different from one place to another when you look closely. Anyway, it looks similar. I think the heart of nations is different, however; their hearts are different. I ask him, you should make your daughters do the vacuuming. In Brazil that is what the daughters do.''

"He could ask the sons to do the vacuuming, for that matter," said Marybeth.

Ouida laughed. "The men and boys don't do nothing, except with more rich people, then none of them don't do nothing, boys or girls either, in Brazil.''

"Anything," said Theo.

"Well, anything. They have many servants, but that is changing, though, as there are not so many servants any more and modern mothers are not so indulgent. But Mr. Griggs says, 'My girls don't do nothin and they just like they mother.' '' Her voice deepened in imitation of Griggs.

If she can imitate Griggs, why can't she imitate standard American speech, thinks Theo. Is it just a matter of imitation? Is it something more?

They try to say encouraging things, to cheer her about Griggs. Is not Griggs, after all, the answer for Ouida? He doesn't sound too bad to Theo—at least Ouida appears to like his sofa and his lamp. Presently Ouida sighs and takes her leave. For a young woman she walks up stairs very slowly.

Theo has noticed this often.

"Can't you be better to Ouida?" Marybeth said suddenly. "She's not a fool. She deserves respect. She's done a lot with her life. Did you know she was a schoolteacher in Brazil, a kindergarten teacher, and she got her education against all odds!"

"Well, of course, we're very fond of Ouida. You don't feel we are kind to Ouida?" Theo asked, astonished.

"You should speak more slowly, and explain things to her, the expressions she doesn't understand. She shouldn't have to marry Griggs. People shouldn't yield to these old tyrannies."

"I don't know," Theo said. "It sounded better than I had expected. I felt rather relieved. The sofa, the lamp."

Oh, what will become of Ouida when I give myself up, thought Marybeth.

"Teddy," Anton said, "I think it's getting late. We've had a difficult day. I think we should turn in." It was said firmly in the tones of a camp director or leader, or just someone who was weary of disputation. Was the se-

cret of Anton's nature a wish not to be disturbed? Was
inertia the sacred center of art? Theo considered.

"Yes, let's call it a night," she said. "We can talk in
the morning."

"Who is that in the kitchen?" Anton asked.

"Ouida has come back downstairs," Marybeth said.
"Tomorrow is her *festa*, all the people coming to eat her
feijoada, she probably has a lot of work to do."

"Tomorrow is a day we should all go underground,"
Anton said.

16. *Wilted Violets*

They wait silently until the others have gone up; then
Chuck goes upstairs with Marybeth and into her bedroom, and closes the door behind them and begins to
take off her clothes right away, with the assurance of a
prince or a conqueror, and he understands all buttons and
zippers, and all the smooth electric places of Marybeth's
body.

How has he learned all this? What has he been up to
since leaving Bettendorf, Iowa? Did he know these things
back then, behind the gym, or down Terrier's Ravine?
All that Marybeth knows about pipe bombs, incendiary
techniques and detonating devices is as nothing beside
the hot things Chuck knows. She gratefully gives herself
up to his ancient knowing, and his inspirations. On the
eve of prison, yet she has never been so pleased.

Chuck is so strong, so inexhaustible. How fleeting a
night of love, and yet slow, time for all caresses, all
confidences, all pleasures, whispers. They keep the light
on. It burns far into the night, as though for some forlorn
insomniac.

"Oh, my darling, my beautiful Marybeth," Chuck is

saying, his fingers, his lips again caressing the nipples of her breasts. Once Marybeth, at her moment of greatest pleasure, hears a kind of clangor, as of metal gates, and her shivers turn to tears, and she whispers, "Oh, Chuck, what are we going to do?"

"Oh, beautiful Marybeth," whispers Chuck all night, his lips now against the polished ridge of her collarbone, now against her navel: "Don't worry, everything will be all right, it doesn't matter; whatever has happened doesn't matter now."

Can that be true? Does Chuck know, or can he somehow control what has happened—its significance, the future? Marybeth, lying in his arms, wonders. Oh! Sweet Chuck! Marybeth feels like the winner of a lottery, her heart uneasy with disbelief at her undeserved good fortune. Maybe he's right about things. She can feel his heart beating.

Chuck is so strong, so inexhaustible, vigilant as a prison guard, and into the toils of the night when Marybeth dozes exhaustedly off will watch over her. She can feel this as her lids settle, as she lies within his arms. If she opens her eyes, his will be thoughtfully open watching, he will be thinking what to do. Then he will begin to kiss her again.

Chuck looks like the Viking hero in a book she had once, who wore a dragon on his leather jerkin and had a golden beard like Chuck's, and a helmet with horns that stuck out fiercely like the horns of a bull or goat, only Chuck's horn, of course, stuck out differently. Ooooh. His fingers burn gently along her thighs. His whispers are as alluring and consoling as the whispers of gods in the ears of maidens; the maidens are like lilies and crocuses swelling in the moist springtime, and bending and swaying to the winds, and to the will of ardent gods.

* * *

Later she is awake again. Now Chuck has fallen asleep.
They are still lying in the soft night light, on her bed,
which is kind of crowded because it's a single bed and
Chuck is so large, Chuck is so beautiful. Chuck is so
beautiful, thinks Marybeth, looking at his naked body, no
parts you have to skip over, nothing too skinny or too
small, and anyway what the hell, if you are going to prison
you have a right to have everything beautiful, even if it's
only for one night and can't be forever. The only thing
surprising is that it was, is, perfect. Tears spring to her
eyes, thinking not of prison but of Chuck's perfection.

How can they be like that, all energy and hardness,
like engines one minute, not themselves, crying and
catching you to them with strong inhuman arms and
teeth? How did Chuck find me? Was it grace, or a last
torment? Oh, God, it was probably a last torment. In the
nights, in her prison cell, she will remember his love
words, the little sigh he makes now in his sleep, and she
will never sleep.

But it is hard to think of herself or of tomorrow. The
fascination of Chuck's breathing compels her like the
swaying of a watch before her eyes. She is still mesmer-
ized by desire. Will he wake up again? Can he do it again
so soon? Will he wake up if I just touch his tip, very
gently, just to see? The tip of it as velvet as a butterfly
wing or petal of a flower, the colonnade—Greek temples,
she thinks of, and pillars of strength.

Sex on the air. Funny how it gets on the air and fills the
whole house with its slightly noxious vapor, waking Theo
by seeping into her room. She thinks of the little African
violets on the living-room whatnot, imagines them pressing their petals fastidiously closed. It is obvious that love
is being made somewhere in the house. No breathings
and bedsprings, not any embarrassing moans, but just
. . . Would Ouida sense it? Would Anton wake?

Perhaps it only wakes the mistress of the house, whose rights, somehow, are being transgressed; love being made in her house, but not by her.

Funny how it is just *there*, on the air. She wonders now if the time or two she brought a man home, long years ago, up to her room—Warren Peterson was one— with what silence, with what secrecy, they thought—did Mother waken in this way, to this same little sour draft, the slight chill of one's own solitude?

It is so quiet, thinks Ouida, wakening anxiously. Something is happening. But as she lies waiting, nothing does happen, so she goes to the bathroom, and then goes back to bed and sleep.

Anton does not wake. Will Anton wake, wonders Theo. How chagrined he will be if he realizes what is happening. I hope he doesn't wake.

An idea of Marybeth comes into her mind, naked but wearing long black stockings, the costume of the girl on the dirty-magazine covers you can't help seeing at the newsstand. She can't quite imagine Chuck. She tries not to imagine either one of them, of course. She tries to go back to sleep.

Chuck like something by Praxiteles, she thinks. The girl's heart beating like a bird's. How strange, with troubles like hers, to seize at pleasure, the illusory comforts of the body. Saints say illusory, but who listens to them. Well, foolish girl, but perhaps that is what one does in the jaws of death, seize at life; I don't know too much about it. My life has contained no crisis of this kind.

How do they know I won't have my face lifted and give some recitals? Anyway, Chuck won't let her go to prison; you can't make love to a girl and then escort her to the prison door. He has ideas, he has a plan, he's bound to save her.

This comforts Theo off to sleep, but with the covers thrown back a little, the air slightly too hot, the dark a queer violet color.

Crossly she is awakened yet again, later. I am turning insomniac. Soulless acts of sex. Though of course you mustn't think of it that way; that's just how in our day we thought of it, sex without love. We had to be "in love"; that's what we always were.

She thinks of an article she read somewhere. All this business about orgasms now—you would think from magazines it wasn't even the same sensation we used to experience. A memory floats into her mind, of herself, half falling off her bunk in some stateroom, sailing somewhere, sobbing with the violent intensity of some sensation attained with difficulty, and the lover already crept off. Who would that have been? Probably André Thierry. How many lovers have I had, after all? What marvelous lingerie we wore then, nighties of chiffon; even after nylon came in I wore chiffon a long time.

She wonders what time it is. The red eye of the smoke alarm does not reveal it. She cannot see her clock. She turns on the light. Two. How thin her arm is, scrawny old arm; she does not like to see it, and turns the light off again.

Is it still going on? Making love before prison like the last meal, she supposes. Does anyone really feel hungry for his last meal? In the prison, the girl will feed forever on her memory of her lost love. She thinks of Marybeth in a sort of cage, mournfully sad, thinking of Chuck forever.

Now, an odd thing, she hears them; they are going downstairs, tiptoeing in the dark, whispering on the stairs. They're going down to the kitchen, probably. In the violet darkness, night truck noises are heard on the freeway, droning away. Somewhere a dog barks in a panicky way. Won't everyone here be awakened by what Theo hears now, the sound of the piano in the living room? How peculiar. Who is playing it? And why is the sound so muffled?

Probably they've slid the doors to, those doors that are never closed. It is the cavatina for which the music has lain on top in the piano bench for years, probably decades; someone is playing it at last, the happy little melody played by Theo at her own childhood lessons. She never plays now.

Anton hears the far-off music without really waking, but thinks or dreams of the story in which the man says, "I would sleep but thou must dance." In his dream someone is saying this to him, and he tries to move his feet to dance but they are too heavy in hiking boots to move.

I wonder which of them plays? Theo thinks, tossing.

It was Chuck and Marybeth in the living room, but then they were starving and went to the kitchen to make chicken sandwiches. They had everything to talk about. It's funny, Marybeth thought, how you don't forget to talk, but feelings and thoughts become words as naturally as to a child; the truth just rose naturally to her lips as if she'd been telling it all along. She didn't even mind that she was wearing the dingy nightie she'd taken out of the closet, one that she'd been going to abandon, but just pulled on to come down here, and now she realized in the kitchen light how sordid it looked, a smear of blood on its hem. Chuck will know everything about me; I want him to, she thought; I don't care. I am someone who wears nightgowns like this.

She told him all the things, all the secrets, the by now

frayed ideas and wishes she had given up on; it was nice to leave them with someone, not much of a legacy to leave a loved person, but all she had. He seemed to know that they were important to her, for he heard them rather gravely. There was such a grave sweetness about his smile.

"Look, Marybeth," Chuck interrupted her. "Sometime you're going to have to tell me about it—what you actually did. Theo didn't tell me that."

"She didn't tell you?" How could he not know? They had all of them acted as if they knew. Her stomach churned. Knew *all*, Theo had said. Marybeth could imagine the kind smiles slipping off their faces, Chuck turned to cold stone. But she wasn't surprised at this turn of things in the torture plan.

"She told me as much as she knew, but she didn't know just exaclty—the circumstances," Chuck said.

Marybeth went on spreading mayonnaise. "Of course I've lived with it myself for a long time; it doesn't even sound so bad to me any more. I mean there's no feeling, there's just a knowing. I guess I'm used to it. You can get used to a surprising lot." To excuse her calm tone; he would think she was a monster of coldness.

"I know," Chuck said.

"It was in college; I went to Ohio. I—with some other people—we blew up a laboratory that was developing another kind of napalm, and there was a man working in the lab—it was at night—and he was killed."

She watched Chuck closely. He didn't seem surprised or appalled. She supposed he had been expecting something like that.

"What would they charge you with? What about the other people?"

"Only one was caught, and he was charged with first-degree murder, and convicted of second-degree, and he got twenty years."

"You didn't *mean* to," Chuck said.

"But the government is incredibly more vindictive than just the daily system of criminal justice—about political crimes, I mean. And still, after all this time. Someone was caught a couple of weeks ago, a Sharon Armbrewster, her situation was similar to mine, and she . . ." What did Chuck really think? Even a long-ago and inadvertent murder was a kind of slime. Impossible to associate it with someone of Chuck's peculiar radiance.

She watched him for a sign of his disgust, and he, understanding her scrutiny, said, "It doesn't make any difference to me. I knew it was something like this. It doesn't make any difference."

Doesn't it? Marybeth wondered. Can that be true? How terrible.

"There's something else besides," she said, a sensation of confessional frenzy building up that she had never felt before. "I'm not sorry. I'm not really sorry. When I'm old like Theo, I'll look back and have that. I think everyone who made napalm should have been blown up. That man sitting in his laboratory, making something to blow up children with, I don't care what his circumstances were, or how he rationalized it, I'm glad he took his terrible secret to the grave, if he did, or even if he didn't."

Strangely, Chuck laughed at this.

"And there's something else. We could have telephoned to give him a few minutes to get out of there. Well, we thought we had. That is, everybody thought someone else had. But no one had."

Chuck nodded.

"And I think, besides, that there was a moment when *I* realized that no one had, and I could have. But I didn't. See, that's what I have to pay for, that moment of knowledge."

Chuck shrugged and picked up his chicken sandwich. "And the idea you have to pay at all. That's kind of cute. Where'd you get that? God makes you pay, or who?"

"Not *God*," objected Marybeth. He must think she's kind of dumb or something.

"The President? Mr. Policeman? You think that justice always triumphs?"

"Not justice," said Marybeth. "I mean, it doesn't seem to exist. Oh, I don't know."

"Look, Marybeth, you give yourself airs, kind of— don't you think?—talking about 'paying' and all that because you caused a death. That's something people have to bear all the time. What about wars and accidents? Where's your head? You're just run down by the fear of consequences. Your compunctions about life are rather after the fact, so what good is it to go sit in jail? Especially if you're not sorry." He laughed. "There are more useful forms of atonement, anyway."

"Don't make light of it, Chuck. That's what I'm talking about. If we make light of it, then what was the use of it?"

"Well," acknowledged Chuck. "Well, I'm not making light of some guy getting his head blown off, no."

"You don't know how much I've thought about it in six years. Well—I haven't thought about it as much as I should—you just get so numb and live day to day. But when I do think about it I always come to the same conclusion, that my guilt is deeply important to me. Maybe it's even the best thing about me. But it's taken me all this time to see that I have to give myself up and go to prison for it, for it to mean anything . . ."

Chuck put down his sandwich and drew her to him and kissed her. "This isn't a good time to talk about it," he said.

"It's not that I *want* to go to prison," she said.

"Beautiful girl," he said, and traced the line of her lips with his finger.

Ouida woke in terror. It is the goat, she thought. No, it was a bad dream, and she waited till her heart calmed before she tried to remember it. It was a bad dream in which she was speaking in English at a large church, in the pulpit, her arms covered with the white robes of a priest. She could see the embroidered cuffs of her robe as she glanced down at her notes, which had suddenly disappeared. She continued as best she could to communicate the message she had brought the congregation. She burned with the sensation of it urgency. Then her English left her. She could think of no more English words.

Her message was urgent. She was obliged to continue in Portuguese. But the congregation, despite the fact that she was their priest, began to move and murmur, then to jeer and shout and wave ribbons. Angry ribbons encircled her. It was a bullfight. "Where is your license? Where is your visa?" they cried. Then the ribbons became pieces of paper, a horrible litter of paper fluttering down entangling her. Her hands had turned bright orange and she dashed from the ring.

She calmed herself; it was only a dream, only a tension in expectation of the *feijoada*, or a memory of the Sacramento school. She got up to look at the clock on her dresser, to see if it was time yet to get up and start the beans cooking. She had planned to get up at five but it was still only three. She ticked off in her mind all the steps of the *festa*, the decoration, the method she had settled on for selling tickets. I was a fool to think they would give me a driving permit without a visa, it crossed her mind. Something else crossed her mind she tried not to think of, the lips of Griggs searching her lips, the dry pressure of his hand brushing her breast.

Marybeth and Chuck sneak back to bed. There he will take her again. His joyful greediness seems like a miracle of nature to her, dissolving her. "Oh, God, Chuck," she whispers, almost unbelieving, at his new embraces.

When Marybeth next awoke, it was in the pale light of the morning before sunrise. Her first sensation, as always, was terror, but as she lay patiently under it, waiting to throw it off with her shivers, she became aware that it was not the customary terror—police, prison—here was a different terror, tantalizing in its novelty, challenging her. This one had nothing to do with her life, for a change. She reorganized her thoughts.

There, taking up most of the bed, was Chuck. She remembered. All was changed. He slept so beautiful and calm. Oh, now she saw the face of this terror all right. It is the terror that must wake everyone in the world but her, until now. She is always so slow to catch on to things.

Tears rose and slipped down her cheeks but she didn't move her head. Chuck, so beautiful and strong, would get cancer and die; his bones would be eaten away. They were bound to be. I must be going crazy, she thought, what's the matter with me? Chuck is perfectly healthy. Chen-yu will die.

She couldn't shake this off. What should she do? She was so powerless she couldn't even will the awful words out of her mind, she couldn't do anything but shiver. Over the bureau the paper towels printed with bloody feathers—could they bring a charm to bear? Could anything avert horror? Could anything avert anything? She resorted to her childhood prayer: Dear God, please don't let anything happen.

Slyly she wrested the pillow from Chuck's sleeping grasp and mashed it around her head, trying to block out the light, press out the terrible icy pain, but it was as if a new place, exquisitely sore, had been found on the surface of her brain, a place she never knew about, scored, laid open, raw, ready to receive the searing prod,

the cruel goad of these new thoughts: at any moment the
fragility of those you love can kill you with pain. It was
like her fear for Chen-yu, but even worse. Things got
worse and worse. What had laid open these new places
in her brain? Gasping, alone, in the dim morning, she
didn't know if she could bear to live now that she knew
this new thing.

She'd get up. Things are always better when you get up
and move around and don't lie there drowning in gall.
She put the tattered nightgown back on, and went downstairs; it was stupid to lie there trembling, the hell with
it. What was the matter with her brain, was she weak-
brained?

But the sadness didn't go away in the kitchen, it just
changed again. I must be going crazy, she thought. She
poached an egg in the electric egg poacher. Hers was
just sadness, with no cause or name. Who wouldn't feel
sad going to prison? Of course Chuck would die, so
would she, so would Chen-yu, so would everybody, and
you can't worry about it from second to second. Maybe
this sadness was just the normal sadness after love that
everybody is said to feel, and she had never felt till now.
Maybe the sadness gets stronger, the stronger the love.

She dropped the egg getting it out of the little metal
cup. The yolk broke and ran along the counter. She
sopped it up with bread and ate it, and threw away the
white.

Oh, she knew that you're supposed to live from day to
day, for the moment only, for pleasure and beauty and
let tomorrow come what may—but what good was that
kind of advice for persons of a serious nature? How to
drive away the shadows of the future? It's Chen-yu I'm
worried about, she thought, what kind of life has he got
to look forward to? It's Ouida, someone's got to help her,
and no one will if they put me in prison. She only *seems*

to understand English, she doesn't really, she's going to fuck up; no one cares around here as long as she gets the dishes done.

Thinking of Chuck asleep upstairs, now a certain anger stole into her heart, replacing the sensation of absolute pain and coming therefore as a kind of relief. God damn Chuck, how could he just sleep like that?

How could he sleep? How could he take her over that way with his calm and largeness, and light her up and turn her into some kind of melted radiant object pulsating beneath magisterial fingers? She could imagine she was becoming something really abject, like a doe in a whole herd of does just waiting and grazing. Is that what she was supposed to do while he just slept, just dropped off to sleep leaving her throbbing and chilling down and catching terrors, and she would just have to wait around till he woke up again, as if he were a car with some kind of capricious mechanical problem that would just stop, just shut down until it was ready to start up again, and besides he was keeping a number of things in his head that she bet he wouldn't tell her.

Yes, those things in his head made her feel dismayed and excluded, he would never bring them out; maybe things about war, also art, which he had thoughts and plans about, and she was not artistic. He wouldn't want to tell her lots of things, and she wanted to tell him everything, and that was another of the many things that were not fair. The idea of unfairness was better than dread, and made her hungry, so that she ate some cold potato salad out of the fridge.

Maybe, she thought, she'd go wake him up and tell him everything after they made love again. Maybe he'd be waking up a little right now, and be ready. She could just tiptoe up and see. She'd have a piece of toast first, and honey, heart breaking, not understanding why. Why did she feel so mad at Chuck, when he hadn't done anything after all—or rather he had, and he had done it perfectly?

Now here in the growing morning light came Ouida, in an old terry-cloth wrapper, without her glasses on, her eyes narrow slits. Through her glasses they looked like great big eyes, were perhaps now puffed with sleep or tears.

"Ouida! It's only five-thirty. Did I wake you up?" Marybeth said.

"No, oh, *meu Deus*, I have so much to do, for it is the day of the *festa*, and I have to begin the beans at this hour, for they must cook at least six hours with the *carne seca*, and then I have so much else to do—chop the onions, seven dozen onions, and slice four dozen oranges, shred five bunches of collard, the decorations—oh, so much to do, and I think the crowd will be a big one, for yesterday I have learned that a professor at Sacramento State will bring one entire class of Portuguese One. What is Portuguese One?"

"Beginning Portuguese."

"Oh. Also I have put so many signs, at the bus and at churches and the Co-op, I am beginning to be afraid who will arrive. What if too many arrive?"

"What can I help with?"

"You are up early, too," Ouida said.

"Yes."

"I almost do not know where to start. There are the paper plates and cups to put out, and we will decorate the tables with the colors of Brazil. Many things are done already. I have made the tickets, and name badges to show who has paid. I learned these techniques from the First Presbyterian Church, and I have already cooked the pork and sausage. But so much has to be done all at once, at the moment. In Brazil we have many people helping all at once at a *festa*. It is hard to make a *festa* alone.''

''Just show me what you want,'' Marybeth said, sitting on the kitchen stool. Ouida, smiling gratefully, piled oranges in front of her, a huge pile of oranges to slice, and handed her a serrated knife. ''Slices like this, this thick; then we peel away the outside, like this, or if it will not peel, then make little stars, like this, by cutting the peel away.'' Ouida showed her. Marybeth set to, peeling, peeling, not thinking about anything. At about six-thirty she realized she was still sitting there in her ragged nightie and others would be getting up.

''I'll come back later and help some more, Ouida,'' she said. It didn't seem that the pile of oranges had gotten smaller at all.

SATURDAY

17. Ill Humors

It is working, getting large and hard and ready. Is Chuck awake, too, or just *it*? He seems asleep. She snuggles close in upon him and bites his earlobe. His eyelids stir. "Chuck, Chuck," she whispers, "*you* have to wake up, too." Chuck so wonderful he can do it in his sleep. Her pique diminishes, she can hardly remember her cross feeling. She wants him to wake because she wants him to remember every beautiful thing they say and do together.

His eyes open and for a minute his face is frozen in panic or confusion; he doesn't know where he is. Then he does, and it's all right, and he groans. Gets up and goes to the bathroom. Marybeth lies on her bed and listens and marvels. Gallons and gallons.

He comes back and lies down again, eyes blank and yearning to close. He puts an arm over his eyes and sighs sleepily. Marybeth would like to pinch him but strokes his arm instead. It is her freedom that is ending, yet it is Chuck who seems to be leaving, laid out on his bed like a barge, like King Arthur going to Avalon, eyes dreamily unknowing. Her own eyes fill. She wants to pinch him.

"Did you dream?" she asks. "Do you ever dream? Do you ever have nightmares about the war, or bad experiences? Do you ever cry out in your sleep?" She tries to imagine him in his military uniform, far away thinking military thoughts, or rescuing little Vietnamese kids. She wonders if he slept with Vietnamese whores, desperate thin girls in their little slit dresses—would he do that?

She must have everything about him, to take with her to jail.

"No," he manages to answer. Never dreams.

"Tell me about the war. Did you really fight? Did you kill anyone? Were you ever scared? How could you? How *could you*?"

Presently he takes his arm off his face. His eyes are open and more alert. He sits up a little. His mind is focusing, his expression resumes sentience. His expression assumes purposefulness. He reaches under her nightie and strokes her thighs and gathers her to him. Marybeth sighs and fondles his wonderful cock. It is bliss, of course. Still it isn't the same as an answer to those questions.

Theo wakes with the strong sense of someone in the room with her, or of someone who has just stolen out. Could someone have looked in on her—perhaps Anton, worried that she'd had a stroke? Has she overslept? She looks at her clock. Overslept a little. How deeply one sleeps in the morning after a restless night, as if drowned. She remembers how as a little girl—they slept in what was now Ouida's room, and Mother slept in here—if Mother looked in on them, Theo could feel her, even lying with her eyes closed, could feel her there. She hates remembering this.

She supposes there will be no place to change at the prison, so she dresses in her leotards and tights now, and over them puts her black skirt with the ruffle at the bottom, noticing again how rusty it has gotten to be. Still, she will just appear as she is, rusty skirt and all, and not try to appear more worldly or exotic than she really is;

she will have to be enough for Fontana as she is. But she'll take along her stick, which, besides being a legitimate tool of her trade, lends an air perhaps of authority, of experience, of art and the world.

She would not dare, and perhaps would not be permitted, to tap the knees and ankles of the prisoners, of course not. A young woman could not go among the prisoners at all.

Standing at the bureau, Theo thinks of their plan for saving Marybeth. She thinks again, Why shouldn't the girl be Esther Lundberg? A child sunk without a trace, and the parents living in Europe. Who would know? Then she notices her aventurine beads on the corner of her mirror and puts them in her pocket, thinking that they have never been becoming, but that the girl could wear them very well. I'll see if she wants them, she thinks.

She looks in her bureau drawers for her old journals of travels, where she was sure she would find a useful record of that terrible sea voyage, the terrible event that marred it, some clue, some information that would help. She is puzzled to find that her journals aren't there, then remembers reading them over, a few years ago, down in the library; that was before Anton had come home, when she could leave her journals where she pleased around the house.

No smell of smoke on the stairwell, but a strong coffee smell floating up. It would be a hot day. The heat began these hot mornings collecting in the lower hall on the sunbeams that came through the glass prisms on either side of the door. Halfway up the stairs already and it was not eight o'clock. Marybeth was making the coffee, and Chuck was with her, sitting on a kitchen stool, large as a stevedore, not the build for dancing, and suddenly too proprietary to suit Theo. He was gazing at Marybeth. They were riveted by the bond that everyone could guess. Still, Theo supposed, he would save her. They looked at each other endlessly. But, she now noticed, curiously, there appeared to be a matter of dispute between them.

"It just pisses me off, that's all," Marybeth was saying as Theo came in, and Chuck saying, "Why would you want me to harrow you with terrible things I'd rather forget, assuming my mind was filled with harrowing things, which I'm afraid it isn't. Still . . ."

Poor Ouida was there, looking as though she'd been up for hours, toiling at the sink, her hair bound in a pink nylon scarf, her expression panicked. From sounds in the breakfast room, Theo heard that Anton had gone in there—perhaps to spare himself the sight of so much toil, so much bliss?

In the breakfast room Anton had set up twenty or thirty large photographs on the chair rail around the room, and was standing among them, turning this way and that, squinting his eyes at them.

"Oh," she said, "time for the calendar."

"Once again," he said. Every August he had to select pictures for the Sierra Club Anton Wait calendar for next year. Then they would spend the next few weeks—Theo helped—finding bits of poems for epigraphs. It was not too different from the illustrated magazine they had put together as children. Perhaps nothing changes.

"That's a lovely one," she said, pointing at a field of boulders with mountains behind. "Where's that?"

"Mount Williamson," he said.

"Some autumn month. It has a look of autumn."

"It hasn't the look of any month at all, I'm afraid," he said. "I'd about decided against it. It was taken last spring, in fact."

"Oh, what's the difference, as long as it has the look of something or other?"

Anton smiled. "There are people who could tell you from the length of the shadow what month it would be."

"Well, ask the others," she said. "I'm not sensitive to trees, as you know. They all look quite lovely of course."

"So today is your prison festival," Anton said, in that tone she disliked—patronizing, or so it seemed to her.

"You'll have a productive day of course, in your darkroom."

"That's my livelihood," he reminded her.

"Come have breakfast in the kitchen," she said. "Leave the photos there and we'll get the others to help choose them, too. Has anybody fed the chickens?"

In the hall the leafy sound was heard of letters falling through the slot of the door. Theo picked them up. Two letters for Anton, which he opened in the kitchen. One was a bawdy birthday card. He looked surprised and puzzled. It wasn't his birthday. One from his daughter Emily—lined notebook paper covered with her childish round hand. "Dear Daddy," it would begin. Anton put it on the kitchen table, unread, an act of carelessness so emblematic of his general indifference, it seemed to Theo, about feelings and people. How irritable one feels after a restless night, she thought.

"Marybeth," Theo said, "you could pretend to be the little girl who went overboard, you know. It would work. Her name—did I tell you her name?—was Esther Lundberg. Presently I'll go find the passages in my journals, to make sure of everything. How old are you?"

"Twenty-seven," Marybeth said crossly. "Older than you thought, right? I know. Most people by my age have got their lives together. Only—only it sets you back to lead a life like mine."

"Anyone could say that," Theo said, but thinking
again, Yes, the profile, the dark marks under the eyes,
tiny lines at the side of the eyes, older than I thought.
She had supposed all girls were twenty or twenty-one,
washing their hair a lot, all dressed alike in jeans and
Indian gauze blouses. But of course Marybeth would be
older. Could she pass for as old as Esther Lundberg would
have been?

"Esther Lundberg would have been born in about 1946.
Forty-five or six. But some people appear younger than
they are."

Marybeth shrugged in a sullen way. She was making a
piece of toast for Chuck. It was Chuck who was interested in Esther Lundberg, and had thought of more questions to ask Theo.

"Just let me get the journals," Theo said.

In the library, she opened the desk drawer where her old
diaries were and brought them out. Some, written in pencil, had faded until they were hard to read; in others the
ink had run. Somewhere in the early fifties they stopped,
but she had been good about them till then, faithfully
recording the names of hotels and what the food was and
things about pretty little foreign streets, Russian dancers,
the intrigues of the artists, complaints. She sat at the
desk and slipped into them—they were still interesting,
she thought; other people might be interested, too, in the
record of a ballet dancer in the forties. She should pub-
lish them.

The crossing was in 1949, in March, found without
difficulty, and legible. On a ship you had plenty of time:

No one *nice* at my table worse luck, and now too late to change
that. A Swedish couple, from St. Charles, Minn., v. attractive—*he* is attractive but a bit too much like the minister in
Rosmersholm, no? They say they don't want to raise their chil-

dren in America. I wonder what they expected, and why they went there? But won't ask. But they are quite nice.

And then, two more days with no mention of them except of the storm. Then:

A terrible tragedy. The Lundbergs' little girl has fallen overboard. Everyone searched all day, and there isn't a trace. Everyone is weeping openly. Those poor people. How curious the way a tragedy brings people together.

That was all. Stupefied, Theo leafed forward a few pages, backward. They land in Copenhagen. They are going to Aarhus on the train. The child's name was not even mentioned; was she right that she had been called Esther? But she was sure of that. How was it that this bitter evidence of arbitrary misfortune, of predestined malice— the most powerful experience she had ever had and that she had never forgotten and that had retained its power to wake and frighten her after all these years; had seemed, indeed, almost to have happened to *her*—how was it it had made so little impression at the time? A few lines— on to the Danish herring, on to the color of a tutu . . . No mention, no mention of the dread at all.

"I'm sorry," she said, coming back to them. "It's a curious thing, but I seem not to have written very much down. My mind, I suppose, my heart was too full of it perhaps. But my memory is very exact. The major things, I suppose, you don't need to write down, the traumas in your life, and such. I suppose I ought to be thankful I wrote down as much of the trivia as I have. Otherwise it would be just gone. Pages and pages of things I have no memory of. People's whole lives gone like that. Millions and millions of people, nothing left of them—Anton, of course, those handsome photographs, that's a kind of record really, Anton, of where you went, if not what you thought about.''

''My pictures are certainly a record of what I thought about,'' Anton objected, sounding irritated.

''Not entirely. Obviously you think about things you never take pictures of. You never take pictures of people, yet you think about them, at least I guess you do, and . . .''

''Teddy, you don't know what I think about! I wish you'd stop going on about my pictures and about my life; you don't know anything about them,'' Anton said. ''What a nag you are really—how lucky that you didn't marry.''

Theo hardly knew what to say to this touchy remark. ''Oh, you are a success,'' she said. ''A famous man.''

''You always act as if photography were just a lame-brained thing; well, dancing isn't so fucking intellectual,'' Anton went on.

''Uh—I suppose we can't help what we're called to,'' Theo said. Had it been real anguish in his voice? How embarrassing that they should quarrel in front of these young people. The young man staring with feigned pre-occupation at the contents of Julie Burnham's envelope— a newspaper clipping, two Xeroxed pages, a looseleaf sheet of handwritten notes. The girl was looking at her and Anton aghast. Had she thought them models of something or other—courtesy, or satisfaction, or common sense?

''I'm aware of my failures in life,'' Anton was saying. ''I don't need you to remind me, I feel them better than you can—you don't even know what they are . . .''

''Now at my age,'' Theo said, striving for a reasonable and mollifying tone, ''I never think of my life at all. Except for moments, as yesterday, for some reason. But mostly I no longer think of it. When I was younger I did, I thought of it as a thing, like a souvenir or a diamond ring, that I owned. What should I wear to set it off, where will I take it, to whom shall I give it? It seemed like something I owned, it had hardness and depth. Shall I give it up to art? To love? But now I never think of it at all, it's taken me over. I just do what it says.

"I'm sorry," she said, to their silence, "all this carrying on. Morning garrulity is never appreciated, I know. But I'm so harried by peculiarly oppressive memories and awful dreams all night—surely it's just biochemical, something eaten yesterday—sardines—or those folk tales about cucumber and milk; since yesterday—memories reeling around unbidden, certainly unwanted. What makes them come back? How can you keep them away? How can a man live, for instance, having been to war— how does he know when he goes to bed at night that gory memories won't come back on him? Memories ready to pounce, so terrible . . ."

"Repression," Marybeth said, with a meaningful look at Chuck.

"And my memories are nothing much, either, compared with some people's, and yet I dread having them back. Tepid memories indeed, and yet they're too much for me. What do people do who have really horrible ones? Well," she turned to Marybeth, "wouldn't your memories be perfectly horrible?"

"Oh, Teddy," Anton said, in an admonitory tone.

"No, I've never done anything I couldn't stand remembering," Marybeth said. Could that be true? Not exactly. "Not like being in a war," she said.

"Don't you find men touching?" Theo said, turning to the eggs and the stove, trying to raise the level of the conversation. "So bravely, so uncomplainingly do they do things—for instance, go to war or sea. Centuries of men going to sea, little boys even—in the nineteenth century. Haven't you seen those little carvings that the whalers did while off at sea—little wheels for cutting pastry with? I find that very touching. All those months, long cold months away, thinking of pie. Don't you hate to think of lonely sailor children thinking of their mothers and of pie?''

She could not go away like that, she thought, to sea. The realization subdued the gesture of her arm. To say nothing of going to war. How could men? And the way they try to do things for themselves, brushing their own shoes and coats. What do men think of? It's hard to imagine the mind of a man, she thought, minds lacking the rich fullness of a woman's mind, all kinds of ideas cut off from them, no ideas about sewing or the colors of things. Gently she lowered the egg into the water, which was at the rolling boil, lowered it slowly so as not to crack it.

"All that trying men have to do," she said. "How often they must be cold and afraid. Think of being a soldier of Napoleon, a common soldier, with frozen feet. How horrible." It was true she didn't find Anton particularly touching. He was more of a woman to her. A great artist, it was said. Well. It was true his pictures had always turned out, even when they were both little and had Brownie cameras. And none of her pictures ever turned out. She could still feel the tiniest sting of resentment over this.

"What gets me is how little I do remember," Marybeth put in, caught by her own thoughts. "I might as well have led my life in a trance. Is everyone like that? My mind keeps wandering. But I guess you'd need an inner eye like a laser beam to keep it focused on one bad memory all the time. A bad memory is more a kind of—I don't know—a fishhook that catches you suddenly."

Yet the oddness of talking about memory at all brought back memories from everywhere; it was like sitting under a leaking roof, no protection from sudden new leaks. She did suddenly remember every betrayal and lie, every glassy look of inattention that would transfix the faces of supposed friends the instant they recognized they could not go along with you. You were bad news. You saw it hit them. It was different here, with everyone interested and kind.

"Some things I can't remember when I try. I can't remember all my names any more. For about three years I would make up new names all the time, then forget them. Sometimes I would treat myself to a pretty name, as if that could pretty up my situation."

"I always wanted to keep my own name," Theo said. "Anton, shall I boil you an egg, too, while I'm standing here? A nice, old-fashioned boiled egg." She took up another egg in the spoon. "What a strange morning this is. Why have we been quarreling?"

"It is the drought," Ouida said suddenly, looking up from her peeling. "If it would rain, many things would be better. Only I hope it does not rain on my *feijoada* day."

"You think you bear the weight of the world on your shoulders, you think it's kept afloat by your concern alone," Anton said to Theo. "Such self-importance."

"I? An indolent, disaffected woman? But now we have Marybeth's plight—Ouida's plight—we *do* have a lot to worry us."

"I can do the worrying about my own life," Marybeth said, resuming her surly tone, her surly glances at Chuck. Class president. Wing commander.

"Yes, you're young, that's a time to worry about life," Theo said, now thinking that she would really like a big breakfast, with orange juice and bacon. But if she fixed it, she'd have to fix it for all. What an undertaking. Better not.

"She has a more than worrying practical problem," Chuck said, looking up as if she hadn't been listening until now. "Marybeth."

"Teddy, have you written your lecture?" Anton asked. "It's nearly nine. What time do you leave?"

"Ten-thirty. I've given that lecture dozens of times. I guess I'd better put it in order, though. There are some parts that might not be suitable at a prison."

I'd like a few slices of bacon and some orange juice, but now here I've cooked the egg too soon, she was thinking, the thin sensation of petulance relocating itself in her stomach, making her feel hungry, absolutely starved. Resentfully she ate her egg, then excused herself and went into the library, her emotion now wedged in her throat like a bone. But she felt a little calmer when she pulled out her collection of slides and peered in the drawer where the little 16-millimeter films on reels lay; she'd done this lecture many times, and yet the beauty of their leaps, the tension of the still figures poised to leap, would still surprise and thrill her. Here is the great Nijinsky. That is Pavlova, with Diaghilev. Now we'll see a little film of Martha Graham. In Paris in the 1930's they . . .

A lecture in a prison could of course have nothing of an academic cast. It must have something to do with the prisoners. My life has had an academic cast, no temperament for performance, never had to have an abortion, never placed a bomb.

Still, my life has been exciting, compared to most lives; how is it I feel so disappointed with it this morning, she thought, looking at a photograph of the marvelous Lermentovaya, and herself just visible behind in the corps de ballet, not that she had always been stuck in the corps. Whereas most people are always in the corps, so what had she to complain of? People with—with large appetites—she thought, must always be hungry. Oh, but I don't have a large appetite, I'm a picky eater.

* * *

What can she tell them, to begin with? It doesn't matter to me what you've done? But of course you can never say that. She has heard that you are to make no reference to the circumstance that they are there, for any reason whatever. Someone from the Friends Outside group has briefed them on this. "I know you would not be here to learn about the dance if you did not sense its relevance to . . ." Oh, hell.

Hell, they will have come out of desperation, because of the monotony, the ones that don't go to the painting or writing workshops, or who can't get into the foreign film festival; probably they'll all want the foreign films, unless you get sick of movies in prisons.

She can tell them about the inner peace conferred by the deeply meditated movements and perfect command of the body. Ten minutes of slides, twenty of film and ten of demonstration, then more if they are enjoying it. She lays the slides in the little rack in the case she keeps for lectures of this kind. Then I'll try to get them to stand in fifth position. They won't be able to do it—it will intrigue them. Or else they will. Graceful strong men. Dancers the greatest athletes, stronger and fleeter than quarterbacks—be sure to tell them that.

Particularly vivid to her imagination is a tall man in black tights, probably a Negro, very strong, taller than principal dancers usually are, but with the breadth of chest and neck to maintain the proportion, to give an impression of force. Perhaps he will not have danced before; under her guidance he will execute the first few steps, then step out, leap, and then soar; the gift of grace. She knows he will be there, this man, yet she does not know what she is thinking of really; she supposes it to be an artifact of memory, brought up by the old photos. She'll know when she sees him where she has seen him before.

* * *

Chuck goes off home for some clean clothes. Out in the
yard, Anton feeds the chickens, Carlyle snuffling along
behind, and Ouida is trying to set up the phonograph.
Fragments of loud music start up and then groan away.
The amplified shriek of a needle sliding across a record
makes Theo jump, then clench her teeth. A cowboy sings:

> *The good days all are over now,*
> *Dear girl, my heart is sinking fast.*
> *What was can never be no more,*
> *In vain do we regret the past.*
> *Come back, come back, O days of love,*
> *Let not my life as withered be*
> *As them that never kissed at all,*
> *Or lay beneath the laurel tree.*

It seems so apt to Theo, so pertinent to her fragile mood,
that she might suspect pointed cruelty, did she not know
Ouida to be incapable of that.

18. *Vegetables*

The others came for Theo. They came in a Dodge van
that said "Jesus loves you" on the side.

"Why is it the idea of riding to Fontana with people
who love Jesus worries me a little?" Theo said, pulling
back the front curtains to peer out. She recognized the
driver, Clarence Harter, a Co-op board member, but she
hadn't known he felt that way about Jesus.

Anton, coming downstairs with his cameras, saw her
standing one-legged in the hall, like a stork, a sign with
Theo of apprehension.

"Will you be gone all day?" he asked, picking up her
slide projector to help her out with it.

"Late afternoon. I suppose we may stop for supper on

the way home, so don't wait. I hope everything will be all right here? You won't let her—do anything—while I'm gone. Marybeth.''

"We'll try to maintain the status quo, whatever that may be," Anton said.

"I don't know either. I feel so kind of filled with thumps," Theo said.

Anton smiled.

"You should be coming along, Anton. It would do them more good to do photography, you know, something more realistic that they could continue with when they get out. They can't go on to become dancers, after all.''

"There are plenty of people to teach them photography. I'm sure they already have a program set up."

"You think you're above working with prisoners or students.''

"True," Anton agreed.

"Well," Theo said, "so long. If you were nice, you'd stick around here today and help poor Ouida with her festival.''

"I mean to lie low until the food is served," Anton said.

"Ouida," said Marybeth, sitting on the kitchen stool peeling oranges and piling little towers of slices, slowly, for it seemed to take forever, "do you think you'll marry Mr. Griggs? I mean, do you think that's your destiny? Do you think that people have a sense of their destiny?"

Ouida frowned. "I am afraid they do not."

"What did you expect to be when you grew up?" Marybeth asked. Ouida shook her head, thinking of herself as a little girl, thinking of a school photo of herself, smiling, wearing her sailor tie and hat. How changed things were.

"Nobody knows what happen to them when they grow

up. There is no prophecy, that is only superstition. Christian people do not believe in prophecy.''

"Schoolteacher, airline stewardess—I knew some answers I would dishonestly provide, but I never really thought they would happen to me. I suppose those were my first lies. I didn't think—I didn't think of destiny at all.''

"I never thought I would come to the U.S.,'' Ouida said. "How I came here makes such a tale, I could not have known.''

"Once in high school, a teacher told everyone's fortunes, on the last day, and he wouldn't tell mine. I should have known then. He wouldn't. He just sort of shook his head and said, 'Oh, Marybeth, you'll be all right.' Do you think he can have known, and didn't want me to know what really would happen?''

"No,'' Ouida said, and after a while: "Sometimes I think of the little girl Ouida there, and I do not think this woman here can be her. I was noticed by the Presbyterian missionary—that I did not expect—and took to Londrina for education. That is how I went to the lycée, and my brothers also receive scholarships in this way. One is a pastor, one an advocate. My father's farm was very poor, we did not expect to be singled out by fortune in this way. My brother thanks God in his prayers for it, but sometimes I forget that prayer. And sometimes I say to myself what if I had had the misfortune to be born in India? We cannot control, we must give thanks. And yet . . .''

"Well, you could have been born Jackie Onassis, too,'' Marybeth said. "You have as much reason to feel resentful as to feel grateful, exactly.''

"A person would not want to be that poor woman, her husband shot. Why would a woman want to be that? Would *you*?''

"Yes,'' Marybeth said.

"In our school we have a little book when we finish,

and all our friends write in this book, the teachers also. Many friends of mine put in 'Lots of babies for Ouida, nice husband, ten kids,' things like that, so you see prophecy is not the same as truth. Those things are but wishes.''

"If you married Griggs, you'd have a bunch of kids in a hurry, instant family.'' Marybeth laughed, meaning to scare Ouida with that idea. "But no, of course I know there's no such thing as prophecy.''

But she had done the *I Ching* a number of times and meant to do it again.

The driver, Clarence Harter, introduced Theo to the others. She sat in the middle row of seats next to a Darrell someone—she hated to ask them to say their second names over again. There were three young people in the seats behind—the girls, younger and prettier than Theo thought would be allowed—then Clarence in front driving, and next to him a Lillian Maddox, whom Theo knew also, who did silkscreen prints. Behind these people, in the very back on the flat bed of the van, there were easels and boxes, and a basket of jams and jellies, exactly as though they were going to a country fair.

Theo still had her misgivings. Why were any of them here? What sort of people go smilingly into prisons? What a nerve to imagine they could just go in and lift the sore and blighted spirits therein; shouldn't they just be left to themselves, those poor men?

But it was she who wanted to be left to herself. She was too old. There was no one of her age here; even Lillian Maddox must be only around forty. The young people behind her maintained an odd, elliptical conversation, probably trying to clean up their accustomed language for her benefit. That annoyed her.

"I wonder if the—ah—uh . . .'' they said.

"Yeeeaaaaah,'' they would say. The young man sitting

next to her—Darrell—said that he had been corresponding with a number of the prisoners and that there was a lot of talent there. Needed formal direction, he felt, but definitely talent there. Many of the Orris faculty were interested in the prison thing, he said.

Oh, God, Theo thought, I'm not, I really am not.

Just let it be over, she thought, the Valley so damned hot this time of year, even so early in the morning, they could have at least gone up in something air-conditioned, and the hills so brown, like tinder this time of year; it's even an ugly business getting there.

"They say the paintings are very good," Lillian said, turning back to Theo, with her arm over the seat. "I know people who bought pictures there last year at the festival for their own homes."

Voyeurs is what we are, meddlesome do-gooders, Theo thought.

"I don't hold out much hope for it, do you, really?" she said.

"Hope?" they said. They seemed puzzled that she should mention it—almost as if hope were not intended. What *was* intended?

"Hope that it will change the lives of anyone," she went on, knowing she should not. "You have to get people when they're young. I have a pupil only eight, his mother a wise woman, I think, after all. But for the rest, it's simply too late, isn't it? If we're being honest. There isn't any use. These self-congratulatory expeditions, do we really think . . ."

The others said nothing, simply stared at her in a shocked way, as if they had no idea what she was talking about. She wasn't so sure herself. Stupid old woman. Shame made her go on talking: shame, irritation, indignation.

"She means the *ballet*," said Lillian Maddox at last, obviously relieved. "If you don't start people early, then they really can't expect to make much progress. That's what she means.''

Oh. They nodded. Theo tightened her mouth and said nothing the rest of the journey.

In the sunshine, moving in and out of the old house, through the kitchen, through the rich smells of beans and onions and garlic and steaming meat, Marybeth felt nothing could be wrong. Her spirits were perfectly buoyed up on wafts of strange delicious food cooking. Perhaps you couldn't turn yourself in on Saturdays; the appropriate authorities wouldn't be there; and no doubt Anton was right about getting a lawyer and waiting till Monday.

Ouida thought Mr. Griggs might come to help with moving the chairs and tables, but he didn't. Chuck helped. Ouida was puzzled about Chuck, how he had come to stay as if a member of the family. Who was he? How beautiful his golden hair was.

"Pretty, sort of like Vlaminck," said Chuck when they had the tables all set up, all covered with red, white and green. The umbrellas gotten out from the garage, old canvas ones, had faded to a beautiful rose.

"It'll be too hot," Marybeth said, hating the ruinous sun and not knowing what Vlaminck was.

"No, it is good for Brazilians, see, it will seem more *acostumado*," Ouida said.

When no one was around, Chuck would draw Marybeth to him and kiss her, in the kitchen or back yard, wherever they were, and once Ouida saw them, and whirled her face around as if ashamed.

But sometimes, pausing in the shadow of a rose umbrella for a moment, Marybeth would feel the touch of sadness, like a spirit hand. Maybe it would have been easier, it would have been better, not to have found all this—happiness and love—just at the end. It's the cruelest thing of all, she thought. And yet she would not have wanted to miss them, that was the paradox, that was the puzzlement. Her sense of completeness belied the unpleasant prospects of her immediate future. She would have the rose umbrellas to sort of bloom in her heart against the gray prison walls. And you *can* remember kisses, in a way; you can remember that you had them.

And at other times, looking at Chuck from across the yard or out the window, she would be seized by a vertigo of panic and despair. What misery to be here happy with Chuck—it was like the last few moments of a scented, soothing bath, fast draining, soon to leave you shivering on the tiles.

And at other moments she would look at the envelope Julie had left, which Chuck had put on the counter again, just curious to know—what would the name have been? Would it be a name she might have kept and fondly become? But she didn't touch the envelope or ask Chuck.

Theo thought the prison disappointing. Like monsters, like terrors when viewed close up, it had a shabby, accessible aspect. There were comparisons; it was like a neglected army base or a camp of mobile homes. She hadn't really expected—no, of course not—the appurtenances of a storied prison, iron bars, and sweating stone walls, escarpments, crenelations. Even so, bungalows painted yellow but peeling were disappointing. Bougainvillaea waved off the roof of one, perhaps the home of a guard.

Yes, you could see there, up on the water tower in the middle of the large yard, guards with machine guns. That was serious, that was prison. She shivered, despite the scorching heat, sighed deeply. Clarence announced them. "Friends Outside," he said importantly. He was talking to the guard at the low chain fence, showing papers and passes. They were to drive into that yard to unload their easels and projectors there.

"Then you go to processing before proceeding to the recreation area. The ladies will understand about the search procedures?" The guard had thrust his face against the window and was looking at them all—it seemed to Theo extra intently, as if to memorize their features. Perhaps memorization was his job. They stirred and twittered. They would understand. All this politeness was somehow offensive, Theo was thinking. "The guard will meet you in the yard to assist with . . ." So military, Theo thought, remembering a ride in a jeep with a colonel in Germany after the war. Miss Wait the dancer. That is the Officers' Club over there, there the noncommissioned officers' (you will never see that), there is the General Headquarters. She had laughed, her hair had blown, now here she was. Strange she couldn't remember if she'd gone to bed with that colonel. How could you not remember something like that?

"It is good that Miss Wait has gone to help the poor prisoners. I am ashamed that today all my thoughts are for my own benefit. In helping others, poor prisoners and men, is a woman's nature and her fulfillment. It is a woman's nature to be a helper and peacemaker, you see," Ouida said as they chopped the onions, their eyes streaming tears.

"It says in many religious beliefs that a woman is the principle of calm and staying still, stillness. For instance, a man might be a horse or a tiger, but a woman is a flower or a vegetable."

"Oh, yeah? Like a tomato, I suppose," sniffed Marybeth.

"Yes, some fruitful vegetable, or a tree—for instance, the pomegranate, or a peach."

"Peachy," Marybeth said. "Really, Ouida, you aren't

rooted to the ground—you can be and do and have force." But Ouida didn't think that Marybeth understood what she meant. These were merely symbols of woman's nature, they did not mean you were really rooted like a tree. Although without a passport you might as well be rooted to the ground like a tree. Complicated explanations in English defeated her.

"Ouida, don't you mind being compared to a fruitful vegetable? That's just the trouble, with your brothers, and things you've told me about in Brazil, that they go along thinking that you're just a tomato."

"But we are not *really* vegetables." Ouida laughed, thinking Marybeth sweetly simple about matters of symbolism. "It is only a manner of thought."

They have driven on into the yard.

"You should back that van against the ramp to the kitchen building," the guard is saying. Someone tries to garden at this prison; Theo notices the little flower beds with shriveled petunias stuck in them, men with no feeling for flowers perhaps—or why would they be in prison? Flowers could save you from prison, surely, if flowers can do anything. Someone has bordered the parched flower bed with stones but what it needs is water. Strange they are allowed stones. Stone soup, thinks Theo.

Strange, Theo is thinking; she is beginning to feel rather dazed by the heat inside the van and the shuffling of papers through the window and the instructions which, however, Clarence seems to understand, nodding and nodding his head. Or perhaps she says aloud that it's strange they are allowed stones.

"Those are the most trustworthy of course," says someone.

The tailgate is opened and someone looks at the easel,

the little jars of jam and jelly marked "Plum + Apple 1975" and the red checkered tablecloths they have brought to make the dining hall festive, like a bistro.

Of course, they say. No one around. Where are all the people? Where are the prisoners and the cells? Someone joins them, a man in a green suit, like a hospital orderly, and leans back to Theo and Darrell and then suddenly hands a paper to Lillian Maddox and tells her to take it back to the guard at the gate. Theo, who has just been looking out the rear, suddenly now does not see Clarence Harter any more.

The orderly is a Negro whose white eyes shine, his face shines, and he breathes with deep sounds as he inhales; he sounds like a creaking pier. Perhaps an asthmatic. He leaps into the car where Clarence Harter was a second ago.

Some of the people are getting out of the bus, though Theo does not know who has told them to. All the people in the rear seats—Hildy, Nancy and Jess, they were called—have gotten out. Where are they? It seems to Theo she has only turned away for a second, for a second's reverie about that colonel; now she and Darrell sit there, sit still in the second seats, and this orderly is speaking to them, but because of the impediment of his voice Theo doesn't clearly understand him.

It's a great thing, thought Marybeth, how the heaviest cruel rusted weights and cleavers hanging over the head lose their power, in the course of a morning of helping to move chairs and kissing on a bright summer's day, lose their power to make you miserable and fill your every instant with dread. She forgot about herself for long moments at a time, while moving chairs and kissing Chuck, and stirring Ouida's big vats of beans to keep them from sticking. The vats said "First Presbyterian Church" on them. Ouida was in despair. She'd gotten the idea that no

one would come. They had to work hard to keep her
cheerful.

At noon they ate some of the beans themselves, and
the meat—pork ears, Ouida teased them, and laughed
when they made faces. Masses of people will come soon,
they told her.

Chuck said to Marybeth, "Let's go up to your room for
a while before the people come; I want to tell you something," which, she knew, would be about love, so she
went right along. They made love with the windows open,
unheard in the clatter downstairs—the agitated cackle of
the hens disturbed in their coop, the pans, the record
player which Ouida could not adjust to suit her. After-
ward their wet bodies dried off in the hot breeze, cooling
them.

"Chuck," said Marybeth, "do you think I'm over-
sexed? Oh, I know there's no such thing, everybody has
their own pace—all the same . . ." She's thinking what
a tragedy for someone bound for prison.

"Yes, you maniac," said Chuck.

"Would you believe me if I told you that I had decided
not to give myself up till I got laid?" Marybeth asked.

"Yes, I would." Chuck laughed.

"I suppose someday you'll go on about the horror of
war, of death, of things I don't know about," said Marybeth presently. Chuck noticed that this was her first reference to a future.

"Why would you want me to? No, I wouldn't. Anyway, why should I? What do I know? What do you think
I know?" Chuck said.

"Men think women keep women's secrets is all, to do
with wombs and such, but they keep worldly secrets,
too," said Marybeth, thinking of the shed all filled with
bombs.

"Of course they do, my darling," Chuck said, lifting

her above him on the bed so that the tips of her breasts brushed his chest, and then kissed each one, and then the place between where their sweat had made her both sweet and salty.

19. *Without a Trace*

Someone Theo does not see walks down the ramp again and opens the rear gate of the bus, and three large cartons are lifted in. These shift and sway in a living manner. The bus is started again; Theo sees that Clarence Harter is slumped to the floor in front with a bloody cut over his ear. The orderly has started the van, and now backs it up. He kills the motor, utters something, starts the motor again; they shiver falteringly forward.

Now they are driving out the gate. There are shouts, there is an air of desperation and pursuit. Where have all the others—Lillian, Jess, Nancy and Hildy—gone; it is only she and Clarence and Darrell who are being driven out. Darrell, next to her, childishly begins to cling to her. Theo half expects shots, machine guns. But there's no shooting, only shouts. A siren begins. As they pull out the gate, Theo looks back and sees prison guards standing in the prison yard shaking out the red checkered tablecloths, like waiters in a garden. She is not frightened, or is too frightened to feel so.

"They won't fuck with us now, they know we got high explosives here," says a man with an authoritative voice who bursts out of one of the boxes in the rear. Now there are many sirens.

This Darrell someone has his face buried in Theo's shoulder, and is saying, "God, oh, God." But fright, or the flurry of activity, has dimmed Theo's sight so that the shapes and words are all gray, flickering by. Miles

go flickering by, minutes flickering by, and they roar
along in the comandeered van.

She can't quite see or tell where they are, but on a
road, not a freeway but a fast road; cars are coming toward them and pass by. Should she wave, try to catch
someone's attention? She should do something, no doubt,
but what? They seem to drive on and on, with sirens
wailing behind them.

Time passes but Theo can't tell how much time; she is
not sure of their speed. People talk but it is hard to tell
who talks to whom. The other two boxes burst open, so
that now there are three new people in the back of the
van, all dressed like orderlies in green—that must be
prison dress. Their voices are muffled and tentative. They
talk of a greasy guard—what does that mean? Someone
makes suggestions about the driving, and at one moment
the driver slows and says, "Drive it your fucking self."

They turn down a lane, going slower, so that she can
begin to collect her wits and try to gauge her whereabouts and the situation: what is happening? They go
down the lane, an unpaved road. She has the impression
of fences and ruts, trees on either side, and presently the
curious sound of sirens from all directions at once, as if
they were in an echo chamber.

"Shit, oh, shit," say the men in green clothes who had
burst out of the boxes, and, "They won't fuck with us
here, they know we got hostages, they know we got high
explosives here." Who are the hostages, Theo wonders.

"*Careful!*" someone screams as the car tilts in the rut
of the road. The deep scudding sound of tires stopping
on dirt, the squealing of brakes. Theo and Darrell, clinging, lurch forward with the impact of the stop, and then
Theo's vertigo clears up a little. They have come to a
stop on a rise of ground, not on a road at all but on open
ground, in a field, stopped still right in the middle of a

field. Over there in some trees she sees the gleam of metal, has a sense of shapes, men moving around.

"Let us out," she says to the strange man in the front seat; but she knows from the pale gray color of things, from the muffled unsaid things, that they aren't going to.

Naked, Chuck stood in the bedroom, planning to get dressed, noticing the library books on Marybeth's dresser. *Lorna Doone, The Man in the Iron Mask, The Longest Journey.*

Marybeth half dozed on the bed. He came and kissed her fingertips, the knuckles, the flat of the palm, and squeezed her thin little fingers as if trying to judge their strength.

"Poor little hands," he said. "Poor scared girl. We'll be together, and everything will be all right with you, don't you know that now?"

Marybeth wished, longed for it to be so, but it wasn't so, she didn't think, so she turned her face away.

"It's nearly one o'clock and people will come soon," Marybeth said reassuringly to Ouida.

"Oh, I am feeling so worried," Ouida said. "I have spent all my money for this, and the *carne seca* was very expensive, also the mandioca for the *farofa*. What will I do if nobody comes?"

"People *will* come," Marybeth assured her; but she got worried, too, when nobody did come, at first. Then, at around two, three Brazilian women came, and Ouida hugged Marybeth and said, "See, Brazilians are always late, I almost forgot that of my countrymen."

The women were colorfully got up in flowered dresses and bright necklaces, joyful at the prospect of *feijoada*.

"How hungry we were for *feijoada*," they said. "This is indeed to be in Brazil again!"

Ouida put Marybeth at a card table in the side yard, where people had to pass. It was her job to sell tickets to those who came, and collect the tickets of some who had bought them already from Ouida at her churches. Marybeth gave them little badges to pin on when they had paid. She drew the badges with flow pens: round red tomatoes for women, and smiling sun faces for men.

"Ouida has a lot of organizational ability," said Chuck, standing behind Marybeth, talking to her and eating his fiftieth plate of black beans.

"I have brought my three children here," said a man, coming up to them. "Is there a half price for children?"

"We'll have to ask Ouida," Marybeth said.

A new flurry of arrivals—that group must be Portuguese One, people in their teens and twenties in American clothes, mostly jeans, and their instructor in a Hawaiian shirt, salt-and-pepper mustache. Some black people no one knew, not students of Portuguese or members of Ouida's churches.

"Well, is it a public gathering?" asks a woman. "You sellin tickets to all?"

"Sure," Marybeth says, imagining Ouida will be pleased. Ouida isn't too pleased; she peers into the vat of beans.

"Sixty, I hope it is right, I hope no more," she says tensely.

Somebody turns up the record player, which has been discreetly leaking tunes at low volume behind them and now can be properly heard. Brazilian music Ouida has found records of, and mariachis. It is festive. There is much laughter, much muttering guttural sounds of Portuguese unintelligible to others. Individually the members of Portuguese One come up to Marybeth at her card table and say, *"Bom dia!"*

Ouida dashes back and forth from the kitchen with kettles. Chuck helps with the heavy vats of beans. Anton has come out of his studio, and he helps, too. He naturally ranges himself on the side of the proprietors of this *festa* instead of with the guests, in the adversary relation that is developing, like faintly turned meat, between them and the guests. Some people throw beans and *farofa* into the chicken pen.

"Isn't there some other kind of music?" Marybeth hears people ask, and she feels irritated at them. Brazilian music is very nice.

"Laughter in other languages has a different cadence; it's a little different in pitch or something," Chuck observes. "It doesn't sound like we're in America."

When there is a lull in arrivals, Marybeth leaves her post to go over and collect paper napkins which have blown off the table and are stuck up against the chicken wire.

"My God, delicious, this is delicious, wonderful, Ouida!" cries a man, and throws his arms around Ouida. A beautiful dark brown couple in Brazilian costume are dancing to a samba.

"It is a proper samba," whispers Ouida reverently. They know they are watched by all. They have the impassive faces of professional dancers, beautifully concentrating; their bodies, slim as snakes, perform the ripples and glides.

"Ouida! Let's hear it for Ouida Senza!" cries the professor of Portuguese One.

"That is Meesis Aheem," whispers Ouida to Marybeth of a woman in a sari and tennis shoes, smudged red circles between her deep dark eyes. Other people from Ouida's school have come, too; it is a kind of token of affection. But not the Chinese girls from typing class.

"It's like the United Nations," Anton says, his tone ambiguous.

"Oh, I think it's great," Marybeth says. "The food is great, everybody likes it, Ouida is so happy."

The chickens run senselessly around in their enclosure, maddened, it appears, by the phonograph. A little boy watches them. It is Chen-yu. His mother Julie hovers near him, looking obsessively at her watch. Chen-yu waves and calls to the chickens.

"Ouida, darling," cries a man, "it's a triumph," and closely embraces Marybeth, pressing against her breasts, sliding his hands down her buttocks.

"I'm not Ouida," she says.

Anton, not usually attracted to human subjects, goes to get a camera. It is irresistible, the beautiful array, the flags, the rose umbrellas, the gold earrings flashing, the flashing smiles, the quite improbably ruffled skirts swirling, like something out of *National Geographic*, and the beautiful dark eyes. Carlyle the dog begins to bark maddeningly from the upstairs window, where they have locked him in a bedroom.

"That's someone on the phone," Anton said, coming out of his studio in the garage to find Chuck. "They tell us to go to Fontana, there's some trouble, a prison break, involving Theo." He said this almost conversationally to Chuck; Chuck could see he was stunned or unbelieving.

"Who called?" Chuck asked.

"It was the police, I guess, or the sheriff."

Chuck drew Marybeth away from the row of bowls she was ladling rice into and told her this. She gasped. "I'm coming, too. Of course," she said. "I don't care whether police are there or not. Ouida—we'll be back—can you get along here?"

"I'll drive my car," Chuck said, taking them around into the street.

"I knew she shouldn't fuck around with prisons," Marybeth said.

"They didn't explain what they want with us. Still, we should be there. Of course we should be there," Anton said in the car. Too tall a man for the back seat of Chuck's Camaro, so that his knees stuck up under his chin. He had his camera bag on his lap, and his arms folded over his camera bag.

"This is a terrible thing," he said in the same tone, rather without conviction. Did he mean by this mild indictment that it was not a terrible thing, or that he didn't know why it was a terrible thing? Marybeth, crawling with urgency, squirmed and tried to imagine what awful thing could be happening; but she felt constrained from mentioning anything. She understood Anton's pale, blank face.

"Tell me the turn off for Fontana," Chuck said when they were on I-80. "Is it marked?"

"I don't know how to feel," Anton said suddenly, as if asking for advice on it. "Worried, of course, but how worried ought I to feel? How did they know to call, unless Theo told them to? That must mean she's all right. Perhaps she's a hostage, I keep thinking of that. She—she hasn't got the temperament for that. She's the sort of person who would do something foolish, excitable, I'm afraid, likely to lose her head in a situation—she hardly understands the desperation, the seriousness—things . . ."

"She'll be all right," they were saying to him soon. "The police know what to do about these things." You'd say anything to relieve the contracted expression of worry on the poor man's face.

Theo knows she must make some effort to understand her situation. Four convicts have seized the van in which she is riding. They have knocked out Clarence Harter and now he lies on the floor unconscious. Or does she see him stir? She leans forward to watch for him stirring, and the convict in the driver's seat pushes her back again into her own seat, as if she were a menacing person.

They have driven somewhere and are surrounded, it must be by police. The young man next to her, Darrell someone, seems to have known this was going to happen. What did he know? Seems to have known and now objects. Objects to what? She tries to listen and understand.

It seems that the pots of jelly and jam in the neat basket in the rear of the van are what he is objecting to. "Be careful, you fucking idiots, you were supposed to leave that stuff inside," he screams at the others, over and over, apparently referring to the jelly and jam. So it must not be jelly and jam at all, or why would he care? Not really jelly and jam in the jars. There is a strange smell. She believes she could get it all straight if only this Darrell would stop screeching.

Ah. Jelly and jam really explosive, something known to Darrell, who wishes they had left it behind. I certainly agree with that, thinks Theo.

"They won't do nothing, we got hostages here," the convicts are saying.

Well, that's us, Theo thinks, Clarence and I. Darrell, too? Or is he in it with them?

"That explosive was to be left inside, you fucking idiots, you weren't supposed to drive it out. It was to liberate the prison with," he says again and again.

Still, it isn't clear who is in charge here. They need a leader, Theo thinks. It might as well be me. They are surrounded by people, police and others, who want, no doubt, to capture the convicts and rescue her and Clarence. Darrell, too? Even though he is somehow in league with the convicts? What about the others, she wonders, the ones who got out?

Here her powers fail, sunk by the snuffles and quavers in all the throats of her companions as they peer out the windows into the field. She feels a tremor in her throat, the trembling inclination to scream. I'm not a screamer, she thinks; still . . . She can imagine the high, clear imperative of her own screams, but she can't really produce them. Too inhibited.

"Look here," she says instead, irritably, to Darrell, "you knew about this, how stupid can you be?" But she sees that reproaches are not helpful now, and she falls silent.

Out in the back yard with people dancing all around her, Ouida sees that her *festa* is a success, yet it does not seem like a success, for the people do not seem happy, though the *feijoada* is delicious, and Roberta's husband, even he likes it, his eyes bluest blue.

Someone went boldly right into the house, to use the toilet, despite Ouida's pleas and remonstrances. "No, no, we cannot go inside, it belongs to the people who—I promised that no one would go inside."

No, it is not like a *festa* in Brazil, where everyone dances and claps and laughs loudly, for here, although there is laughter and music, yet there is an aimless standing around on the part of many, many people who do not dance. Perhaps they do not know how. Perhaps, Ouida thinks, it is only in Brazil that everyone can dance.

Roberta hugs her and says it is delicious, it is a success. Two children scuffle and cause the legs of a card table to buckle, so that the kettle slides and Ouida only catches it in time.

Many strangers here. At first she was glad, it meant more money—maybe even enough money to be convincing to Colonel Pacific. But she does not like the strangers—they have a dangerous careering aspect, as if they could pick up the *festa* and run away, taking it where it does not want to go. They do not regard her. They demand food and refills.

Ouida tries to explain that she has planned for each person one generous portion only. They do not regard her.

"I hope there will be enough; there will not be enough," she says to Roberta, and to Mrs. Phyllis, a white Presbyterian lady, formerly missionary in Brazil and fond of *feijoada*.

"Maybe we should boil some more rice; that will always stretch the meal," Mrs. Phyllis says, surveying the crowd, the kettle with practiced eye. "I'll go boil the rice."

Some African students come, in dashikis and pillbox hats. They pull out drums. "Oh," says Ouida, tears in her eyes, pressing her knuckles to her lips, "that is not the music of Brazil," but no one regards her.

Two large women come, in print dresses and heavy shoes, and white frizzy hair, and they have only one ticket. Ouida tries to explain to them: one ticket for each person, each ticket four dollars.

"Well, ah brought man fren, and I done bought this ticket already, you didn't say it wasn't for a fren, too." Then they crash right in—right by Mark, the nice boy who was manning the table to sell tickets—crash right into the yard and they don't know anybody, nobody greets them, and they don't care.

Two children, fighting again, tip chairs over.

It seems to Theo they have been here a long time. Over beyond, at the rim of the field where the trees thrust up as on a shore, as if it were the shore and she on a ship departing, except for the stillness, the awful immobility with which their vessel sits, no soothing rocking but the stillness instead of piers—over there suddenly Theo can distinguish Anton and Chuck and the girl on the shore. It is not surprising. Their little orange faces, their waving arms—they look like people who have been left behind. She presses her face past Darrell to the window. They don't see me, she realizes.

* * *

Chuck has taken the girl's hand. She clings to his arm. Anton is waving his arms, and a policeman in helmet and boots tells them something. Anton stops waving. He's been told to stop waving. Perhaps they fear to startle the prisoners. In the bus, the one now slumps over the steering wheel, watching with bright eyes like a sick fox.

Those guns, the forest bristling with guns. Theo feels the excitement of guns, the something exhilarating. The heart races.

"We got to talk to them," says one in back, "got to get someone up here to talk about it." But the watchers do not approach. They don't see us, not really, Theo thinks. From all the watches of the forest come sirens like hunters' horns.

"Wave your arms. Wave a white handkerchief," Theo says to them. You're supposed to tear off a piece of your slip, but I'm not wearing a slip, she thinks. I'm wearing black. Why don't they do something? They sit so still, these men; men are supposed to do something. These are so unmanfully daunted—why? Destroyed already. "*I* will wave," she says, but a man in back catches her arm.

"Careful. We got to get someone up here to hear our demands, we can't alarm them."

"Trigger-happy pigs is what we got to deal with," says one of the men, who has pink hair.

It's the feeling of playing hide-and-seek, Theo thinks. It's like being frozen in a dark corner, not daring to breathe; so we sit here not breathing. They seem, all of them, to be suspended in some thick medium like water-glass; the air is transparent but somehow viscous.

"Let me out," she says. The hand on her shoulder gets firmer.

"I'll go tell them." But they don't release her.

She feels stifled, she has to force back the heavy air in order to speak or breathe; their hoarse breathing presses upon her lungs, the solid pressing faces of danger impinge upon them from the perimeter of the field. Anton has his two hands clasped together at his breast, Theo notices; is he having chest pain? She notes this, wonders, cannot, curiously, care.

The girl standing there among all those police—isn't she frightened? Worried for her own safety? When will they grab her: we know you, we're coming to get you. This is California now. The girl tosses her hair and stares into the field looking for Theo.

How brave she is, thinks Theo admiringly. She is touched, and full of love at Marybeth's risk. The pressing slimy feel to the air increases.

"As far as we can tell," a detective in a felt hat says to Anton, taking Anton's arm and strolling him along behind a patrol car conspiratorially, "as far as we can tell, two hostages—your sister and we don't know the identity of the other one, some kid, maybe a student, or maybe mixed up in it, too." His tone is not censorious, is brotherly.

"Too?" says Anton. Marybeth and Chuck crowd closely along behind.

"The others—the other Friends Outside—they left the van when it arrived at the prison; that's when the prisoners got in. We're trying to find out how much they know. They all got out except for one, Clarence Harter, who was driving the van, and maybe he's still in it, but we can't see him. They may have him on the floor."

"Who?" asks the confused Anton.

"Who the outside contact was, we aren't sure. Maybe the whole bunch. And someone must have greased a guard."

"What difference does it make? What are you talking about!" Anton suddenly shouts. "Christ, what's the difference? Just tell those people to let Theo out."

"Dangerous, desperate men," says the detective. "We're waiting for the word on their exact identities. They're checking to see who's unaccounted for at Fontana. Then we'll get the personality profiles, we'll get the psychologists in here.''

All of us together only yesterday, thinks Theo—only this morning—and now how far away they are, with their little mouths, little round O's like Cheerios, framing unheard shouts. Can they see me? It seems they can't see me. We are too far away. The shore recedes. She sees the girl bury her face in her hands, a gesture of uncharacteristic anguish. Theo tries to wrest her own arm free to wave; she means nothing more than to wave.

The girl's anguish and Anton's arms across his chest, more than her own surroundings—this cozy little van in the pretty field—increase Theo's sense of danger. It is like a little electric shock at her fingertips, the realization: this is real, then; Anton is here. How did he know to come here? Perhaps the alarm has gone off, the smoke alarm, its red eye following her to Fontana.

Now her choices are arrayed before her—to be fearful or to be brave—in a moment of clear decision; she gets the idea that the danger doesn't matter, she doesn't care, because it has always been there, you're always in danger, that's the meaning of life. At this thought the air lightens immediately, as if sprayed with aerosol something, and she can breathe deeper, though the man in the front seat still cannot; he still labors over his breathing like something broken or punctured.

For some reason she suddenly has the clear memory or conviction that she indeed did lock her hotel room against the Finn all those years ago. That was something she was never sure about until this moment. Yes, she did lock it. Precautions are of no value. Smoke alarms. No, there's nothing you can do.

This is one of the things that happen, she thinks, the kind of thing that has always followed me around, that's all. How deep, how calm her satisfaction that she is at least right about this, and besides it doesn't matter.

She peers across the field again. Anton is clutching his chest. It would be like him to have a heart attack at a time like this; that's how he is.

Theo puts her hands on her knees. She feels their familiar knobbiness, not really good legs for a dancer, but better than most; some people have to overcome worse handicaps—say, the handicap of a slight bow. Her knees reassure her. If that man would only clear his throat, or blow his nose; his breath is like someone's who is stretched on a torture rack, she thinks. His arm, bare, sticking out of the short sleeve of his green prison suit, is seamed and scarred with horrible welts, as if he has indeed been tortured in his life. Seeing it, Theo remembers something else that has not struck her before, yet now she can visualize it clearly, and understand it, too. She sees in her clear memory the hand of little Charles on the barre, and across the wrist and top of the hand rows of welts like these.

"Are you an asthmatic?" she asks the convict.

A policeman with a loud voice, who had moments before been shouting directions on every side, now came up to Anton. The policeman was embedded deep in his plastic and leather gear, his voice muffled beneath a gas mask.

"It's imperative that you tell us what you know about your sister's involvement with this escape plot," he said.

"What?"

"Escape plot. We know—good intentions. Well-meaning—these people don't understand. May help save her life now, whatever you can tell us."

"Excuse me?" Anton said, in a faint voice.

"She wasn't mixed up in anything that we know of," Chuck said.

"That you know of," said the doubting voice. "Please,

Mr. Wait, we aren't going to hassle you. You can see it may help her.''

"No, I don't think Theo was mixed up in it," Anton said. "She was not enthusiastic about going to Fontana at all.''

"Naturally," said the policeman.

"An innocent victim," said Chuck loudly. "Why can't you get her out of there? You haven't even spoken to the people in the van there.''

"Where is the gas team? Bring the gas people up here," the policeman said to others, turning his back on them in disgust.

The big woman who has brought her friend in free rolls her sleeves above her biceps like a sailor and hoists a heavy case up on a card table, which totters under the weight. "Look here, give me a hand with them legs there," she says, and her friend kicks at the legs.

"Look at here," she says loudly to everybody. "Genuine Indian jewelry. Now is the time to invest in this. Worth a fortune, people is discovering the beauty and value of jewelry made by genuine native American craftsmen.''

She unfolds the four sides of the case, which are lined with silver bracelets and necklaces with turquoise stones. People come up to look.

"This is not the thing," whispers Mrs. Phyllis to Ouida. "These people shouldn't do this." She says to the woman, "The other people came here to eat and dance.''

"We ain't stoppin them eatin and dancin," says the friend.

"Heritage designs, you can't get these in no store," says the woman to the assembling crowd.

The allure of the smoldering silver in the sun stops the eating and dancing. Mrs. Aheem, strong little woman, shoulders the others aside and pushes close to peer, and rub the bracelets.

"Just lookin, no touchin," says the woman, knocking her hand away. "You see somethin you like aks me and ah'll show you."

"Sisters," says a black man, so tall, standing behind the others, that the peddler woman can meet his eyes over the heads of all the people. He wears a big white hat. Like the hat of a television sheriff, thinks Ouida. "That fine-lookin merchandise looks hot to me," he says, his smile so merry and full of light, so attractive that Ouida would have touched his sleeve if she were closer. But the peddler woman curses him.

Her curses fill the air. Her friend fills the air with operatic protests. His smile, so full of meaning, never changes. A shuffling chorus of people backs off, opening a little path from the man to the women; people scuttle off.

Ouida does not understand, but senses the discord, the gathering trouble or the gnawing and churning of generating panic, and she, too, backs away.

Large sounds, grandly amplified, come to the sitters in the van. "You are to come out. Come out with your hands up. You have five minutes to come out with your hands up."

"What then? What then?" Theo cries. All are still, rooted.

"Oh, no!" Darrell cries. "They'll gas us, they'll get us all; let us out, let's get away from this bus."

"Shut up! Now hold still, they know we got hostages, they got to talk to us. They ain't even talked to us."

"You are being warned" comes the voice from a great horn like His Master's Voice.

Yes, thinks Theo, always being warned, ever mindful of the warning. Theo, come out of there; Theo, come home, come out with your hands up. She the most timid of creatures, always mindful of every warning; suppose she doesn't pay any attention now?

That girl, boldly heedless, has acted, risked herself, now this minute, by standing around elbow to elbow with police. Perhaps she has never been warned. Girls nowadays. Theo becomes aware of a weight in the pocket of her skirt, her aventurine beads, warm from her body, as comforting as a rosary—she supposes rosaries are comforting. She's forgotten to give them to the girl, and now she'll never get them, she thinks, and, with the next instant, why did I think that?

It doesn't matter because now the young man will warn and protect her. The girl's face is hidden against his shoulder and his face is turned, unblinking, bravely, toward Theo's van. Theo waves, little jabs of assent to him, and no one stops her hand this time.

Perhaps he can't see her. He doesn't wave back. "Stop that," her companions now say.

How do men get the ability, the presence, to stare right at danger and peril and discomfiture without looking away? Is it nice? Is it right of them? How disappointing that the girl, supposed to be so bold, so political, now hides her face on Chuck's breast, and it is Chuck who boldly stares. An agreement between them, Theo supposes, a stupid agreement, division of labor, staring and hiding.

Now Anton begins to wave—no, to beckon, as if she could just come if she would. Why does he not get out his camera and photograph this?

She turns her attention to the faces of her companions, strange faces with the usual components—lips, noses, eyes—but none come together to form a recognizable person. No one here to form an agreement with, but just bodies and gibbering voices, the wail of Darrell, the coarse sighs.

They know each other no better than when they set off. Do they know her? Do they even know her name?

"Theodora Wait," she says. They pay no attention to her.

"Jet airplane," someone is saying.

"My name is Theodora Wait." But they do not hear her, no matter what she says.

Irritated, exasperated with them, she stirs firmly. "Let's get out." But she is weighted, too, with the leaden sense of futility; these people with their cement feet, how could she have supposed they could dance? Anyway, suppose they do get out and hobble across the hot burning field through that thick smoky air, pushing their way—to what, toward whom, why? That armed ring of strangers bristling with metal rods and aerials and guns, wands, appurtenances, faces covered with masks and armored heads and eyes shut behind mirrors, not really people at all.

The faces of Marybeth and Chuck are turned toward each other and have nothing to do with her, nothing whatever; and Anton—who is he, anyway? Someone she knew briefly when she was little, who has led his life elsewhere. How sad that everyone should turn out strangers; whom does she know? Who knows her? How hollow, how brittle is the living self, so like the shell of a locust, about to shatter, with nothing inside.

"Well, shit, I'm gettin outta here. Open the windows, you know what they gonna do."

"Talk, they'll talk, they'll talk to us."

"They know we got hostages here, they know we got high explosives here." Do they know? Do they care? Who are they?

Oh, questions of inconsequence, it comes to Theo. Who cares for answers? You don't finally care.

"Two minutes," say the voices, and she still cannot bring herself to a sense of consequence; other things are so present, so immediate—the heat, and now a terrible smell filling the van compels her attention.

"Somebody got to get out and get them over here to hear our demands. Why don't they send somebody?"

"Shit, they think we got explosives, see, they don't dare—would you? We got to speak to them."

"Wave something," Theo says. "Have we no guns?"

"They know we got innocent people in here. What can they do?"

"Well, get out and holler at them."

"Hell, they can't hear. We hear them because they got a bullhorn."

"Let's put the old woman out, she can go tell them."

"Me! Put me!" cries Darrell.

Theo feels her interest wane. They seem to be speaking from afar.

"Everything is being done," says a fat sheriff's deputy in a leather jacket. He shows them a gun. He waves at all the guns. "Those there are .270 rifles. That's a big-game weapon, that can hit a five-inch target at a thousand yards, and we got the man who can do that, too. Those there are Ithacas, twelve-gauge. The Ithaca's an anti-vehicle weapon, you could level a wall with it when it's loaded with rifled slugs. Those are the CS canisters."

Chuck and Anton stare at the guns, but Marybeth turns away.

"Some of the men here, they prefer to use their own weapons. That's why you see the different ones. Everyone wants to put a stop to this kind of thing, rest assured," the deputy goes on.

"Stand back sister, can't you?" says another man,

pushing past Marybeth. "Do we need these people here?"

Marybeth does not want to watch now anyway. Cannot. Whatever happens. She hears Chuck's angry voice, remonstrating, shouting. She withdraws into a sunny patch and sits down on a warm stone. She tries to hear inside herself, tries not to hear the men's voices. Of course she is very frightened, of course she is. But there is also within her something flat and calm, like a warm stone to be listened to. She can almost hear it.

In the front seat of the van the driver turns around and looks at the others.

"Shall I honk the horn?"

"Hell, what good'll that do?"

"What are our demands?"

"Getaway car and some lead time."

"No, we'd never get away in no car—we need a jet airplane take us to Cuba."

"You crazy asshole, they can't get no jet. They know we got innocent people here, they ain't gonna do nothin."

Now, across the field, Theo can see the girl clinging to the man, as if she cannot go on, hiding her face and clinging. You can go on, Theo thinks severely; I went through with it, you can go through with it.

"Endanger the innocent."

"Jet airplane to Cuba."

The terrible smell is perhaps the smell of her own resentment, or of someone's fear.

"Innocent people in here."

Innocence, what an idea, as if there were such a thing, she thinks. Innocence, justice—what ideas. Fairy tales for men. Only the warm worn knobs of her knees are familiar and reassuring, so that her last feeling is one of reassurance, and then a tear-gas bullet—as they must have known it would—detonates all the explosives inside the van.

20. Bank of America

Ouida knew it was anger that stole over her and threatened to smother her heart—she had felt it once, twice, a number of times lately, and here it was again. But she battled it. Her head ached with unshed tears of anger, and also fear. She was afraid of what they would say when they came home. She knew they were kind. She knew they would not scream at her or turn savage, or turn her out. But did she? Would they? Like a hurricane, like the deadly tidal wave, the powerful force of evil passion had engulfed the *festa*. Might not some of the left-over savage spirit infect them, too?

She had promised safekeeping to Miss Theo, she had assured them, but nevertheless they would come home to find wreckage. She tried to calm her anger. It was not *all* the people. Most people are good. She told herself this again and again. And now the chickens flew squawking, loose, lost, and a table was broken, the leg broken right off, also a large crockery bowl that had been Miss Theo's nice bowl, just the right size for rising the bread, and now broken to bits.

She wasn't sure how it had begun. Was it the students from Portuguese One? Perhaps it had been they, they were young and thoughtless, or the two quarreling children, the children that shrieked and quarreled out of control—where were the mothers? Or the peddler woman with her jewelry who ran cursing at the tall man when he tore the money from her hand. How had it begun?

All the good people vanished in a flash. Most people are good in their hearts. She could not blame the good people; just one or two bad ones are all it takes to make a wreck, to make a shambles, to make a rising hell of crashing noises and angry voices. Oh, why could not the bad people be good and see the light in their hearts? What good did it do them to be bad? Why? She had heard the reasons, had read all the reasons, and yet she did not know. The bitter idea stole over her, but she forced it away, that no one did know and that all people were bad.

In the hall she watched a trickle of water from the bathroom leak along the side of the rug runner. The toilet was stopped up, and she'd better do something. Already a stench; sodden paper wads were floating into the hall. She hurried through the back yard to the garage to find the rubber plunger, chilling at the squalor there. People had taken the phonograph records; only a few were left on the table, and one lay broken on the ground. There was no food left, only some sections of orange, and limp shreds of collard browning in the bowl. The chicken wire was wrenched apart.

It is Americans, she thought. It is that Americans do not know how to make a *festa*. It is in their nature to quarrel and they do not dance. She should have known, but she had thought only Brazilians would come.

In the garage she could see into Mr. Anton's study, where the pictures were, the beautiful pictures of icy streams and snow like clouds lying on the black mountain rocks, and she reassured herself that some Americans were gentle and good. Many, doubtless, were good. Would the heart of Miss Theo break with sorrow at the fate of her big crockery bowl?

Her own heart speeded up again with fear. She got the plunger and hurried back to the house. First the bathroom, then the kitchen, then the back yard, in that order; she must not lose control but must work vigorously before they came home. She must not permit tears or anger to rule her. She must not expend the spirit—it is profitless to exhaust the spirit with negative emotions; negative emotions will not get this mess cleaned up.

She had forgotten that Mr. Griggs was coming. She had promised to vacuum his house. At the sound of his step on the porch, at her memory, she almost cried aloud. It was more than she could bear. But here he was, and just when he had said he would come, not wearing his uniform but in a shirt with red and green stripes.

"My God, girl, you got a mess here! What happened?" he asked, though it was plain enough. The water trickled faster into the hall. He took the plunger from her and peered in at the mess. Her heart swelled gratefully, also painfully, from embarrassment at the disgrace in there. Embarrassment that they now shared knowledge of certain bodily things. She told him what had happened. If *he* had been here, she boldly thought, a security officer, it could not have happened.

"You let them walk all over you here," he said, as if he read her thoughts exactly. "Why didn't you call the police?"

"I did not like to," Ouida said. "I did not think the people meant any harm, only . . ."

"Only you don't call this harm? Where are the people that lives here? Where was they?" He was reproaching her, but yet he was employing the plunger, which was very kind. She had a strange feeling of weakness, lightheadedness, which made her afraid, for a moment, to get down to clean the water up, her head swam so funny. She knelt in a dry place and tucked up the edges of the hall runner, and began to sop up the stinking water with her sponge and squeeze it into the bucket, but her hands felt like leaden weights on the ends of her arms; she could hardly lift them.

"The people all went away in a rush, I do not know

why. They said they would help with the *festa*, but they went away, and I was alone here, and then the trouble came over the *festa*, some anger or quarrel that I did not understand. Roberta and Mrs. Phyllis stayed to help me for a time, but Roberta and her husband had to leave because they had told the baby-sitter. Then Mrs. Phyllis, she . . ." Ouida could not remember what had happened to Mrs. Phyllis, where had she gone?

"Call the police in here, that's what you should have did right away," Mr. Griggs said. He flushed the toilet several times. They listened gratefully to its successful operation.

"Oh, I am not one to call the police," Ouida said finally. "I am afraid their attention will be turned to me. I am sorry you did not come early to help, for you said you might." She could not restrain this ungenerous reproach, and for the man who had unplugged the toilet so kindly. "But you never come when you say," she added unavoidably.

"Haven't you got a mop? Don't put your hands in that," he said. "The police ain't got nothin against you."

She stood up dizzily. Why could he not remember? It was as if he had not ever heard a thing she said to him. Perhaps he did not listen to a woman, or perhaps the American men did none of them listen to a woman, or perhaps no man anywhere listened to a woman.

"Colonel Pacific has my passport," she told him again, "and now I have received a letter telling me to appear for my visa."

"Well, that ain't nothin beside my case. You reprobatin me without rememberin that I got plenty on my mind. There never was no man as vexed as me." His tone frightened Ouida; she had reached his crazy subject, that was plain from the sudden loudness of his voice. Do not all men have a point on which they are crazy?

* * *

They were working in the back yard, picking up the broken things and scattered paper napkins, and Mr. Griggs was trying to mend the fence so they could once again confine the chickens. The others drove up in a yellow car that Ouida didn't recognize and parked the car in the alley by the garage. Ouida breathed deeply with resolution, telling herself again and again that they would not be angry, because they were good; and indeed they were not angry. They did not seem to see her at all, but wandered like people under the evil spell of *macumba*, like the people who are said to rise up at midnight and walk together without speaking into a marsh or riverbed to their death and no one ever knows why, or the ones that lie in an open grave which the diggers have prepared for someone else on the morrow, lie there with staring eyes and die soon after. Ouida had seen before those staring eyes, those same attenuated steps. They did not seem to notice the desperate chickens sprinting around their feet. She shivered with her intuition of their horror; it blazed out of their eyes.

Their voices were so soft as not to be heard. They went into the kitchen. Miss Theo was not with them, so Ouida would not yet have to confess the fate of the crockery bowl. Mr. Griggs, *graças a Deus*, had fallen silent, ceased for the moment his complicated and fatiguing explication, some story that was on his heart, but which she could not understand, and which made her head ache inside. He ceased his harangue now and watched the strange gait of the others, and took note of the way their hands were knitted together, all three clinging together as if bound together like a chain gang: the girl and the young man, one on either side of the old one.

We must make an explanation, was Ouida's guilty thought, hoping they would understand and not be too angry, we must explain, and followed them into the kitchen, bearing in either hand the shattered fragments of the blue crockery bowl.

* * *

The men were sitting at the kitchen table, and Marybeth
had put the kettle on and was staring into it as if it contained secrets. Ouida sensed but could not explain the
thick gravity of the air. Perhaps a madness had settled
over this place, had maddened the guests at the *festa*,
benumbed Mr. Anton and the others, crazed the agitated
Mr. Griggs, who was again shouting excitedly at her of
his case.

"We should have made them let us stay; we should
have watched them, listened. We have to let this be
known," Anton said. No one said anything in reply.

"They didn't try to save her, they didn't care. 'We have
to show these people.' I heard an officer say that. 'We
mean business.' I heard him say that over and over.
'These people, these people,' they said as if that were
Theo."

"Mr. Wait, they may not have realized there were explosives in that van; it was just tear gas, they meant to
use just tear gas to get them out," Chuck said, in a voice
not convinced. Anton shook his head.

"No, no coffee," he said presently to Marybeth. "I
think I'll go up and lie down for a half-hour. I'd like to—
to just compose myself. Then we'll think what to do."
His eyes filled; he covered them and walked away.

"Chuck!" cried Marybeth when Anton had left. "You
don't believe that, do you, that they didn't know? They
knew! I could tell they knew something!"

Chuck shrugged, as if vainly trying to shake off horror
that clung. "I think they knew," he said. His face was
pale and angry.

"In a case like mine," said Griggs, coming in, speaking
where he had left off, "you just got to keep after it, day
after day. They all think an old black man is just gonna

shuffle off and forget it; they think he'll forget all about it or get discouraged, but that ain't my way, and I ain't goin to forget, although I am plenty discouraged. It ain't just the three hundred dollars, either, so when you all the time complainin when I ain't right there to take you hither and yon in my car, you might consider the time I got to put in on this case.''

"I don't wish to complain," Ouida protested, humiliated at his idea of her, for she was not a complaining person. "It is just that in our country we depend on a person when he says. I do not wish to be a complaining person . . .''

Mr. Griggs looked at Marybeth and Chuck. "Let me tell you somethin about my case,'' he said. "This girl here can't get it through her head.''

Chuck and Marybeth looked at him passively. A black man about fifty, grizzled, wringing his hands and scratching his neck in a state of indignation.

"That first girl—she was a white girl, too, they all in it—she done said to herself, 'This old coon don't know nothin,' and she made me sign the paper, but she never give me the money order.''

"You'd better start at the beginning," said Chuck.

"Yeah," said Mr. Griggs. "Yeah. Well, it concern the Bank of America. That Bank of America versus Griggs, and I don't need to tell you who won.''

Ouida tried to follow his words, because she could see that it was settled. She would marry him. By their attentions he could tell that Marybeth and Chuck considered it settled, too, or something in his story compelled their attention, for they listened to what he was saying with great solemnity, but she herself could not. She could not understand him. Was it wise to marry when you could not understand? Was it important? But it was settled, in any case, had been settled by his hand on the plunger, by his striped shirt of red and green, by the letter in her pocket, by the ravening screeches of the disorderly guests, by—oh, a number of things before she was born, in other lives, no doubt, and by the things that were to come. The old saying came to her: The ending is written in the first line.

"I went to buy the money order, see, for three hundred dollars, to pay for Lonnie's treatment. Let me tell you. She never give it to me. I signed the papers, and all them copies, and I give her the money right at the bank with the people standin there watchin, and she shoves all them papers back at me, and I goes out. Then I ain't gone a block without realizin it—I say to myself, *"Now I ain't got that money order."* That's right—I look around in all my pockets, and all along the curb, and in the magazine—I'm carryin this magazine—and I ain't got it. I catches on *immediately* that she ain't give it to me. So I go right back. I ain't been gone ten minutes, you understand, and I tell her I ain't got it. Them people standin around saw me go; they says, 'Oh, you put it in your magazine,' but I ain't, that was only the carbon paper. She only *give* me the carbon paper."

Ouida was somewhat reassured by the attention that Marybeth and Chuck gave to him. So he was a good, serious man, worth attending.

"Now the bank man—she went and call the man—he say, 'All right, all right, we can put a stop payment on it, that's all right,' so they done. But they say, 'We can't give you your money back yet.' That's right, you done give us your three hundred dollars, we don't give you no money order nor yet no money. And we are the Bank of America."

"That is a very fine bank," Ouida said.

"And they ain't put it in my account, either, if that's what you thinkin," Griggs said, smiling a little in triumph at the mystery here. "They jus kep it. They say, 'We goin to put a stop on it and then after a while you git your money.' But after a while, see, this dude come in and cash that money order and they don't stop it at all, they done pay him the money. Some dude I never seen."

"He found the money order?" Chuck said.

"Not him, some other dude found it, and took it to this other one, the one that cashed it, he runs a clothin store, see, and the dude that found it buys some shoes and some rags and pays with this money order, and then when I go checkin up I find all this out. If I hadn't stuck to it right from the beginnin, I never would have found out nothin. They thought I'd forget about it, see? They thought I wasn't goin to come back checkin, see. An old darky, Old Black Joe here, ain't supposed to do that, but I done."

"Three hundred dollars," sighs Ouida aloud, thinking that that is half enough to fly to Brazil on scheduled airlines, maybe even some over, enough to bring a present to each of her nieces and nephews, each one, and to her brothers and their wives, and many other benefits. Then, with a little start of guilt at indulging this thought, she remembers her promise to vacuum Mr. Griggs's house, and he will want to be starting soon, so she goes off to get the vacuum.

"I done demanded they tell me who cashed the check. It's not a funny business to me, I went around there every day, and I ain't goin to let it drop. Well, you bringin that vacuum cleaner?"

"Yes, it needs a vacuum cleaner there, but first I must vacuum here, because the people came inside and have left much disorder, and I promised Miss Theo this would not happen."

"How can they do that?" Marybeth asks. "A stopped check is a stopped check. It's the clothing-store man that's out."

"Oh, no, he ain't out. I done took him to court, the judge say he ain't out. But that's later. First I took the bank to court."

Ouida, hearing and understanding this as she carries the *aspirador* into the carpeted breakfast room to get the crumbs there, is impressed. It is true that Griggs must be sound, must be strong and important to undertake to sue a bank. A tiny hopeful spark kindles. "The bank permits this?" she asks over her shoulder.

"It's America, ain't it?" Griggs says. "It ain't up to them to say if they get sued. Anythin under five hundred dollars you can take to small-claims court, that's where it go, and that's what I done.

"Course it's all conspired against me. I should have knowed that. Well, the *first* thing I done, right after the incident, I went to the police and made a lost report. Then, when I am gettin my case up, I go back to the police to get a copy of my report, seein that it's important that I did cover myself that way. But they don't have nothin, no copy of my report, I might as well have save my breath as go in to the police."

Marybeth and Chuck look at him with extra attention.

"See, the teller is a white girl, that is the explanation," Griggs says. He has an apologetic note in his voice but he faces them firmly. "See, when I first goes to the police to make the lost report, I tell them then I thinks the teller has kep the money order, and the girl takin the report—she a white girl also—she say, 'What race is the teller?' and I say white, and she say, 'Well, you must have made a mistake, you must have lost it yourself.' Now what is it to them? Is it or ain't it their job to keep a copy of my report same as other citizens, and what is it to them the race of the teller?"

* * *

Now, all at once, Marybeth has begun to cry. Ouida does not know why. Is it the story? Is it a sad story? She cannot shake the feeling that all evil passions are awhirl in here today, all forces of disorder and antagonism unleashed. By what? If only she knew, or had words for this sense of the evil toils of a snake wrapped around your arms and legs, sitting on your tongue so you cannot cry out. She is losing her English, she can understand less and less of their words; it is as if the toils of the snake have squeezed them right out of her mind, or perhaps the words were a magic gift that vanished in the new day.

Mr. Griggs pauses, in apparent embarrassment, and Marybeth takes deep gulps of air to quiet herself.

"They all in it together with they lies," he said presently, "because they all think no black man gonna pursue this. But I do, I take the Bank of America to court, for not stoppin the check, and there I hear all the names, the name of the dude that bought the clothes, and the name of the dude that run the clothin store, who brought in the check to the bank. The first one he's called Frank Bekin, Becker, somthin, he's the dude that bought the clothes. Course the judge, a white man needless to say, he judges for the Bank of America."

Mr. Griggs was growing more and more upset, Ouida could tell as she watched from the doorway. She could tell because he worked his fingers together in a lattice and pulled and cracked them. He could make his fingers creak and crack like dried bones. That seemed a strange trick. His fingers so dark they were purple or dusky blue on the backs, pink on the fronts. But she could not understand what he had said, that last part—his accent, the rapidity of his words.

"Now it ain't right for them to stop the check and then pay out the money, and plenty of people have told me it ain't."

"It isn't right, that's right," Chuck agreed, with a fascinated expression, that same expression of dazed and stunned fascination they had all worn since they came home—even Mr. Anton, who had gone upstairs. Like people touched by the *macumba*, thought Ouida again.

"Will it be on the radio? Will people call and come over?" Marybeth suddenly said to Chuck.

"Not for a while," Chuck said. "I don't know."

A sudden sting of shame made her rub her eyes. Could they tell? Did it show that her grief was not simple but subtle, complex? It seemed to her that Chuck was staring at her. It seemed to her that winged creatures, a pack of them at her back, hounded her, tearing shreds of clothes off her, stole from her pockets with their curved beaks, yet left her strangely lighter.

"Oh, it's just that I always thought it would be me," she said. "And now I don't know how to feel."

"It isn't your fault," Chuck said, as he had said at first, in the field, holding her. She did not quite understand. Of course it wasn't her *fault*.

"There was never anything anyone could do, was there?" Marybeth said.

"I don't know. I keep thinking if we'd spoken up, made them realize that we were . . ."

"I mean ever, anytime," Marybeth said. How had she ever thought otherwise? "I mean from the first."

"No," said Chuck, with a hard edge to his tone; without saying, however, how he had found this out.

Her eyes stung so. "I just want to be with you."

He nodded, rather abstractedly.

"Let's not ever leave each other," Marybeth said. No, he did not seem to be listening. New compunctions, doubts, appalled apprehensions had made him for the moment a trifle vague, she supposed, but she did not mind too much, and derived comfort from the press of his hand.

"I don't know if the Bank of America done pay off the judge or what; anyway, I seen them after court, all laughin and they arms around each other," said Mr. Griggs, angrily cracking his knuckles.

Ouida suddenly decides against plugging the vacuum in, with him talking and cracking his bones like the rattling bones of the *macumbeira*. There is something not nice about drowning him out when his emotions are strong, for he waves his arms, rather like Miss Theo when she is excited, and tears stand in his eyes, though Ouida does not know why. The possession of English is like a possession of mercury which sometimes slithers away leaving you only elusive droplets of understanding. "Judge," one word she understands, and "court," and some others, not all. Will he snap his fingers at her? Will he ever put his hands gently on her head or shoulders? She has certain questions, certain fears she could ask Marybeth about if these men were not here.

But her friend Marybeth, she thinks, does not seem that she would want to hear, not just now, her cheeks just like roses; some Brazilians also have that fair skin with the black hair, but seldom do they have the blue eyes. Marybeth's eyes are blind-looking since she came home. If she were to try to reach out the hand of fellowship to Marybeth, Ouida suddenly feels, some power would arrest her hand; some pale or invisible shield has gone up around the girl like one of those dome-shaped glasses inside which are put blossoms or a clock. It is not the girl's misery altogether—she has got up from the

table and withdrawn a little way not to interrupt Mr.
Griggs with her sobs, she sinks against the kitchen wall
in sobs. There is a change, other changes.

It is a thing with all religions and faiths, that they want
you to help yourself, all faiths have that, Ouida thinks, the
cold alone feeling stealing within her, and hoping that she
has the faith within herself, loneliness like drowning in a
jungle pool, faith like a perishable blossom.

Mr. Griggs has a thin mustache like a Brazilian man,
thin over the upper lip. The mustache of Griggs is gray
and white. Her ears strain to understand him, but he
might be speaking backward in Chinese. The others appear to understand him and find his words of interest and
importance. Something stiff inside her, like the straight
back of a chair, now sinks, slumps, crumples, unresist-
ing. She toys with the plug of the vacuum but fears to
plug it in.

"Then I sues the other guy, the clothin-store dude, his
name is David Schimmer. I been thinkin maybe *he* got
to give me my money back if the bank don't, but that
second judge, he just say, 'Man, you got screwed, you
go back to the first judge and make an appeal! And he
tell me how to do it. He tell there ain't nothin he can do,
but tell me how to make the appeal. It ain't the fault of
this David Schimmer, he says.

"Well, there ain't no sense in me goin back to that first
judge, he in it for the Bank of America, I told this second
judge that, and I told him three hundred dollars, Your
Honor, that is a lot of money to me, that was all the
money I got, and I starts to tell them about Lonnie. But
then I think, Hell, they'll think that I am makin that up
about his back to gain their sympathy. He need treatment, the treatment he got now ain't workin anyway, and
his back is gonna be as crooked as a snake's ladder. Lon-

nie is my boy, he has a curvature of the spine, he got to
have a different treatment from what they give him.''

Lonnie. The word sticks out intelligibly for Ouida from
this difficult monologue. Lonnie is the little frail boy, a
good boy only twelve who will need affection because a
crippled, such as you often see in Brazil but not so much
here. Ouida plugs in the *aspirador* but doesn't turn it on.
  Lonnie a nice little boy but then all those bad daughters, well, they are nearly grown is one good thing, and
if she marries with Griggs they will not be at home long,
for they are almost old enough to have families, and in
America, she has noticed, the children go off young, and
do not live at home with the family until marriage.
  ''In Brazil,'' she says aloud, having listened with particular care to the words surrounding Lonnie, ''there the
poor people can get excellent medical care—operations
and everything, as I have had on my teeroid, and it costs
nothing at the university.''

''White, they all white, you can't get no doctor to tell
you the truth,'' says Griggs. ''You white, you don't know
what I say is the truth.'' Tears rush to his eyes and trickle
down his cheeks. ''I got to buy him treatment and they
think I'm makin it up to gain they sympathy.''
  She must turn on the vacuum, of course, but at the idea
her heart fills with grief. It is not precisely housecleaning
that brings on the grief, but it is a memory of voices far
away speaking so you can understand them, and to which,
for reasons she cannot understand, she cannot return.
She *wishes* to stay, but a person never gets over love for
his own language, she thinks.
  A scatter of crumbs lies on the breakfast-room carpet,
perhaps from the *feijoada* guests, perhaps only from their
own breakfast, Miss Theo gesturing with her toast. This

is a nice carpet, and the carpet of Mr. Griggs is not so nice but maybe she will like it better when it is vacuumed. If it were allowed, she would put the carpet of Griggs outside his front door, but it would not be allowed. She thinks of it, lying in the center of his front room like a round pond, herself walking around and around it, thinking safe thoughts, for married to Griggs neither Colonel Pacific nor the immigration nor her brothers nor anyone could do anything against her. She is startled at the loudness in the voice of Griggs.

"I'm thinkin, shit, I ain't gonna tell them about Lonnie, they goin to do me justice for reasons of justice. I read up on that. They gonna do me justice for reasons of justice. They don't give a shit about any black child, be he crooked or straight."

Ouida, hearing the sobs of Marybeth, the sobs of Griggs, impulsively flips the switch of the *aspirador*, which fills the breakfast room with a solemn swooshing noise but not so loud they cannot go on with their talking as she, Ouida, goes on with her vacuuming, which seems to give her a kind of space or hollow place for her own thoughts, a space in which to repair them and store a little bravery up, for her spirits are failing.

What do I care about the next life? The treacherous thought comes stealing into her mind in English. She does not know where it comes from.

She is brave, she knows, to come an unmarried woman to a strange land and then bravely to leave her protectors and Colonel and Mrs. Pacific when she is mistreated, whereas another person less self-respecting would have abided. And then to have learned so much English and taken driver's training and typing and much more. Yet it is in the face of her immense ignorance that she feels daunted, she loses heart.

"I have figured it out, see, they all in it. The teller and her boyfriend. That's Frank Bekin, Baker, I figure he's her boyfriend, she give him the money order, he cashes it at the clothin store. I don't know if this David Schimmer is in it, maybe he jus cash the check. But I can't prove it. I can prove it if I can see them together, that's why I'm followin Frank Bekin, but it take time, it's time-consumin. I ain't caught them together yet, I been workin nights mostly, I ain't had the time to put into it but . . .''

"Oh, poor man, stop! There's no point in going on with it, what good does it do?'' cries Marybeth. "They'll just kill you, they always win,'' but the young man shushes her, does not seem to wish to listen to her just now.

Ouida thinks of bridals, of the groom in his wedding shirt and bright sash, in his smart boots, dancing, leaping, his knife at his belt, his long mustache. She sees him so clearly, hears the music so clearly. Curious a thing it is that the mind can look in upon itself and bring out the memory of music. She can hum the wedding song, but without the guitars and drums it has a mournful, slow sound. Her childhood entirely a memory of happy weddings, the people running barefoot along the street. That was before Londrina. There cannot have been as many people in her village as wedding feasts she could remember, as if the people had got married over and over again there. The mind can bring back a smell, roasting pig and mandioca root. She hums a little of the wedding song to herself as she pushes the *aspirador* back and forth.

Meu Deus, think Ouida, for she cannot protect herself; she feels she has lost the ability to do this and stands as on the edge of the densest jungle full of snakes and the nectar of poison flowers and things you must not eat and horned animals such as the goat who will leap upon you— you will see their shadow a second or two before they pounce and rend you; you will know but it will be too late, and other dangers there, too.

She is on the edge and in she will plunge, and cannot hope ever to correct herself, for she is ignorant of so much—she counts things that come rushing into her mind. Of what to say to judges, and to which—the husband or the wife—the carpet will belong, and if they catch you and send you back because they think you have not enough love, will it be by scheduled airlines? Will Griggs want the matrimonial rights, or is he too old? How old is too old? How old is Griggs? Evil daughters have been known to poison the new stepmother, this is even common. In the voice of Griggs, mysteriously, a wail, the sound of tears rising as he is talking again about his boy Lonnie. Where has the conquistador gone, his eyes streaming tears? Why are they all crying—the young man and the pretty girl? Who *are* they all? Where is Miss Theo? What *are* the matrimonial rights?

About the Author

Diane Johnson is the author of six novels. Her collection of essays, TERRORISTS AND NOVELISTS, was nominated for the 1983 Pulitzer Prize and her biography of Mary Ellen Peacock Meredith, LESSER LIVES, was nominated for a National Book Award in 1973. A frequent contributor to the *New York Review of Books*, Ms. Johnson lives in San Francisco and teaches at the University of California at Davis.

Heartwarming...
Heartbreaking

NOVELS BY
ALICE ADAMS